DARKNESS FALLS

BOOK 1 OF THE NATURE'S FURY SERIES

*When Mother Nature reaches her breaking point,
humans have no choice but to face her fury.*

A.E. FAULKNER

INDIEOWL
PRESS

4700 Millenia Blvd.
Ste #175-90776
Orlando, FL 32839

info@indieowlpress.com
www.indieowlpress.com

DARKNESS FALLS

Cover design by Michelle Preast
Indie Book Cover Design / Michelle-Preast.com

Interior layout by Vanessa Anderson
at NightOwlFreelance.com

Manufactured in the United States of America

ISBN-13: 978-1-949193-98-5

For Cinny

Without you, the sun doesn't shine as bright as it once did.
Sixteen years with you wasn't even close to enough.

Miss you *every* day. ♥

"For this world in its present form is passing away."

—*Corinthians 7:29-31*

Contents

Contents

Contents

DARKNESS FALLS

Chapter 1

A shrill scream pierces the night. Shadows dance along the walls as my eyes widen, darting back and forth. Paralyzed with fear, I shrink under the flimsy blanket.

Riley and I duck away from the windows during the day and keep the lights low at night. No sense in inviting unwanted attention. For a wishful moment, I pretend that the TV in the living room is tuned to a horror movie and it's just the actors' dramatic shrieks assaulting my ears.

But the only sounds in the trailer are Riley's deep breaths, my stifled gasps, and a charged silence. Retreating farther under the blanket, every muscle in my body tenses with anticipation. As I silently wish the night away, the next, and last, cry I hear is abruptly cut short. I'm not sure which is worse—the sound of someone's pain and fear, or the silence of their extinguished existence.

Since we got to the trailer a week ago, my sister, Riley, and I have spent most of our time absorbing the endless streaming news reports. As low-tech as the 19" Toshiba is, it has been our only connection to the outside world. Thank goodness Aunt Grace insisted on getting it.

In what felt like an instant, our little world had shattered. And that was just the ripple effect from a greater tragedy that had destroyed many more lives. I am teetering on the edge of what has become a repeated loop of internal despair this week.

Sleep had been my only escape from the heartbreak, but now it brings no respite, only fresh nightmares. Squinting at Riley, jealousy trickles through me. She is practically unconscious; escape comes quickly when she closes her eyes. I can't grasp peace like she appears to have—least of all, at night. Deceptive silence and sobbing have imprisoned my mind in a perpetual state of sleepless overdrive.

Focused on purging my mind of all thought, the tension seeps out of my body. Sinking into the squeaky mattress, my eyelids once again flutter closed. My mind drifts to happier times, but I'm powerless to stop the flashbacks of unwanted memories.

I'm back in my old bedroom, carelessly tossing clothes on my bed. Riley is next door in her room, doing the same except with much more restraint. I'm sure she's over there carefully folding each shirt, tucking a coordinating bra and underwear set inside the fold. I'll just be happy if I have enough clean clothes to pack.

"Try to finish up, girls," Mom calls up the stairs. We're setting our alarms for 6:00 a.m. so we can get an early start. *Ugh.* I know it's a vacation, and we're all looking forward to it, but why on

Earth do we need to wake up as if it's a school day? We're staying at my aunt's trailer in Delaware near the beach, so we can show up as early—or late—as we want.

Riley responds first, "I'm done, Mom. Just rechecking my bags to make sure I didn't forget anything." Of course, she is. She probably started packing weeks ago and just refolded everything for fun tonight.

"Yeah, I'm done, too. I just wanted to make sure I didn't forget Riley's zit cream or foot powder," I add. No one acknowledges my snark.

"Alright, I'll see you girls in a few hours. Goodnight, Riley. Goodnight, Quinn," Mom says.

"Goodnight," Riley and I both call at the same time.

Once again, I'm jolted awake, this time by a dream of the family I no longer have. I shake my head, trying to erase the dream. Another night has become a sleepless cycle of sorrow. I volley between shifting from one uncomfortable position to another.

Flipping to my other side, I peer in Riley's direction. The ratty yellow blanket drapes over her thin frame just as it did the last time I woke, as if she hasn't moved in hours. Strands of her long brown hair scatter across the pillow.

While Riley's mind is probably journeying to a faraway world right now, I'm just waiting for oblivion to sweep me back under its dark veil. Reality wraps its spindly claws around my brain and replays the local news reports of our first days here over and over, like a playlist on repeat:

> *In breaking news, the Eastern seaboard suffered major damage today when a record-breaking, 8.2 magnitude, earthquake struck. While the West Coast has seen more than its share of earthquakes, this is not a common occurrence along the Atlantic Ocean.*
>
> *Classified as a great earthquake, this seismic event has sent Delaware into a state of emergency. Additionally, Rhode Island, Connecticut, New Jersey, and Maryland have also declared states of emergency. Massachusetts and New York suffered damage as well.*
>
> *Locally, Route One has sustained unprecedented destruction. A record-setting earthquake for the northeast region triggered the Chesapeake & Delaware Canal Bridge to collapse, plunging chunks of the bridge, as well as the vehicles on it, into the canal. Responders are still attempting to locate survivors.*
>
> *Emergency crews are working day and night to dismantle the massive pileup, facing significant cracks and fissures in the asphalt. As part of the state of emergency, Route One is closed until further notice. It has not been confirmed, but we have received reports that most of the state highway's 103 miles are in some way obstructed.*
>
> *Unstable ground and road damage paralyzed traffic on the highway, causing mass confusion. The situation worsened when towers and sound barriers shifted with the land, some crashing into roadways. The resulting damage*

has left pockets of the region without cell phone and land-line telephone services.

First responders from surrounding states are sending assistance for Delaware's rescue and recovery efforts, and the Red Cross has set up temporary shelters to aid victims of this devastating disaster. Also, military bases throughout the region are accepting those who have been displaced. Stay tuned for more information.

Reports got a bit more specific as the week went on, but mostly just kept repeating the same information. Eventually, Riley and I agreed that our minds had become numb to the news, and we could no longer keep processing the regurgitated reports. We turned the TV off at that point and unplugged it for good measure. Since no one in the trailer park knew we were coming, we decided to keep it that way for as long as possible. We stayed inside, avoided the windows, and used only faint lights at night, mainly the cracked red flashlight Aunt Grace stored in the junk drawer for emergencies.

Neither of us wanted to venture back out to the highway. For me, at least, if I didn't have to see where our vacation had ended before it began, it was all a little less real. *Maybe it was all a horrendous nightmare that I could still wake up from at any moment.* Not even the lure of finding our cell phones, both missing since we got here, could drag us out to the wreck.

The trailer's fake wood-paneled walls might as well have been prison bars. When your mind is swamped with grief, you don't really care if your life is standing still. While we find some small comfort nesting in the trailer we've vacationed in with our parents for our whole lives, the reality that we can't stay here forever has been bubbling up in our whispered conversations.

Caught somewhere between teenagers and young adults, neither one of us has taken charge of our situation. I'll be turning seventeen in a few months, yet I've never felt so young, helpless, and afraid as I have these past few days.

At this point, we're almost out of food, with no idea what the immediate future holds. I think Riley's been counting on someone—anyone—to come rescue us. Mom and Dad can't come back. Ever. Who knows what's really happening in the rest of the world. It only took about 20 seconds for ours to crumble.

I force my eyes closed and settle back into the bed, praying for another day to be over.

Chapter 2

A thudding sound jars me from sleep. My groggy eyes land on the front door just as the pounding pauses. When Riley jumps up, scrambling to the living room, the doorknob starts shaking vigorously. Her alarmed brown eyes meet mine as realization dawns that our visitor is morphing into an intruder. With trembling hands, she wedges a finger between two mini blinds and peeks out. "Quinn, it's Jim," she whispers.

Ugh, Slim Jim. He's a year-round resident who lives two lots away from our aunt's trailer with his brother and their dad. His brother, Dan, is a nice guy. Their dad oversees maintenance for the park. Somehow this makes Jim think he owns everyone and everything within a one-mile radius. I throw my feet over the side of the bed and slowly rise, trying not to picture the greasy black hair that clings to his wide forehead, or his beady eyes that glare at me more times than not.

Motioning downward with my hands, I whisper back, "Let's just ignore it. He'll go away." Cocking her head to the side, she contemplates my idea for a moment. When she scrunches her face in a pained expression, I know she's surrendered to opening the door.

"He's not that bad," she says quietly. "And besides, we may need his help sometime…soon."

As I open my mouth to object, Riley tugs on the door and hesitantly greets our company. "Uh, Jim, hi."

He takes that as an invitation to come in and struts right through the door.

Riley awkwardly shuffles backward and bumps into the kitchen wall, eyeing me as she straightens herself.

His eyes rove to the kitchen and the other bedroom.

"I didn't expect to find you here," he says, rubbing his chin. "How the hell did you even get here?"

Stepping into the living room, my welcome is not as gracious as Riley's. "Well, hello, Jim. Just make yourself right at home, why don't you?"

At the sound of my voice, his shoulders sag noticeably.

We've never gotten along. Even as kids, Jim and I used to fight all the time, settling our disagreements with fists and force. I think I won more times than not. Not that he would ever admit that.

"Quinn," he says sharply, nodding at me in acknowledgement. He mutters under his breath, "You're here too," but his words and message are clear. He's always tried to avoid me while seeking out Riley, which is absolutely fine by me. I think it's mostly because they are closer in age. Jim's gotta be about twenty-two now and

8

Riley's almost eighteen. It might also have a bit to do with the fact that she may be just a tad nicer to people in general.

Turning back toward Riley, Jim leans forward, resting an arm on the wall above her head.

She must be uncomfortable being that close to him. I'm ready to jump out of my skin just seeing him that physically close to anyone.

"So, Riley, when did you all get here? You know, with everything that's been going on out there," he says, jabbing a thumb toward the front door.

Riley cocks her head to the side, glancing at me nervously. *How are we going to explain that it's just the two of us here?* We haven't said the words out loud yet, and Jim is the last person I want to talk to about it. "Well, um, Quinn and I got here a few days ago."

He looks perplexed. I imagine he wears that expression several times a day. "It's just you two?" He runs a hand through his slick hair and smooths out his mustache, which is so thin it should really be called a microstache. "Everything okay?" He looks back and forth between us, raising his eyebrows.

"Yeah, Jim, we're fine," I answer stoically.

Riley's deep brown eyes drop to the floor.

We don't need his help and we don't need him thinking that we do. What we do need is for him to get out of here. "So, Jim, what's going on? Did you need something?" He's used to me being rude, so there's really no reason to disappoint him.

"Well," he answers, "Dan and I are going around checking on everyone. You know, we thought everything settled from the quake, but now we gotta watch out for the aftershocks."

"What?" I ask before I can stop myself. He smirks in my

direction. He loves this. I actually want information that he has. "Well, Quinn, after the quake, the aftershocks caused even more damage and deaths. Responders can't keep up with it all," he pauses for effect, drawing out the conversation. "You mark my words, Quinn. This is just the start. The start of all hell breaking loose."

Riley's breathing betrays her rising panic; her normally pale complexion fades to a ghostly white. "What? Jim, why would you say that? You think it's going to get worse?"

I tug my hyperventilating sister to the couch. As she plops down, I shoot Jim a look that screams "*Shut up!*"

Following us to the couch, Jim settles in on Riley's other side. "Hey, Riley, I didn't mean to upset you. I'm sorry. There's just a lot going on and…I really just came over to make sure everything was okay here."

At least he has the decency to sound apologetic.

Suddenly, my mind flits to last night and the shrill scream that woke me. I can't ask about it in front of Riley. She's already upset. *Maybe I can find Dan later and ask if he heard anything.* But first, I've got to get rid of Jim.

"Everything is fine here, Jim. Thanks for stopping by," I say as Riley raises teary eyes my way.

Jim places a hand on her leg, turning her attention back to him. "Now, Riley, I hope you know that I'm here if you need anything. You know where to find me, right?"

Ugh. Message received.

I know Riley sees right through him, but she's too nice to show it. I don't mind being the one to rush this conversation. "Jim, thanks. Really. It's nice of you and Dan to check up on everyone. I think we're okay here, though. If we need anything, you'll be the first to know."

With that I stand, hoping he'll mirror my movement. A drop of luck splashes in my direction and he rises from the cushions. Striding toward the door, I yank it open expectantly.

"Alright, then," Jim says awkwardly. Walking backward toward the door, his eyes remain fixed on my sister. "Riley, you should probably stay put. You know, try and keep a low profile."

She nods slowly, brushing long, thin locks of hair away from her face.

He crosses the threshold, calling out a final goodbye as I promptly swing the door closed. Turning the lock and leaning against the door, my gaze settles on Riley. When her narrowed eyes meet mine, I have a feeling I'm about to get a lecture.

"Quinn, you know Jim was just trying to help us. Why can't you just try to be polite? Just a little bit."

Riley attempts to wield guilt my way, but I'm immune. I keep my tone even; I don't want to fight with her. "Riley, I don't trust that guy or his dimwitted brother. They just like to throw their weight around. They aren't checking in with everyone to offer help, they're just being nosy—probably eyeing up supplies to steal." *How can she disagree with that? She's got to know I'm right.* "And," I add for good measure, "I really don't care if I hurt that slimeball's feelings right now. I've got my own feelings to deal with *and yours!*"

"Quinn, why do you always have to expect the worst from people? Why can't you just take what Jim says at face value? You know, we might need him and Dan to help us figure out what to do. I just think you could be a little nicer."

Okay, Riley clearly doesn't get it, and I'm not going to waste my time trying to make her see. I hop off the couch and head to the bathroom. Breezing past her, I mutter, "I'm gonna hit the shower."

The hot stream of water evaporates my tension. By the time I'm dressed and done in the bathroom, my anger has dissipated, like the steam on the mirror, replaced by an idea blooming in my mind. I'll need a quick change of clothes, and I probably shouldn't have showered just yet, but it's worth it.

Riley glances up from her book when I spring into the bedroom. Tossing last night's PJs onto the pile, they perfectly peak the mountain of laundry climbing up the corner. Digging through my suitcase, I pitch the articles I don't need right now with no regard for where they may land. *Why not? It's not like there's much left in there anyway.*

"What are you up to?" Riley asks lightly.

I can tell she wants our latest spat behind us, too. And I know what I need to lower my stress level a few more notches. Now that Dan and Jim know we're here, we aren't exactly invisible anymore. Initially, Riley and I needed to overcome our shock from the trip down here. Now I can barely stand to spend one more second hiding inside this wood-paneled prison.

"I need a run. It'll feel good to stretch my muscles and burn some energy." I answer, tugging my long brown hair into a ponytail. *And maybe, just maybe, it will distract me from the recent memory of all I've lost.* "Why don't you come too? It would be good for you to get outta here for a little while."

"No!" Crossing her arms, Riley is adamant. "We should keep a low profile. We can't take any chances of someone else seeing us." Dropping my running gear, I stride out to the kitchen and grab a breakfast bar. Riley trails behind me. *Why can't she ever just agree with me? Why does everything have to be a fight?*

"Take any chances!?" My earlier anger bubbles up to the surface before I can cork it. "How about a chance to take a look around and see what's going on out there? How about a chance to breathe some fresh air?" Now that the flood gates have opened, a tidal wave of words spills out. "Riley, I know we agreed to hide out, but what does it matter now that Jim and Dan know we're here?" Planting my hands on my hips, I await her response.

"Quinn, I'm scared," Riley practically whispers, wringing her hands. "I don't know what to do. I just want to wake up from this nightmare." She plops down on the couch, freeing a few dust particles that dance in the sun's rays.

Her confession instantly melts my anger. In one breath, she drives me nuts, like only a sister can, and in the next breath, I just want to protect her. Even though she's older, she's always been the meeker one. And I can't wait for her to jump in and lead us. I'm not sure she ever would.

With no intention of liberating more dust, I carefully lower myself onto the green floral sofa. Sitting close enough that my knees brush hers, I grab Riley's shaking hands. Meeting her eyes, I relent. "Look, I feel the same way. I don't know what to do either." Digging deep for a confidence I don't feel, my tone is soft but steady. "We may be safe right now, but we can't stay here forever. And besides, we aren't invisible anymore. Now that Jim and Dan know we're here, maybe we should go visit Benny."

"Quinn, maybe we should go back to the highway—try to find someone from the Red Cross to help us." She eyes me anxiously, as if willing me to agree.

"Riley, I don't think that's a good idea. We're still minors. What would they do with us? I'm not willing to give up my freedom and have some stranger decide what happens to us."

Her glassy eyes hold mine as she processes my words. I can almost see the thoughts flitting through her mind. "Alright, maybe we should try to gather more information before we decide anything," Riley says cautiously. "Let's start with Benny and see if he knows what's going on and who's even here."

"Yes," I wholeheartedly agree. *Maybe I can try to figure out where that scream came from last night.* "Let's draw a map and we can ask Benny who lives in each trailer. We can make notes and—"

"Quinn, let's just go to Benny's now," Riley says, interrupting my plans.

"Riley, calm down. Here's what we'll do. I'm going to go for a run. I *need* to go for a run. While I'm gone, you grab some breakfast and draw a map of the trailer park. When I get back, we'll visit Benny and see what he knows."

Thankfully, she doesn't argue. Eyes downcast, she slowly nods. For a moment I wonder how she's not dehydrated from all the tears she's cried this week. I haven't cried as much as she has, but my heart still feels like an open wound, festering in grief.

"Riley, it's okay. I'll be back soon. I'm just gonna take the Pine Trail. You know that one's short. Just work on the map, so we're all ready to go when I get back." She nods again, and I rise slowly, returning to the bedroom to retrieve my gear.

After tracking down both sneakers, I park myself on the

couch to steal a few glances her way as I lace up. Her movements are robotic as she shuffles around in the tiny kitchen. When she starts digging through drawers, I crack open the door, my eyes searching for movement. Satisfied that no one is watching, I slip outside.

Chapter 3

Rushing out the door, I draw in a deep breath, filling my lungs with fresh air. It's so freeing to escape our self-made cocoon, even for just a short time. Since we got here, we've been slogging through the motions of living. I found myself standing in the shower or sitting at the kitchen table countless times, not remembering how I got there. Or maybe just not caring.

Darting behind the trailer, I position myself between the overgrown hydrangea bushes. My dad always complained about the unwieldy blue and purple blooms, but now they provide the perfect cover to block me from prying eyes. *If none of this happened, I wouldn't be worrying about hiding behind some stupid plants. I'd chop them all down in a heartbeat if it meant I could have my dad back.*

Bending at my waist and lowering my palms to the ground, I walk my hands forward. My weakened muscles wake with each stretch. The familiar movements spark a surge of electricity through my limbs. After a few more stretches, off I go, lightly jogging down the path I've run a hundred times. I revel in the lush trees and wildflowers surrounding me.

I haven't been outside since our escape from the cars and trucks choking the highway. That makes skirting around the plants snaking onto the trail a welcome change.

For the first time in a week, my eyes feast on their surroundings. The mostly tan and white homes all stand at attention in perfectly symmetrical lines. Most of the owners live here year-round, and it shows. Those homes boast freshly-painted shutters and smooth siding. Not like my aunt's trailer, which could use a design overhaul and furniture from this century.

My feet practically glide over the winding asphalt. After a short run through the trailer park, I take a detour down the dirt path to my left, Pine Trail. Ducking my head and shoulders to avoid the tree overgrowth, I nearly lose my balance, my steps stuttering briefly. It's been too long since I ran like this. My legs relish the strain.

While I typically run solo, loneliness chases my every stride. Maybe the reality that I'll be returning to exactly what I left niggles at the back of my brain. All I've had is Riley, and we spent half the time silently mourning our former life, arguing, or barely suppressing our mutual hostility after an argument.

Shaking the negative thoughts from my mind, I push my legs harder, each foot pounding the ground as it briefly touches and launches again. My lungs keep tempo with my stride, a dizzying rush of air sweeping in and out of my body with every inhale and exhale. After about a mile of dodging overgrowth on the path, I'm nearly out of breath. That would be unheard of just a few weeks ago, during track season. Before summer started, a five-mile run was an easy workout for me.

Approaching an opening in the path, I slow my pace and alert my senses. With too many unknowns right now, I can't be too careful, especially being out here alone. As the wooded path spills into an overgrown yard, about a dozen felines linger in the grass, splayed out in various states of slumber. The white ranch house with sagging maroon shutters must be their home. Cats line the sidewalk and entryway like lawn ornaments.

Life abounds outside, but no shadows pass beyond the lifeless windows. Slinking around the side of the house, I hunch down in case anyone inside decides to peer out. Since I could use a little breather anyway, I plop down on the grass to see what the cats do. Most barely throw a passing glance my way, but a few wander over. A short-haired black cat with sparkling emerald eyes butts her head against my bent knee. I rub her neck just beneath her green collar and extend my hand to a brown tiger-striped cat with striking yellow-green eyes. The tiger rolls on his back and I can't resist grabbing that furry belly.

The four-legged fuzz balls remind me of the only family member who didn't make this trip. Whenever we go on vacation, our rat terrier spends the week with my mom's sister, our Aunt Robin. This time was no different. If this trip had gone as planned, we would be heading home and picking Snickers up tomorrow. Turning my attention back to the pets before me, I block thoughts of him wondering where we are and why we aren't coming back.

Scratching the crook of the tiger's neck, his reflective yellow collar sparkles in the sunlight. The glare targets my squinting eyes with laser-like focus. Leaning closer to cast a shadow over that blinding collar, baby-talk is about to spill from my lips when a soft squeaking noise draws my attention.

Rising slowly, I creep toward the noise, staying close to the house. Peering around the corner, I spy a man in khaki shorts and a navy-blue T-shirt squatting down at the hose, turning on the spigot. Crap. I've stayed too long and now the homeowner is outside. I don't want him to see me on his property, grabbing his cats' bellies.

I slowly lift my left leg, gently pitching backward. My foot is promptly greeted with a hiss and a swipe as I nearly plant it on the tiger, who must have followed me to the corner. *Dammit.* My eyes dart to the man but he hasn't even flinched. I guess hissing is a pretty common sound around here.

That gentle squeaking sound drifts my way again. Whatever that guy is doing, he doesn't know I'm watching. This emboldens me to spy a little longer. Crouching down, I peer around the corner to see him filling water jugs from the outside spigot. Why would he be doing that? Maybe it's for the cats and he doesn't want to fill the jugs up inside and lug them out. The furball I've decided to name Tiger flops down at my feet, rolling onto his back, exposing that fuzzy white belly again. Instantly forgiving the hiss and swipe, I am at this cat's mercy. Once again, I reach down and gently stroke the soft fur while stealing another peek at the stranger.

This time, he's facing my direction, but his eyes slide over each water jug as he tightens the caps. More teenager than man, he looks younger by the minute. I'm guessing he's probably eighteen or nineteen. When he finishes capping the bottles, he runs a hand through his messy black hair, sending small tufts of it out like antennae. He narrows his eyes and scrunches his forehead as he stares at the water. I'm certain he's debating how he's going to carry four full water jugs with two hands.

Hands down, he makes for a better view than the trailer's fake-wood-paneled walls. Just as my legs start to cramp, Tiger decides he's had enough of my gentle hand and attempts to keep a chunk of it for himself. The fuzzy little demon wraps his paws around my hand, drawing it to his sharp teeth as his feet bat my arm. A gasp escapes my lips in reaction to the jolt and pain of claws and jaws sinking into my flesh. *Dogs don't do this.* I yank my arm from the cat's grasp and take an instinctive step away. I earn myself a nice scratch for selfishly wanting to keep my hand and arm intact. Realization dawns on me that I've probably drawn some attention my way.

My eyes shift to the stranger. His shoulders hunker as he meets my gaze, his crystal blue eyes widening.

Chapter 4

Bravo. Since I left the trailer park, I've managed to trespass on someone's property, announce myself to said property owner, serve as a scratching post for a temperamental cat, and probably worry my sister. I told her I'd be right back, and here I am, frantically searching for something to blot the blood trickling down my arm. I can't ignore the guy, though. I should apologize for being here.

The handsome stranger stands abruptly and stares for a moment. He's as unsure as I am about what to do. Cradling my scratched arm, my eyes follow the few cautious steps he takes toward me. *At least he's not yelling at me to get off his property.*

He stops about three feet before me and practically stutters, "H-hi. Are you, are you okay?" He glances at my cradled arm. A gentleness in his eyes conveys genuine concern.

"I'm fine. It's just a little scratch," I say flatly, knowing that an apology is probably in order for trespassing. *I wouldn't be standing here like an idiot if I had just minded my own business and stuck to my run.*

"Oh, right," he sounds even less comfortable than he did a moment ago. Shifting on his feet, his eyes focus on the ground.

"I'm sorry," we both blurt out at the same time. Our narrowed eyes meet, expressions mirroring each other. "What did you say?" I ask him. He looks at me like I have a trail of fire blazing from my arm, which it sure feels like right about now.

"I said I'm sorry. Look, I didn't mean to help myself to your water. I just needed to replenish my supply and I saw all these cats around and thought whoever lived here is probably a compassionate person and might be willing to share a little bit of water with someone who needs it." His explanation pours out in a flood of words.

"Wait, you don't live here?" I ask before the floodgates burst open again. Scrunching his eyes and pursing his lips, he responds, "No, I thought you lived here." He pauses for a moment before crossing his arms and asking, "If this isn't your house, what are you doing here?"

I turn my toe around in the grass and explain, "I'm staying down the road a bit and went out for a run. I stopped here to take a little rest and pet some of the cats. I didn't expect to see anyone else, and I didn't expect one of the fuzzballs to try and scratch my arm off."

He lets out a surprised chuckle. "I'm Aidan," he says, extending a hand.

I thrust my good hand toward him and give his a squeeze. "Quinn."

"Well, Quinn, it's nice to meet you. I'm going to have to get going, though. I've got to get this water home before anyone else catches me stealing it." A twinkle flashes in his eye as he smiles at me.

"It's nice to meet you too. Stay hydrated," I say as I turn back toward the wooded path.

He calls out to me, "Until the next time. If there is one."

I stride over the familiar wooded path back to the trailer park with a renewed purpose. I've got to reach Riley before she panics. Loping with an awkward gait, I stanch the bleeding by clasping one hand over my injured arm. When the yellow, white, and gray trailers appear, I shift to a cool down mode, easing my muscles, and slowing my heart rate.

Nearing the trailer, a face hovering in the window catches my eye. I'd know that scowl anywhere. Riley's angry gaze follows my movements. *Great. Why is there always a layer of tension lodged between us?* Stopping when I reach the small gravel patch that serves as a tiny front yard, I plant my legs astride and stretch my arms to the ground. My mind launches into calculations. *How long was I gone? It couldn't have been more than forty minutes.*

Riley stomps out the door, launching into an interrogation. *So much for keeping a low profile.* "Where have you been!?" Her ragged voice borders on hysteria. "Why did you take so long? What were you doing?" Taking a deep breath and straightening up, I talk myself out of losing patience. *She's scared. This is her fear pouring out. Maybe she was afraid that I'd never come back.*

Reaching an arm out to her, resting a hand on her shoulder, I meet her eyes. "Riley, I'm so sorry. I totally lost track of time. Please don't be—"

Before I can finish begging for forgiveness, she seizes my arm. "What happened to you?" Her demeanor immediately softens.

Glancing down at my souvenir from the day, I explain, "Oh, I came across some kitties on my run. I stopped to pet them, and one didn't exactly return my love."

Riley gently turns my arm; her eyes trace my injury. "There's a first aid kit inside. I saw it when I was looking for paper and a pen to make the map. You should go clean that, so we can patch it up."

After a quick soapy scrub, I'm almost ready to go. In between blotting the scratch with toilet paper, I slip on the last clean set of clothes I packed. Quietly emerging from the bathroom, my eyes seek Riley. They find their target quickly. She sits at the kitchen table, wringing her hands as her eyes slide across the hand-drawn map. My heart aches witnessing her nearly-constant dejected state. Physically, we have survived the last week just fine but emotionally, our spirits fade a little more each day that we wake up to this nightmare.

Riley and I have stayed in this trailer every summer for the past ten years, but this is the only time we've been here alone, just the two of us. Free from my recent but chronic haze, I gingerly step toward Riley. "Hey, sis, you ready?" I ask with over-exaggerated enthusiasm. Riley squints up at me, doubting my sunny tone.

"Come sit down," she says, motioning to the bench seat she occupies. "I'll clean that scratch." This is where Riley excels. Right now, her gentle, comforting demeanor is exactly what I need. She swabs an antiseptic gel over the scratch, triggering a spontaneous inhale of air that sounds like a hiss. A little ironic that *I'm* hissing because of that cat. "Oh, sorry," Riley says. "Almost done."

She carefully affixes a clean bandage over my wound and re-packages the first aid kit. Gathering the trash, I rise from the table and attempt to deposit it in the overflowing garbage bin. *We're gonna have to do something about that. But not right now.* "Ready to go?"

Riley doesn't meet my eyes. "Quinn, I was so worried about you. I drew the map and I thought we'd go out, but I really don't feel like it now. Let's just call it a day." Her shaky voice radiates defeat. *It's my fault for leaving her alone for too long.*

In a flash, I'm standing before her. "No, Riley, it's not too late. We can still go visit some of the others. Getting out a bit would be good for you," I plea. "You pick where we go first." I don't wait for her to refuse. Grabbing her hand, I pull her up out of the seat. If she thinks about this for too long, she'll abandon our plan and just give up. That's the last thing Mom and Dad would have wanted us to do.

Chapter 5

Riley reluctantly follows me across the door's threshold. Surrendering to my resolve, she quietly murmurs, "Alright, let's start with Benny. He's really the only one I want to see anyway. Maybe he'll know what we should do."

"Yes—that's a great plan!" I say, once again reverting to exaggerated enthusiasm. "Let's leave the map here and mark it up when we get back. Don't want anyone to think we're taking notes or anything. Even though we are," I joke, flashing Riley a cheesy grin.

Her half-smile rewards my effort, and gratitude swells within me. *As awful as our current situation is, at least I'm not here alone.* Both of our parents were gone in the blink of an eye. It just as easily could have been Riley, too. Although life is pretty crummy right now, at least I still have my sister.

The moment our feet hit the pavement, my stomach grumbles

with hunger. The near-silence just amplifies it. Remembering the breakfast bar I grabbed from the kitchen before my run, I dig around in my pockets but come up empty. *I must have left it in my pocket before I showered again and changed clothes.*

We navigate through the park, my eyes searching every home for movement or any signs of life. Shifting my gaze back and forth in slow motion, I scrutinize our surroundings.

I've never seen the trailer park so vacant. No residents outside watering their plants or walking their dogs. No kids zipping through people's yards on their bikes or skateboards. Not even Jim's dad out tinkering in the storage shed. I thought I would be relieved to get out and see people, but this may be more depressing than sitting around in the trailer with Riley.

The gravelly path crunches under our sneakers. We follow it to Benny's place, the last lot on the perimeter of the park. Benny's lived here as long as I can remember. He doesn't come out much, but he is getting to be pretty ancient. He's got to be in his seventies now.

Climbing the three steps leading to his olive-green door, we pause for a moment before Riley gently knocks. After a few moments, scuffling feet stop in their tracks, and a familiar ebony face appears through the window. Benny's gray eyes scrunch at the corners as a smile splays across his face. He unclicks the lock and tugs the door open, greeting us with a deep baritone voice. "Well, if it isn't the Whelan girls," Benny booms. "Come on in. It's great to see you!"

For a brief moment, I forget everything that's happened. Reality quickly returns when Benny's eyes wander over our heads, searching out the family members that won't be joining us.

Benny wraps us both in a hug before we all take a seat at the circular oak kitchen table. He has no need for idle prattle. I like that about him. He jumps right to the point. "Girls, I'm glad to see you're okay, but what are you doing here? You should be home right now. I don't mean home like at Grace's, I mean at home with your parents."

Riley and I glance at each other. Her doe-like eyes glaze over with a thin sheen of tears. This is too hard for her. I'll have to do it.

Struggling to keep my voice steady, I recount how traffic went haywire on Route One. "We almost made it here when rain came out of nowhere and hammered the car. Sometime between Pennsylvania and Delaware, it felt like the Earth was tumbling off its axis." I grasp the table top for support and continue. "We had no idea what was happening. As if the rain wasn't enough, the ground below us roared and bucked, sending cars sliding and smashing into each other. There was nowhere to go." Tears flood my eyes, threatening to spill. "Dad tried. He was trying to stop, to get away. But it was like slow motion. Cars flew toward us from every direction." Recounting that highway of death and destruction leaves me queasy. When I pause to take a deep breath, Riley takes over.

"I think I blacked out because I don't remember much about it. I remember Quinn's tear-stained face hovering over mine. When I saw the front of the car, it was just…gone. I couldn't speak. I just wanted to disappear into myself at that moment." She stops, her eyes focusing on the wood-grained table.

Benny's dark eyes volley back and forth between us. "And your parents?" he asks gently. His wrinkled face sags with genuine concern.

28

On warm summer nights my dad would sit with Benny for hours, drinking beer and reliving their younger days. I'm pretty sure those were some of my dad's favorite times here. Mom would send us over to retrieve Dad before we went to sleep. Benny always plied us with spiced gumdrops. He seemed to have an endless supply. We never told Mom about our pre-bedtime sugar rush but were always willing to visit Benny. He's been like a long-distance grandfather to us.

"Girls?" I shake myself out of the memory and answer Benny. "A red pickup truck flipped over directly in front of us. Behind it, some sort of black SUV lost control and slammed into the truck. The force of the truck…it didn't slow until it rammed into our car. It completely crumpled the front half."

Benny's eyes drop and remain fixed on the floor when he speaks. "So, there's no chance—"

I'm not going to let him finish that sentence. I really don't want to hear the words. "No. There's no way," I interrupt.

Benny's watery eyes meet mine. "Oh girls, I'm so sorry. You did the right thing coming here, to Grace's trailer."

With that, we fill Benny in on the past week. When the car finally stilled, confusion prevailed. Limping, crying bodies emerged from smoking vehicles. Alarms blared from immobile cars and trucks. Luggage spilled from vans and SUVs.

Squeezing my eyes shut did nothing to hamper the nightmare erupting around me. Cracking my eyes open to the crushed nothingness of the dashboard and steering wheel, I forced my splayed fingers to trace the vertical lines running down the seat's fabric. Just a moment before, my dad was on the other side of that seat. Seconds later, it was consumed by metal and glass. Just like the passenger seat where I last saw my mother.

Crumbling inside and out, I succumbed to the intense sobbing my body couldn't contain. After what felt like hours, I pushed through the shock and turned my unfocused gaze in Riley's direction. Slumped toward the window, her head was cradled against the seatbelt. For a terrifying moment, I thought she was gone too. When my puffy eyes couldn't locate any rise and fall in her chest, I grabbed her shoulders, fiercely shaking her limp body until she responded.

Rubbing my eyes, I explain how we pilfered what we could from the car. Thankfully, our suitcases and the food coolers were on wheels. We had to maneuver about a mile from the car to the trailer. Mindlessly, we did it, not muttering a word. That first night we locked ourselves in the trailer, unpacked the week's worth of meals, and settled in the flimsy beds, hiding beneath the shabby blankets. Since then, we haven't done much besides sleeping. We only eat when our feeble appetites demand it. My eyelids droop by the time my lips close.

Riley sits quietly, a pained expression painted on her face.

Benny rubs his eyes with the heel of his palm. "Girls, how about some food? You humor an old man and eat something?" We break into weak smiles in unison and nod. *How could anyone say no to that?* Besides, now that he's mentioned food, my stomach recalls how empty it feels.

"That sounds great, Benny," Riley confirms. "Quinn, you go rest and I'll help Benny." Slowly rising from the table, my legs feel like lead. Meandering to the living room, I drop into the brown plaid recliner that my dad relaxed in dozens of times. Riley must have found her voice again. I'm thankful she keeps

Benny company so that I can decompress.

Talking about the crash renews my sense of grief. *I guess it's mine until my own death causes someone else's grief.* A wave of anguish courses through me, numbing my limbs and shooting a surge of pain through my heart. Between this and the run, I'm drained. When my eyes flutter closed, reality gently slips away.

A muffled voice pulls me from the black void of sleep. A steady tapping on my arm accompanies Riley's soft words. "Quinn, wake up. Dinner's ready." Arching my back and stretching in the recliner, my groggy eyes wander to the kitchen table. Sure enough, Benny is already seated before the steaming bowls of rice, chicken, and broccoli that await us. Rubbing my eyes, I peel myself out of the recliner and mosey over to the table.

"So, Quinn, while you were catching some ZZZs, I was asking your sister about your plans," Benny says. "Sounds like you two got none."

Riley glances at me apologetically. I reach my hand across the small table and place it over hers. "She's right, we haven't done much beyond getting through each day," I answer somberly.

"Well, on the news, they're calling this area a recommended evacuation zone." He raises his eyebrows and pauses. When I just stare at him, he continues. "Because of the damage along the highway and concerns that older people won't be able to access food and medicines they need."

"So, what does that mean exactly, a *recommended evacuation*," I ask.

Riley's eyes stay focused on Benny, and I'm guessing she heard all of this while I slept.

"It means, if you want to get out and get help, now is the time to do it," Benny says, rubbing the white scruff on his warm brown chin.

"Some of the residents have been talking and they're gonna try to reach a military base not too far from here, just until the highway is cleared," Benny says. "Maybe you girls should go with them."

"Wait a minute, why are you saying *them* and not *us?*" I ask. "Aren't you going?"

Leaning back in his chair, he releases a sigh and rubs a big hand over his ebony face.

"Girls, I'm an old coot. I'll just slow everyone down," Benny explains. He raises both arms and waves them in the air. "Besides, I'm not leaving my castle here without its king. But you, you girls should go to the base. See what the government is fixing to do." He eyes us warily, shifting his gaze between us, awaiting a response.

Maybe Riley's had a little bit of time to consider this new information, but I haven't, and we shouldn't rush into any decision.

"When are they leaving?" I ask. "We have to discuss this and consider all of our options."

"What's there to discuss," Riley asks nervously. "We don't *have* any other options."

Thankfully, Benny jumps in again. "The group leaves in three days. Talk and think about it. Come see me again before then. I'll find out more in case you decide to go." He pauses for a moment before raising his graying caterpillar eyebrows, sending dark creases along his forehead. "And girls, you have to think beyond today. Grace's trailer isn't a sustainable home. Whatever you decide, I'll help you, but you have to figure out what you're gonna do."

I have so many questions, but my brain is firing in too many directions at once. I just can't process any more information right now. We finish our meal and help Benny clean up. While Riley clears the table and I start washing dishes, Benny invites us to gather our belongings and stay with him. Surprisingly, Riley agrees with me that we should stay in Aunt Grace's trailer for now. As grim as the past week has been, the trailer has been our safe haven. Besides, Riley and I need time alone to talk this out. While she may latch on to any solution right now, I'm not so sure we should join the group. It would be an easier decision if Benny were part of this pilgrimage.

About a quarter of the trailers are vacation rentals, like our aunt's. We've met some of the permanent residents in passing, but other than a few names here and there, the only others we know are Jim, Dan, and their dad.

Chapter 6

The walk back to our trailer is hurried. We want to be behind locked doors before darkness falls. Rubbing my arms, I attempt to counteract the chilly air that's uncharacteristic for June. Once safely inside, words spill out of Riley's mouth, "So, what are you thinking about the military base?"

"I'm not sure," I say slowly. "If Benny were going, this would be easier. I just have so many questions and doubts. Like, what if it's not some safe haven? What if we can't just show up and knock on the door? How far is it? If the highway's that bad, how is this group going to get there?"

Riley sinks into the sofa, eyes focused on the floor. She wrings her hands in her lap. "Quinn, we can't stay here forever. We have to do something. Go somewhere."

"I know, but Pennsylvania's a long way without a car." *Not like a car would do us much good with the highway being one big traffic jam.*

"The military base is probably our only hope," she says. "I really just want to go home, but you're right. We don't have a way to get back to Pennsylvania on our own right now. Maybe people at the military base would let us call someone?"

Aunt Grace cut the land line service to the trailer when pretty much everyone in the family had a cell phone anyway. Except I'm pretty sure mine hurtled across the highway in the impact, and we didn't find Riley's, although we didn't exactly pore through the car before we left it.

"What if it isn't safe?" I ask. "And we don't even know the people we'd be going there with. I mean, how can we trust them?"

"Unless Dan and Jim are going," Riley starts. "Maybe we should ask. We can just stick with them."

"Riley, we do *not* need them! We can figure this out without them," I counter.

Riley's tear-filled eyes meet mine. "I just don't know what to do, Quinn. I…I wish someone was here to decide for us."

"Look, we're both exhausted. Let's call it a day and talk more tomorrow. We could use some sleep," I say.

Sometimes our dreams are sweet fantasies and sometimes they are flashbacks to a hell we never want to remember. Since the accident, my dreams typically feature the latter. I hate how little control we have over the images our closed eyes display.

As my body rests, my mind replays the morning we left for vacation. Our drive to the trailer should have taken about four hours, maybe a little longer if bathroom stops were necessary. This time, it took us nearly six hours just to make it to Route One, which runs right past the trailer park. The morning started out pretty typical, except for waking up with the first rays of sunlight. Shortly after tumbling out of bed, I caught my family's excitement and allowed it to overtake me. All four of us were dressed, completely packed, and finished with breakfast by 7:00 a.m.

From the hazy fog of my memory, I watch us load the car with a week's worth of belongings before the sights and sounds of the trip return. Ear buds pumped Imagine Dragons and P!nk into my head as the rolling hills of Amish country flashed past my window. My mind replays when my body crumpled into the seat, lulled to sleep by the car's motion.

As I helplessly re-live that day, my mind remembers the tinny echo of rain that pelted the roof and pulled me from the nap. I rubbed my eyes, then turned my gaze out the window to find the scenery blanketed in rainfall and fog. A torrential downpour curtained everything beyond the lane next to us. Mom practically shouted to be heard when she asked my dad, "Should we pull over and wait the rain out?" When I glanced over at Riley, she was asleep, not even stirring. That girl could sleep through a bulldozer crashing into a dynamite factory.

Dad had answered confidently, "We're so close. I hate to pull over now. Just a little bit farther and we'll be at the trailer." I watched as my mom gently placed her arm on his in solidarity. True partners, right to the very end.

I turned my attention back outside to watch for a break in the rain. My eyes widened in horror when my ears identified the distinct grating sound of car smashing car, metal crumpling upon impact. Mom screamed and Dad slammed on the brake, but it did no good. Once again, my mind replays our car sliding on the rain-slicked road, along with all of the other vehicles around us. Red and black masses flashed past our windshield. The snapping crunch of metal filled my ears before the world fell eerily silent.

When my body starts shaking uncontrollably, my eyes fly open. Riley is hovering over me, saying the same thing over and over. "Quinn, wake up!" She releases my shoulders when she sees I'm awake. I shake my head, as if that could rid my mind of the images it refuses to forget. "Quinn, are you okay? You were screaming in your sleep."

"Sorry I woke you," I say between gasps. "I was just having a stupid dream."

"Sounded like a pretty bad nightmare," she says. "And you didn't wake me. I was reading. Are you okay?"

"I'm fine, Riley," I lie. "Let's go back to sleep." Of course, my sister sees right through me. Tugging gently on my hair, she draws out my name. "Quiiiiiiiiiiinn. I know you're lying. Tell me about it."

Huffing out a deep breath, I relent. "It was about the crash. We were on our way here and the rain was falling and…I had to see it all happen again," I whisper.

Wrapping gentle arms around my trembling figure, Riley whispers back, "I'm sorry, Quinn. We shouldn't have had to go through that once, let alone again and again."

Tears trailing down my cheeks, I nod numbly.

"Quinn," she says into my hair. "Do you want to know what I dream about?" Unwilling to use what I expect would be a wavering voice, I nod into her shoulder again.

"Well," she starts. "Since everything happened, my dreams have been filled with memories. Wonderful memories. And I love it. I love seeing them again and remembering the happy times."

"Doesn't it make you sad knowing that those things can't happen ever again?" I ask, pushing my voice to work through the tears.

"As much as that part sucks, memories are all we've got now. And I don't ever want to forget them, so I love dreaming about them, allowing my mind to go back to those places." She pauses for a moment. "I think you'll start to feel that way too, Quinn. Just try to focus on the good as much as you can, even though the bad is pretty much reigning over everything at this point."

"Thanks, Riley," I say genuinely. "I'll try. I really will." With that we share weak smiles.

"You wanna try to get some more sleep?" she asks. When I nod, she rises and ambles back to her bed, tugging on the flimsy blanket.

I lay still, listening for the moment when Riley's breathing slows and steadies. Flopping from one side to the other until I can't stand it any longer, I check my watch. It's 2:33 a.m.

Quietly climbing out of bed, I tiptoe to the kitchen window. The street lights throughout the park illuminate the area. Grabbing a bottle of water from the counter, I untwist the cap and take a swig. Our remaining four bottles stand like soldiers at attention, although they make a puny army. Glancing back out the window, a quiet calm settles over the trailer park. With nothing to do out here, I set the water bottle back on the counter and replace the cap. Just as I turn back toward the bedroom, movement outside the window catches my eye.

I instinctively duck below the window, slowly creeping up to expose as little of myself as possible. A man darts through the shadows. My eyes follow his path as he zig-zags from porch to bush to shed. He takes cover as he moves swiftly and deftly from home to home. I'm so busy watching him that I almost miss the face that pops up at the kitchen window. The one I'm hovering just below. I freeze in place, but I know I'm visible from his vantage point. I'm sure of it because our eyes lock in that split second.

Chapter 7

My temporary paralysis thaws as recognition dawns across both of our faces. It's Aidan! The guy who was filling water jugs at the cat house. He's not exactly a friend, but I don't believe he is a threat either. Although, he is slinking around the trailer park in the middle of the night. *What the hell?*

I maintain eye contact with him between windows as I scramble to the door. I quietly unlock it and slip outside. Aidan strides across the porch with light steps and meets me. His blue eyes are wide. "Scratch, is that you?" *What?* Narrowing my eyes, I cross my arms. He glances at my bandaged limb and awkwardly points to it. "Um, Quinn, right? You got scratched by a cat the other day when we met, right?"

Oooohhh. *Well, if he's going to give me a nickname,* "Yeah, it's me. How are you, Jugs?"

"Jugs?" a male voice barks out from behind me before it

evaporates into laughter. "Who the hell is Jugs?" he asks between snickers.

It's too dark to tell, but I wonder if Aidan's face flushes red. He speaks while I stare at the newcomer. "Jeff, this is Quinn. I met her a few days ago when I was out getting water," he explains. "She got a nasty scratch from a cat that day, so I thought Scratch would be a good nickname for her. I guess since she saw me filling the water jugs, she's apparently taken to calling me Jugs."

I smirk and extend my hand to Jeff. "Nice to meet you. And I prefer to be called Quinn, by the way." He returns my grin and shakes my hand. His muscular arms practically jump out of his short sleeves.

"Well, it's nice to meet you too, *Quinn*. I'm Jeff. Please don't judge me by the company I keep." He barely finishes speaking before he chuckles again. His demeanor puts me at ease immediately. Comfortable enough to ask the question burning in my mind.

"So, Jeff, Aidan, what the hell are you doing sneaking around here in the middle of the night?" Jeff's smile slides off his face. They glance at each other, shifting as if they are uncomfortable in their own skin. Aidan speaks first. "Well, Quinn, we're kind of looking for things. Things that people aren't using anymore so that we can…borrow them." Jeff nods quickly in support.

"Oh, I understand," I say, my arms sliding down to rest on my hips. "You're here to steal stuff."

The guys nervously glance at each other. Jeff points to the trailer door. "Is this your place? Maybe we should go inside, and we can explain." Um, not a chance I'm inviting two near-strangers into our only sanctuary while my sister is getting some much-needed sleep.

"That arrangement isn't going to work," I say sternly. As Aidan steps toward me, words spill from his mouth. "Look, Quinn, we're not bad people. We're just stuck. There was a bad accident and our car was wrecked. We're trying to make it down to Virginia and...we're just stuck." His eyes skim the ground dejectedly.

Oh my gosh. They got caught in that Route One accident, too. My doubts about them dissolve as my heart seizes in response to our similar circumstances. I reach out and place my hand on Aidan's arm. "I was in that accident, too. Our car was totaled," I say, my eyes misting. *Please don't let me start crying right now.*

"Aidan, man, we should probably get going soon," Jeff says, pulling me away from the threatening spiral of memories. His interruption is a welcome distraction.

"You're right," Aidan says, his eyes locked with mine. "But before we go, Quinn, you need to know, you're not safe here. Do you have somewhere else to go?"

"What are you talking about?" My head volleys back and forth between the guys. Jeff runs a hand through his short brown hair and exhales a sigh. He leans in conspiratorially and says in a hushed voice, "Look, we've been checking out the unoccupied homes around here. You know, just borrowing things to help us get by. But one of the trailers we went to, we thought it was empty..."

Aidan finishes for him. "Quinn, one of your neighbors is dead. We thought the trailer was vacant, so we went inside. We grabbed some canned food and other stuff from the kitchen and then we went to the bedroom to see if there were any blankets and pillows."

Tag-teaming again, Jeff continues. "We thought the smell was some food rotting. But… we found her just lying there on the bed, lifeless. Looked like she was stabbed. There was blood on the sheets and blanket." He pauses momentarily before breaking the silence. "We would have helped her if we could, but she was gone."

I raise a hand to cover my gaping mouth. The scream I heard the other night. That must have been it. *Why didn't I think to go see what was happening?* Maybe I could have helped her. Maybe I could have stopped it.

"Guys, which trailer? Where did you see this?" I don't know many of the permanent residents, and if it was someone who is only here for vacations, there's no chance I know her.

Aidan steps to the edge of the porch and points, "Two homes down in that direction. The one with the wishing well in the front yard." I wrap my arms around myself to contain the shiver running through me. The guys exchange a look and I know what's coming next.

"Look, we gotta go," Aidan says. "How about we check on you tomorrow? Would that be okay? Just make sure you're alright." Before I can filter my thoughts, they escape my lips. "That would be really nice. Yeah, I'd like that."

"Okay," Jeff says, nodding. The guys eye each other, silently communicating. They hesitate for just a moment and then Aidan speaks again. "Quinn, just keep a low profile, okay? Try to keep yourself hidden. We'll come back tomorrow night after it gets dark and we can talk more then."

"Okay," I say. "Thanks. I'll see you tomorrow. Or, today I

guess." The guys watch me head inside the trailer. I lock the door and peer out the window, watching them leave. I barely know them, but I sense they're like me and Riley—good people trying to navigate their way through a bad situation.

As I tiptoe back to the bedroom and settle under the covers, I vow to tell Riley everything. She deserves to know we could be in danger here and she needs to meet Aidan and Jeff. Maybe they are our ticket out of here.

Chapter 8

"Rise and shine, sleepyhead," Riley calls in a sing-song voice that immediately grates on my nerves.

I pull a pillow over my head and burrow under the blankets. "Go away, Riley. I'm tired."

A knock on the door startles us both. *Are Aidan and Jeff back already? Did Benny come to talk?* Riley jumps up and rushes to the door. Paranoia speeds through my brain like a race car. If it is Aidan and Jeff, she'll freak out. I forgot to tell her about meeting Aidan on my run. She has no idea yet that two guys know where I'm staying and plan to come back.

Panicked, I jump out of bed and rush toward the door. Riley's already there, and as she slowly opens the door, Slim Jim crowds the threshold trying to look casual, leaning one arm against the doorjamb.

I release an uncontrollable, audible sigh. *Okay, I'd much rather see Aidan, Jeff, and Benny all at the same time if it meant Jim wasn't here.* Plopping on the couch, I fold my arms, impatiently waiting for him to turn around and march himself out.

"Oh, hey, Quinn," he says, clearly disappointed by my presence, as usual. "Hi, Jim," I reply sternly. Riley cuts through the tension. "What's up, Jim?" she asks. After a quick glance my way, Jim leans conspiratorially toward Riley and paints a goofy smile on his face. "I just thought you and I could talk for a minute. Maybe step outside with me?" He bows a hand, motioning out the door, as if he's presenting her with a magical castle.

A small giggle escapes her. It quickly dissolves when her eyes slide over to my glowering glare. "Sure, Jim, I can talk for a minute. I'll be right back, Quinn," she calls.

Okay, I guess she's not so worried about keeping a low profile now. I might as well grab a shower. If she wants to talk to Jim alone, that's fine. She can have it. I'll just lose myself in the soap and steam.

When I twist the squeaky shower handle off, the trailer is silent. Jim better be gone. I leisurely dry off and dress. We definitely need to figure out this laundry thing. I hate putting on worn clothes after a nice hot shower.

Returning to the bedroom to ditch my dirty clothes, I spy Riley curled up in her bed. She glances up from a book just as I toss my rank pajamas in the ever-growing mountain of laundry in the corner. "So, what did Jim want?" I ask.

Riley answers, keeping her eyes glued to the pages of her book. "Um, just wanted to invite us to dinner." She cringes as soon as the words escape her mouth.

"Why on earth would we want to have dinner with him and his moron brother? I'd rather offer up my good hand to Tiger, the little demon that tried to claw my arm off," I say.

Riley closes her book, tosses it on the bed, and rushes over to me. Words spill out of her, matching her body's pace. "I know. I'm sorry. I told him we'd be there at six."

I look at her incredulously, waiting for an explanation. I don't have to wait long. "Okay, look, he keeps stopping by to check on us and asking questions about Mom and Dad. Let's just get this over with. Besides, we need to figure out if we're going to the base or not. We're running out of supplies. We can't stay here by ourselves forever."

She's right. We haven't quite figured out much beyond right here, right now. I've been waiting out the storm inside my head, but in reality, we have no idea what tomorrow will bring. We have to stop living as if we're already dead.

"You're right." I surprise us both by agreeing with her. "We have to figure out what we're gonna do. No one's coming to rescue us. Mom and Dad are gone and we're not little kids anymore. We need to take care of ourselves."

With that, Riley leans forward and wraps her arms around me. I reciprocate, savoring the instant comfort a simple hug can bring.

Our stomachs guiding us, Riley and I search the kitchen cabinets for breakfast. We take seats at the booth-style table and split the last pack of strawberry Pop-Tarts. After devouring every last crumb on the plate, I exhale a calming breath. "Riley, we need to talk," I say. She rushes to respond, "I know, we need to figure out what to tell Benny."

"No, Riley, it's more than that," I explain. "You know how I went for my run yesterday?" She nods in acknowledgement, watching me intently. "Well, I got scratched by that cat, you know, but I wasn't the only one there." Her eyes widen. "What are you talking about?"

As I explain meeting Aidan and our early morning reunion, as well as my introduction to Jeff, she absorbs every word. She folds her hands as if in prayer when I tell her about the body Aidan and Jeff say they discovered. Before I even finish, she starts wringing her hands and firing questions at me. "Do you think they were telling the truth? Who would do something like that? Should we tell someone?"

Scooting closer, I take her hands in mine. "I don't know. I think Aidan and Jeff are good guys, but I'm not ready to trust everything they say. I think maybe we should make sure they're telling the truth."

Her eyes open wider. "You want to go find the body?" Her voice rises with each word. She starts shaking her head back and forth, her body slightly trembling. "I don't want to see that. Maybe we should tell Jim and Dan. They're in charge of the park; it's their job, not ours."

I gently rub Riley's arm. "I *need* to see this for myself. I need to know if we can trust these guys or not," I explain. "You don't have to go inside. Just come with me and be my lookout in case anyone shows up."

She nods her head quickly, keeping her eyes downcast. "Let's get this over with," she says.

Chapter 9

Paranoia consumes the trailer as we prepare to investigate a murder. Worried that someone will see us breaking into the neighbor's home, and maybe accuse us of hurting her—if what Aidan and Jeff say is true, we take every caution before venturing outside.

Starting at opposite ends of the trailer, Riley and I slink along the walls, peering out each window. As we work our way toward each other, we quietly call out status updates.

"No movement out there."

"I don't see anyone."

"Nothing happening outside."

When we reach the living room, facing each other, our eyes lock. I give Riley one curt nod, silently saying *let's do this*. I lead the way outside and to the neighbor's. My thankfulness for the deserted park dissolves as I realize how wrong it feels. I have never seen this place so desolate. I miss the sounds of music playing, kids laughing, and dogs barking. Now I would be surprised to see anyone around. I've got to ask Benny where everyone is.

The walk to the trailer is short. A rickety wishing well adorns the front yard, confirming we're in the right place. Moving quickly, we focus on the canary-yellow front door. Each step that brings us closer to the entrance also answers how we'll get inside. The door is barely pulled shut. A strong breeze could push it open. *Maybe Aidan and Jeff jimmied the lock and now it hangs on its hinges with no ability to hold shut.*

Riley slithers down the porch wall, propping herself up next to the door. When I slowly push it open, the putrid scent of rot bombards us. Riley wrinkles her nose as I step inside. The door opens into the living room, which is cloaked in darkness. Curtains shroud the windows, blocking the sun's rays I pinch my nostrils closed and force my feet farther into the uninviting home.

While there's no sense in wandering around, my brain wrestles with my body. I want to get this over with, but fear hampers every movement. Deathly silence hovers in the air. Even in the dimness, I can tell that the layout mirrors Aunt Grace's trailer. My feet slowly amble down a hallway opposite the kitchen. I'm betting it leads to the bedroom.

The first door I pass is a bathroom. Nothing looks amiss in the pink room with no curtains. The white mini-blinds are closed but the bright glow of sunlight behind them breaches the otherwise dim interior. Towels hang neatly on a rack, and a soap dish rests on the sink. Unfortunately, any fragrance the pastel seashell-shaped soaps may emit is overpowered by the aroma of decay.

The next door opens to a bedroom. Once again, the curtains are closed, and I can only make out the outlines of a dresser, bed, and nightstand. I exhale with short-lived relief. If the guys are telling the truth, and my nose is accurately corroborating, there is another bedroom waiting for me.

The door at the end of the hallway stands at attention, sealing me from whatever secrets it holds. Raising my hand to knock, I pause before slowly dropping my arm back to my side. Silence and darkness permeate this space. I can't imagine anything alive awaiting me on the other side of the door. I reach for the handle and turn it in what feels like slow motion.

The rotting stench slaps me in the face when I swing the door open. My hands fly to my face, equally trying to cover my gasp and my breathing passages. This room is dark, but my eyes quickly adjust to the dim light and hone-in on the lump on the bed, fully covered by a white sheet stained with dark splotches. I've come this far. I can't stop now.

My lead-filled shoes resist each shaky step. Leaning toward the top of the bed, I gingerly grasp the sheet between my thumb and pointer finger. Slowly, I drag the sheet down to reveal exactly what Aidan and Jeff described. A thin woman with shoulder-length gray hair lies stiffly on the bed. Her skin bears an unhealthy gray pallor. Her wounds, which once erupted red, look black in contrast with the white sheet.

She's definitely gone. She must have been the one I heard scream the other night. I gently replace the sheet and walk backward toward the door, keeping my eyes on the woman, as if she might suddenly snap back to life. I leave the door open and turn on my heel in the hallway.

Swiping away the tears trailing down my cheeks, I trudge out to the living room and scan the surroundings. A large, blue plaid couch and matching recliner overpower the room. Bookshelves and end tables sit untouched, displaying an impressive collection of dust. Not finding what I seek, I stride to the kitchen. This room has clearly been ransacked. Cupboards hang open while silverware, plastic lids, and napkins lie scattered about the floor.

My eyes land on a cylindrical white vase that sits proudly on the window sill overlooking the sink. Perfect. Its artificial bouquet of brilliant yellow daffodils will never wither. Maneuvering around the mess, I extend my arm and grab the vase, emptying its contents. Turning back toward the bedroom, I stumble over a coffeemaker that was probably knocked down when this place was looted.

Graceful as ever, my kneecaps break the fall. My palms plant the floor a moment later, scoring an assist. Raising my head, I'm greeted by the wooden door of a bottom cupboard. It differs from all the others in that it's the only one still closed. Curiosity overpowers the distraction of my throbbing knees and I tug it open. The small cupboard is crammed with boxes and cans neatly organized. All of the food is organic, the bright packaging heralding its contents' healthy virtues.

"Quinn! Are you okay?" Riley's voice practically startles me right out of my skin. "I heard a thump and you've been in there for a long time."

"I fell. I'm okay. There's no one here, um, I mean there is

someone here, but she's…"

"So, they were right?" Riley asks. "What Aidan and Jeff told you is true?" I nod gravely. "So, what are you doing? Can we go?"

"I just need to do one more thing. I promise I'll be quick. Just give me two more minutes," I say, holding her gaze. Riley nods and steps back out the door. I pick myself up and rush down the hallway, daffodils in hand. I place them on the bed, lean down and whisper, "I'm sorry this happened to you. I'm sorry I didn't try to stop it. You deserve so much more, but this is the best I can do right now. I hope you're in a better place. I hope you have peace."

With that, I rise, leaving the corpse and her crypt, gently closing the bedroom door behind me. I pause for just a moment to brush the tears off my cheeks. Guilt overcomes me. I might have been able to help that woman. But I didn't. I hid under the covers, feeling sorry for myself. I wrap trembling arms around my body, trying to contain the regret seeping out. Rushing outside to the porch, Riley's eyes meet mine as she scrambles up and follows me back to our place.

Chapter 10

Catching up to me, Riley places a gentle hand on my arm. "Quinn, are you okay? Do you want to talk about it?"

"Let's just get back," I say as my eyes bounce from home to home. Whoever did this could still be here, just waiting to hurt someone else. My heart lurches and my feet stagger when movement catches my eye. Tilting my head toward the short, bald man shuffling toward us, Riley's eyes widen.

As our paths cross, the man barely gives us a passing glance. "Hello," he says, disinterested, continuing on his way.

"Hi," Riley replies.

At least we know we aren't the only ones in this whole trailer park besides Jim, Dan, and Benny.

Back at the trailer, Riley and I plop down on the dusty old couch and I breeze over the details of my discovery. As I replay everything in my mind, one detail feels off. "Riley, why would one cupboard in the kitchen be packed full when everything else in the room was a mess? Do you think whoever ransacked the place missed that one cupboard?"

"I saw that kitchen when I ran in to check on you," Riley says. "I can't imagine whoever did that left anything unturned."

"But that's the thing," I counter. "The other rooms were fine. It was just the kitchen that was torn apart."

"Well, that just shows that whoever did this wanted food and didn't care what they had to do to take it," Riley says. "Maybe they just couldn't carry it all?"

My mind slides more puzzle pieces together. "Riley, if whoever did this took the time to organize, and maybe even inventory that cupboard, then that means they're coming back for it."

Feeling unsettled, we decide to check in with Benny. We were supposed to be thinking about going to the military base, but too much else has cluttered my brain since we last talked to him.

As we tug the front door closed behind us, I think about how once again everything has shifted. After a week of isolation, we're spending more and more time outside the trailer. During that time right after the crash, I kind of forgot that life continued on outside of these walls.

Our quiet walk to Benny's is interrupted by what sounds like motorcycles revving to life in quick succession. Turning toward the commotion, we see two riders. The first wears a black helmet with a tinted shield that covers his whole head. It matches his solid black bike. It's smaller than a motorcycle; it must be some sort of dirt bike. When the second rider comes into view, it's clear who it is.

Jim's brother, Dan, doesn't bother to wear a helmet. His bug-like goggles must block the wind, but they certainly won't do him any good if his head meets the asphalt. The guys glance our way as they pass. Riley gives a quick wave and Jim throws a slight nod in our direction. Thankfully, they continue on their way, so we do the same.

Ambling up Benny's familiar front steps, we knock on the door. When he doesn't answer, my heart flutters with panic. *What if someone hurt him just like that woman?* I knock long and loud this time, not caring if anyone hears. *I need Benny to hear. I need Benny to be fine.*

After several long minutes, the sound of shuffling feet travels toward the door. Benny peeks out the window, his wrinkled face relaxing in recognition. Swinging the door open, he waves us inside. "Hi girls, come on in."

He moves stiffly. His chestnut face looks pale, and the wrinkles around his eyes are more pronounced than they were just yesterday. Riley touches his arm once we're inside. "Are you okay, Benny? We were worried when you didn't answer the door right away."

He waves her off. "Oh, I was just taking my afternoon nap, that's all."

"I'm sorry we woke you," I say. "Want us to come back later?"

"No, not at all," he says thoughtfully. "I've been thinking about you girls a lot, about your parents, and I'm glad to see you. I've always got time for you two."

The three of us settle into the living room and talk. We fill

Benny in on our discovery. He listens in silence, a fist to his mouth. I'm not sure if he's using it to hold his words or his emotions inside. Maybe a little bit of both. Guilt flickers through me when I realize how much grief and pain we have brought him over these few days. I know he cares, but maybe it's unfair of us to unload all of this on him.

When Riley and I finish, Benny looks between us. "That sounds like Mrs. Adams," he says, rubbing his chin in thought. "People make bad decisions when they're scared. I'm glad you girls have each other, but I still think you should be staying here with me." He pauses briefly, as though he wants to say more. "Have you girls thought about leaving? Going to the base?"

"We honestly haven't talked much about it," I admit. I'm not sure what else to say but Riley jumps in, voicing a thought I whole-heartedly agree with. "Benny, what if all three of us stuck together? What if we all go to the military base? Things aren't safe here anymore and we don't want to leave you behind."

Benny chuckles a hollow laugh. "Oh, girls, I just don't get around like I used to. I'd slow everyone down. I'd make the trip more difficult for everyone."

His argument has changed. I need some facts if he's going to play this card. "Benny, how far is it to the base? How many people are going and how are they getting there?" His steely gaze tells me he doesn't like my challenge, but he must know we're not going to just forget about him.

He releases a long exhale and rubs his forehead. His deep voice is strong. "There's a group of about 20 going. They're headed north to Dover Air Force Base. It's about 30 miles from here." I cross my arms and raise my eyebrows, waiting for him to answer the rest of my questions.

"They have cars, but they aren't sure how far they'll be able to drive." Riley and I look at him questioningly. Benny splays his hands in front of him as he explains. "With the Route One wreck, they might not be able to get through. And even if they do, there could be more wrecks along the way, blocking the road." That's right, of course. Who knows if the smashed and stacked vehicles have been cleared or how far their clutter reaches. They must block a good portion of the highway. In our single-minded goal to reach the trailer that first day, we didn't pay much attention, but I vaguely recall feeling like a tiny boat surrounded by a sea of cars and trucks. *It probably wasn't our smartest move to boycott the news.*

"Benny," Riley starts. "Who is planning to go? We've barely seen anyone around here."

He scratches his chin and answers. "There's about a dozen residents, permanent residents, that are going. They're packing, getting ready to leave. It's a little early in the season, you're the only ones I know of that came for vacation." He leans back, eyes bouncing back and forth between us. "The ones that can get around better have been making trips to the highway, trying to get a feel for a direction to head. They're gonna take four cars and make a caravan, sticking to the shoulder where the roads aren't cleared enough yet."

Scrunching my eyes and tightening my crossed arms, I eye Benny warily. "So, let me get this straight. You would just have to sit in someone's car for a few hours and tag along for the ride, but you don't want to go?"

Benny immediately adopts the face my dad would get when I challenged his authority. A flicker of heartache washes through me. As if on cue, my tag-team partner jumps in. "Benny, if you cannot give us a good reason to stay here, then we have to insist that you come with us." I'm impressed. For Riley, that is a forceful statement.

Backed into a corner, Benny's gray eyes shift between us as a smirk tugs on his mouth. "I guess saying that no one wants an old man tagging along won't help?" Riley and I rise in unison and wrap our arms around him. "No!" I say, smiling. We've won him over.

"Ugh. You girls wear me out. I think I need to get back to that nap you rudely interrupted," he says, grinning.

Now that we know he's going with us, even though he didn't exactly say it, I can freely laugh at his little joke.

"Benny, I'm really glad you're coming with us," Riley says softly. Her words are tinged with emotion. No doubt she feels as I do right now—Benny is the closest thing we have to family here and neither of us wants to let him go.

"How about we come back tomorrow to help you pack things up?" I suggest. Still grinning, Benny nods once. "That would be real nice, girls. I'll see you then."

Riley and I give Benny one more hug and then say our goodbyes. It's early afternoon but I'm emotionally drained. We plod back to the trailer and grab a quick, and late, lunch. We weren't very hungry after finding Mrs. Adams' body, but now my stomach is demanding sustenance.

Raiding the cabinets, we find one lonesome can of spaghetti that must have been hiding during our previous searches. After we scarf it down, I inform Riley that I'm following Benny's lead and taking a nap. She follows me to the bedroom, and as my eyelids grow heavy, the last thing to cross my vision is Riley settling into the other bed with her Kindle.

Chapter 11

Talking to Benny must have eased much of the burden on my mind because peaceful dreams dominate my sleep. Visions of Riley, Benny and I at the military base flash through my consciousness. As we enjoy a salty breeze on a sunny afternoon, a cocoon of safety envelops us. Gently, my mind eases out of the dream and my eyes flutter open.

My eyes sweep the room, landing on a Riley-shaped lump in the other bed. She fell asleep too. Glancing at the wall clock with starfish representing every other number, I confirm my suspicion. It's 5:30 and we've got to get ready for dinner with Slim Jim and Dim Dan. A root canal sounds more fun right about now.

After gently waking Riley, I splash some water on my face and tug a brush through my tangled brown locks. Just as we're ready to leave, Riley insists that we bring something with us, like a host gift. I am certain Jim and Dan have no idea what a host gift is and thus there is no need to bring anything. Riley's manners win and together we scavenge the kitchen for any food we can afford to share. Our stores are dwindling and the best we can do is a box of expired saltines.

Forcing my feet out the door, I trudge behind Riley for the short walk to Jim and Dan's trailer. Before Riley can even raise her arm to knock, Jim swings the door open and brandishes a sly smile. "Thought I saw you heading this way," he says.

"Thanks for inviting us for dinner, Jim," Riley politely answers.

He motions for Riley to enter. I follow her, sealing my lips in hopes that I can avoid saying something rude.

Dan buzzes around the kitchen, overseeing the stove. Steam pours from a medium-sized pot and the aroma of barbequed meat penetrates the air. Spatula in hand, Dan throws us a wave.

"Hey, Dan," I say. Dan's a decent guy. His biggest flaw is being Jim's brother.

After some idle chit-chat and the presentation of our unimpressive host gift, we settle at the table and begin passing around plates of food. Dan has prepared what looks like chicken, buttered noodles, and creamed corn.

Piling noodles on my plate, I start asking questions before Jim can. "So, where's your dad?" When silence greets me, I assume my question sounded a bit blunt, maybe because I've said about two words since I arrived.

Jim's expression darkens, but before he can respond, Dan answers, "Um, Dad passed last fall. Heart attack. Went to sleep one night and…never woke up."

I hold Dan's gaze to convey my sympathy. "I am so sorry. I had no idea."

Riley speaks up, "I'm sorry too. Your dad was a good man. I bet everyone misses him around here."

Their mom left when the boys were very young, so that means they're on their own now. *Just like me and Riley.*

Jim's face softens, but it looks forced. "Well, Dad had a good life. Now Dan and I watch over the park and everyone here." My face flushes as I remember how Jim's been coming around to check on us. If they took over the property maintenance for their dad, then they really did come over just to check on us. *Why do I always have to be such an ass and expect the worst from people?*

"Well, come on now, let's dig in," Dan says, his eyes volleying around the table. "Might as well eat while it's still hot." With that, he forks a small slab of meat and pushes it onto his plate with his finger. Ever the gentleman, he passes the plate of meat to me when he's done serving himself. The barbeque scent makes my stomach rumble, but the meat looks really stringy. I take a shot at asking nicely.

"Dan, this smells really good. What kind of meat is it?" It doesn't look like pork or chicken. Dan and Jim exchange a knowing glance, and Jim answers me. "Well, Quinn, Dan and I went hunting a bit today. Down the road there's a…chicken farm, and we went and got ourselves a chicken to cook." Dan chuckles under his breath.

"You stole someone's chicken?" I blurt.

Riley kicks me under the table.

I'm not sure this is chicken but whatever it is, I'm not eating it.

"We didn't *steal* anything," Jim says. He swipes away the trail of barbeque juice running down his chin. Dan holds a bowl out in front of me, "Quinn, have some noodles." It seems like every conversation we have ends up with Jim and I at each other's throats.

"So, Riley," Jim starts. "What's your family planning to do now that the highway is a shit storm?"

Riley shoots me a quick glance and stumbles over her words, "Well, it's really just me and Quinn now. Mom and Dad...We got into an accident on the way down here and Mom and Dad..."

I finish for her, explaining that, between the hammering rain and the shaking ground, we were powerless to avoid landing in the middle of what felt like a NASCAR smashup. Jim and Dan listen intently as I describe how the front half of the car was crushed, yet Riley and I were able to walk away from the backseat physically unharmed.

"Oh damn, Riley, you were in the Route One wreck last week?" Jim straightens in his chair, genuine concern overtaking his features.

Riley stammers, "Y—yes. Quinn and I walked to the trailer and kind of laid low for a while."

"Oh man," Jim says. "Dan and I heard all kinds of commotion that day. We hopped on our dirt bikes and raced over to the highway. It was just bumper to bumper metal and glass, people and cars everywhere," he says. "I wish I knew you were there. I would have found you, Riley."

Um, I was there too. It's as if I've completely disappeared from this conversation. Dan must feel left out as well because he chimes in.

"It was a mess," Dan interjects, as if our memories and Jim's recount aren't clear enough. He starts counting off what happened on his fingers. "So, first a nasty rain storm hit, then the ground started shaking from that earthquake. A few days later, they started talking about some franking accident because of the aftershocks."

Riley asks before I can, "What? What are you talking about?"

Jim jumps in to translate for us. "He means fracking. Didn't you hear about this? It was all over the news."

All over the news? Of course. Jim and Dan have actual cable TV. Our small screen has just a few static-tainted local channels. Aunt Grace doesn't bother with cable since the trailer is only used a few weeks each year. And, it didn't exactly help that we turned the TV off after the first few days. I'm guessing Jim and Dan have a really good home entertainment set-up to compensate for what I imagine are pretty flimsy social calendars.

For once, Jim has my attention and I want to hear what he has to say. "Jim, what are they saying? What happened? And what's happening out there now?" I jab a thumb toward the door.

Jim takes a big bite of meat and leans back in his chair. He loves feeling important. It probably doesn't happen too often. He's going to savor this moment, along with that stringy white meat he just shoveled into his mouth.

After a nice long pause for effect, Jim wipes his mouth with the back of his hand and finally explains that three days after the wreck, right about the time Riley and I tuned out the news, there was a fracking accident in the river basin. He rests his elbows on the table and steeples his hands. Apparently, this was controversial because months before some environmental group—"tree huggers"—as Jim calls them, were fighting to ban fracking anywhere in the state. A judge disallowed the proposed ban and a company swooped in and started drilling into rocks. While the initial earthquake didn't appear to impact the fracking site, aftershocks did. "Anyway, this company was out there, pumping thousands of gallons of water into the drill site when a pipe sprung a leak, dumping contaminated water into the basin," Jim concludes.

"So, this is all related," Riley says with a pained expression.

"That's right," Jim says, facing her. "Some random ass earthquake happens in the Atlantic, then its aftershocks screw up a fracking site. And we're kinda sitting in the middle of it."

Riley and I face each other, the same questions racing through both of our minds. *What about home? How far did the aftershocks reach? I vaguely remember the news mentioning Pennsylvania, but I was half-zombie at that point.*

Riley voices our fears. "Jim, did they say anything about Pennsylvania? Was there a lot of damage there?" Jim slips on his imaginary concerned mask to answer her. He reaches over and rests his hand on hers. "Riley, the news is saying that thousands of people are dead or missing. Between the highway accidents and bridges collapsing—"

"And more bridges could have fallen," Dan says, hunching his shoulders in question. "I bet all kinds of buildings could have toppled like dominoes."

"Government's stepping in," Jim says. "They're telling everyone affected by the earthquake to go to designated shelters throughout the state. This thing ran up the East Coast, but Delaware got hit pretty bad, no doubt about that."

I'm not sure if I'm more shocked by this information or by the fact that I actually want to hear what Jim has to say. "So, Jim," I start, "do you think it's all over now or do you think it's going to get worse?" My eyes meet Riley's as understanding washes over us. This is so much bigger than us.

"Well, I do think things are about to get worse," Jim says. "I think that earthquake was just the beginning of a shit storm."

Chapter 12

The rest of dinner is pretty quiet as Riley and I contemplate this newly-acquired information. My brain battles between wanting to ask more questions and wanting to shut down. My inner sloth wins, and I stop asking questions.

Once the guys clear every last crumb of food from their plates, I stand and start clearing the table. This conversation has wiped me out, and I'm tired of pushing the gristly meat around my plate. Before I even make it to the sink, Jim pipes up, "How about you girls clean up while Dan and I have a beer?" And I'm suddenly reminded why I don't spend more time with the Masters brothers. I have enough manners to help clean up after a meal, but I don't appreciate the whole *women clean the kitchen, so the men can sit and drink* expectation.

Riley stands, shooting me a keep-your-mouth-shut look. She responds before I can. "Sure, Jim. Thanks again for dinner, guys. We appreciate it. We'll clean up."

The guys stop by the fridge and grab a six pack before they head outside. Riley and I swing into action. I beeline back to the table and stack the remaining dirty dishes while Riley fills the sink with warm, soapy water.

While she starts scrubbing plates, I gather the empty packaging Dan left behind when he tore open the noodles. *Organic Pad Thai Rice Noodles.* Hmmm, I don't picture Dan and Jim the type to buy healthy foods. They're more beans-and-weenies kind of guys.

"Quinn," Riley whispers in my direction. Confident she's captured my attention, she continues. "What do you think that meat was? It was really greasy."

I didn't notice she actually ate it. "Riley, I didn't eat any. I didn't like the looks of it, so I ate the noodles and hid the meat under my napkin."

"I wish I thought to do that!" Riley says. "Let's finish up and get out of here."

"Sounds good to me," I say, suddenly remembering the scream I heard the other night. With all of our dinner talk about the disasters, I'd forgotten to tell Jim and Dan about the body and ask if they saw or heard anything suspicious. "Hey, you keep going in here and I'll go out and check on Jim and Dan. You know, see if they need anything."

She narrows her eyes. I get it. *I would never offer to do something nice for Slim Jim.* "Look, I need to take the trash out. I don't want that rank meat from my napkin to stink up the place. If they smell it, they'll know one of us just pretended to eat."

"Okay!" Riley returns her focus to the sink. "I just need a few more minutes here."

With that, I grab the trash and scurry out the front door. Jim and Dan are settled in their green and tan lawn chairs, guzzling away. Jim looks surprised to see me, his eyes shooting to the garbage bag in my hand. He jumps out of his chair. "What are you doing taking the trash out? That's a man's job. You go back to the kitchen." He reaches to grab the bag, but I side-step him, abruptly slamming into Dan. I drop the bag in surprise and its contents spill. In my rush, I neglected to tie it shut.

"Jesus, Dan. I'm sorry. I didn't see you," I stammer. Before Dan can respond, Jim curtly commands, "Go back inside. Dan and I will clean this up."

In that instant I decide I don't care if they see the uneaten meat. They are more than welcome to pick up the trash with their bare hands. I scan the mess, barely visible in the fading daylight. Just as I turn to step back inside the trailer my eyes land on a shiny yellow collar.

Flashbacks of my run flicker through my mind. The cat-infested yard. Tiger's squishy belly and scythe-like claws. A yellow collar. I remember the shiny flecks that shot tiny glares into my pupils. Slowly walking back inside the trailer, I fumble over my own feet. The heat of Jim's gaze bores into my skull. I stumble back inside the trailer, a little dazed.

"Hey there," Riley greets me. "All done in here. Ready to go?"

I nod my head quickly, meeting her eyes.

"Quinn, what's wrong?"

I shake my head and whisper. "We'll talk at home. Let's get outta here."

We breeze past Jim and Dan, thanking them in passing. Riley

70

mumbles something about us wanting to get home before it gets too dark outside. When I glance back, Jim's eyes follow us intently. He knows we're spooked.

As soon as we make it back to the trailer, we slip inside, lock the door, and plop on the couch. Riley turns sideways, facing me. "Quinn, what is it? What's wrong?" I unload my suspicions slowly. I can't just blurt out that I think Dan and Jim caught and served up Tiger on our plates tonight. Riley's face morphs from disbelief to disgust. As I speak, her hand flies to her mouth.

"Quinn, I ate that meat tonight! Are you telling me I ate a cat?"

The living room lamps are pretty dim. Since people know we're here now, there's no point in keeping them off anymore. Even in the dim light, Riley's complexion tinges green. I can't lie to her. "Riley, I'm sorry, but the more I think about it, the more I think I'm right."

Riley jumps up and races to the bathroom. In this small space, I can clearly hear her retch and then rinse her mouth. A few minutes later, she returns to the couch, slinking into the cushions. Her face looks gaunt, her skin paler than usual.

"Why don't you just lay down and relax while we wait for Aidan and Jeff to show up?" I urge. Thankfully, she humors me. When she curls up on the couch, I grab a thin blanket from the bedroom and cover her. Her back faces me, so I can't tell if her eyes are open or not. Either way, I think some quiet time is just what she needs. I decide it's a good time to inventory what's left of our measly food provisions.

Chapter 13

In the rapidly fading sunlight, I remove every consumable crumb from each cabinet and drawer. I move systematically from left to right, placing all of my finds on the kitchen table. Our stash consists of two cans of fruit cocktail, three cans of tuna, one very dusty can of beef stew, a partially crushed box of spaghetti, a six-pack of pineapple juice, and about a dozen single-serving sized water bottles. We gave the last of our saltines to Jim and Dan, so no more crackers.

I drop my head and rub my forehead. We don't have much food left. Luckily, our appetites have been nearly non-existent, but we do need to think about the future. I'm startled out of my thoughts by a sharp knocking. I glance over at Riley, who is sitting up on the couch. *Was she just sitting there watching me?* I rush to the door and peek out. Sure enough, it's Aidan and Jeff. I open the door a little wider and motion them inside.

"Hi, guys," I say in greeting. "Looks like you found us again with no problem." They both stare as their eyes fall on Riley. "Us?" Jeff questions. "I didn't know someone else was here."

As Riley rises from the couch awkwardly, I quickly step between her and the guys. "Yes, I guess I didn't mention it before. This is my sister, Riley." She extends her right hand and the guys reciprocate. She gives each a nod, telling them it's nice to meet them.

Jeff's eyes twinkle with amusement as he glances around the trailer. "You hiding anyone else in here?"

"Just our two pet Dobermans, but they only attack on command. Oh, and when they're hungry. And did I mention we're almost out of dog food?" My tone remains steady as each lie rolls off my tongue.

The guys shift uncomfortably and watch me carefully. The moment my eyes meet Riley's, we both burst out laughing.

Jeff rubs his chin and Aidan pastes a smirk on his face. "Boy, Riley, I didn't know your sister was such a comedian," Aidan says.

We dial back our laughter to quiet chuckles and give the guys our full attention.

"I'm sorry, I just needed a little humor," I explain. "Seriously guys, would you like to sit down?" I motion to the couch. They eye it as if it's a hungry Doberman for a moment before cautiously shuffling toward it and easing onto the dusty cushions.

Riley and I sit in the recliners on either side of the couch.

Aidan is the first to speak. "So, Quinn, I assume you filled Riley in on...uh, what we found yesterday?" I nod. "Yes, we actually went and confirmed what you saw," I say.

Aidan eyes us both incredulously. "You went there? Just the

two of you?"

Riley and I look at each other and then turn back to Aidan. "Yes, we went. We had to know you were telling the truth. I had to see it for myself," I explain. "It looked like someone ransacked the place for food. Did you see the kitchen?"

"Yeah," Jeff says. "Looked like they tore it apart. Took every last crumb."

"Actually," I correct him. "They didn't take everything." Both Aidan and Jeff lean toward me. "We found a cupboard, one cupboard, and it was packed with boxes and cans of food."

"So," Jeff begins casually. "What did you do with all that food?"

Riley and I glance at each other. *Dammit. I didn't think to grab any of it. I wanted to get out of there as fast as possible after I paid my respects.*

"We fed it to the Dobermans," Riley says.

A genuine laugh escapes my lips.

Aidan and Jeff narrow their eyes at us. "You left it there, didn't you?" Aidan scrutinizes.

"We did," I say. "We were kinda freaked out; we just wanted to get out of there."

Jeff runs a hand through his hair. "I guess it's kinda up for grabs then, right? I mean, technically, Aidan and I found it, and you wouldn't have even gone there if we hadn't told you about the…situation."

I narrow my eyes and open my mouth, but before I can spew a retort to remind Jeff that the only reason he was even here was to steal, Aidan raises his palm before me. "Look," he says, shifting his gaze between us, "that food doesn't belong to any of us, but it's not doing any good just sitting there. And whoever did that to that woman, well, they don't deserve it. I say we split it. It might as well go to good use, and we deserve it more than some thug does."

I glance at Riley and she gives me a subtle nod. I meet Aidan's warm blue eyes. "That sounds fair."

We all turn toward Jeff, who rubs his chin and nods. "Alright then," Aidan says. "That's settled. Now, on to the next order of business."

Riley raises her eyebrows and crosses her arms. "And what would that be?"

The guys glance at each other before Jeff answers. "What's your plan? Do you live here?"

Riley and I take turns telling the guys about our failed vacation. We skim over the car accident and explain how we've been hiding out at the trailer since then. The guys listen intently. When we finish, they volunteer their story.

Aidan explains that he and Jeff are college roommates. Childhood friends, they decided to attend Temple University in Philadelphia together. As the end of their freshman year neared, they made plans to break up the summer with some road trips, their first one to the Florida Keys. They were headed south when they got caught in the Route One wreck that ended our family trip.

"So," Aidan explains. "We would like to continue south, but we have no transportation. We've just been biding our time here, trying to figure out our next step."

My mind wanders as a hazy plan forms in my mind. A plan that involves Jim and Dan's dirt bikes but not Jim and Dan. I blurt out, "I have an idea!" All three of them turn their surprised expressions my way. I need one piece of information first. "Where do you guys live, when you're not at school? Where is home?"

Jeff answers for them both, "Columbia, Pennsylvania."

Riley meets my eyes, questioning my intent. I flash her a smile and understanding washes over her face. "We're from Pennsylvania, too," Riley says. "Lancaster."

Everything's clicking into place. If we stick together, maybe the four of us can get back home a little easier.

"Guys," I start, and the words flow out of my mouth almost faster than I can think them. "I know where we can get two motorbikes. Why don't we gather our stuff and get the hell out of here? Forget about going south. Let's all go home. We can make our way around obstacles and drive through woods if we have to. Let's just do whatever it takes to get home."

I'm practically jumping out of my seat in anticipation, but Aidan looks away, running a hand through his hair, sending black tufts in every direction. In silent communication, he turns to Jeff, who's scratching his chin. After an uncomfortable moment, they look from me to Riley.

"So…it's not just the two of us," Aidan says slowly, motioning between him and Jeff. "We're actually travelling with some friends."

Chapter 14

I just stare at them blankly. It never occurred to me that they were travelling in a group. There's no way Jim and Dan's dirt bikes can carry more than two people each. Even that would be pushing it when you consider the weight of our backpacks. My hope deflates as the plan crumbles.

Jeff leans forward, running a hand through his hair. "You could meet them, you know. Maybe we can all come up with a plan and travel together. You know, safety in numbers?" He gives us a weak smile.

Aidan's back stiffens, and he interjects, "How about we take this one step at a time? Jeff and I can talk to our friends about you. But right now, how about we get that food before someone else does?"

Riley glances at me and answers for us. "Yeah, Aidan, that's a great idea." I finally find my voice. "We actually need to tie up some loose ends here anyway. A group is heading to a military base, and we have to decide if we're going with them or not."

Aidan's chiseled features turn serious. "Alright, let's get the food, we'll take our share back to our *camp* and tell our friends about you."

His emphasis on the word camp piques my interest. "Where are you guys staying?" I ask. The guys glance at each other again. I know we're entering into an uneasy partnership here, but it's not like we're going to take our imaginary Dobermans and hunt them down.

Jeff nonchalantly nods at Aidan, consenting to share the information. Still, Aidan is vague. "We're staying at a campground just down the road. When we crashed, we needed a place to stay, and we didn't want to hoof it all over the place looking for shelter."

Good enough. *At least they answered.* "Alright, so when do we get this food? I don't really want to go at night, but I think the sooner, the better. The longer we wait, the more likely someone else will take it."

"Agreed." Aidan and Jeff say in unison.

"Look," Aidan starts. "There's no sense in all four of us going. It would just make us more likely to draw attention to ourselves." He motions to me and Riley. "Why don't you two wait here. Jeff and I will get the food and bring it back to divvy up?"

Riley and I answer him at the same time, although our responses couldn't be further from identical. Riley squeaks, "That sounds great," while I state, "No. One of you should go and one of us should go."

Riley shrinks at my words.

There is no way I'm sending her over there, but I'm also not taking handouts just because we're females—and who knows if these guys will bring our half back.

Jeff raises a brow. "You sure? You don't have to do this, Quinn."

"Look," I say, "If this is some kind of partnership, we need to be equals. I'll go. Riley will stay here. Which one of you two wants to come?"

Aidan speaks first, beating Jeff by about a millisecond. "I'll go with you." When he holds my gaze, I wonder if admiration lurks in his eyes, or maybe that's just surprise at my stupidity. In the seconds it took to settle who's going, I've morphed from brave to terrified. The last thing I want to do is walk into a dark trailer harboring a dead body with a guy I just met.

In one fluid motion, Aidan stands. "Let's do this," he says. Rising on shaking knees, I chant a silent prayer that my mind can propel my body forward. If Aidan notices my hesitancy, he's decent enough to keep it to himself. "Do you two have any flashlights we could use?"

Riley nods and rises, striding toward the kitchen's junk drawer. Jeff stands and eyes me warily. I have to prove that I'm useful. "I'll grab a bag we can use to carry the food." As I head toward the bedroom, the guys' whispered words float through the air, but I can't make out what they're saying.

Just a few minutes later, the four of us are once again facing each other in the living room. Riley hands Aidan and I flashlights. Patting the empty beach bag slung over my shoulder, I announce, "Okay, I think we're ready."

"You two hold down the fort," Aidan says. "We'll be back soon." Tugging the door open, I lead the way outside with Aidan following close behind. We walk briskly and speak quietly. A chill dances through the air, and goosebumps erupt on my bare arms.

"Let's not use the flashlights until we get inside the trailer," he starts. I can tell he's gauging my reaction, appraising my willingness to let him lead. I nod my head in agreement. Although night has fallen, and the path is draped in darkness, we stay close as we move. I can see him clearly, so I'm guessing he saw my assent.

Glancing over at me, he whispers, "I need you to stand guard. We can't risk both of us going inside and not seeing someone approach. You stay low right outside the door while I run inside, grab the food, and get out of there." *Oh, thank you, Jesus! I really, really, really didn't want to go back inside there.*

Shrugging, I try to play it cool. "Yeah, sure. I can do that." He flashes me a warm smile and returns his eyes to the path. The wishing well comes into view, and we both know it's not far now.

When we reach the door, Aidan gives me a slight nod and pulls it open, slipping inside. I take my lookout position, hunkering down against the doorjamb. As I wait, my mind flashes back to the evening's events. It doesn't feel like we just had dinner with Dan and Jim tonight. I involuntarily shake as I recall my suspicions. Rubbing my arms to soften the goosebumps, I'm pulled from my thoughts by the sound of Aidan shuffling inside the trailer.

I trace a finger over the nearly-healed scratch on my arm. My souvenir from Tiger has almost faded. And just like that my mind drifts back to what I swear was Tiger's collar in Jim and

Dan's trash. A thought strikes my mind like lightning. I shoot to my feet just as Aidan slips out the door, bloated beach bag in hand.

Meeting Aidan face-to-face, I grab his arm, unable to control my need for information. "Remember the day we met? Remember all the cats at that house?"

He exhales a chuckle and runs a hand through his hair. "That's not what I expected you to say just now. You're kind of…intense sometimes, huh?"

I grab his shoulders, shaking him slightly. "Listen to me." I may be bordering on lunacy here, but I'm powerless to stop myself. He wipes off a smirk and replaces it with a serious look. I think he's humoring me, but I'll take it. Inhaling a deep breath, I ask, "Do you remember the cat that scratched me?" He nods. "Do you remember if he had a shiny yellow collar?"

He busts out laughing, quickly covering his mouth to suppress the noise when he remembers we're supposed to be sneaking around out here. When I cross my arms and glare at him, he has the decency to feign slight remorse. Swiping a hand over his mouth, it settles there as if to clamp down a response. Before my eyes, he turns on the charm. "I'm sorry, I thought you were joking," he says, guilt overtaking his features. "Um, what are you asking?"

I struggle to tamp down my annoyance. "Do you remember if any of the cats were wearing collars? You know, the cats we saw at that house the day we met." The words sound condescending as they fly out of my mouth, but I feel the need to be as specific as possible.

He scrunches his face in thought, narrowing his eyes, and

answers my question with a question, "They were wearing collars?" *Ugh. I give up.*

"Look, just forget about it," I say, frustration oozing out of each word. *I give up.* "Let's get going. I'm sure Riley's worried about us by now." I turn and lead the way back to our trailer. We walk the short distance in silence.

Chapter 15

Once we reach the familiar porch of my temporary home base, I hold the door open wide for Aidan and the loot. He plops the beach bag on the kitchen table, and Riley and Jeff practically sprint over from the couch.

She's wringing her hands as she rushes over. "I was starting to wonder if something went wrong," Riley confesses. "I wanted to come after you."

"Oh, nothing to worry about," Aidan reassures her. "Quinn rushed right in there and cleaned the place out. I slowed us down carrying all of this stash back. I probably should have just let her carry it. I think she would have been faster." He gives me a wink.

Why would he say that? But if he wants to make me look good, I'll take all the help I can get! Okay, maybe I can forgive his earlier discretion— flaking on the cat details. Flashing him a smile, I focus my energy on preventing my cheeks from flushing.

The four of us hover around the kitchen table, dividing the food into two equal piles. The conversation is easy, and Jeff's humor keeps the mood light. When we finish, my eyes wander over the stack Riley and I will share: four boxes of brown rice, three pouches of lentils, two boxes of dried pasta, two cans of tuna, six single-serving mixed fruit cups, and a canister of mixed nuts. It's a big improvement over the box of almost-stale saltines that was the highlight of our food inventory before tonight.

"Wow, guys," Riley says. "Thanks so much for bringing this back. I hate that we had to take it from someone's home but more than that, I hate that she doesn't need it anymore."

I gently rub Riley's arm and turn to the guys. "Let's get your half packed up. You can use the beach bag."

Riley helps me pack their share and I hand the bag to Aidan. "Thanks," he says, almost shyly. "Want us to bring your bag back tomorrow? I think there's more to discuss." I glance at Riley and the hint of a smirk on her face tells me she's fine with that. "Yes," I say confidently. "Why don't you come a little earlier though? If we are going to come meet your friends, I don't want it to get too late."

With that, Aidan flashes a perfect smile. The guys start walking toward the door and Jeff calls over his shoulder, "Nice doing business with you." Aidan throws us a small wave and says, "Until tomorrow."

As soon as we close and lock the door, I exhale a deep breath and announce my intent to catch some ZZZs. Riley agrees, and we ready ourselves for some much-needed rest.

Morning arrives way too soon. When sunlight illuminates my eyelids, I know it's time to start the day. Glancing across the room, I spy Riley in her bed, propped up on one arm, reading a book. I watch her for a few minutes, thinking about how we haven't even stepped foot in the trailer's other bedroom. I can't even count how many times Riley and I burst in there when the first rays of sun spilled into our room. We'd rouse our parents from sleep, so we could greet the day with sand and seagulls.

Maybe someday I'll be able to smile when I recall those memories, but right now they just renew the pain. Riley shifts her position and glimpses me watching her. "Hey, Quinn. Stare much?" My embarrassment pulls me from my thoughts. "Sorry, just waking up."

Riley switches off her Kindle and stretches. I restrain from criticizing her for using it again when I see her dig out a charger and plug it into the wall. It must be getting low on its charge by now. "Wanna grab some breakfast and check on Benny?" she asks.

"That sounds great, Riley," I say just before I rise and attempt to shine.

After we dress, we clear off the sand-colored kitchen table. We were so tired last night after Aidan and Jeff left that we didn't bother to put the food away. When I present a fruit cup to Riley, she nods and marches to the utensil drawer, retrieving spoons for us.

As we both peel off the thin plastic lids separating us from our tiny feast, Riley eyes me. "Quinn, why did you ask Aidan and Jeff about driving north with us? I thought we were planning to go to the military base since we finally convinced Benny to go with us."

"Honestly, Riley, I don't know what I was thinking," I admit. "I was just excited by the prospect of going home, but you're right. I don't want to leave Benny."

She smirks. "Are you sure it didn't have anything to do with Aidan and those sky-blue eyes? Or maybe Jeff and his muscular arms?"

"Wait, Jeff's got muscular arms?" I ask.

She doesn't even bother to answer me. "I knew it!" she exclaims. "*Quinn likes Aidan,*" she chants in a sing-song voice. We both collapse in a fit of giggles. For a brief moment, it feels good to just be a girl who can laugh about her latest crush.

We finish our breakfast and squirrel away last night's food bounty in a cupboard. No matter what, we won't be staying here for much longer, but if whoever ransacked Mrs. Adams' trailer decides to peek in our windows, I don't want to leave a bullseye sitting right out in the open.

As I slide the last box of rice into one of the lower cupboards, the word *organic* catches my eye. That's right, all of the food I saw in Mrs. Adams' trailer was organic. Flashbacks of cleaning up Jim and Dan's kitchen last night come to mind. The noodle packaging I threw out—it was organic rice noodles. At the time I thought it was strange that Jim and Dan would be in possession of healthy food. I shoot to my feet in one swift motion.

Startled, Riley gasps and casts her wide eyes at me.

My hand flies to my mouth as I rethink my accusations.

"What—what's wrong?"

Thoughts rush through my brain like a roller coaster plunging downhill. Grabbing Riley's hands, my intense gaze latches onto hers. "Riley, I think Jim and Dan are the ones that killed Mrs. Adams. I think those noodles Dan cooked last night came from her trailer."

Riley shakes her head no and slowly backs away from me, out of my grasp.

"No, Riley, just listen to me. I didn't tell you, but the other night I heard a scream. I didn't say anything about it because I didn't want to scare you, but then when Aidan and Jeff told us about what they found…I thought maybe that was what I heard."

Riley brings her hands together to cover the lower half of her face, but at least she's stopped shaking her head. I take it as a sign to continue. "And remember what I told you last night? About seeing that collar in the trash bag after we cleaned up from dinner?"

She nods.

"I think Jim and Dan killed Tiger and Mrs. Adams."

"That's quite an accusation," Riley starts, pausing for a moment. Her eyes narrow as she processes my words. "I guess it could make sense, though. I would have never thought…" she trails off, shaking her head.

As much as I detest Jim, I never figured he was capable of something like this.

"Although…" Riley continues. "Their dad is gone, and he probably kept them in line. Now they're in survival mode, only thinking about themselves."

"Let's take a walk and visit Benny," I say. "We should fill him in on what's going on and see what he thinks. And no matter what, we need to make sure he's been packing." Riley nods in agreement.

Chapter 16

The trek to Benny's house is largely silent as we're both lost in our thoughts. My sister and I are the same in this respect. We need to slide all the pieces of this puzzle around mentally, trying to decipher what truly makes sense. When we reach his door, I raise my fist and rap my knuckles on it.

We hear fast-shuffling feet approach the door. When it cracks open, a middle-aged woman, slightly taller than me, peers out. She opens the door wider when she recognizes us. The funny thing is, I have no idea who she is. "You must be Quinn and Riley," she says, smiling.

Riley and I nod slowly, gawking at the woman. "Girls, come on in, I'm Benny's friend," she says, stepping aside and motioning us forward. Crossing the threshold, we both search our surroundings for Benny, to no avail.

"Come sit for a moment, girls," the woman says, leading us to the couch. Once we're all seated, Cindy introduces herself and fills us in. She's a longtime resident of the park, and also a longtime friend of Benny's. As a nurse, she makes a habit of checking in on the elderly residents. When she stopped in this morning, Benny was out of breath and sweaty, exerted from answering the door. After quizzing him on how he was feeling, she ran home and got her blood pressure cuff. When she checked Benny's reading, it was sky high.

As she speaks, I take in her appearance. Stray gray hairs mingle with the midnight black mane that drifts to her shoulders. I wonder if those follicles display the worry she feels for the older residents like Benny. Shaking myself out of distraction, I return to the conversation.

Cindy explains that she spent the day watching over Benny to make sure he took it easy.

Riley and I sit politely and listen, but we both grow antsy as the words we have to say threaten to spill out. It's great Cindy's taken care of him, but we're here now.

"Girls," she starts. "I know Benny talked about going to the Air Force Base with you, but he really needs to stay put until we're sure he's okay." She pauses and looks between us, waiting for a reaction. My heart plummets. "But we're just going to sit in a car, he can do that," I counter.

"Oh, honey," Cindy speaks softly. She adjusts her glasses and her warm brown eyes meet mine. I know that we all want the same thing—what's best for Benny. We just have different definitions of what that is in this moment. "He has to relax to keep that blood pressure down. I know the group is leaving tomorrow for Dover Air Force Base. Benny told me you girls were going to come by today. He's resting, and I don't want to wake him, but he told me that he wants you girls to go with the group."

I start to shake my head no, but Cindy gently places a hand on each of our shoulders. "Girls, I promise you both that I will bring Benny to that base myself as soon as his blood pressure reading is normal." She looks back and forth between us. I don't know her, but Benny does. And I believe he trusts her.

Riley nods her head. "Cindy, you're right. We want Benny to be safe. When you think he's ready, we'll be waiting there for him."

Shuffling gravel as we go, Riley and I trudge back to the trailer, deflated from our visit to Benny's. "I guess we should start packing, huh?" I murmur.

Riley doesn't even look my way when she mumbles, "Yeah."

In near silence, we gather our dirty clothes. Digging into my impressive mound, I separate out like articles to form smaller piles. Apparently, Riley was folding her dirty clothes the whole time we've been here, so her bags are packed in record time.

Riley plops on her bed and watches me fold. She speaks slowly, as if she's thinking out loud. "Quinn, you know how you said last night about maybe *borrowing* the dirt bikes from Jim and Dan?" I forgot that thought even crossed my mind. She must be cooking up an idea.

"Yeah, of course," I respond. "Well," she continues. "If they really hurt that neighbor and the cat, then maybe they deserve a little payback. Maybe we *should* take their bikes. It'll put them out of commission for a little while and it could help us get out of here faster."

Electricity shoots through my veins. I didn't think Riley had it in her to support a plan like that. "I'm not against it, but what do we do once we have the bikes?"

"Let's go home," she says, defeated. "I'm tired of trying to figure out what to do, where to go. I don't want to go to some military base. I just want to go home."

She's right. We've been through enough. Home won't be the same, but it's where we belong. "Me too. Let's do it."

"Okay, good," she continues. "I have a plan."

Chapter 17

Riley and I finish up a simple dinner of tuna and mixed nuts just as a knock thuds on the door. True to their word, Aidan and Jeff arrive before dark. I let them in while Riley quickly clears the table.

"Evening, ladies," Jeff greets us.

Aidan gives a slight nod.

"Hey, guys," I say.

"So, you ready to come meet our gang?" Jeff asks.

Riley and I glance at each other before she responds. "Why don't you guys have a seat? We have a little proposition for you."

Jeff rubs his hands together and smiles. "Woohoo, this sounds interesting!"

Aidan chuckles and they both step to the living room area and sink into the couch.

Riley and I explain our plan. If the guys are agreeable, Riley will go visit Jim and Dan, luring them to our trailer. I'll be hiding outside of their trailer, and I'll run in while they're distracted and find the keys for the dirt bikes. Once I have the keys in hand, I'll hoof it back to our trailer as if I just came back from a run. I'll turn on the rude to try and get them to leave. Once they're back home and settled, the four of us will sneak over and wheel the dirt bikes out of the trailer park. After we're a distance away, we'll start them up and drive back to Aidan and Jeff's camp.

Aidan rubs his chin and squints. "Let me get this straight. You got all judgy because Jeff and I were collecting food from vacated trailers. But now you want to steal dirt bikes from your neighbors? How is that okay?"

Oh my gosh. After everything we said, *that's* what stands out in his mind? "Aidan," I start. "These guys are bad news. I'm pretty sure they're the ones who killed the woman you guys found, and I'm pretty sure they killed and cooked one of the cats from that yard where we met." I pause to let the information sink in.

"No offense, Quinn, but you're starting to sound a little crazy," Aidan says.

I drop my head back on the couch cushion and groan. *He can be so frustrating sometimes.*

"A little?" Jeff adds. "I'd say you're being kind with that estimate."

Riley speaks up. I watch in awe as my meek sister commands the conversation. "Guys, Quinn's right. Jim and Dan are showing their true colors. They don't care who they hurt as long as they have what they need. We can't trust them, and it's not safe to stay here any longer. I can't think of a better escape than taking

94

those bikes, weaving through the wreck blocking the highway, and high-tailing it out of here. You guys have your friends and you have a plan. But Quinn and I, all we've got is each other."

Pride rockets through my chest. I've never heard Riley speak so firmly. The mood shifts in an instant, and the guys wipe the smirks off their faces.

"Not to sound like an ass," Jeff starts. "But what's in it for us? I'm not saying we won't help you, I'm just wondering what our role is besides pushing the bikes out of here for you?"

"We only need one bike," I explain. "You guys can take the other. I know it's not just the two of you, but maybe you can use the bike somehow?" I know we're making a lot of assumptions here—like the bikes will have gas in them and won't break down, but the more Riley and I talked about her plan, the more we felt the need to share one bike. We won't be able to carry as much with us, and we won't have a backup bike, but at least we can't get separated this way.

Jeff looks to Aidan and he finally speaks. "How about this," he rubs his chin again in thought, "We'll help you get the bikes, but then the four of us head back to our camp. You meet our friends and together we'll all figure out what to do next."

Looking to Riley, my thoughts reflect in her eyes. *Why should we go to their camp and meet their friends? We have our plan and, once we have transportation, all we need is each other to carry it out.* Riley throws me a subtle nod and I know we're both thinking the same thing. *If this is what it takes to get that bike, we'll do it. It's just a brief distraction from our goal.*

"Deal," I say confidently.

Aidan raises his hand to shake mine and I slowly take hold

of his. Eye to eye, we seal the deal with mutually firm grips. I silently pray that my face isn't flushing as my brain recognizes that we just briefly held hands.

Jeff stands, thankfully taking the focus off of me and Aidan. He claps his hands together once and says, "While I thought this arrangement was going to be much more interesting, I see we have a plan. Let's do this."

Riley and I grab the backpacks we filled earlier and hand them to Jeff and Aidan, who promptly sling them over their shoulders. We can't exactly carry backpacks around with us if Dan and Jim are going to believe our story. Riley unfolds our crude map and shows the guys where Jim and Dan's trailer is— and where they keep the dirt bikes. I run outside to turn the trailer's water off. The plan is for Riley to tell Jim and Dan that she thinks a pipe burst because our water just stopped working. We don't want to cause any real damage to the trailer, so I'm just switching the water off, something I've seen my dad do at the end of every vacation after we loaded the car to go home.

Dashing back inside the trailer, I wave to the guys as Riley leads them out the door. She's going to point out some hiding places for them while I change into my running gear and sneakers. When she returns, we meet in the kitchen for one last pow-wow.

"You ready for this?" I ask her. She doesn't have a dishonest bone in her body. I'm still shocked that she ran with my idea. She nods with determination. "We're gonna do this, Quinn. We're getting out of here, and we're going home. We'll figure out something to tell Benny, but he'll understand."

I've never seen this side of Riley, but I like it. Her newfound confidence comforts me. Maybe I don't always have to take the lead. Tugging her into my arms for a quick embrace, she reciprocates before pulling back. She gives me one sharp nod, as if saying, "Go!"

Chapter 18

I walk outside and start stretching, just in case any wandering eyes catch my movement. After a too-brief warmup, I start jogging at a slow pace. I follow the dirt path that leads all the way around the park and duck into the wooded area at the far end, opposite Benny's trailer.

Thankfully, the sun is setting and a dim curtain spreads over the park. The surrounding trees, their mature branches already sheltering the area, throw shadows in every direction. I slowly slink to the hiding spot where Riley positioned Aidan and Jeff.

Jeff sees me first. "Quinn, I like your outfit. You should wear that more often." *What an ass.* My running tights are just that—form-fitting for ease of motion. My shirt is equally body-hugging, designed to pull sweat from my skin and keep me cool.

"It's my running gear," I say condescendingly. "I wear it for function—not form or to impress *you.*" Jeff raises his hands in surrender and says, "Hey, no need to get all worked up. I'm just saying that you won't offend anyone here if you want to wear stuff like that more often." Aidan shushes us with a quick swipe of his hand through the air.

Riley throws a sly smile our way as she marches to Jim and Dan's door, knocking frantically. When Dan yanks the door open, she slides on a mask of concern and pleas for help. He motions her inside, and she follows compliantly.

The three of us meld into the bushes as best we can. Watching intently, it's not long before Jim throws the door open and leads the way to our trailer. "Oh guys, thanks so much," Riley purrs as she trails Jim.

"Why do I need to come?" Dan mumbles to himself.

Jim throws him a stink-eye before slowing to match pace with Riley. "So, Quinn's gone?" He sounds hopeful.

Riley answers, "Yep, she went for a run. I wanted to take a shower, but I can't get the water to work. We can't stay here without water."

As they continue walking away from us, Jim says something about Riley staying with them. *As if any female would want to live with those two.*

Jeff whispers, "Sounds like they're not part of your fan club, Quinn. How's that possible?"

Before I can shoot back a snide remark, Aidan whispers, *"Quinn, go now—and hurry. Just get the keys and get out."*

I run full-speed toward the door, feeling self-conscious that the guys are staring at my butt. *No time to worry about that now.* I fly through the door, realizing we didn't have a plan for if the guys locked it. Luckily, that thought didn't occur to Jim and Dan either.

Although I was just here yesterday, the place is considerably messier. Empty snack bags and dented beer cans litter the living room end tables. Video game controllers sit idle on the coffee table, cords snaking out from behind the wooden entertainment center. Not a speck of dust on those. I'd bet they provide nearly constant companionship for Jim and Dan.

I shake my head to rein in my focus. Keys. I need to find the keys. I scan the wall on both sides of the door, searching for hooks or a key holder. Nothing. If the keys are anywhere on the end tables, I'm screwed. Besides not wanting to dig through the trash strewn about, I don't have time to waste.

Striding to the kitchen, I fumble my hands along the counters, pushing mail, dish towels, and pens out of the way. Finally, at the end of the counter, the bounty awaits. A round orange ashtray cradles two sets of keys. I have no idea what a dirt bike key looks like, so I'll need to take both keychains.

I swipe the ashtray and stash it in a cupboard on the opposite side of the kitchen. Maybe I can delay Jim and Dan's discovery that the keys are missing if one thinks the other misplaced the whole ashtray. With that, my work is done. I sprint to the living room and peek out the window. Seeing no movement, I slowly open the door, peering out one last time for good measure, and then dash to where Aidan and Jeff wait.

"Good job, Quinn," Aidan says, eyeing my bulging fists. I couldn't hide the keyrings even if I tried to right now. "Thanks," I say, slightly out of breath from the adrenaline rush. "Alright, phase two." I hand the guys the keys and they start walking casually away from Jim and Dan's place, taking a roundabout way back to our trailer.

Once again, I break into a jog along the gravel road, winding my way back to Aunt Grace's. All this adrenaline will support my story. Wiping the nervous sweat from my forehead, I look the part of someone who just finished a run. Within a few minutes, I'm right back where I started. Reaching the trailer's front yard, I bend forward, stretching my supposedly tired muscles.

Jim struts out the door, leaving it wide open. Riley follows him a moment later. "Everything looks good in there, I don't get it," he's murmuring.

Riley sees me first. "Quinn, hey, the water won't turn on, so I got Jim and Dan. I thought they could help us figure out what's wrong."

Jim's heading toward the water valve access panel.

I make a quick confession before he finds the sabotaged switch. "Oh, Riley, that's my fault. I'm sorry, I forgot to tell you," I explain, "I shut the water off. Nothing's wrong. I can turn it back on."

Clearly annoyed, Jim turns toward me. "Now why the hell would you do that?" he asks. As if it's any of his business.

"I just…with everything going on, I thought we should conserve water. I figured I'd turn it back on when we needed it."

"Well, nice if you would have told your sister," Jim snipes. *I've sufficiently annoyed Jim, so my job here is done.*

Dan wanders outside and Jim motions for them to leave.

Riley calls to them as Jim storms off and Dan hustles to catch up with his brother. "I'm so sorry guys. Thanks for coming over. Sorry to bug you."

Before a laugh escapes me, I dash into the trailer.

Riley follows and tugs the door closed.

We both collapse in a fit of giggles. I can barely breathe as I mock Jim. *"Nice if you would have told your sister!"* A fast knock on the door startles us both.

Riley jumps up and answers it. If Jim's back, he may lunge at me if he heard my impersonation.

Chapter 19

As soon as Riley cracks the door open, Jeff and Aidan push their way inside. "Forget about anything, ladies? Or should I say *anyone*?" Jeff says indignantly. Riley closes and locks the door as we both burst out laughing again.

Aidan and Jeff patiently wait while Riley and I expel the last of our laughter. Once we've calmed down, we head back to the bedroom to grab two more bags. The guys hid our backpacks from earlier with the bikes. Now we've got to load up. Riley and I don't plan to come back to Aunt Grace's trailer. It's too risky if Jim and Dan ever figure out that we had anything to do with their bikes disappearing. We've got to get word to Benny, just so he knows not to expect us at the base. Maybe we can figure something out after we talk to Aidan and Jeff's friends. We may have to make a quick stop at Benny's trailer before leaving town.

Gathering the last of the belongings we can feasibly carry, we make our way to the door. I turn to give the trailer one last look. Hopefully, it's goodbye for now and not forever. Until things get back to normal again—at least for the rest of the world. I have a feeling nothing will ever feel normal again for me and Riley.

After locking the door, we slink off through the night to where Aidan and Jeff hid the bikes. We all agree the guys should drive. They both claim they've ridden dirt bikes before, and Riley and I have no idea where we're headed anyway. We wheel the bikes out to the highway, into the center of the traffic mess. When we feel sufficiently concealed, Aidan and Jeff each hop on a bike and look at us expectantly.

Riley gives me a knowing look and hops on the back of Jeff's bike.

Heat sears across my cheeks as I walk to Aidan's bike and plant myself behind him.

Aidan and Jeff wear our backpacks across their chests so that we can hold onto them.

Trying to wrap my arms around Aidan is awkward, if not impossible, with one bag tucked across my chest and another slung over my shoulder, readying itself to bounce along my back the whole ride.

He turns his head toward me, our faces dangerously close. "You ready?"

With a big gulp and zero confidence I reply, "Yes." It's all the confirmation Aidan needs; he starts the bike and takes off.

Jeff follows.

I cringe when the engines roar to life. *Let's hope Jim and Dan are busy, caught up in some netherworld realm battling each other with medieval weapons.* I envision them sitting on their couch, a beer in one hand and a video game controller in the other.

Jeff and Riley follow close behind. We ride single file as we weave around both crashed and parked cars. Less than two miles down the road, the gaps widen, and the vehicles become fewer and further between. After a right turn, we hit open road and the guys drive the bikes parallel, as if they're fighter pilots in formation. The guys' giddiness increases along with the bikes' speed. Unfortunately, the added wind and motion leave Riley and I struggling to hang onto our flailing belongings and our drivers.

Thankfully, a few minutes later, the guys decrease speed and pull off the road. After taking two rights and a left, I think we've reached a dead end. A crumbling pavement path leads us through a gap in the trees just wide enough for a small SUV. The dirt bikes' headlights shine ahead, spotlighting a decrepit wooden sign dangling from a scraggly oak tree. White letters carved into the green sign welcome us to the Rustic Shores Campground.

The guys switch off the bikes' headlights and slow to a crawl. The engines are much quieter at a snail's pace.

In the moonlight I can make out the shapes of small buildings, cabins probably. They form a small village. The closer we roll toward the center of the space, the more structures come into view. A soft orange light flickers, bouncing off the external walls of a few cabins.

Aidan and Jeff stop the bikes, planting their feet firmly on the ground.

"We're here," Aidan announces.

Chapter 20

This place must have closed years ago. The ramshackle cabins look more like oversized sheds about to collapse. The road, or what is supposed to be a road, bears giant cracks with weeds choking out of every opening. I keep my thoughts to myself. As I climb off the bike, I reposition my bags, so they no longer dig into my shoulders and back. I notice Riley doing the same.

Aidan and Jeff switch our backpacks from their chests to their backs and then turn, watching us.

I take a deep breath and run my fingers through my hair, which is now completely wind-blown from the ride. Surrendering to the fact that it isn't going to get any better without some heavy-duty brushing, I shrug and say, "Ready."

The guys lead us along a narrow path winding around the back of the nearest cabin. It appears to be the largest structure in the cluster. When we round the corner and near a flickering campfire, I'm shocked by the size of the "group." Aidan said they were travelling with some friends. I expected more than two.

One girl and one guy, both seemingly around our age, sit on logs flanking the fire. Unless others are inside the nearby cabins, four people barely constitute a group. I clamp my lips shut before asking "Is this it?"

The guy and girl stop talking. Their eyes shift nervously from their friends to the strangers invading what is probably the only safe place they've known since the crash that stranded us all. As they rise to their feet, Jeff closes the gap and clasps his hand around the guy's shoulder, saying, "Hey, man!" The girl watches cautiously.

As if brokering a deal, Jeff maintains his position between *us* and *them*. "Jasmine, Wes, I'd like you to meet Riley and Quinn."

I throw a weak wave in the air and mutter a half-hearted, "Hello."

Always polite, Riley gives them both an enthusiastic, "Nice to meet you." Her words spring from a genuine smile. I can hear it in her tone.

Aidan moves past us toward Jeff. "Why don't we all have a seat and maybe get to know each other a little better?"

Riley and I move to the nearest log and lower ourselves onto it.

The guys each take a separate log, and Jasmine settles in next to Jeff. The orange glow of the flames illuminates her high cheekbones and full lips. Her dark, cautious eyes scrutinize me, resulting in a fierce expression that would be better served flaunting the latest shade of eyeshadow in a commercial or magazine. Curly black locks hover just above her shoulders, framing her face, and her golden-umber complexion appears flawless in the dancing shadows.

As if Jasmine's perfection isn't intimidating enough, her posture is stiff and uninviting. Jeff must notice too. He clamps a strong hand around her knee and gives it a shake. She jumps slightly but rewards his effort with a sincere smile. Okay, maybe she's just nervous around new people. I need to put aside my high school girl mentality. This girl isn't a threat to me. In fact, after tomorrow, I won't ever see her again. Riley and I will be on our way home. While one nightmare will be behind us, another will be just beginning.

I'm not sure how life will go on without our parents, but we have to try. Just as I'm about to mentally conjure up a list of which relatives we should try to get a hold of first, Wes breaks the silence.

"You guys did good," he says, nodding toward Aidan and Jeff. The flickering flame dances across his full lips and wide nose, giving him an eerie quality. "We haven't eaten all day and these two look like they'll be tasty!"

Chapter 21

My heart thunders in my chest as I steal a glance at Riley. Mouths hanging open, we gawk at each of the four people sitting before us.

Jeff and Aidan burst into laughter.

Jasmine grins with amusement.

"I'm just kidding, ladies," Wes says, breaking into a wide smile. "Just thought we could use a little icebreaker."

Riley and I glare at him.

"Sorry," he raises his hands in surrender. "Why doesn't someone else talk now?"

With that, I let myself relax a little. Conversation flows more easily, and we learn that Jasmine just completed her first year at Temple University. She plans to major in environmental law, using her education to defend and protect the environment. I can respect that.

Wes and Jeff are both part of Temple's ROTC program and they met in a military science course. While Wes plans to eventually join the Air Force, Jeff's aiming for the National Guard. Their military courses will prepare them to become officers in their respective branches.

Aidan proves to be the least predictable. He's majoring in geology and, based on how animated he becomes when he talks about land formations, he has a weird fascination with caves. I'm not really sure what the point of a degree in geology is, but I don't ask.

After the others share brief snippets of who they are, Riley tells everyone that she's seventeen but she's less than three months away from eighteen. Because of school registration date requirements, she'll be a senior in high school this fall. She's always been one of the oldest kids in her class, falling on the mature-end of the spectrum. She plans to go to college after graduation and become a child psychologist.

I nod in support. She has a very nurturing personality, and I think she'd make an amazing therapist.

We clearly share the same genes, as evidenced by our matching brown hair and eyes and average builds. But that's pretty much where the similarities end.

When it's my turn to speak, I admit that while I am sixteen, and clearly the youngest one here, I turn seventeen next month. I force myself to swallow the emotional abyss swelling in my throat at the thought of spending a birthday without my parents.

Riley gently takes my hand in hers and gives me a slight nod of acknowledgment.

I continue, telling the group that I'll be a junior in the fall.

Before anyone can ask, because they always seem to question why Riley and I are so close in age, I admit that I was a surprise to my parents. They always knew they wanted at least two kids, they just never counted on number two coming so soon after number one. So, for about five weeks out of the year, Riley and I are both the same age. My parents used to joke that we were twins for those few weeks.

A dark cloud of melancholy grasps me. No one asks about our parents, so Aidan and Jeff must have told them. Doubts and despair flit through my mind. *Is finishing high school out of my grasp at this point? Will Riley and I have the luxury of choosing career paths?* My little introduction was so automatic that I didn't consider how ridiculous it sounds when you add a healthy dose of reality to the equation.

I vaguely catch the conversation floating around the fire when Jasmine asks, "So, what are your plans now?"

Riley and I glance at each other before I answer. "We kind of *borrowed* a dirt bike, so we're gonna head home. To Pennsylvania."

"That sounds like a good idea," Jasmine says. "When are you leaving?"

Okay, I guess the chitchat is over, and she just wants to know when she can be rid of us.

Riley answers for us this time. "Tomorrow. We're leaving in the morning."

"Yeah, about that," Aidan starts. "Are you sure you want to make that trip alone? I mean, just the two of you?"

Jeff backs him up. "You know, we're heading south to drop Jasmine off, but then we're going home to Pennsylvania. We could all stay together and watch each other's backs." The flames

111

illuminate the scathing look Jasmine shoots Jeff. He's completely oblivious.

While it's really nice of them to offer, there's no way we're taking all that time to trek south and then backtrack north. And especially not with Jasmine. She's about as welcoming as a scorpion. While I wouldn't mind traveling with the others, she is seriously not someone I would ever choose to spend time with.

Riley replies, "Thanks, guys, but—"

Aidan cuts her off, "Just sleep on it, okay? Think about it. We should all get some sleep anyway."

Chapter 22

Wes offers to show us to a cabin. From the looks of it, they're all void of human occupants but very likely occupied by rodent and insect communities.

Aidan and Jeff call "Goodnight" to us as we follow Wes to the cabin just twenty paces from the fire.

Wes sweeps open the unlocked door, freeing an invisible cloud of musty air.

I swear something small and dark skitters across the floor as we enter. Its footfalls are soft, but a slight scratching sound reaches my ears as the intruder escapes.

Wes stops in the doorway, flips on a dim light, and turns to us. "Ladies, your chateau for the night." He runs his hand across his close-cropped brown hair. He looks pleased with himself, but I'm not sure why. This shack makes Aunt Grace's trailer look like a penthouse suite. *I can't believe I ever criticized that place.* The walls here are real wood, though—none of that fake paneling stuff like at the trailer. Except real wood rots and these walls have more cracks and crevices than the Grand Canyon. From a few feet away, they look slightly stronger than popsicle sticks.

I cross the dusty floor, ignoring the metal-framed bed, and study the wall. Squinting in the faint light, I see at least a dozen small holes punched in a six-inch square area. *Are those termite holes?* I turn to see Riley patting down the mattress on the bed closest to the door. *Maybe she's testing it for mice or spiders.*

She jumps back with a yelp when a volcano of brown bugs erupts from its center. She stumbles to the door backwards as the oval-shaped beasts spill across the bed. "I think those are bedbugs," she cries, pointing toward the offenders.

There's no way we're spending the night in this shack. The bugs were here first, and in my opinion, they've got dibs. "We can't stay here," I say, striding toward the door.

Wes' smile falls as he looks between us and the amber stream of insects. "Do you want to check out another cabin?" Riley and I both shake our heads vigorously.

"I gotcha," he says, smiling. "Let's get out of here."

He pulls the door closed, which is a pretty meager barrier between us and the cabin's vile inhabitants. As we wind our way back to the fire, I notice that Jasmine is gone. *Yes! Maybe she went to sleep.*

Wes interrupts Aidan and Jeff's conversation. "Hey guys, the ladies here would prefer *not* to stay in a cabin this evening."

Three sets of eyes land on us, seeking an explanation.

I glance at Riley as she pushes a stray lock of brown hair behind her ear and answers. "It's just that we've never really gone camping before, like rustic camping, and so we're not exactly used to it."

Leave it to Riley to soften the blow. It's good she spoke for us. I don't think I could have been that nice.

"They don't call this place *Rustic Shores* for nothing," Jeff quips.

"Honestly," Aidan says. "The cabins are all pretty much the same. It took us some getting used to but it's all we have. We don't even have a car to sleep in."

Okay, I officially want to go back to Aunt Grace's trailer. I didn't have to share my bed there with any six or eight-legged creepy-crawlies—at least none that I was aware of.

"How about we just curl up by the fire?" Riley says. My face snaps toward her as questions pour from my mouth. "You want to sleep on the ground? Outside? All night?" I have to clarify because her words make no sense.

"What other option do we have?" she asks calmly. "We can't just roll back into the trailer park with stolen bikes."

I know she's right, but sleep on the *ground?* "And Quinn," she adds. "We've got the fire. Maybe it will keep the bugs and animals away."

"Look," Aidan interrupts. "In our scavenging," he says, gesturing toward Jeff, "we found some blankets. They're all yours." He turns and strides toward the cabin next to the one they attempted to give us.

"Well, looks like this situation is under control," Wes says. "I'm gonna hit the hay. See you all in the morning." He turns and walks to the cabin Aidan entered.

Riley and I call, "Goodnight."

Jeff saunters over and leans in toward us conspiratorially. "So, ladies, just one more thing you need to know for tonight…" He pauses for effect, glancing back and forth between us. "The ladies washroom is just around the corner." He jabs a thumb toward a wooded area behind him. "Jasmine tells us it's just a few steps down from the Hilton."

"Great. I can't wait to check it out!" I say.

Aidan returns with two blankets and thrusts them toward us. He looks back and forth between us. "Do me a favor and wrap up tight. And sleep close to the fire. It's been getting really cold out here at night. Like, really cold."

"Yeah," Jeff adds. "Sure as hell doesn't feel like summer at the beach around here at night."

I give them both a salute, and after a final round of goodnights, the guys disappear to the same cabin as Wes. I wonder if Jasmine is inside that one too. I guess I wouldn't want to sleep alone in one of these rodent shacks if I were her.

After a quick trip to the bathroom, which is too kind a term for the windowless cinder block hovel, Riley and I wrap ourselves in the blankets Aidan gave us. Riley hands me a sweatshirt from her backpack to use as a pillow. My tired body seems to protest every position I try.

Eventually, I surrender to the inevitable, and as I gaze at the fire's dying glow, my eyelids start to droop. The sharp crack of a branch snapping sends my eyes wide open and my heart racing. Swiveling my neck back and forth, I search out the source of the noise.

When my eyes land on Riley, she is unsurprisingly still and probably nearly unconscious. *Why did she get all the good sleep*

116

genes? The blanket of darkness beyond the small radius of light surrounding the fire reveals nothing. Although my ears remain on high alert, there is no chance I'm leaving our nesting nook to investigate the noise. I settle back into my blanket.

Chapter 23

Anytime you try to make yourself fall asleep it just does the opposite. I try to clear my mind of everything that happened today and focus on breathing in and out. The crackling fire emits a soothing blanket of warmth along with the lulling sound of flames devouring wood. Attempting to find a comfortable position, I will my body to descend into a dreamless oblivion.

Just as I'm about to flip to my left side, soft rhythmic thudding announces approaching footsteps. This time I don't dare turn my head toward the sound. Whispering voices float through the air toward me. *Is someone talking to me?* My senses on high alert, I tune out the rest of the world and listen intently.

"So," a hushed male voice says. "Quinn's kinda cute, huh?" Oh my gosh. No one is talking *to* me. They're talking *about* me. Who is it, though? I haven't spent enough time with any of these people to differentiate their voices. Well, except for Jasmine. Like nails on a chalkboard, her voice grates on my last nerve. Maybe just because she doesn't seem to have anything nice to say. To me, at least.

"I don't know. I mean, I'm just trying to get back to my family. I really hope she gets back home, too, but I've got bigger things on my mind."

"Yeah, totally. Me too. I definitely didn't notice that the scenery improved around here tonight." I hear them both exhale a quiet chuckle and the footsteps start to trail off. I bet they're going to the washrooms. I stay perfectly still. No need for them to know I overheard their conversation.

As I focus on inhaling and exhaling deep calming breaths, my body relaxes into the soft blue blanket separating me from the ground. Soon enough, exhaustion overtakes my body and propels my mind to a quiet oblivion.

The sun's golden rays peek through the surrounding trees, announcing a new day. I try to stretch the kinks out of my neck and back, but they aren't going anywhere. It doesn't matter. Today we go home. It will never be what it once was, but at least Riley and I have a plan and we'll be together.

When I roll over to check if Riley's still sleeping, only her crumbled red blanket greets me. She must be at the bathroom.

After a few minutes, impatience overtakes reason. I de-blanket and rise to my feet. Might as well head to the washroom. I can catch up with her there and freshen up a bit. I take a moment to stretch my cramped legs and then break into a slow jog down the same path we followed last night.

Inhaling the fresh morning air, I truly observe my surroundings. Although the buildings are eyesores, the landscape is stunning. Lush green grass and plants smother the dirt path. An army of trees stands at attention, some boasting white flowers, others displaying lush leaves. The campground is breathtaking.

I finally have a clue as to why the group chose to hole up here. It's a completely different place in the daylight. With a renewed spring in my step, I cross the threshold of the washroom. It's quiet, so I bend down to search for feet in one of the stalls. No one. "Riley?" I call out anyway. Nothing. *Maybe I just missed her.*

Splashing water on my face and running fingers through my tangled hair, I ready myself for the day. Retracing my steps, I dash back to our blankets. Still no Riley. The others are starting to emerge from their cabin. Wes and Jeff throw me nods as they stumble down the path to the washroom.

Aidan slowly approaches me. "Morning. You two sleep okay?" He runs a hand through his tousled black hair, but it's going to take a lot more than that to tame it.

"Um, last night was fine," I start, my heartbeat soaring like a cheetah hunting prey. "But I... I can't find Riley. When I woke up she was just gone."

"She's probably just in the bathroom," he says calmly. "Did you check there? I mean, what kind of weirdo doesn't need to use the bathroom as soon as they wake up?"

"No, Aidan," the words rush out as my panic rises. "I already checked there. She isn't there. She's gone."

He rests a hand on my arm and leans his face toward me, intently meeting my eyes. "It's okay, Quinn, we'll find her. She's gotta be around here somewhere."

Jasmine gingerly steps out of the cabin. *Yep, they all stayed in the same one last night. And my first impression was right…In the daylight, her caramel skin practically glows.* "Morning," she calls as she strides toward us. I know that greeting was for Aidan because her bright eyes skim past me.

Awkwardness fills the air as Aidan turns to her. "Jasmine," he says. "Have you seen Riley, Quinn's sister?"

Her eyes shift back and forth between us. "No, I haven't seen her since last night. What's going on?"

Just as Aidan's about to fill Jasmine in, Jeff and Wes return from the washroom. I stand next to him numbly while Aidan tells the group that I haven't seen Riley since we went to sleep last night. When he finishes, silence surrounds us like a dense fog and the weight of eight eyes lands on me.

"Let's take a better look around," Jeff says. "I'll start checking cabins." With that, he dashes away from us with Wes trailing after him.

"Wait up, man. I'll help," Wes calls.

Aidan cups his hands around his mouth and walks along the trail calling, "Riley." I stand next to him mutely.

"Hey," Jasmine tugs on his sleeve. "I'll check the area around both washrooms."

"Thanks," Aidan says. When he turns to me, his blue eyes flash with worry. "Quinn, it's okay. We're gonna find her. Maybe she just went for a walk in the woods and lost her bearings."

I nod stupidly as my limbs grow heavy and numb.

I start wringing my hands, just like Riley does when she's worried. My nervous energy erupts, and I stride to a block of cabins. I rush from cabin to cabin, my stringy hair fluttering behind me like a cape. The winds are picking up. It can't be much past eight o'clock but the sun is already scorching. *How was it so cold last night and less than twelve hours later it's sweltering?* I ignore the warm breeze as it licks my cheeks and forehead, leaving behind beads of sweat.

Within a few minutes, the group gathers at the fire ring. I drag myself over to join them but tune out their voices. Their dejected looks confirm they have not found my sister. I stumble to a log and lower myself down to sit.

Brushing away the silent tears blazing down my cheeks, I sweep my head back and forth. There's no sign of Riley. Not that I can see much through the watery veil blurring my vision. The world around me tumbles out of focus as my breathing skyrockets.

I mutely glance at the others. Their voices echo as if resonating from the bottom of a canyon, not just a few feet away from me. While a fog descends over my mind, I retreat further into myself.

Chapter 24

I am utterly alone. I don't even know these people and they are all that I have at this moment. Crushing pains shoot through my chest as the weight of this knowledge sinks in.

Aidan kneels on the ground in front of me. He places a hand over mine and our eyes meet. He opens his mouth to speak, but before he can utter a word, Jasmine's voice rings out above the hushed conversation swirling around us.

"We cannot go after her," Jasmine insists, looking pointedly at the guys. "We have to worry about ourselves. Besides, we have no idea where she is…and if she went willingly—"

The roller coaster I'm riding retreats from sullen emptiness and crests raging fury. "Are you kidding me!?" I practically shriek, standing and facing her. "You think she just went off and left with no note, no goodbyes, nothing?"

Our relationship has gone from apprehensive to acidic in about five seconds. Red hot blood surges through my veins. Anger spills from my body in sharp breaths while my heart slams in my chest.

"Look," Aidan rushes in between us. "We can't leave someone behind. She could be in danger. It doesn't mean we change our whole plan, it just means we take a little detour and then get back on track."

"Take a detour for how long?" Jasmine snipes. Her brown eyes narrow. "One day will turn into two days and two days will turn into a week. Maybe she doesn't want to be found."

I lunge at Jasmine. We're all on edge but Aidan has the fastest reflexes. He comes at me from the side, wrapping his arms around mine, suspending my forward motion. Jasmine's eyes narrow. *What is her problem?*

Wes jumps into the conversation. "Guys, even if Riley is fine, and I'm sure she is, we need a plan. We should check the whole area around where she slept and make sure she didn't leave a note. What if she saw something on the way here last night that she thought we could use? Maybe she went to find it and she'll come back? What if she came back here and we were gone? We've got to consider all the possibilities."

Jasmine grins.

Goddammit. I'm going to slap that smirk right off her face. Attempting to swipe at her, I realize Aidan's arms still encase me. "I don't have time for this. It's just taking me away from finding my sister."

"If I let you go, will you keep your hands to yourself?" Aidan asks, condescension oozing from every syllable. I give him a sharp nod, so he'll back off. He eyes me as he takes a cautious step back.

Shifting the focus away from me, Aidan cuts into the sudden awkward silence. "So, Jeff, man, you're up. Quinn and I vote for going to find Riley. Jasmine and Wes want to see if she comes back on her own. What do you say? We need a tie-breaker."

Jeff's hazel eyes shift around the group, but the hesitation I see in them has nothing to do with uncertainty. His mind is clicking a plan into place. As he runs a hand through his mussed brown hair, Jasmine crosses her arms, preparing to protest. Jeff holds her gaze, but I know he's talking directly to me even when his eyes shift around the group. His ROTC training shows as he takes charge of the situation.

"We don't know what happened to Riley. We know she wouldn't just get up and leave for no reason," Jeff proceeds cautiously, "but, we also have no idea where she went. Like Wes said, let's slow down and look for clues—anything that can help us figure out which direction she went."

"Slow down?! We don't have time to slow down. We need to find my sister NOW." My voice rises with every word. Maybe getting mixed up with these people was a bad idea.

"Quinn." Aidan takes a guarded step toward me, like I'm a cornered viper poised to strike. "Just stop and think. We have no idea where to go. Can you track Riley? Cuz I can't, and I don't think any one of us knows how to do that. We have to stop, think, and make a plan." His tone says this argument is over. Before I can respond, Jeff takes the forefront again and starts ordering everyone around.

"Wes, why don't you check Riley's blanket and the area where she slept?" With a confident nod, Wes breaks away from the group and examines our makeshift beds from last night. Jeff commands confidently. "Jasmine, come with me. We're going to circle the camp area to look for broken twigs, flattened grass, anything that might point us toward a path or direction she might have taken."

"What should we do?" I call out before he takes off. Instead of answering me, his gaze shifts to my side. "Aidan, interrogate the last person who saw her." I scrunch my face in confusion. *What?*

As the others focus on their tasks, Aidan turns his attention to me. "Quinn, can I talk to you for a moment?" Now that everyone is at least doing something, my pulse slows and my ears open. "Sure," I answer, holding his gaze. My brain bounces between anger that this is happening, fear that I'll never see my sister again, and awe for the strangers who are helping me get a handle on this awful situation.

His bright blue eyes resemble tropical waters. Clear and honest. Struggling to focus on his words instead of his physical features, I silently scold myself for allowing this distraction. "Quinn, can you think of anywhere Riley might have gone?"

I'm at a loss. "No, my sister is chronologically older, but she doesn't have a brave bone in her body. She would never leave the group behind and go anywhere alone." I cringe inwardly at the harshness of my thoughts when they translate into spoken words.

"Okaaaaay," Aidan stalls, "Did you two go anywhere besides the trailer park? Do you have any other relatives or friends in the area?"

"No." I'm adamant. "The only place we have ever stayed down here is at my aunt's trailer. After we…got to town…we headed to the trailer and planted ourselves there."

Just then, Wes steps back over to us. "I really didn't find anything out of the ordinary, except that it looks like she didn't take anything with her. She left her bag here. That tells me she didn't plan to go far."

"And, Quinn, you didn't hear anything?" he raises an eyebrow in question. "No! I would tell you if I knew anything. I'm the one who wants her back the most." Taking a deep breath, I continue, "I guess I've just been so tired from the past week that I finally just passed out and… Wait! I think I heard a branch snapping just before I fell asleep last night. But I guess it could have been an animal or really anything…"

Wes rubs his smooth chin, asking again, "But you didn't see anything?" I shake my head in defeat. Looking between me and Aidan, he asks, "You guys got any ideas of where to look?" I explain that the only place we know is the trailer park.

Jeff and Jasmine appear, sweaty and breathless from running circles around our camp. "Hey guys, we really didn't see anything out of place in any direction," Jeff says disappointedly. Scratching his head, he adds, "How is that even possible? No clues anywhere." *Great. So we really have no idea where she is.*

Jeff turns to Wes, asking between pants, "Hey, man, find anything in her stuff?" Hooking his thumbs in his shorts pockets, Wes mutters, "Nothing."

Jasmine shifts, crossing her arms and cocking her hip to the side as if to say, "I told you so." She chimes in with her own idea, "Maybe we should just stay here in case she comes back."

Why couldn't she disappear instead of Riley?

"I don't know, Jasmine," Wes says. "I don't like that we don't even know how long she's been gone. It could have been as soon as Quinn fell asleep last night."

"Alright, guys," Jeff directs, motioning for everyone to gather. He's caught his breath and ready to move things along. "Let's pack up and clear out. We'll head to the trailer park where Riley and Quinn were staying. We don't know anywhere else Riley could have gone, so right now that's our only lead."

"And what if she isn't there," Jasmine challenges. "Do we waste more time looking for her, or do we stick with our plan?"

Just when I think her dislike factor has peaked, she opens her mouth again and ups it a notch or two. Before my lips part to respond, Aidan diffuses the tension.

"Jasmine, let's take this one step at a time. We can't go searching all over creation, but we can go to the one place we know that Riley has been before. Let's focus our energy on that right now."

Chapter 25

Riley's bag rests at the foot of a log, just where she left it last night. Shouldering my own backpack, I leave hers. It will wait right here for when she returns. One by one, the others gather around the fire pit, bags slung over their shoulders.

Five heads bob in affirmation when Aidan simply asks, "Ready?" He and Jeff lead the way around the run-down cabins, along the dirt path leading to the campground's entrance.

Technically, I was with them when they parked the bikes last night, but between the shadowy trees obscuring our path and my jittery nerves, I'd be lucky if I could find my way out of Rustic Shores at all. I'm glad I'm not captaining this voyage.

Scanning our surroundings in hopes of spotting a clue that will lead me to Riley, my eyes stall on the horizon. Just a short time ago the rising sun was shining bright. Now the sky casts a sickly greenish-yellow hue. Maybe a storm is brewing, preparing to wage war with the sunrise's pleasant blue sky. *That's fitting. It perfectly captures my mood.*

I'm so consumed by my inner thoughts and blindly following the group that I don't even notice when Aidan stops abruptly. I plow into him before my mind catches up with my body. "I'm sorry I didn't see—" I start, but Aidan raises a hand in the air and cuts me off. "Where the hell are the bikes?" Jeff just stares at him, slack-jawed and silent.

After a brief discussion, we agree on one conclusion. Jim and Dan must have figured out we stole their bikes, tracked us down, retrieved their bikes, and snatched Riley.

Jasmine *kindly* points out that it's too much of a coincidence that someone found their camp the same night Riley and I joined them.

It is too much of a coincidence, but how the hell could they have tracked us down? Can they sniff out a trail? We were so careful. And why would they take Riley? They'd have to know I'd come looking for her.

Without wheels, our only option is to walk back to the trailer park. When Jasmine complains, I *sweetly* suggest that she stay at the campground and wait for us there.

Shooting daggers my way, the guys remind us both that it's safer to all stick together. Like the bikes, Riley didn't just evaporate into thin air.

As our feet meet pavement, the clouds overtake the sun. The humidity is almost unbearable, even for a summer day in Delaware. It saps my fleeting energy. I'm sure our proximity to the asphalt only fuels the heat simmering around us. Digging into my bag as we walk, I discover an elastic band hiding in the seam at the bottom. I'm not sure how long it's taken up residence there but it's getting a new home. I pull my hair back into a tight ponytail and secure it with the band.

Weaving through the cluttered highway is easy on foot, but it requires concentration to avoid looking too closely inside the immobilized cars and trucks we pass. The last thing I want to see is anything that resembles our car. And what happened to it. The wind rushes around us, sharing our path and pushing us forward.

I turn my attention to the trees lining the highway. Massive trunks rise high above us, their emerald foliage dancing in the breeze. Being out here makes me think of running and the exquisite escape it provides my brain.

I'm quickly returned to the present by a soft crinkling sound.

Wes digs some trail mix out of his backpack and offers it around. I pass but the others start munching.

Aidan drops back to keep pace with me. He thrusts a water bottle toward me. "Here, why don't you at least drink?" he offers. I shake my head, but he lifts my arm and wraps my fingers around the bottle. "You know what I went through to get that water. I would be extremely offended if you rejected it."

"What exactly did you go through?" I ask, turning my head toward him to gauge his answer.

"Okay, when we ran out of drinking water, I had to find and *borrow* water jugs, so we could keep refilling our water bottles. Once we used those up, I had to navigate my way through kitty city to refill them. Then I met some crazy chick who started calling me *Jugs* because of it." He waves his hands in the air as he speaks, fake indignation oozing from every word.

I laugh. I actually laugh. It's the last thing I would have ever believed possible right now. My resolve builds just enough to propel my feet a little faster.

Chapter 26

As the outskirts of the trailer park come into view, I steal a glance at my chest, half-expecting to see my shirt billow and cinch as my heart thunders in my chest. I can't slow my brisk pace. Raising my shaking hands, I force them to smooth the sweaty, loose strands of hair away from my face. My ponytail put up a good fight, but it could only contain my straggly brown locks for so long. The swirling wind didn't exactly help that situation.

Aidan glances my way. His weak smile whispers apprehension. I throw him a slight nod and avert my focus back to the highway. I need confidence right now, not pity or confirmation that my fear is about to come true.

The whistling wind and crunching of gravel beneath our tired feet have been the only sounds for most of the trip. Thankfully, Jeff breaks the near-silence. "Guys, we're almost there! Where do we look first?"

"Geez, Jeff, could you sound more excited?" Jasmine comments.

How do these guys deal with her attitude?

Shouting echoes in the distance, competing with the rumble of a revving engine. We all stop short, alarmed eyes searching our surroundings.

I suddenly feel very exposed walking along the highway.

"Guys," Jasmine says quietly. "Maybe we should try to blend in with the tree line?"

We all nod in agreement and dash toward the surrounding vegetation.

Slinking through the wooded area, we're careful not to venture too far from the road.

From this distance, bodies swarm through the trailer park. That's not a good sign, considering it's the complete opposite of what Riley and I experienced all the days we were there.

Jeff stretches his arms out and motions "down" with his hands. In a single movement, we comply, forming a quiet huddle among the shade and shelter of the pine trees. Aidan aims his deep blue eyes my way and whispers, "Quinn, is this normal? The few times Jeff and I have been to the park, it was like a ghost town."

I shake my head, shifting my eyes around the group. "No, Riley and I stayed there for a week and barely saw or heard anyone else. Something is really wrong."

Aidan leans back on his haunches. I can tell he's uncertain what to do. It may not be safe to walk in there like we planned, but he must know I'm not just giving up and leaving.

Beside me, Jeff drops one knee into the dirt and addresses

the group. "Guys, you stay here. I'll go on a recon mission, find out what the hell is going on, and be back in a few," he says. Flanking Jeff's other side, Jasmine clutches his arm. "No! We don't know what's going on. We aren't sending you into a dangerous situation. The only reason we're here is because of *her*," she gestures toward me. "She should go!"

Aidan raises a hand to calm the imminent argument, but Jeff jumps in before anyone can speak. He casually drapes one arm over my shoulder and the other over Jasmine's. "Now ladies, I know there's some tension. Just promise me, if you decide to have it out, please let me be right here in the middle of it."

A genuine laugh escapes me. Jeff's ability to diffuse a potentially explosive situation makes him that much more likeable.

Before anyone else can chime in, Wes speaks. He's so quiet that I sometimes forget he's even here. "Hey, I'll go. I'm like a ninja. Sending Jeff is like sending Godzilla to sneak up on Tokyo. They'd be all over him in no time, but I can slip in and out of there before anyone even blinks."

Silence descends as eyes shift back and forth.

Aidan addresses Wes, "Are you sure you're up for this?"

Wes gives one brisk nod.

Aidan looks at us each in turn. "Does anyone object?"

Again, silence.

Wes slowly stands, stretching his legs. "Alright, everyone wait here and stay quiet. I'll be back in a few." When his eyes catch mine, I send him a silent *thank you*.

As Wes dashes off toward the trailer park, we settle into the overgrowth.

I keep my head down as Jasmine's words replay in my head. It *is* my fault they're all here. I have no right to put any of them in danger. Before my mind can wander too far, Jeff pulls me out of my thoughts.

"Sooooooo…anyone up for a little game of Truth or Dare?" he asks, wiggling his eyebrows. Jasmine and I both answer at the same time, "No!" In the brief second our eyes meet, daggers erupt from her brown irises.

Not sure what exactly I did to offend her, but it looks like we won't be doing each other's hair anytime soon.

Hunching my back to stay low, I amble toward a nearby rock. While its flat surface invites me to sit, the rigid exterior is unwelcoming. When Jeff leads Jasmine toward a rock several feet away from me, I lower myself onto my new seat.

Aidan scuttles over and plops down next to me. He casually rests his arms on his knees. "How are you doing?" he asks quietly.

"I'm okay," I lie. Lowering my voice, I lean toward him. "Aidan, what are you all doing here?"

His eyes widen as if I actually expect him to answer that question.

"I mean, finding Riley is my problem. I have no right to ask anyone else to help me find her. Jasmine's right. I'm the only one who should be here." With the last few words, I drop my head into my hands so that he can't see the tears threatening to spill. The universe seems determined to remind me that I am utterly alone now.

In one swift movement, he places his hand under my chin, turning my face and effectively capturing me with his kind blue eyes. "Quinn, you didn't ask anyone to come here with you. We chose to come. I know Jasmine can be a little…disagreeable sometimes. She just worries about everyone and I know she's really anxious to get to her family…I mean, we all are."

My gaze turns grateful and a tear tumbles down my cheek. *Dammit.* Aidan tenderly wipes it away. My eyelashes flutter as I try to contain my soaring emotions. Wind rushes around me, a cool breeze snaking down my spine. *When did the temperature nosedive?* Maybe it's because we're shaded by the trees. The cooler air soothes my clammy skin.

"Hey, you two, what's going on over there?" Jeff calls in a sing-song voice. "Do you need some alone time?" I squeeze my eyes shut as my face flushes red.

"Actually, what we really need is some food," Aidan says. "How 'bout you two run to McDonald's and pick up some burgers and fries?" My embarrassment dissolves into envy as I observe the easy camaraderie they share.

Rolling my eyes, they land on a shadow prowling through the trees. I reach out, tugging on Aidan's arm, and nod in that direction. His eyes slide to where I indicate, and a small smirk plays on his lips. "I'd know that ninja anywhere," he says and stands.

Chapter 27

Jeff and Jasmine turn, rising to their feet, so I do too. As promised, Wes glides quietly toward us. He's got to be at least six feet tall with a muscular build. *How does he move around so stealthily?* If I hadn't seen him approach, I never would have heard him.

"So," Wes starts. "It seems the natives are restless."

We form a small circle around him as he elaborates. "It looks like the residents are arguing about evacuating the park. People are loading up cars and trying to convince others to come with them."

"Are they going to Dover Air Force Base?" I ask.

"I think so." Wes nods. "They're saying something about going to the military and taking cover. Sounds like something is coming, something they're trying to outrun."

I know it's unlikely, but I have to ask. "Did you by any chance see Riley?" I draw in a breath, trying to fill my chest with air instead of hope.

"Quinn," he says as he leans back on his heels. "I only met Riley once and it was dark. I didn't get a good look at her, but I remember thinking you two look alike and I didn't see anyone there who looked like you."

I release my breath, both physically and mentally deflating. Aidan scratches his chin and asks Wes, "Any idea what's got them all worked up? What's making them hightail it out of there?"

"I saw one old lady keep looking up at the sky like she was expecting it to fall or something," Wes hunches a broad shoulder up. "Maybe they know this is gonna be a nasty storm? It sure feels like something's brewing."

"Speaking of this weather, we can't exactly sit around here just waiting for a storm to hit," Jeff says. Aidan, Jeff, and Wes eye each other, communicating wordlessly.

"Alright, if something's going on to get everyone all riled up, maybe we should find out what it is," Aidan says.

"And, if something is coming," Jeff adds. "We should find some cover."

"Look," Jasmine states calmly. "I agreed to come here and help look for Riley, but if we're not looking for her, I want to go back to the camp. It's not much, but at least there aren't people running around screaming at each other there."

Hmm, I guess she forgot about my little outburst earlier. No need to remind anyone of that.

"You know what," I start. "You guys should go back. I'm going to our trailer. I'll look for Riley there, and if I can't find her…I'll think of something." I turn my attention to each of the guys individually, letting my gaze slide past Jasmine completely. "Thanks for coming with me. Really. But you guys go back. There's really nothing else you can do."

Relief flashes over both Jasmine's and Wes' face. *That's right,* I think to myself, *I am officially letting you off the hook.* This traveling as a group thing is slowing me down anyway.

"How about this?" Aidan proposes. "Jasmine, Jeff, and Wes go back to the campsite. If Riley does show up there, she'll panic if she can't find anyone. Quinn and I will stay here and figure out what's going on. We'll stay in the trailer and meet up with you guys in the morning."

"Aidan, you don't have to stay," I start. There is no way I'm leaving here until I know where my sister is, but this is my problem, no one else's. Somehow Jasmine's earlier words lit a fire that I won't allow to extinguish. Before I can finish my thought, he cuts me off. "I know I don't have to, but I am going to," he says with finality.

Jasmine raises her brow and smoothes her curly hair back but, thankfully, keeps quiet. When she turns on her heels and starts back toward their camp, Jeff and Wes stumble to catch up with her. They throw quick waves to us over their shoulders. "We'll be back in the morning," Jeff calls.

"Well," I say. "That was awkward."

Aidan smirks at me. "Just a little," he agrees.

A roar of thunder echoes in the distance. The leafy treetops meet an ashen sky. Facing me, Aidan asks, "So, you up for going to the trailer park?"

"Yes!" I answer. "I don't know many people there, but I have every right to be there. I just hope we don't run into Jim and

Dan...unless they have Riley...ugh. Let's just go."

He follows me as I slink through the woods toward the outskirts of the park. I do have the right to be there, but I really don't want to be accused of stealing any dirt bikes. Even though I did do it. I like Aidan's choice of the word *borrow* better.

We tiptoe into the park near Benny's trailer, creep up the steps, and gently knock on the door. When I press my ear to the door, no movement echoes inside. Aidan taps me on the shoulder and whispers, "Someone's coming over here."

Turning, my eyes fix on Cindy, who moves soundlessly toward us. Adjusting her glasses, she raises a single finger to her lips, as if to say, "Shh." When she's close enough, she grabs my hands. "Quinn, are you okay?" she asks. "Who's this?" She jerks her head toward Aidan.

In hushed tones we exchange information. I explain that Riley is missing, and Aidan is helping me look for her.

She confirms that she hasn't seen Riley, but that it has been chaotic. *So, technically, Riley could be around here somewhere.* My eyes uncontrollably wander over Cindy's head, searching out movement. Cindy snaps my attention back to her at the mention of local police officers riding into the trailer park on motorcycles, calling an impromptu meeting with residents. Amid an arsenal of questions, they briefly explained that the highway was about halfway cleared, but the reason for their visit was to alert residents of a tornado warning.

Scrunching my face in confusion, I ask, "Is that better or worse than a tornado watch?"

Before she can answer, Aidan pipes up. "Well, if a watch is bad, consider a warning super-bad."

141

When I glare at him with narrowed eyes, he elaborates, "A tornado watch means that a tornado could form. But a warning means that a storm-cycle likely to cause a tornado showed up on radar—or one that caused a tornado somewhere else is now headed this way, so it's pretty likely to happen here as well."

I want to question it even though he sounds pretty sure of himself. *I know, it doesn't really matter.* The wind is starting to bat green leaves through the air, and every now and then a small branch bounces off me. It's getting stronger.

Aidan rolls his eyes and Cindy grabs my shoulder. "Quinn, you have to get to shelter. Don't stay here. Trailer parks are like magnets for tornadoes. It's not safe," she pleads.

"And what about Benny?" I ask. Just yesterday she told me Benny couldn't leave, so how is he going to be safe?

She straightens her glasses and pushes a lock of shoulder-length raven-black hair behind her ear. "Some of the neighbors loaded him up to take him to Dover," she says. Worry radiates from her deep brown eyes. "Quinn, we just don't have a choice anymore. The officers told everyone that a path is clear now along the highway's shoulder. We can use that to reach the Air Force Base. I'm going with him, but they'll have medical staff and equipment there. When it's safe, we'll come back as soon as we can."

She looks at me sadly. I know what's coming next. "Why don't you and your friend—" she starts, but I don't let her finish.

"No," I say firmly. "Cindy, take care of Benny and tell him I'll miss him. Aidan and I have to go now. I need to find my sister."

I don't resist when she pulls me in for a quick hug. She

whispers in my ear, "Be safe, honey."

Pulling away, I give her a quick nod in acknowledgement and then turn away and stride toward Aunt Grace's trailer. I don't look back.

Chapter 28

My brisk stride quickly morphs into a full-fledged run. I can't help myself. We're so close now. I don't even bother sticking to the gravel road; I run through people's yards, hurdling over plants and dodging lawn chairs. I can hear Aidan trying to keep up with me.

I slow down only when I'm steps away from the porch. Digging in my bag, my fingers grasp the green flip-flop keychain that's always held this key. I fumble to unlock the door and then bolt inside.

"Riley," I scream, tearing down the hallway. I throw open the bedroom door and sweep my eyes across the room. *No.* She's not here. I turn and retrace my steps, peeking in the bathroom before I shuffle past the kitchen toward the other bedroom.

Aidan stumbles into the trailer, panting. "Thanks for waiting," he huffs, leaning over to rest his hands on his knees.

I brush past him calling, "Riley! Are you here?" The other bedroom door is already open, and when I peer inside, it's just as we left it. The pink floral quilt lays smooth over the queen-sized bed. This bedroom has a small closet, but when I yank the wooden bifold door open, all that greets me is the dusty old upright vacuum cleaner and a spare yellow windbreaker, sagging limply on a hanger.

Dammit. Somewhere deep down, I believed she'd be here. Next stop: Dan and Jim's. I whirl around and start down the hallway to the living room. Aidan is sitting on the couch, staring out the door he left open. I move closer and search his face. Although he's caught his breath, shadows linger under his eyes. I didn't notice them before, but I haven't really looked that closely until now.

"Hey," I say, "Riley's not here. I need to run over to Dan and Jim's. You know, see if she's there." I bend down to meet his gaze at eye level. "Why don't you stay here and rest for a few minutes?" Just as I finish speaking, a rush of wind from the open door pushes past me, blowing stray wisps of hair into my face.

I yank the ponytail holder from what's become a bird's nest of hair. It's completely failed me. Swiping the hair away from my face, I focus on Aidan's narrowing eyes. Their brilliant sky blue turns icy as he watches me intently. "Seriously, Quinn?" He pauses as if I'm supposed to know what his problem is.

I mirror his narrowed eyes and wait. "There's a freaking hurricane out there," he roars as he points to the open door. "We. Have. To. Leave. Now!" As if on cue, glass shatters down the hallway. I'm so startled I scream; something just crashed through a window. Flinching, I shift back on my heels. I guess he's right, but it feels like giving up. I'll never stop searching for my sister. Taking advantage of my momentary stupor, Aidan grabs my hand, pulling me along with him as he stands. *"Come on,"* he says in a husky voice. With that, he leads me out the door and stops abruptly. I watch mutely as he pulls the door closed tightly and turns the key I left dangling in the knob. Shoving it into his pocket, he grabs my hand and tugs me down the steps.

Wind beats against us as we run along the gravel road. Aidan leads us toward the wooded path that I ran the day I met him. *Maybe he wants to retreat from the open space within the trailer park.* I don't question where we're going, I just follow him blindly, dodging flying debris.

Our pace slows as swirling pebbles and dust muddy our vision. Booming thunder erupts. I'm not sure if my heartbeat or the wind rages in my ears. Whichever it is, it's loud. The warm, wet air clings to my skin.

When we break free of the trees' cover, the white house with maroon shutters comes into view. Aidan points toward it. At this point, I really don't care where we go, as long as we get out of this storm. The yard is feline-free now. *I guess the cats are smarter than us.* They probably sensed the storm coming and took cover hours ago.

Aidan finally releases my hand. He must know I'm not a flight risk anymore. There's no way I'm heading back to the trailer park in this storm. I follow on his heels as he charges up the sidewalk right to the front porch. My eyes land on the wooden porch swing, jolting back and forth. Its chains are powerless to the wind, which easily jostles the whole swing.

When he starts pounding on the door, I glance at the sky.

Any hint of sun has been subdued by a menacing wall of clouds. The looming gray haze exhibits a sickly green tint. As the door swings open, Aidan grabs my hand again, propelling us over the threshold.

Chapter 29

We burst into the house a dripping, breathless heap of limbs. I hear the door close behind us and my eyes search for whoever let us in. A silver-haired woman in a wheelchair watches us curiously. Still breathing heavy, Aidan reaches toward her with a hand extended. "Ma'am, thank you so much for opening the door," he says.

Our arrival has stirred up the four-legged residents. An orange tabby rubs up against my legs but backs away in disgust when it realizes my legs are wet. A black and orange calico sniffs my shoe.

"I reckon you two kids are looking for somewhere to ride out the storm?" the lady asks gruffly. Her curly hair hangs just above her chin. She makes no move to cover up her white cotton nightgown swimming in pink flowers. When Aidan starts to answer, she cuts him off.

"It's gonna get worse before it gets better," she says. "Follow me. We'll get you dried off."

We jump out of the way as she drives her electric wheelchair past us and down a hallway. "I'm Rose," she says in passing.

The front entranceway is tidy, but as we follow her through the house, I notice that most of the rooms are stuffed with piles of boxes. I raise an eyebrow at Aidan. *Maybe this woman's a hoarder. She obviously likes to accumulate cats. Is she one of those people who can't throw anything away?*

Other than the boxes, the house is a cheerful blend of pastel walls with perfectly-matched carpets. Each room we pass bears a floor-to-ceiling color theme—from the blue living room to the yellow kitchen to the mint-green dining room.

When we reach a cotton-candy pink bathroom, the woman stops and points inside. "There are towels in the closet. Go ahead, grab some and dry off. Might want to clean those shoes too," she mutters as her eyes track the mud trail our shoes left on the carpet.

I make a mental note to clean our muddy tracks before we leave.

A boom of thunder startles all three of us. Aidan and I hurry into the bathroom and dab our dripping hair and skin as best we can. Stark lightning flashes through the window, spurring us to finish up.

When we rush back out to the hallway, Rose starts wheeling toward the door where we entered. "You kids better get down to the basement. Storm's getting worse." We follow her as she speeds past the living room. Maneuvering around a stack of boxes, she stops and swivels around to face us. Pointing at a door adjacent to the one we first burst through, she directs us. "Down there, kids. Basement's the safest place in a storm like this. I'll holler down when it's passed."

Aidan and I glance at each other before he says, "You're coming with us."

Rose chuckles. "Sweetie, I can't go down there." She pats the wheelchair frame. "This would make for a pretty bumpy ride, don't ya think?"

Another roll of thunder rumbles and glass shatters in a nearby room, wind screaming through the now-open space.

I pull the basement door open as far as it goes and switch on the light. Aidan gives me a nod and we position ourselves on either side of Rose and bend down. "I wasn't asking. I was telling you. You're coming with us, Rose."

We each wrap an arm around her back and use our other arm to lift a leg. Rose lets out a startled cry. I swear I hear her say, "Jerry!" under her breath. *Probably one of the cats. Oh well, he'll have to fend for himself right now. There's no time to search for him.* We carefully lift her out of the chair but clumsily stumble down the steps. After we set her down on a dusty floral couch, Aidan races back up the stairs and slams the door closed.

We both drop our backpacks to the floor and take a moment to catch our breath and assess our surroundings. Although it's still audible, the thunder is muffled down here. The lightning is hindered by the lack of windows. The gray cinder block walls make for a beautiful, secure site.

Aidan plops on the couch next to Rose, freeing the largest dust cloud I've ever seen. "So, in the last ten minutes, I've been more intimate with you two than I've been with anyone since my husband died," Rose says casually. "I think it's about time I know your names."

A nervous giggle slips past my lips as I slide into a nearby captain's chair. Aidan extends a hand and says, "I'm Aidan." After a proper handshake, he motions toward me, saying, "And this is Quinn."

With nowhere to go, we all settle in, allowing our conversation to drift from the distant past to the painful present. Rose explains the boxes cluttering the first floor. For years, her daughter Emily has been trying to convince her to move to a senior living community.

Rose was able to stand her ground until she literally couldn't any longer. After a fall last year, she ended up in the wheelchair and every day seemed to be harder than the last. Caring for the house and cats had started to overwhelm her.

Last month, Rose finally agreed to move, so Emily and her husband started packing up her belongings and making arrangements for an animal rescue group to help find homes for all the cats.

"Well, Rose, that's a relief," Aidan starts. *Where is he going with this? She's clearly emotional, don't make it worse.* "I was starting to wonder what else you collected besides boxes and cats."

Rose bursts into laughter and I'm swept up in it too. After a few minutes and a brief awkward silence, the tears streaming down her cheeks release sorrow. *In this short time, she has been nothing but kind to us and I hate to see her upset.* I rush over to the free side of the couch and place my hand on Rose's back, trying to comfort her.

"Oh, kids," she sobs. "I don't know how I'm gonna leave

them all. My daughter, I know she loves me, but she's got her own life. She's busy. But these cats, they need me. They're always here for me. And now I'm just gonna leave 'em." With that, she presses the palms of her wrinkly hands to her eyes, trying to blot the tears away.

I turn a panicked gaze to Aidan, but he doesn't even glance my way. He confidently slides closer to Rose, wraps an arm around her and sits like a sentry as she falls to pieces. He doesn't say anything, he just comforts her while she cries. I guess that's the best we can do for her right now. We're all travelling along a path of loss. We can't truly understand the depth of another's despair, but at the very least we can offer simple human contact. Unspoken comfort.

After a few minutes, Rose tires from the emotional outburst. She starts to apologize but Aidan shushes her and tells her to rest. I jump up and help Aidan get her settled on the couch. Her eyes look glassy as she thanks us and lets her body relax into the cushions.

Chapter 30

Aidan grabs my hand and leads me around a corner toward a section of the basement that I didn't notice until now. This part looks like storage central. Shelving units line the cinder block walls and dusty plastic tubs fill the shelves.

A rug rests on the floor in front of the shelving units, inviting us to sit. The tan rectangular carpet is thin, but at least it's softer than the floor. Other than the couch and chairs we just left, there's really no other furniture we can sit on. With nothing else to do, we plop down across from each other.

"So," I start. "You were really good with Rose, you know?"

Running a hand through his hair, his downcast face makes him look shy and uncertain. "Yeah, well, I grew up with two younger sisters. I guess I learned how to console them when they were upset."

I can tell he doesn't want to talk about his family. And I don't blame him; it's not like that's a happy subject for me these days.

"Well, I just wanted to thank you for jumping in. I wasn't really sure what to do." And, even though it crossed my mind since we showed up here, I decided not to tell Rose that Aidan and I have both been here before, at least *outside* the house.

"I thought about telling her a joke to cheer her up, but I wasn't sure if she would appreciate that or not," he says.

"What was your joke?" I ask. My tone borders on flirting. He must not mind because he smiles broadly and proceeds. "Why was the sedimentary rock extra cheap?" Oh geez, here comes the geologist in him. I narrow my eyes and try very hard not to scrunch up my nose.

"Because it was on shale," he says, unable to contain a hearty chuckle. I force a fake laugh and say, "Thanks for not saying that to Rose when she was upset. She was already suffering enough."

"Oh, look who's the comedian now," he says. "How about we just agree that we both have a good sense of humor!" I giggle and nod, realizing that my emotions surge and recede so quickly these days. One minute I'm angry that Riley is gone, the next I'm terrified of a storm, and when I have a moment to breathe, I just want to flirt with Aidan.

"Hey, you hungry?" he asks. "I'm starving." With that, he hops up and strides back the way we came. He rounds the corner a moment later, carrying our backpacks. Depositing mine at my feet, he drops to the floor, emptying the contents from his bag.

He dumps out a sweatshirt, a set of keys, a pocket knife, an unopened water bottle, and a can of beef stew that he gazes at lovingly. He catches me smiling at his love-struck expression and asks, "So, what do you got?"

Suddenly, I don't want to show him what's in my bag. "Um,

you know what," I say lamely. "I didn't really bring anything, so let's just use your stuff, okay?"

He shakes his head. "No deal. I showed you mine, now you show me yours." My incredulous look only slightly delays the inevitable and earns me a stern head shake.

I slowly unzip my backpack, gingerly reaching inside. Sliding a small plastic bottle of hand sanitizer out, I place it on the ground in front of me. Aidan raises his eyebrows and gives a brief nod of approval. I huff out a sigh and reach back in the bag. This time I pull out my makeup bag. I set it on the ground quickly and reach back into my backpack.

"Wait a minute, what's that?" Aidan asks, pointing at the sparkly silver pouch. "It's just my makeup," I mumble. "Nothing important." He stifles a laugh and motions for me to continue. His face turns serious when I pull out my cell phone charger.

"You've got a working cell phone?" he asks, anticipation oozing out of each word. I roll my eyes before answering. "No, I lost my phone in the car wreck. I don't know why I still carry the charger around with me...habit, I guess." He narrows his eyes in confusion. *Ugh.*

I reach back into the bag with both arms and pull out as much as I can. *I want to get this over with.* I unceremoniously dump my possessions on the floor in front of me – nail polish, lip gloss, a pack of gum, and a blue hairbrush.

He scrunches his face up and crosses his arms. "You got anything else in there?" I answer by pulling out my high school team's cross-country sweatshirt and the water bottle I use for running, which happens to be empty. Then I make a show of upending the backpack, proving that it's empty.

"Alright, well your bag of tricks is really helpful," he says. "But I'm gonna take a quick look around here and see if there's a utility sink or something we can use to wash up."

After a brief exploratory mission, he returns defeated. "Nothing. Looks like we're eating right here. At least we have your hand sanitizer, right?"

"Why don't we just run upstairs, wash our hands and run back down?" I start. "Or better yet, we can check out the kitchen and see if Rose has anything we can just grab and bring down here to eat. We can even grab food for her."

"Gee, Quinn, that's nice of you," he says. "Willingly bringing something back for Rose that you found while snooping around in her cupboards…while she slept."

Embarrassment flashes across my cheeks. "Well, I didn't think of it that way." I try to shrug his words off.

"Look, that storm can't be over yet. We need to stay put. We'll eat and then we'll try to sleep." *Geez, who died and made him the supreme commander?*

"Aye, aye, sir," I say with a salute.

"Now, now," he says, a smile quirking on his full lips. "No need to salute, but you can continue to call me sir. I like the sound of that."

I roll my eyes but can't hold back a giggle. We settle in next to each other, sitting cross-legged on the thin carpet. Aidan pulls the tab off the can of beef stew. We have no spoons. He holds the can out to me. "Here, you eat first. Use your hand to scoop out your half." He says it matter-of-factly, like he's done this a million other times.

Eating beef stew with my bare hand sounds nasty but there's

really no other option. I'd kill for a bathroom right now, or even just a full-fledged sink with water and soap. I grab the sanitizer bottle and scrub my hands until they're pink. After I set the bottle in front of Aidan, I reach into the gooey brown sauce and retrieve a piece of coin-shaped meat. My rumbling stomach confirms it's the best thing I've ever tasted.

With all the restraint I can muster, I finish my dinner and hand the half-empty can to Aidan. He digs in, polishing off his stew in minutes. We both lick our fingers clean and apply a fresh coating of sanitizer.

"Let's try to get some sleep," Aidan says. "I think we're gonna have a big day tomorrow."

"Good idea," I say. I'm emotionally exhausted and there's really nothing else to do. He holds his sweatshirt out to me. "You want this? You can put yours on and use this as a pillow."

"No," I say, "But thanks for offering. Thanks for everything." My voice cracks, but I push the words out. My mind flashes to Rose's earlier emotional display. We all endure loss. And we are all, ultimately, alone to face it. I'm worried about Riley. I don't want to get all sensitive right now, but I'm glad Aidan is here with me. I curl up on the rug, wrapping my arms around myself. Aidan whispers, "Goodnight," and I close my eyes, willing this day to be over, so I can get back on track and find my sister.

For a short time at least, sleep finds me and lulls me into a dreamless state.

Chapter 31

I'm jolted awake by what feels like thunder striking my chest. My grandpa John's face flashes through my mind. He died of a heart attack when I was in elementary school, but I remember his face from pictures my mom kept around the house. I worry that the suffocating pain consuming my chest is my heart vying for oxygen. Or maybe my heart is literally breaking. I shift positions, trying to lessen the pain.

Momentarily forgetting where I am, my eyes widen. They sweep across the shelving units surrounding me and land on the lump lying just a foot or two away. The sight of the same blue T-shirt and khaki shorts I've seen for the past three days slow my pulse. A smile tugs at my lips as I search his face. Aidan's features look softer, younger, as he sleeps.

I lean toward him, just a little closer, to get a better look. I stifle a giggle when I see the a tiny dribble of drool along his chin.

Satisfied that I got a good look at him, and terrified that he could open his eyes at any moment and catch me staring, I shuffle back to my side of the rug.

Just as I settle into a comfortable position, a crack of thunder cuts through the calm. *That must have been close.* The storm has largely been muted up until this point. When the basement goes dark a moment later, I know we've lost power.

Thankfully, that's the only strike not muffled by the cinder block walls. After a few deep breaths, the ache in my chest weakens and I'm ready to drift back to sleep.

As my mind fades in and out of a dreamless haze, a creaking sound pulls my senses back to reality. I open my eyes to an empty rug. After quickly stretching out the creaks in my neck and shoulders, I rise on wobbly feet.

Walking toward the steps, I find Rose sitting on the couch, looking rested. "Good morning, dear," she says. "I'm afraid I haven't been the best host. I hear you and Aidan had to sleep on the floor last night."

I kneel down in front of her, resting my hand on her arm. "Rose, we can't thank you enough for giving us a safe place to wait out the storm. You have been the best host possible." I smile at her before my eyes canvass the basement. I guess it's pretty obvious who I'm looking for.

"Oh, sweetie, he went upstairs to see what we missed last night," Rose says wistfully.

"Are you okay down here?" I ask.

"Well, this sofa's gonna smell pretty bad if I don't get to a bathroom soon," she says. "But seeing how the only one's upstairs, I'm gonna need my somewhat clumsy houseguests to assist me with that."

A chirp of laughter escapes me, and I pat her hand. "I'll go retrieve clumsy houseguest number one."

She winks at me.

I jump to my feet and dash up the stairs.

Pushing open the basement door, I'm amazed by the difference last night made. In the living room, Rose's neatly stacked boxes have toppled and tumbled. Any floor space open enough for her wheelchair to pass through is covered in cardboard.

I scan the hallway we walked through just last night. Thankfully, it's mostly clear. When the front door opens and closes, I turn to the noise. Aidan eyes me cautiously.

"Rose has to use the bathroom, so we've got to get her up here," I inform him. "Soon, I think."

He nods and takes a step closer. Speaking quietly, he updates me. "Quinn, it's a mess inside and out. Winds must have blown out the windows and knocked stuff around in here. Out there, trees are down, and debris is scattered everywhere I can see."

I nod slowly. "Just what we need, another challenge," I say scornfully.

Grabbing my shoulders, he intently meets my eyes. *Can he see I'm on the verge of spiraling into insanity?* "Look, this isn't gonna stop us. Let's get Rose settled and head back to the trailer park."

When I manage a slight nod, he releases my shoulders and leads the way to the basement. We awkwardly carry Rose up the stairs, desperately trying to keep our footing steady. Her death grip is surprisingly strong.

Thankfully, her wheelchair sits where we left it, just behind the basement door near the wall. It looks somehow unharmed. *One small miracle in this mess.*

Once she's safely seated, Rose visibly relaxes. "Oh, I missed ya, Jerry," she says, patting the arm rests. I try to stifle a giggle. "You named your wheelchair?" I ask.

Her smile reaches her watery eyes when she says, "I sure did. Jerry was my husband. He was my home, and now he still is." A sappy smile spreads across my face.

Chapter 32

Aidan pulls us out of the moment with practicality. "Alright, Rose, how about Quinn and I clear the path for you, so you can drive Jerry to the bathroom?"

With that, we spring into action. Retracing our steps from last night, the hallway remains pretty clear. Just a few random obstacles stand in our way, which we promptly relocate. On this floor, the living room took the worst of the damage. Strong winds must have poured in through the large picture windows. Rose is actually lucky that some of her belongings were packed away in boxes. That probably protected them last night.

Once Rose is behind a closed door, we huddle to discuss our plan. "So," I start, "We should probably head back to the trailer park and look for Riley. Who knows how long it will take to get there if trees are down. Our path could be totally blocked."

He stops me before I can say anything else. "Quinn, we can't leave just yet. I want to find Riley and I want to make sure my friends are all okay, but we've got to make sure Rose is safe here before we can leave."

My eagerness deflates, but I know he's right. Just as silence veils our conversation, the bathroom door opens and Rose wheels out. My stomach takes that moment to share how empty it feels right now. A loud growl moans from my mid-section.

"Well," Rose says. "How about I rustle up some breakfast, and then you two can be on your way? I've got to start feeding the cats anyway. They were probably hiding all night and want last night's supper by now." She turns the wheelchair and rolls to the kitchen. I hear her muttering along the way, "And who knows how long it'll take me to coax the scared ones out of their hiding places."

She seems to have made up her mind, but Aidan calls out to her. "Sounds great, Rose. Thank you. While you're doing that, Quinn and I are going to patch up your broken windows and just fix things up as best we can, okay?" She throws a muffled, "Sure" over her shoulder as she continues on to the kitchen.

It's comforting to know that she isn't going to beg us to stay. I was worried she would need more help, but she seems eager to return to a solitary routine.

I throw my arms up to motion "after you," and Aidan leads the way to the living room. First, we forge a path through the fallen boxes, restacking them as we make our way toward the shattered windows. Once he assesses the damage, Aidan looks around for something to cover the openings, while I find a trash can and vacuum to remove the glass shards.

163

While Aidan heads back down to the basement, I go straight to the kitchen to ask Rose for the supplies I need. Informing me that the power is out, which I should have figured from the brief report Aidan gave after his glimpse outside this morning, Rose directs me to a trash can, broom and dustpan. Not my ideal tools for removing glass pieces from carpet, but I guess I'm old-schooling it today.

As I head back to the living room, the cats slowly meander toward the kitchen. They must realize their meal ticket is back and ready to be at their service.

It takes me a good ten minutes to pick up the largest pieces of glass. My efforts to sweep the remaining pieces with a broom are useless. Aidan returns just in time to question my progress. "Having much luck there?"

I chuckle in spite of myself. "I'm striking out here. What did you find?"

"Well," he begins, "I couldn't find any plywood, which would have been ideal. So, then I thought we could unhinge some of the inside doors and nail them up over the windows." My eyes narrow in confusion. *I can't even clean up glass and he wants me to help hang a door over a window?*

"But," he continues, "I don't think that'll work with the picture window." He pauses to scratch his head. "So, I found some tarps in the basement. I say we hang those around the windows and then stack all the boxes in front of the tarps. Whatever we come up with is a temporary fix anyway, and I think that's the best we can do."

While I attempt to extract as much of the glass from the carpet as I can, Aidan checks with Rose to make sure she's okay with us nailing a tarp to her living room wall. After she waves him away, instructing him on where to find a hammer and nails, we set to work. I guess she figures she won't be living here much longer anyway.

About thirty minutes later, my arms are tired from holding up the tarp in awkward positions while Aidan affixed it to the walls. It takes us another twenty minutes to arrange stacks of boxes in front of the windows, our lame attempt at securing the openings.

Just as we're about to collapse on the plaid sofa, Rose calls to us from the kitchen. "If you're done destroying my living room, I've got some breakfast for ya!" We smile at each other before walking down the hallway. With each step, my nose picks up more scents. And none of them are good.

When we reach the kitchen, my eyes lock on the source of the odor. Half a dozen cats have emerged from hiding and sit before various-sized bowls of brown and tan mush. "Sorry, I had to get some of my babies started on breakfast," Rose says, smiling. She adds, under her breath, "And I've got a lot more to do still."

She wheels up to the table and motions for us to sit. We dig into heaping bowls of yogurt, granola, and fruit chunks. She must have opened the refrigerator to retrieve the yogurt. I hope the power comes back on soon, so that everything else inside doesn't spoil. The mixed fruit obviously came from a can but it's absolutely delicious.

After a quick cleanup, we're ready to leave. Aidan asks Rose if she's sure she'll be okay.

"Now don't you worry about me, kids," she says. "I've got

to take care of the cats, and with this power outage, that'll delay Emily from coming here for a few more days. I've got lots to do and I've got lots of company."

After quick hugs, we say our goodbyes and weave through the cats, now intently grooming themselves.

Chapter 33

We step into a world of browns and greens. Tree branches, leaves, lawn ornaments, and trash can contents litter the ground as far as I can see. Aidan tugs me along to the path behind the house that leads to the woods.

Our trip today is much slower as we dodge downed trees. Everything feels so wrong. Maybe we were cocooned in Rose's house for too long. It felt like things might actually be okay in the short time we stayed there. Now, it just feels like the world has changed once again and we're struggling to keep up with it.

After what feels like hours, but couldn't possibly be, we reach the tree line that surrounds the trailer park. Reality slaps me across the face.

As I take in the scene, my eyes swell with sorrow and my heart burns with rage. *How do things just keep getting worse and worse? Haven't I been through enough already?*

Lawn chairs are strewn about the pathways. Porch railings lie splintered. A few of the trailers closest to the woods bear the brunt of fallen trees, their roofs slouching under the weight.

I stop in my tracks, raise both hands to my head and slowly turn from right to left, digesting the panoramic view. I can't speak. I can't express the emotions vying to escape my body. I feel battered, like one of the lawn ornaments destroyed during last night's storm.

Aidan snaps me out of my stupor. "Quinn," he says softly as he places a hand on my shoulder. "Let's keep going." I barely know him, but, once again, I'm thankful he's here. I waft between feeling like I couldn't do this alone to knowing that this is my problem and no one else's to deal with. I force myself to pick one foot up and place it in front of the other. I focus on taking one step at a time, following the gravelly path toward Aunt Grace's trailer.

The wooden steps have caved in on themselves. Aidan jumps up onto the porch and holds a hand out to help me up. Physically, I don't need his help, but emotionally a feather could knock me down right now.

I gratefully take his hand and let him pull me up. The trailer's door dangles on only its top hinges. Aidan steps in front of me and pushes the door aside. "Riley? You here?" His voice reminds me that I have one too. I push past him into the trailer.

"Riley!" I call. "Riley, we're here. Where are you?" Aidan points to the bedroom Riley and I shared, "You check out that end and I'll take the other end." With that, we separate. My eyes scan the upturned end table and a floor lamp that lies sprawled across the living room. I step over fallen shelves and the old-fashioned trinkets that peered out from them for as long as I can remember.

I push the bedroom door open as I half-heartedly plea, "Riley?" I stop mid-step when a shadow dashes across the room toward the window. "Riley?" I say again, but the shadow crouches. Riley wouldn't try to hide from me. Which means whoever is in this room isn't my sister.

The first part of my body to wake from its temporary stupor is my vocal chords. A scream rips from my throat. I think Aidan calls my name, but I don't answer. I just keep my eyes on the figure crouching by the window.

Aidan brushes past me, following my gaze. "Hey there," he says to the stranger calmly, both hands raised in front of him. "How about you come on out and we can introduce ourselves?"

The stranger slowly rises, and I'm shocked to see that when he stands at full height, he doesn't even reach my shoulders. A disheveled boy stands in the room with us. My frightened brain interpreted him to be a seven-foot-tall grim reaper. I stifle an inappropriate giggle. I imagine it would sound heinous, like a serial killer laughing at her own sick joke.

"Hi, I'm Aidan and this is Quinn," he says, motioning toward me. "Who are you?"

The boy pushes shaggy blond hair out of his eyes. "I'm Chris," he says quietly. "What are you doing here?" I step forward and answer him. "Um, technically my aunt owns this trailer, so I should really be asking you what *you're* doing here."

"Oh," he scratches his head and flashes us an innocent smile that has probably gotten him out of trouble in the past. "Well, I was just kind of hiding out."

Aidan takes a step toward him. The boy doesn't flinch, but he also doesn't make any move toward us. "Why don't we go sit down on the couch and talk?" Aidan suggests. The boy nods and slowly emerges from his hiding place. He walks with the anticipation of a kid who was just called to the principal's office.

We parade down the hallway single-file and plop ourselves on the couch, Aidan and I face Chris. He relaxes into the couch and looks up at us. A smattering of freckles dots his nose and his green eyes exude innocence.

"So, Chris," Aidan starts. "Do you live around here?"

"Yep," he answers, shoving his hands into the pockets of his blue mesh shorts. He's clearly not interested in elaborating.

Aidan rubs his chin and tries again, "So you live in the trailer park?"

"Nope," Chris replies, chewing on the collar of his Washington Capitals T-shirt. *Okay, this is gonna take all day at this rate and I want to get back to looking for my sister.* I jump into the conversation. "Chris, what are you doing here? Aren't your parents worried about you? Don't you need to get home?"

His posture stiffens at the mention of parents. "No one's worried about me," he says. "Look, I got stuff to do. I gotta go." He rises and starts toward the door.

"Alright then, nice meeting you," I say, giving him a wave.

Aidan jumps to his feet. "Chris, wait!" He shoots me a look, as if he can't believe I was going to just watch the kid leave.

I'm not sure what the big deal is. This kid is just wasting our time and we've got to keep looking for Riley.

Chris stops in his tracks, turns back toward us and cocks his head to one side as if to say, "What do you want?"

"Just give us five minutes, okay? Just five more minutes and then we'll leave you alone," Aidan pleads. Clearly annoyed, Chris releases a dramatic sigh and trudges back to the couch.

Chapter 34

While the boys chat, I search the trailer for anything that might come in handy. Their conversation sounds heated at one point, but I don't pay much attention. I dig through kitchen drawers and retrieve steak knives, a lighter, and a small sewing kit. As I shove them into my backpack, Aidan wanders in. Running a hand through his tousled hair, apprehension weighs on his features.

"What?" I ask. "Are you done with the kid yet? We should keep moving."

Aidan leans back against the counter and crosses his arms. "So, Chris wants to come with us."

"What?" I practically shriek. "Five minutes ago, he couldn't get out of here fast enough. What the hell?"

Aidan glances toward the living room and brings his pointer finger to his lips, silently telling me to shush. He takes three fast strides toward me and leans in close, whispering. "Quinn, I think his parents are…not good people."

Narrowing my eyes, I whisper back. "We can't just *take* this kid with us. Even if his parents suck, which we don't really know for sure. I have enough to worry about without adding kidnapping to my to-do list."

I start to turn back to the drawers, but Aidan grabs my elbow, holding me in place. "You didn't hear the venom in his voice when he said he needed a place to go." I'm still not convinced. When Aidan sees that I have nothing left to say, he adds, "Look, I think the bigger issue here is that if this kid is willing to just go off with people he met a few minutes ago, then he'll go off with anyone. And the next person he asks might not be like us."

Realization dawns on me. No one in Aidan's group would hurt Chris. Well, Jasmine might give him nightmares or tell him there's no Santa Claus, but other than that, we are all good people. What if Chris stumbled upon a child predator? I cringe when I think about what could happen to him. And if he is willing to just tag along with strangers, what does that say about his home life? Growing up, I *never* would have left my parents to willingly go off with strangers. Bitterness descends as I'm reminded that I have no choice when it comes to seeing my parents anymore.

Thoughts zip through my head as Aidan stares at me intently. The last thing I need is one more person to worry about. I just want my family back. I know I can't have my parents back but there's still a chance I can find Riley. I don't want this kid to suffer because we leave him behind, but I also don't want him to get in the way of what I need to do.

As Aidan and I stare at each other wordlessly, a small voice sounds from behind us. "Are you the ones who stole Jim's bikes? Cuz he's pretty mad about that."

Okay, that snapped my mind out of its haze. Aidan and I both turn to Chris, our mouths gaping open. "You know Jim?" I ask.

He nods. "I know him, but I don't like him," he says, crossing his arms.

"You and me both, kid." I smile at this kindred spirit. Chris plants himself at the kitchen table and explains that he's been coming to the trailer park for a few weeks, looking for something to do. When Jim noticed him hanging around, playing with some of the kids, he told Chris to take a hike.

Chris didn't listen, of course, he was just more careful about avoiding Jim. He started spending more and more time around the park, making an effort to keep an eye on Jim's trailer, so he knew when Jim was or wasn't home.

Aidan and I listen raptly as Chris tells us about the time Dan caught Chris in the park after Jim made it clear that he wasn't welcome. Apparently, Dan helped Chris sneak away before Jim saw him. *I knew Dan wasn't a bad guy. He'd be so much better off without his brother.*

I can't bring myself to ask what is so bad about home that makes him want to leave. *I'd give anything to be home right now, as long as Riley was with me.* Before Chris can continue, I ask, "So, how old are you?" He doesn't look old enough to be here right now, talking with a couple of strangers. Alone.

"Ten," Chris says defiantly. *What?* My eyes meet Aidan's and I see the emotions I'm feeling flicker through his eyes: surprise, pity, sadness.

"Chris," Aidan starts. "Don't you—"

"I was here last night," Chris says, knowing we're once again hanging on his every word. "I heard Jim and Dan making plans, talking about some girl. I waited and watched." He turns to me and points. "You know, she looked a lot like you."

All air deflates from my lungs and my body feels slack. I worry that my spiking heart will keep rising until it bursts. Aidan handles the news with a composure that I can't muster.

I listen mutely as Chris explains that he saw Jim and Dan last night, sitting around their fire pit drinking beer. Jim was complaining about some girls, saying he thought they were up to something. *It had to be us. There's no way any other female purposely spoke to Jim yesterday.*

"Wait," Chris interjects, smirking at me. "Quinn. You're the one he was talking about last night." When I nod slowly, a snort escapes him. I'm guessing he's recalling some choice words Jim must have had for me last night.

"What's so funny?" Aidan asks. Chris has the decency to keep his thoughts to himself. He just shakes his head and continues with his story.

"So, I saw Jim and Dan drinking their beer," Chris explains. "They do that a lot. I think they started to get bored because Jim said they should go for a ride." *Of course, he would think that drinking and driving is a good idea. Dumbass.*

Chris chuckles to himself at the next part. "When they couldn't find their keys, Jim started yelling. They went inside, and I think they were smashing things." He hunches his shoulders as if say, "Oh well."

"I kinda got bored and went home." At the realization that

175

he mentioned home, he quickly picks up the pace of his story. "Anyway, I needed someplace to go, so I came back to the park. I thought I could watch Jim rage. But this time was different. When I peeked in their windows, a girl was with them."

Pausing for a moment, he points at me, saying, "She looked a lot like you."

"Oh, and their bikes were parked outside, so they found their keys," he adds. "I hid in the bushes and watched. All three of them drove away."

I stare at Chris, dumbfounded. He saw my sister right after she was taken. I stare at him, waiting for him to say more but he doesn't. Maybe that's all he knows.

"Chris, did they mention anything about where they were headed?" Aidan prompts. Chris rubs his forehead as if he's willing his brain to remember. We both stare intently at him, waiting.

"Umm, Jim said they were going on a long trip," Chris says slowly. We both nod eagerly. "He said…he said something about landing." I just fix my narrowed eyes on him, but Aidan tries to coax the information out of him.

"Okay, landing. Did he say anything else before or after that word?" Aidan says calmly. I want to grab Chris by the shoulders and shake the information out of him.

"Um, he said something about a base. A landing base. South. They had to go south to get there." He smiles, pleased with himself.

I'm not sure what he's so proud of. He isn't making much sense to me.

Aidan must sense that this is going nowhere because he suggests that Chris go home to gather anything he might want to take with him. Chris looks wary, untrusting, but Aidan bends down to his level and holds his gaze. "Quinn and I are gonna take a look around the trailer to see if there's anything else we need. We are not going to leave here without you. When you come back here, the three of us leave together. Okay?" Chris nods his head and turns on his heel, rushing out the door.

With Chris gone, Aidan grasps my shoulders. "Quinn, you still in there?" I reward his effort with a small smile. "I think that kid's telling the truth. Riley isn't here. Let's gather anything useful and head back to the campground. We'll figure out a plan together."

"Are we leaving Chris behind?" I blurt out the first thought that pops into my mind. "No," he answers sternly. "Of course not, I know it's the last thing we need, but I'm not leaving him." He ruffles a hand through his messy black hair. "I have no idea what we're gonna do with him, but we can't leave him here."

I've got no fight left in me. That kid has no reason to lie about seeing Jim, Dan, and Riley last night. Maybe one of the others can crack the code and figure out where my sister is.

Chapter 35

About an hour later, we've finished scavenging the trailer and even raided Dan and Jim's shed for good measure. We load up two nylon shopping bags we found with our treasures: gardening snips, a pruner, work gloves, twine, and duct tape.

Chris appears, out of breath, a camouflage backpack slung over his shoulder. Other than the small bulge resting at the bottom of the bag, it looks mostly empty. *This kid is leaving home and he's barely bringing anything with him?* Maybe we are right to take him with us. Either he doesn't have much to his name, or he doesn't want to remember the life he's leaving.

"Hey there," Aidan says, smiling at Chris. "Quinn and I found a few more things that could help us, and we're just about ready to go. Are you ready to come meet our friends?"

Chris nods, eyeing us warily, as if he still doesn't believe we're taking him with us. *Oh well, he'll see for himself soon enough.*

I just hope he can deal with Jasmine. We probably should have warned him about her before he decided to come with us.

With one last look around the trailer park and the scattered remnants of homes, I turn my attention to the trek ahead. Once again, we're on the highway, this time heading back to Rustic Shores Campground.

"So, Chris—" Aidan starts.

Chris cuts him off. "Tell me about your friends," he says innocently, looking back and forth between us. Smart kid. I think he just wants to avoid answering any questions about himself.

Aidan shoots me a look over Chris' head but answers the kid, explaining that he and Jeff were friends since they were kids. They grew up together and spent the past year as college roommates. They met Jasmine and Wes in classes. Aidan finishes up by explaining that the guys decided to take a road trip, and Jasmine tagged along to get a ride home for the summer.

When he finishes, Chris turns to me. "What about you? He didn't say anything about you being with them."

I forgot how blunt kids can be. Guess I better get used to being around someone with no filter. Jasmine could use a better filter, but this kid seems to have none.

Amused, Aidan raises his eyebrows, waiting for my response.

"Well," I start, "My family was driving down here from Pennsylvania for a vacation. There was a big accident and our car got pretty smashed up. My parents…they weren't okay. But my sister and I made it out and we were together." I pause for a moment, lost in the flood of memories that I'd really rather forget.

Fire burns in my heart and venom laces my words. "That is,

until that asshat Jim took her." I brace for Chris to push for more details, but thankfully, he doesn't. He latches on to our common enemy. We spend the next half hour sharing less-than-flattering stories about Jim. We erupt in laughter after each story, and the walk feels like a quick stroll.

When we reach the campsite, we see Wes and Jasmine sitting by the flameless fire pit. Jeff is pacing in front of them, talking animatedly with his hands. When his eyes land on us, he stops mid-step and rubs his chin. As a grin spreads across his face, he calls out to us. "Well, it's about damn time!"

All three rush over. Jasmine and Wes wrap their arms around Aidan while Jeff pulls me in for a hug. Awkwardness surrounds us when Jeff moves on to Aidan. Wes shuffles over and gives me a half-embrace. Jasmine throws me a slight nod and zeroes in on Chris. "Who is this handsome fellow?" she asks enthusiastically.

When she leans down to Chris' level, he smiles and answers, "I'm Chris." She spends the next ten minutes chatting with him and joking around. This is the complete opposite of what I expected. *When did a welcoming, caring person swoop in and invade Jasmine's body? We were gone for less than twenty-four hours.*

Ambling over to the logs framing the fire ring, we sit. My legs welcome the reprieve.

Chris practically bounces on his feet. Shyly, he looks to Aidan. "Um, okay if I take a look around?"

Aidan smiles and says, "Sure, buddy. Just don't go too far, okay?"

Chris nods and takes off running. This must be a pretty cool place for him to explore.

With Chris busy, Aidan explains why he's even here. The

group listens intently, eyes following Chris each time he soars past us. By the time Aidan's done speaking, the guys fidget uncomfortably. Running long slender fingers through her curly black hair, Jasmine leans in toward the group and speaks quietly. "You did the right thing. The world is a different place now, and if that kid can just pack his belongings and walk away from home without a glance back, something wasn't right."

The others solemnly nod.

When Chris finally tires himself out and plops down next to Aidan, we rehash taking shelter at Rose's house.

Jeff slips in an eyebrow waggle when he says, "So, you two were just crocheting quilts or something with grandma all night, huh?"

Jasmine smacks his arm, but I wish she would have aimed about a foot higher because he still wears a smug grin on his face.

Ignoring the interjection, Aidan continues. The conversation turns serious when he shares Chris' "spy intel" with the group.

"So where did the guys say they were going?" Wes questions. The dark circles under his eyes contrast with the washed-out pallor of his face. *Maybe he didn't get much sleep last night.* We haven't even asked about how they weathered the storm. I tune out the conversation and scrutinize my surroundings.

The shoddy cabins stand. They're just as rundown as they were the first time I saw them, but they are no worse off. Leaves and branches clutter the paths, but this is nothing like the damage at the trailer park. *Maybe trailer parks really are magnets for tornadoes.*

I'm yanked back into the present when fingers snap in front of my face. Jeff waves a hand and calls out, "Mission control to Quinn. Come in, Quinn."

"Sorry guys," I say, sweeping my eyes across each of them in turn. "What did I miss?"

"Quinn," Aidan's eyes widen as he holds my gaze. "We figured it out. We know where Jim and Dan took Riley. Not *landing base*. Langley Air Force Base!"

Chapter 36

"Oh my gosh! You guys figured that out?" Just having a lead calms my nerves. Never mind that hundreds of miles separate Delaware and Virginia. And we have no transportation. And we're basing this off of a ten-year-old's recollection.

Jeff slaps Wes on the back. "Guess this guy actually paid attention in classes," he says, jabbing a thumb toward Wes.

With a genuine smile, Wes explains, "I'm hoping to be stationed at Langley someday. I've never been there, but it's definitely south of here and the name sounds like what Chris heard. And, not to mention that I, for one, would love to check it out."

Jeff interjects, "We could probably make it there in a day if we can just get some wheels."

"Yeah," Aidan says. "And we were going to Virginia to drop Jasmine off, so this really isn't too out of the way."

I glance at Jasmine. She clearly doesn't share the guys' excitement, but at least she doesn't argue.

"So," I start. "How do we find a car?"

"Why, Quinn," Aidan teases. "Are you suggesting we *steal* a car?"

Crossing my arms across my chest, I rebuff, "Not at all. I just want to *borrow* one."

Jeff slaps his hands on his knees. "I think it was gonna come to this anyway. At some point, we'd have to steal some wheels to get the hell out of here. I say we form a search party and start looking."

Wes immediately volunteers, "I'll go." *He volunteered to check out the trailer park for us too. That must be his personality—putting others first.*

I shoot Aidan a look of concern. Shadows hover under Wes' eyes, and his posture is hunched, making him appear drained. Jasmine must see it too because she says, "Wes, you stay. I'm tired of sitting around this place. Jeff and I will go."

It takes a little convincing for Wes to agree, but eventually he does. After a quick lunch, Jeff and Jasmine are on their way. The rest of us clean up belongings and make sure everything is gathered to make a quick getaway once we have wheels.

After explaining that the tornado completely missed the campground last night, Wes says that they just hung out in a cabin and avoided the rain and wind. Still, he's tired from a restless night of howling wind and cracking thunder; he decides to rest while Jeff and Jasmine are gone.

Before he trudges off to the cabin, he points toward the shack he originally showed me and Riley, when he suggested that we sleep there. "I threw Riley's bag and the blankets you two slept on in there when it started to rain last night. Didn't want anything to get ruined." I touch his shoulder and meet his eyes. "Thanks, Wes. That was really thoughtful of you." *Yep, this guy definitely puts others first.*

When Chris begs Aidan to explore the outer edges of the campground, my heart leaps at the thought of spending some time alone. I've appreciated the group's company, except for Jasmine's, but now that we have a solid plan, a solitude breather sounds great. Anytime I needed alone time in my previous life, I'd slip on my sneakers and go for a run. I don't feel like expending that kind of energy right now, though.

When the boys invite me to tag along on their expedition, I wave them off and instead head to the bug-infested cabin to gather the items Wes rescued last night.

After I've folded the red and gray chenille blankets, I sit on the creaky bed frame and open my sister's backpack. Funny how the last time I was in here, I wouldn't have gone near this bed. Now I'm much more interested in preserving my sister's possessions. If a cockroach family decides to join me, so be it.

Reaching into the lilac bag, I smile as I pull out her Kindle. *There's no way she would have gone anywhere willingly without this.* I empty her bag slowly, examining each item as if I'm seeing it for the first time. Except what I'm seeing is little pieces of my sister. Each prized belonging renews the smile on my face.

I envision her taming her long brown hair with the purple hairbrush. Pulling it back with the black elastic headband. Curling up with the hard copy of *Wanted by You* by Steph Nuss. Probably a backup in case she forgot to charge the Kindle. Romance and flowers, that's my sister.

Grasping her wallet, I flip it open to the pictures. I recognize her best friend, Stacy, smiling alongside Riley in a cast photo from last year's school musical. All of the other photos feature our small family—splashes of memories from vacations and formal portrait sessions. The faces blur as my eyes well with tears. I carefully return each item to its lilac home and set the backpack aside. As I turn away from the bag, it falls on its side and a small package tumbles out. I recognize the black Trolli pack instantly. Sour gummy worms, my favorite. I don't know where she got them, but I know they were meant for me. Riley hates sour candy. The tears fall freely as I grab the package and shove it deep into Riley's backpack. Maybe some alone time wasn't such a good idea.

Chapter 37

After a good cry, I dry the tears on my sleeves and take a few deep, calming breaths. Within a few minutes, I hear a voice calling my name. My cruel mind assumes it's Riley and I jump to my feet and rush out the door.

Aidan and Chris come barreling up the path toward me. Chris calls out, "Quinn, we've been looking for you!"

"Sorry, I didn't hear you until just now," I stutter.

I try to avert my eyes, but I'm assuming they're puffy when Aidan asks, "Hey there, you okay?" The last thing I want to do is explain why I'm so upset.

"I'm fine, really," I lie and turn my full attention to Chris. "What's up? What did you need me for?"

"We heard a stream or river or something and we thought we could splash around in there to cool off. Aidan was worried about you, so he made—" Chris starts before Aidan wraps an arm around his head, playfully cutting off his words.

"So, I suggested that we come back and check to see if you wanted to join us," Aidan finishes. "You know, in case you were hot. Well, I mean not that I'm questioning…" His words die off and his face flushes red.

I'm certain my face mirrors his when I start talking just to shut him up. "That was really thoughtful, thanks. Yeah, I could use a change of scenery. Let's go see this body of water, whatever it is."

I follow the boys past the path to the washrooms and onto the wooded trail. After a few minutes, the trees start to thin and the dirt path slopes slightly downhill. When the swirling rush of water reaches my ears, I know we're close.

Aidan leads the way, but Chris' anticipation seems to build with each step we take. He pauses to throw a smile over his shoulder at me before pushing past Aidan and bounding toward the sound of a bustling stream.

Just a few steps behind, Aidan and I reach the clearing a moment later. We see Chris standing a few feet away from the water. I figured he'd be splashing around in there by now.

"What are you doing?" I ask. "Why did you stop?"

He turns toward me slowly, his expression downcast. "It's dead, Quinn. The water's dead."

As I edge closer to him, my eyes fall to what was probably once a vibrant stream. The water is an ashen gray color with blobs of dirt-specked foam sitting atop it. It looks like a flutter of concrete with murky bubbles sliding over its surface. We can't cool off in this water. We shouldn't even touch it.

When my eyes reach the water's edge, I'm even more disturbed. Death lines the land. Crayfish carcasses and lifeless fish—what's left of them—litter the bank, rocking back and forth from the carpet of bugs feasting. The scuttle of activity is a dark contrast to the death just beneath it.

"What happened, guys?" Chris asks innocently, looking between me and Aidan.

Without taking my eyes off what was going to provide some relief from the grating heat, I solemnly respond. "It's poisoned. We can't touch this."

Aidan meets my eyes. "Yeah, Quinn's right. How about we go splash around in the washroom to cool off? We'll just need to make sure that water still looks okay." *Great, if this stream is part of the campground's water source, the group may have already been exposed to this putrid excuse for water.*

With nothing left to say or do, we trudge back to camp. Chris keeps his eyes downcast the whole time. I feel bad for the kid. We had this one chance to goof around and do something fun with him and just like that, it's gone.

While my body moves on autopilot, my mind wanders with questions. *What turns a stream teeming with life into a sickening display of death? How long ago did this happen? Does anyone know or care about this? Is anyone doing anything to fix it? Is it happening anywhere else?*

The three of us head straight to the washrooms on our way back to the cabins. Chris and Aidan check the water in the men's room while I check out the ladies' room. None of us detect any discoloration in the liquid that pours from the faucets or showers. Aidan explains that the group stopped drinking the water from the sinks because it tasted bad, but that's not all that strange for a campground, especially one that's clearly not been used in years.

We offer to have a splash battle with Chris, though secretly

I don't think it's a great idea to handle this water any more than necessary, but his playful spirit has dampened.

With no clear conclusion and no reason to stay there, we head back to the cabin area. Wes sits on a log around the fire pit. "I was wondering where you guys were," he says, stretching. I can't hide my relief at his improved appearance. "Wes, you look soooo much better. I'm glad you got some rest."

He straightens up and cocks his head back proudly. "Well, thanks for noticing, Quinn. You're looking mighty fine yourself."

I giggle and playfully punch his shoulder.

The four of us sit in content silence peppered with small talk until the rumble of an engine permeates the campground.

Chapter 38

We all shoot to our feet and run toward the sound. Peeking around one of the ramshackle cabins, I spot a cloud of dust fanning out behind a gold car that is quickly approaching.

"That's a Chevy Malibu," Wes says. "Let's hope it's Jeff," Aidan adds.

"Um, just in case it's not, why don't we blend into the scenery a bit?" Wes asks. The serious look on his face conveys that it's not a question. We all cower behind the closest cabin while Wes peeks around the corner every few seconds, keeping an eye on the approaching vehicle.

As the car nears, Wes breaks into a smile and announces we should greet our company. Stepping around the corner, I watch two passengers sway and bob as the vehicle traverses the uneven dirt road. Sure enough, when they park a moment later, Jasmine and Jeff emerge from the vehicle. Slapping the hood, Jeff calls out to us. "How do you like our new ride, guys?"

191

After the guys nod their approval to Jeff, we all meander to our unofficial meeting place, the fire pit log area, and sit. Jasmine and Jeff explain how they happened upon a local used car lot and Jeff used his covert skills to unlock the office door and find the keys. While Jasmine wanted to find a bigger car to better accommodate the six of us, Jeff insisted on a compact car, thinking it would last longer until we ran out of gas.

With everything packed and a set of wheels waiting, we load up our belongings and crowd six butts into a vehicle meant for five.

Jeff rushes to the driver's seat, the only one guaranteed to have a whole seat to himself. Jasmine and I move to opposite backseat doors while Wes slides past her and sits in the middle. I claim the seat behind the driver, satisfied that I won't have to be crammed up against Jasmine. She immediately glides in on Wes' other side.

Aidan opens the front passenger door, glancing at Chris. He ruffles the kid's hair and says, "Well, buddy, looks like you and me get the front seat. That okay with you?" Chris belts out a hearty affirmation while Aidan looks anything but thrilled.

Jasmine insists she can guide us in the right direction. Attempting to follow her orders, Jeff navigates the car south, sometimes off-roading it to dodge obstacles. Avoiding Route One altogether, we make our way to Route Nine and head west. We pass other vehicles now and then, but the most interaction we share with them is a curious passing glance.

Once we're set on a course, Aidan brings up the stream we found at the campground today.

I sit quietly and observe their reactions. My worry reflects in their eyes.

"Do you think it was pollution?" Jasmine asks angrily.

Aidan and Chris both shrug.

"I think that's a good guess. Whatever it was, it killed everything that lived in it," Aidan says.

"And it sure made the bugs happy," Chris says. "I never saw so many bugs in one place."

"Hey, have you noticed, we haven't seen many animals on this trip?" Wes asks. "No deer, no rabbits, no squirrels. How can you be outside for days on end and not see a squirrel?"

"Well," Aidan says. "It feels like the weather's been extreme. Even for summer. We go from scorching days to freezing nights."

"And you think that's affected animals?" Jeff asks.

"Animals adapt to their environment," Aidan explains. "Cave crickets and cave fish are completely blind, but they thrive in their environment."

"What is a cave cricket and how is it different from a regular cricket?" Jasmine asks.

"Maybe it's a regular cricket that just lives in a cave," said Wes. "But you don't call regular crickets yard crickets or street crickets."

"Not relevant to the conversation," Aidan dismisses, furrowing his brow. "You know how blind people can have really good hearing or other senses? They adapt to the loss of their vision. Their other senses become heightened. It's the same thing we're seeing here."

"So, what does that mean for us?" Jasmine jumps to the point.

"Yeah, right. He doesn't know," Jeff teases.

"Well, earthquakes and tornadoes are normal weather

events," Aidan interjects. "But not necessarily for this part of the country. So why would we have two unusual events happen so close to each other all of a sudden? And, the weather patterns have been strange too. We've had weather extremes during the day and at night. That's not typical for the East Coast. It's like… Are these events building off of each other?"

"That actually kinda makes sense," Jeff says. "Maybe it's all connected. But why now? What started it all?" Just as I'm about to mention the fracking incident, Jasmine chimes in.

"I think Mother Nature is finally tired of seeing us poison her streams, rivers, and oceans. Mistreat her beautiful creatures. Destroy her wonder. I think her only answer is to eliminate the source of destruction: us."

Eyes wide, Chris looks to Jasmine with awe. Wes rolls his eyes and whispers, "She'll make a great lawyer, huh?"

Jasmine continues undeterred. "Over and over humans have proved they are unable to regulate themselves. This world is turning on us. Every day rivers are tainted from pollution. Fouled water sources are killing the life that once thrived within them."

I tune out as she drones on and on. Maybe she's onto something here. *If animals consume a tainted food or water source, then wouldn't this contamination work its way through the food cycle? Wouldn't it eventually make its way up to the life form that dominates them all?*

By the time I tune back into the conversation, Jasmine is questioning if Mother Nature is laughing at us now. If she's watching, waiting to see what we'll do. *If she is right about all of this, will anyone realize what's happening? Will anyone try to fix what is broken? Probably not.*

Chapter 39

Conversation swirls through the car, but the hum of the engine and the warmth Wes radiates lulls my eyes closed. My mind transports me back to the day we got Snickers. After months and months of begging for a pet, our parents finally caved and took us to an animal shelter.

The distinct smell of wet dog, combined with the pungent odor of urine, invades my nose as I follow my family through the warehouse-like hallway of kennels. Yelping and crying fills my ears. Anxiety and nervous energy hang in every molecule of air.

When I tug on my mom's sleeve and ask if we can leave, she simply says, "You've only been here for a minute and you want to leave. Just imagine how they must feel." Her soft fleece jacket slips through my fingers as she strolls deeper into the room. Her eyes sweep through each kennel as she passes, pausing here and there to offer gentle reassurances to the most vocal residents.

"Guys, come here," Riley calls, kneeling outside of a

kennel, her fingers wrapped around the chain-link door. Kneeling down beside her, I nudge her over, so I can see. My dad reads the cage card as we watch the small bundle of white and brown fur shiver in the corner of his kennel.

"This is Snickers. He's a Rat Terrier mix. They think he's about two-years-old. He was found as a stray with a broken leg. They believe he was hit by a car. He's been at the shelter for four months." An arm wraps around my shoulder, squishing me into Riley. Squatting behind us, my mom speaks loud enough for us to hear over the chorus of canine voices. "He looks pretty sad, girls. Should we ask him if he wants to come home with us?"

The arm around me tightens and I start to lose my balance. My eyes spring open and disappointment washes through me as I take in the faces surrounding me. They bear no resemblance to my parents or my sister. "Quinn, it's okay," Wes says quietly. "You fell asleep, but it's time to wake up."

Raising my head from the pillow I apparently made on Wes' shoulder, I attempt to wipe the sleep from my eyes and the embarrassment from my cheeks. "Quinn!" Chris practically shouts, "look where we're going!" His little pointer finger shakes in excitement as he motions out the window.

Jeff's broad smile fills the rearview mirror while Aidan nervously runs a hand through his tousled black hair. Arms crossed over her chest, Jasmine sulks in her seat. Wes watches me intently, as if I might bolt from the car. Practically jumping up and down in his seat, Chris is like a sparking firework spinning on the ground.

The neon yellow and green storefront practically burns my retinas and it's not even lit. Its huge orange letters scream its name: Ton O' Fun. Without another word, Jeff loops the car around the strip mall slowly and glides into one of many empty parking spaces. "Looks like it's just us," Jeff says. "We got the whole place to ourselves."

"What the hell?" I ask, my voice rising with each word. Raising his hands in a placating gesture, Aidan explains, "We've already covered some distance. We thought it would be a good idea to stop and rest for the night. Jeff and Chris saw this place, so we thought we'd check it out."

Why on earth would we stop driving? If the roads were clear, we could make it to Virginia by late tonight. Jeff throws a sly smirk around the car as he turns it off and opens his door.

"We are gonna have some fun tonight!" Jeff says. "And if anyone gives me any trouble about it, they're getting tossed in the ball pit." Wes shakes his head, chuckling to himself. My eyes widen when Jasmine actually smiles. Her face didn't even crack in the process.

I don't really want to stop driving, but I can't exactly demand that we keep going if everyone else wants to stop. Besides, the look on Chris' face clearly gives away his vote. The kid is ear-to-ear smiles. What ten-year-old wouldn't be?

Aidan turns toward Wes. "What do you think, man?" Wes nods and says, "Sure, why not?" He glances between me and Jasmine. "How about it, ladies? We could all use a little bit of fun. Blow off some steam." When Aidan casts those blue eyes on me, I answer so quickly that I almost cut him off. "Sure." He hesitates, sensing my disappointment, but turns back to the others. "Chris, I already know what you're thinking."

Chris nods. His eyes wide with obvious anticipation of the

whole place at our disposal.

"Alright then, let's grab our stuff while Jeff rolls out the red carpet."

Aidan catches up with Jeff to assist with a quick recon mission of peeking into the indoor playland's front windows, checking for signs of life. Unloading and shouldering our bags, we stroll along the sidewalk toward our destination. Black and white flyers dot the storefront windows, announcing that the plaza is closed until further notice due to a local power outage.

When we meet Jeff and Aidan at the entrance, their smiles convey confidence that no one's inside. We proceed with our plan. I don't really want to know why Jeff is so proficient with a fork and a screwdriver that he can pick the door lock in less than five minutes. Either he expected to need those tools, or he carries them around with him the way I used to carry lip gloss.

We rush through the door like sardines, bumping into each other's bags and bodies. A hint of mildew and sweat mingle to greet our noses. A rainbow-colored confetti and ribbon design brightens the thin black carpet. Basketball hoops and Skee-Ball ramps line the walls. A maze of video games, pinball machines, and virtual-reality simulators clutter the large space.

I have to admit, this place is inviting.

"Wow," Chris exhales. "Can we play some video games?" His hopeful green eyes widen under the shaggy brown bangs dusting his eyebrows. Jasmine's smooth ebony skin tugs into a grin when she answers him. "Buddy, the signs said the power might be out, so we'll have to see if anything works in here." He quickly shrugs off any pending disappointment as his eyes feast on the ball pit.

As much as I thought this was a bad idea, it's kind of cool being the only ones inside a giant indoor playhouse. I'm still taking in my surroundings when Jasmine calls out to the group. "How about we bunk in the party rooms? They're toward the back of the building, so if anyone walks past outside, they won't see us."

"Great idea," Aidan says. He walks toward the party rooms. "Looks like there are three rooms. Us guys can take one room. Jasmine and Quinn, I'm figuring you want your own rooms?" Jasmine and I both answer at the same time. "Yes!"

My relief that sleeping arrangements have been settled is short-lived when Jeff says, "You know, ladies, if you prefer, I would be willing to stay in a room with you both. I can just be like a bodyguard, make sure you're both safe."

Jasmine turns on her heel and strides into Party Room 2. I take a moment to give Jeff the full eye roll he deserves and then head toward Party Room 3. I drop my bags and sink to the floor, my back propped up against the wall. Resting my head in my hands, I try to tamp down the frustration I feel. I just want to find my sister. *Why couldn't we all just take turns driving? Why do we have to stop and waste hours here?*

I nearly jump out of my skin when I hear a hearty, "Hey, Quinn!" Standing in the open doorway, Chris looks pleased that he crashed my pity party. "Oh, hey, Chris, what's up?"

Sliding down beside me onto the floor, Chris fills me in on the group's plan. Jasmine and the guys have already headed back to the kitchen area to look for food. They're hoping to find some frozen pizzas, french fries, or really anything edible.

Chris takes one of my hands in his and pulls as I stand up.

I willingly follow as he leads me to the kitchen. I'm better off helping round up some food than sulking, thinking about where I'd rather be. Once he's satisfied that I'm going to join the others, Chris takes off running back into the fun center. It's probably better that way. I'm not sure I want a kid handling the food. *Who knows when he last washed his hands?*

Chapter 40

The kitchen is a small gold mine. In a short period of time, the gang has formed an assembly line of sorts.

Aidan stands at one end of a long stainless-steel table, freeing pizza crusts from their packaging.

Wes thrusts a dingy thin pan in front of Aidan for each crust.

Jeff and Jasmine bump into each other as he spreads sauce on each crust and she tosses cheese on top.

Deciding it's time to make myself useful, I stride over to the massive commercial oven, briefly examine the knobs, and set the temperature to 375. I figure that's a pretty basic setting.

When I turn back toward the group, Aidan throws me a smirk as he drops the last pizza crust on a pan.

"What?" I ask, crossing my arms.

"Just glad to see you decided to join us," he says, walking past me. Gripping the mighty oven door, he pulls it open and slides all four trays of pizza inside.

"Alright," Jasmine announces, pushing a lock of silky black hair behind her ear. "Let's find plates and silverware." Conveniently for us, the store must have closed normally one night and then sat in a perpetual mode of awaiting the next business day. We find clean plates stacked in the kitchen and a mound of heavy plastic forks and dull knives wrapped in white paper napkins. Once we've all collected a plate and utensil bundle, Jasmine turns to Chris. "So, little man, where should we eat?"

Without hesitation, Chris shouts, "Ball pit!" Glancing at each other, everyone shrugs or nods. "Alright, bud," Jasmine says. "How about we find some drinks and set those up at the ball pit so we're all ready when the pizzas are done?" He nods eagerly and tears off into the labyrinth of fun.

Jasmine yanks open the large stainless-steel refrigerator. We all gather around the open door, silently taking inventory. The shelves are full of bottled water, juice boxes, bags upon bags of lettuce, and tubs of salad dressing. Jasmine grabs a water bottle and a juice box and moves out of the way. As I wrap my hands around a bottle, Chris runs back into the kitchen. "The soda machines won't work!" he announces. Jasmine smiles at him, actually smiles, and says, "I bet they're shut off, buddy, but that's okay. We found other drinks." She thrusts the juice box toward him. In one swift movement, he swipes it from her hand and dashes back to the electronic playland.

It still shocks me to observe Jasmine being so nice to someone. Granted, Chris is a child, but I would think she'd be more apt to tell him that the Easter Bunny is a fake or that monsters really do hide under beds and in closets. Unless it's just me she hates. *I guess that's entirely possible.*

Wes grabs his drink and heads over to the stainless-steel oven, cracking it open to check on our baking feast. A heavenly smell wafts through the air directly to my nose. My mouth waters in response. "I think they're just about done. Let's find some hot pads," Wes says.

Reminded of the food, Jeff springs into action. He finds silicone oven mitts and slips them over his hands. "Release the Kraken," he says dramatically, gesturing for Wes to open the oven door. Jeff swoops in and pulls the pizzas out, one by one, setting them on the stovetop. Aidan waits with a pizza cutter and starts slicing.

We load up our plates, balancing drinks and cutlery sets, and make our way out to the ball pit. Chris leads the way, practically strutting with pride. He's only been with us for a day, but he already seems like a happier kid. I can't understand how a ten-year-old can just leave his home and tag along with a bunch of strangers on a road trip. I know he'll tell us his story when he's ready, but it's really sad to think that he chose us over whatever family he has out there.

Mimicking Chris, we all sit on the edge of the ball pit, our feet dangling inside. Twilight bathes the parking lot, and thanks to the wall plate labeled "overnight lights" that Aidan switched on, Ton O' Fun is blanketed in a dim, unassuming light. While the storefront is lined with floor-to-ceiling windows, the glass is covered with brightly colored jungle animals. Their massive bodies and cartoonish faces shield us from anyone passing by.

After several return trips to the kitchen to replenish our plates, we bask in the luxury of full stomachs and solid shelter. Several contented exhales later, Jasmine slowly rises. "I'm gonna wrap up the leftovers and put them in the fridge in case we want them for breakfast tomorrow." Jeff jumps up, "I'll help. I loooooooove cold pizza for breakfast."

"You know," Jasmine adds, a momentary distant look in her eyes. "Maybe we should pack up some of the food and bring it with us. Just in case we run out of gas or something tomorrow, at least we'd have something to eat."

"Yes!," Chris says, "And maybe we can find some dessert too!" He takes off running toward the kitchen, mumbling something about brownies and cookies.

Jasmine and Jeff chuckle, following after him.

"Well, I'm beat," Wes says, stifling a yawn. He stands and stretches. "I'm going to sleep." Aidan and I wish him goodnight as he trudges back to the guys' party room.

Awkwardness washes over me when I realize it's just me and Aidan left. I don't really want to make small talk, so I slowly rise to my feet. "Well, I guess I'll head to bed too," I say, gathering my empty plate and napkin. His voice stops me in my tracks. "Quinn," Aidan says quietly. Turning toward him, he's standing just inches away, our faces close. "Thanks for going along with this," he says, motioning his hands around the room. "I know you wanted to keep driving today, but I think everyone needed this."

"It's okay." I shrug. "It's nice to have four walls around us and indoor plumbing, you know?" He nods and smiles, running a hand through his messy brown mane. We pile up the empty plates, napkins, and water bottles and start making trips to the trash can. Just as we finish cleaning up, Chris comes running over to us. "Hey, Quinn, let's go look at the ball pit." He grabs my hand and pulls me with him.

I'm not really sure what we're supposed to be looking at, but I don't have to wonder for too long. Seconds after I register movement in my peripheral vision, a muscular arm wraps around my waist and a solid body collides with mine, launching me off the ground. Before I can say a word, I land in the pool of brightly colored plastic orbs. Laughter greets my ears. While I attempt to find my footing in the shifting flow of balls, Jeff lounges in the pit about a foot away from me. A coy smirk overtakes his face as he awaits my reaction.

I glance to the others, who are still standing outside the pit. Jasmine is bent over, shaking, presumably laughing so hard that she struggles to breathe. Aidan rubs a hand over his chin as if trying to cover his grin. Chris is full-on belly laughing. I half expect him to drop to the floor and start rolling around in giddiness.

Whipping a red ball at Jeff's head, I say, "Hilarious. You guys are freaking hilarious!" Before I have time to decide if I'm angry, Chris runs full speed toward us and plunges into the pit. Aidan and Jasmine follow Chris' lead.

After what feels like hours, we finally tire of swimming, jumping, and thrashing in the mountain of balls. My stomach aches from laughing so much. Thoroughly exhausted, we all lie motionless for a few minutes. When Jeff starts fake snoring, we all slog through the pit and head to the party rooms. It's time to call it a night.

Chapter 41

Taking full advantage of our accommodations, I visit the restroom to splash some water on my face and rinse my mouth. *It's the closest I can get to actually brushing my teeth.* Smoothing out my long brown hair, I gently separate a few minor tangles. As I catch my reflection in the mirror, a smile flutters across my face. I literally feel lighter. Maybe a little bit of fun was just what I needed.

On my way back to Party Room 3, Chris intercepts me. "Quinn, the guys' room is really crowded. Can I stay with you?" I respond, "Of course, buddy." I have a feeling that he is the only reason we came here, so in a way, he's responsible for lightening my mood.

Since Chris has hardly any belongings, I send him to the restroom with toothpaste we found during our second scavenging trip at the trailer—at the very least he can use his finger as a makeshift brush and slosh water around in his mouth to rinse. While he gets ready for bed, I push some tables against the wall to create a small nest of space on the floor for us. I spread the blankets Riley and I used at the campground. They offer little cushion, but at least they protect us from the carpet and the filth from who knows how many shoes that have passed over it.

When Chris returns, he takes off his shoes and crawls into our makeshift sleeping area. I flip the light off, and before he can protest, I explain that I'm leaving the door open. The dim light from the main play area will still shine in our room all night. Although his mouth opens, as if he's about to protest, he keeps quiet. I slide my shoes off and crawl onto the blanket next to him.

A comfortable warmth envelops me as Chris snuggles up against my back. His rhythmic breathing slows almost immediately. I fight to keep my eyes open until I'm sure Chris is asleep, but the darkness overtakes my vision before long.

Swirling thoughts transport me to the last track meet of my sophomore year. The sun beats on my face as I squint toward the fence, seeking out my family. I bend down into a starting stance for the 400-meter dash, and shouts of encouragement float to my ears. Before the gun fires, I flash my parents and Riley a quick smile. The moment the starting pistol thunders into the clear blue air, my feet soar over the smooth red rubber. Even halfway around the loop, I can still hear their feverish chants. "Come on, Quinn!" "You got this, keep it up!"

When I round the last turn and know that I'm going to be first to cross the finish line, my eyes wander to movement on the right side of the track. My mom is jumping up and down, my dad is snapping pictures on his phone, and Riley is full-on cheering, her hands cupped around her mouth to amplify her voice.

Once I cross the finish line, a solid ten seconds ahead of the next runner to place, I slow to a jog and move to the grassy center of the track. Bending at the waist and placing my hands on my knees for support, I catch my breath. In between gasps for breath, I cheer on my teammates with unmatched vigor. When the meet ends, I wave goodbye to the team and join my family.

By the time we pile into my dad's car and the engine purrs, my eyes start to flutter closed. When they slowly crack open again, I'm startled by what's before me. We're no longer driving home from the track meet. My panic skyrockets as I recognize Route One near Aunt Grace's trailer. The rain flows in heavy sheets and my parents are debating whether they should pull over and wait out the storm or just keep going. I start screaming that we need to pull over, but they can't hear me. It's like I'm not even there. Riley is sleeping in the backseat next to me. I clutch her arms and shake her, but she doesn't respond.

With tears trailing from my eyes, I reach toward my mom's seat, begging her to hear me. She doesn't even flinch, but my body starts shaking violently. My eyes fly open and my brain stutters as it tries to comprehend what's happening. Aidan's face is inches from mine, his hot breath sweeping across my flushed cheeks.

"Quinn, wake up," he whispers frantically. I fix my wide-eyed gaze on him, searching his eyes for answers. "It's okay, Quinn," he says calmly. "Try to slow down your breathing, take some nice deep breaths, okay?" I nod slowly and will my chest to stop heaving.

Once my breathing evens out, I quietly say, "Sorry, I just had a nightmare." Aidan's blue eyes overflow with pity when he responds, "It sounded like a pretty nasty one."

Looking around the room, I notice Chris is gone. "Where's Chris? Did he come and get you?" Scratching his head, Aidan answers, "Yeah, about that. I guess you started shaking in your sleep and it woke him up. When you started crying and half-screaming, he got freaked out and ran to our room."

Dropping my head into my hands, shame engulfs me. "Poor Chris, I hope he's not scared of me now." I can't look Aidan in the eyes when I share my worry. "Oh, come on now," he says. "He can't be the first guy to run screaming from you." I can't hold back a genuine chuckle that slows my tears and throws me into a fit of unhinged laughter. My overflowing emotions are uncontrollable.

After we've both had a good laugh, silence settles over us. "Thanks for coming in to check on me," I say. "I'm gonna go wash my face and then try to fall back asleep. You are officially relieved of your babysitting duties." He smirks at me and says, "Nope, you're stuck with me tonight. I promised the others I'd keep an eye on you. You know, make sure you don't try to kung-fu anyone else while they're sleeping."

I give him one more smile before I rise to my feet and pad out the door. Tiptoeing to the bathroom, I find my feet keeping pace with the rhythmic sound of rain pelting the roof. Exhaling a sigh of relief, I realize what a good decision it was to stop here for the night. We could be driving in this downpour or attempting to sleep outside at the campground. I'll take four walls and a civilized restroom, even if it means delaying our trip a bit.

As soon as I wash away the excess mucus just waiting to escape my nose and dry the tear tracks on my cheeks, my mood lightens. *It was just a stupid dream. I'm on my way to find Riley. I'm going to see her again, soon.* The door softly swishes closed behind me as I exit the restroom.

When I reach the party room, Aidan is stretched out on my "bed." He pats the gray blanket, encouraging me to join him. There's no way I'm sleeping directly on this carpet, so I follow his lead and lie down on "my" side. I turn so I'm facing away from him. I can sense when he turns toward me, but I stay still. "Now, Quinn," his voice sounds husky. "Don't even think about trying any funny business. I'm here simply to ensure that you sleep soundly. I'd offer to sleep head-to-toe, but I am not willing to leave my head vulnerable to your feet if you decide to go all WWE on me."

"I'll try to restrain myself," I say with mock seriousness. "Goodnight."

"G'night."

Chapter 42

Light slowly invades my eyelids as I stir from a dreamless sleep. Whispered words carry into the room, but I can't quite make them out. My eyes flutter open and land on the arm draped over my waist. My heartbeat quickens when comprehension dawns on my fuzzy brain. Memories of last night flash through my mind, and the source of the calming warmth emanating from my backside zooms into focus.

My ears hone-in on the whispering voices. "Well, look who's all cozy in here," hisses a snarky, high-pitched voice that can only be Jasmine. "Dang, no wonder he left me with Chris." That must be Jeff. "How long was I asleep? What did I miss?" Wes cuts in.

"Hey, guys! What are you all looking at?" Chris' small voice booms as his footfalls approach the doorway. Thank goodness the noise rouses Aidan. His whole body shudders next to me as he's startled awake. I roll over on my side to face the group as Aidan jolts upright mumbling, "What's going on?"

Jeff's only too happy to answer that question, eyebrows waggling overenthusiastically. "Maybe that's what we should be asking you two." After a short burst of laughter, Jasmine and the guys leave us in awkward silence.

Running a hand through his tousled hair, Aidan rolls on his knees and pushes to standing. "Well, I guess we should get ready and hit the road. Today is the day we make it to Langley!"

After a hearty breakfast of cold pizza and juice packs, we gather our belongings and as much food as we can pack, and then bid Ton O' Fun farewell. The distraction it provided was therapeutic, that is, until my nightmare sent Chris screaming from my room.

A light drizzle follows us through the parking lot. It's not enough to warrant an umbrella—not that we have one, but it's about as annoying as a cloud of gnats. While most of us purposefully avoid the minefield of puddles in the lot, each one in our path beckons to Chris. The raindrops seem to energize the kid as he crashes through puddle after puddle, leading the way to the Malibu.

After tossing the food and our bags in the trunk, we cram into the car, returning to the seats we previously occupied. Humidity overtakes the small space, and the cramped quarters are even less comfortable in damp clothes.

Inserting the key into the ignition, Jeff turns to Chris. "Alright, buddy, what now?" After a momentarily look of confusion, Chris' eyes fly open and a grin spreads across his face. "Driver… start… your… engine!" He exclaims with just enough pause between words for maximum impact.

Jeff takes his cue and turns the engine over, shifting from neutral to drive. He shoots us a smirk and says, "Hold on." With that, he grasps the wheel and slams his foot down on the gas pedal. I clutch the grip handle in anticipation, but instead of shooting forward, the back tires spin and the asphalt drops below us.

Chapter 43

Jasmine's screams fill my ears. I can't be sure if my own screams permeate the car too or if they only echo in my mind. Chris' head volleys back and forth between Jeff and Aidan, his eyes searching for answers.

Jeff revs the engine, punching the gas in an attempt to move us forward. While the front end of the car rises, the back drops like a boulder. Aidan shouts to be heard over the panicked din. "Stop! Stop the car. We need to get out. Now."

Seizing the handle, I throw the door open. The hinges squeal as I steal a quick glance behind me. Wes shoves Jasmine out the other door. Fighting gravity, I push through my open door. For a dumbfounded moment, I gawk at the crumbling edge of asphalt glaring at me. Shouting pulls me out of the temporary stupor.

"Quinn! Grab my hand," Jeff yells, reaching over the cracked edge. The previously puddled water rushes toward me, muddying the exposed dirt. Scrambling on the slick earth, I snag Jeff's open palm. His biceps flex as he eases me up and over the fissure. I flop onto my backside and crab-walk away from the opening.

"Stay right there!" Jeff commands as he jumps to his feet and runs around to the other side of the car. *Yeah, no worries there. I've got no plans to jump back into the hole that decided to swallow our car.*

The two front tires perch on the asphalt while the back end of the car grumbles as it slowly sinks deeper into the dirt. Still comprehending that the car we were just sitting in is being swallowed by the earth, I scan the parking lot, searching for signs that the ground isn't done shaking. My eyes barely register the activity swirling around me.

Jeff leads a gasping Jasmine toward me and directs her to sit down. She's still screeching, "What the hell?" when he turns away, shifting his attention to Aidan and Wes. Chris scrambles around the guys, flanking them like a hummingbird searching for nectar.

Wes staggers, leaning into Aidan. An angry red gash separates several inches of skin just below his right knee. Fueled by a rush of adrenaline, I spring to my feet. "What can I do? How can I help?"

"Let's go back inside. We need to get that leg patched up," Jeff commands, rushing to Wes' other side, taking position as another crutch. Trudging around the building, we return to Ton O' Fun. *I never thought we'd see this place again, but we can't seem to escape it.*

The guys lead Wes back to the party room that served as their bedroom last night. As they gently guide Wes onto a makeshift bed, he starts rambling. "Thanks, guys. My leg's killing me. What happened out there? Was there another earthquake?"

"That wasn't an earthquake," Aidan announces. "That was a sinkhole, and it just swallowed our ride and all of our belongings."

Chapter 44

Silence saturates the room. My brain replays the moment I tossed my bag in the trunk, just a moment before I threw Riley's bag in there. *I can't lose my sister's bag. It's the only connection I have to her right now.*

"I'm going back out there. I have to get my stuff out of the trunk," I state firmly. Jasmine punctuates a perfectly-timed eye roll with a groan. Before the looming argument erupts, Jeff barks out orders.

"Quinn, there's no time for that right now. Go to the bathroom, grab as many paper towels as you can find. Run some under hot water and bring them all out here. Aidan and Chris, find a First Aid kit. Jasmine, go to the freezer and find something we can use as an ice pack."

Once again, before my eyes, Jeff transforms into the ROTC student I imagine he was before our paths crossed. He'll be a great military officer someday. The clack of fingers snapping pulls me back to the present. "Quinn! Let's go," Jeff snaps.

After we've gathered our assigned supplies and reported back to Jeff, he patches Wes' leg up as best he can. Wes guzzles down some water and ibuprofen from the First Aid kit. When the bandages prove they'll stay in place, we leave Wes in the party room to rest.

As soon as the door drifts closed, I announce, "Okay, I'm going back to the car. I'll just need the keys."

Aidan and Jeff share a glance. "Let's not have this conversation here. Wes needs to rest. Let's go to the kitchen and talk while we clean up," Jeff suggests. Turning to Chris, he says, "Buddy, why don't you wait here. Just keep an eye out and if Wes makes any noise, you check on him, okay?"

Chris purses his lips and watches us curiously but doesn't argue. His only response is to slide down the jungle-green wall until his butt lands on the black carpet. The four of us continue to the kitchen in silence. Each step I take strengthens my resolve. They will not talk me out of doing what I need to do.

As soon as we reach the kitchen, Aidan ignites the firing squad. "Quinn, sinkholes aren't safe. You can't just hop in and out of them whenever you want."

Striding to the sink, I wash my hands, letting the warm water run down my fingertips just like I'm letting his words slide out of my thoughts. He quickly takes my place at the faucet when I yank a paper towel from the dispenser and scrub my hands dry.

"Yeah, and the last thing we need is someone else hurt," Jasmine mutters, crossing her arms. Before I can respond, Jeff approaches me cautiously.

"I know you want your stuff," he says sympathetically, resting a hand on my shoulder. "Heck, we all do. Not to mention the

218

food that's sitting in that trunk. But it's not worth what could happen. It's just not worth the risk, Quinn." His eyes beg me to understand. But he's the one who will never understand. I need to get my sister's bag. I have to bring it to her.

I don't want to waste one more moment listening to them tell me what to do. "Guys, it's all on me, okay. If I get hurt or something, just leave me. I'll figure it out." Extending one hand, palm side up, in front of me, I simply say, "The keys please."

With an audible huff of disagreement, Jeff beckons over his shoulder. "They're in the party room with Wes. They were digging into my leg, so I pulled them out of my pocket and dropped them on the floor."

"Thanks," I say coolly. Turning on my heel, I stride to the party room. Anchoring one hand on the toothy hippo painted on the door, I crack it open as quietly as possible. Not quietly enough, as a startled Wes questions, "Chris, that you again?"

"Sorry, Wes, it's just me, Quinn," I say quickly. "You keep resting. I just came to get the car keys. Jeff said he dropped them on the floor in here somewhere." Bending down, I start patting the floor and all of the germs it harbors.

"The car keys," he says groggily. "Chris was in here a few minutes ago, looking around on the floor too. Said he needed to get the keys for you."

Chapter 45

Pushing down a surge of panic, I simply say, "Thanks, Wes, you get some rest. I'll go find the kid," before I sprint out the door. Dashing around the colorful money-hungry video games and token dispensers, I whisper-yell, "Chris!"

I'm greeted with silence, as expected. Charging out the door, I tear through the parking lot until the car is in sight. A flutter of movement at the Malibu catches my eye. "Chris!" I yell, hovering around the edge of the asphalt's gaping mouth.

The kid's straddling rocky ledges lining the dirt wall. Looking up, he flashes me a smile. "Quinn, I'm doing it! I'm getting the bags!" Suppressing my anger, I smile back and say, "Chris, let's get you out of there. Let me do it."

As if I didn't say a word, he crawls into the open trunk. The car releases a metallic groan in response to the added weight. Wide-eyed, the smile slips off of Chris' face. "Quinn, wh-what was that?" he stutters.

"Buddy, just come out, okay? We'll worry about the bags later," I plead. He shakes his head defiantly. "Get ready to catch, Quinn. I'm gonna throw a bag out."

With that, he heaves each bag, one at a time, and tosses it to me. He pauses momentarily between each load to catch his breath and swipe messy blond hair off his sweaty forehead. Sweeping my eyes over the car and the hole that swallowed it, a sense of urgency surges through me. Dropping the final bag at my feet, I instruct Chris to crawl out of the trunk slowly.

"I can't, Quinn," he gasps between gulps of air. "The food is still in here. I have to get it." Shaking my head fervently, I cry, "No! It's not worth it. You're more important. Just come out!"

Disbelief flashes in his watery eyes. "But, the cookies," he whimpers.

"Chris, come out now!" I huff through clenched teeth. Worry wraps its sharp claws around every last thought in my head. Slowly nodding in defeat, he concedes.

Shifting his weight to the edge of the trunk, he starts crawling out backwards. When one shaky foot reaches the ledge, he visibly relaxes. Pushing off of the car, he throws his other foot behind him, searching for a grip.

Just as he stands tall, leaning into the alcove of earth, a sharp cry cuts through the air, startling us both. "Chris!" Jasmine's panicked voice rings in my ears as a scream escapes my own lips. "Noooooooo," I shout as Chris loses his foothold. His little hands scramble over the bumper before he disappears into the plunging darkness below.

Chapter 46

I drop to my knees, reaching into the vast emptiness. "Chris, can you hear me? Are you okay?"

"I'm here," a shaky voice answers. It's barely audible. I hope that's only because he's scared and not because he's fallen halfway to China.

"Stay right where you are," I command. "I'll be right there." As I jump to my feet, Aidan, Jeff, and Jasmine surround me. "Where's Chris?" Jeff asks. Pushing through the barrier they form, I walk around to the part of the crevice closest to the open trunk.

Sizing up the best option to find my footing, I answer. "He fell in the sinkhole." My limbs tremble and my lips quiver. *If anything happens to him...*

"You sent a kid into a sinkhole to get your bags?" Jasmine explodes.

Darting my eyes to meet hers, I start explaining, "No! He did it on his own. I was going—" Before I can finish, the guys spring into action. Maneuvering around me, Jeff eases himself into the gaping maw, landing on the ledge Chris found. His much larger feet slip with each step, sending a tumbling trail of dirt and pebbles deeper into the earth. Aidan drops to the ground, flat on his stomach just above the hole, his right arm stretched straight down along the edge. His fingers grasp the waistband of Jeff's shorts, anchoring the rescue efforts.

Jeff leans as deep into the hole as possible without escaping Aidan's hold. He calls to Chris, who answers almost immediately. After sending a few reassuring words to the kid, Jeff rights himself.

"Alright, I've got to crawl down there. I can't reach him from this ledge," he explains. Aidan gives him one solid nod before backing off. Hesitation weighs in his blue eyes, but he just watches, every muscle of his body tensed and ready to act when needed.

While Jeff disappears into the darkness, Jasmine paces the opening. "I can't believe he went down there. This is all *her* fault. *She* should be the one getting Chris out of there."

"Jasmine, enough. This isn't going to help Jeff or Chris," Aidan says sternly. "We'll talk about this later. Right now, we just need to be ready to help when they need it."

I close my eyes and recite a silent prayer. *This is all my fault. If Chris didn't hear me talking about getting the bags from the trunk, he never would have pulled this stunt.*

Voices echo from the hole, but the words jumble together. After a few minutes, a dirt-streaked hand emerges from the depths. Aidan dives to the edge and reaches toward it. "I'm here, buddy. Just another six inches or so and I can reach you," he calls.

Chris' dusty mop of hair rises from the darkness. When he tilts his head back, the trail of tears slinking down his cheeks leaves a clean path in its wake. Aidan releases a loud sigh and heaves his chest farther over the opening.

Worried that the pit will devour yet another one of us, I scramble toward Aidan's feet in an awkward crab walk. Plopping on my butt, I wrap my arms around his calf. "Jasmine! Help me!" I call impatiently. She rushes to his other side and grabs the other calf. Using our weight as leverage, he plunges farther into the hole.

A moment later he's calling, "I got him! Pull!" Jasmine and I share a quick glance before we struggle to heave two bodies out of the opening. Sweat races down my back as my arms tremble with exertion. *It doesn't matter how much this hurts, I won't stop until they're safe.*

Jasmine's grunting echoes my own. Hot tears trickle down my cheeks and nose, blending with the drops of sweat that pause to sting my eyes before flowing down my neck. Spinning around Aidan's leg like a pole, I plant my feet in the dirt. Using my leg muscles to push back while my arms tug him toward me, I gain about an inch of ground. It's progress, and Jasmine notices. She takes up the same position and we continue to heft Aidan and his stowaway out of the crater.

About half a dozen brush burns later, Aidan's body is completely out of the hole. His arms tremble as he hoists Chris up and onto the edge. Jasmine rushes over to Chris, wrapping an arm around him, guiding him away from the crevice. Tears streak her face as she calls down to Jeff in a shaky voice. "We got him! You coming out anytime soon?"

Jeff responds, "Don't you worry about me. Take the little man back to the arcade. I'll be there soon." Smiling, she eases Chris through the desolate parking lot, toward the front of the building. Their steps are slow, and hopefully Chris' breathing will calm enough to match their pace.

Aidan rolls over on his back, his chest rising and falling as he gulps air. I cringe at the sight of harsh red splotches where his shirt rode up and bare skin gave way to the dirt and rubble. After only a moment's rest, he flips back over to his stomach and reaches his right arm into the hole.

A minute later, Jeff's head bobs in the opening. His cheeks and tussled brown hair bear dusty souvenirs of his trip south. His hazel eyes sparkle with satisfaction, knowing that Chris is safe. Aidan gives a low chuckle and grasps Jeff's open hand.

When the Malibu releases a sudden metallic screech and the ground begins to shift again, the contentment in Jeff's eyes vanishes like a thin wisp of smoke.

Chapter 47

Reaching back into his seemingly never-ending reserve of energy, Aidan hauls Jeff out of the abyss in what feels like a nanosecond. Both guys roll away from the hole and scramble to their feet. I grab the bags Chris retrieved and follow as they dash toward the building.

After we've put a solid ten feet of ground between us and the sinkhole, we turn back to watch the car dive farther into the earth. Jeff shakes his head, saying regretfully, "We didn't even get a chance to name her." Aidan pats his back consolingly. "Next time, man. We'll name the next one."

"It's not too late," I say, my eyes latched on the vanishing car. "Barbie. I think we should name her Malibu Barbie."

The guys solemnly nod. After a moment of silence for Barbie, we stumble back to the arcade.

We take turns in the bathroom and kitchen, washing up as best we can in the meager sinks. Once we've banished most of the grime and dirt, we spend the day in silence, passing the time while Jeff tends to the slash in Wes' leg, courtesy of the sinkhole. Aidan and Jasmine take turns keeping Chris amused while I wallow in my own misery. *How did I end up here? I should be with my family, and at this point, I'll be lucky if I ever find my sister.*

After what feels like hours, I wander into the kitchen to find the others sitting around the stainless-steel table. *What are they all doing in here?*

"Hey, Quinn," Aidan greets me. "We were just thinking we should eat some dinner and go to sleep, so we can get an early start in the morning." He doesn't say it, but I think it: *thankfully we didn't take all the food with us when we attempted to leave this place. Otherwise, it would all be wasting away inside that sinkhole.*

Repeating last night's meal, this time with a cloud of gloom hovering over us, we gorge ourselves on pizza. Jasmine takes a few slices to Wes and helps him eat before he allows sleep to lull him back under a restorative veil.

When Jasmine returns with Wes' empty plate, she sends Chris back to the party room to try and get some sleep. Relief flashes through his eyes and an instinctual yawn escapes him. The kid must be worn out after the awful adventure today brought. Calling out a quick goodnight, he meanders out of the kitchen.

The four of us sit in an uncomfortable silence until Aidan slices through it. "So, Quinn, what happened out there today?" he asks, rubbing his chin.

"I told you. I was going to get the bags back. When I went to Wes' room to get the keys, he told me that Chris beat me to it,"

I explain. "The kid must have been listening to our conversation and took off when no one was looking." Aidan and Jeff nod slowly, understandingly, but Jasmine just eyes me as if I'm a bug she's about to squash under her shoe.

"As soon as I realized what he was doing, I ran out to the car, but it was too late. He had already started crawling into the hole and he wouldn't come out. After he tossed out the bags, he was trying to get out when Jasmine's voice startled him." I shoot my own death glare at her. I owe her about half a million of them anyway.

Ignoring my comment, Jasmine volleys her eyes back and forth between the guys. "I'm glad you're both okay after pulling off that rescue. I was really worried one of you, or Chris, would get hurt."

"Yeah, guys," I say. "Thanks for jumping in. I'm not sure I could have done it without you."

"If you weren't here, none of that would have happened," Jasmine huffs under her breath. Her ebony cheeks bear a tinge of red, which I'm guessing is her anger showing itself. I stand from my seat, resting my palms on the table as I lean forward and meet her icy gaze. "I'm not doing this right now. I'm tired." Turning on my heel, I throw a quick goodnight over my shoulder. "I'll see you guys in the morning."

I swoop by the front of the arcade to grab my bag, and Riley's, before returning to last night's party room. Might as well claim it again. This time I'm sleeping alone.

Closing the door for privacy, I slide down the wall onto the floor. I'm beyond caring if my clothes are covered in carpet germs. Instead of grabbing my own bag, I reach for Riley's.

Digging around in it, my fingers latch onto her purple hairbrush. I stare at the brush as if I can will it into materializing my sister. Gently pulling it through my messy locks, I reach back inside the bag with my other hand, feeling around for any unfamiliar object I haven't inspected yet.

When my fingers trace over a smooth square of folded paper, I snatch it before it tumbles back to the bottom of Riley's jumbled belongings. The tattered edges of the blue-lined notebook paper confirm that it's had a rough ride in the backpack.

Slowly I unfold the paper, not sure what to expect. *What would Riley be carrying around with her?* Leaning forward to flatten the sheet on the floor, my eyes devour the brief message written in slanted penmanship.

> *Riley,*
> *I'm worried about you. So much has happened and everything is going to shit. I really think we can help each other. Dan and I got some plans and I'd love to tell you about them. We should talk – alone – and soon. You know where to find me.*
> *Jim*

Crumpling the paper, I shove it back into the purple backpack. With every last ounce of strength left in my arms, my anger erupts, and I pitch the backpack across the room. It slams into the wall with a satisfying thwack and drops to the floor like a sack of potatoes.

Chapter 48

My frustration builds like the humidity before a downpour. First the stupid sinkhole, then Jasmine's stupid attitude, and now I find out Riley and Jim were communicating behind my back. *Why didn't she tell me Jim wanted to talk to her alone? Did she meet him after he gave her the note? Did she know he was going to come get her?*

A loud knocking at the door stills my swirling thoughts for the moment. "Quinn, everything okay in there?" Jeff calls.

"Fine, thanks," I say stiffly, hoping he takes the hint and leaves me alone. Whispering voices outside the door confirm that I'm not getting off that easily. When a softer knock sounds, I call out an impatient, "Come in." *Might as well get this over with so I can be alone again.*

A small face peers around the opening door, his wide eyes meeting mine. "What was that bang, Quinn? It was really loud," Chris says nervously. *Great, I must have scared him.*

"Oh buddy, I just threw a bag across the room and it hit the wall, that's all it was," I say calmly.

"Wh-why'd you do that?" he asks skeptically. I motion for him to come all the way inside the room. When he does, I pat the floor next to me, encouraging him to have a seat. He cautiously approaches, lowering himself down until he's sitting next to me cross-legged.

"Look, I just got upset and I took it out on my sister's backpack. That's all," I explain, pointing to the dejected purple bag slouching on the floor across the room. "Don't you ever do things because you get caught up in a moment?"

"Yeah," he says with a shy smile. "Kinda like today. I heard you talking about getting the bags out of the car, so I wanted to help and do it."

I turn to meet his eyes. "About that…you really shouldn't have done it. You could have gotten really hurt and it would have been all my fault."

He bows his head down, breaking our visual connection. "I just wanted to help," he starts. "I don't want everyone to think I'm worthless." The last word comes out as a whisper, but it radiates in my head. Instantly, my heart aches for this boy who's worried that someone would consider him worthless. I wonder how many times in his short life he's heard that word.

"Chris, they would never think that. *I* would never think that. And you shouldn't ever think you're worthless." Every word is adamant. I need him to believe me.

His eyes trained on the floor, he swipes a few stray tears from his cheeks. I don't know what else to say so I match his silence. If only Riley were here. She'd know exactly what to say to help this kid feel better.

Silence overtakes the room. *What do kids talk about?* After a few awkward minutes, I open my mouth and chase out the only words that cross my mind.

"So, Chris. Jasmine seems to really like you," I say. Before I can really contemplate if this is wrong, I go for it. "Does she ever talk about me?"

"You? No." He pauses a moment to scrunch his face up, as if he's just caught a whiff of something foul. "But I don't think she likes you very much," he answers innocently.

Leave it to a kid to be the most honest one in our little group.

"You know, Chris, I think you're right," I say. "And I just don't know what I ever did to make her hate me so much."

"You don't know? Really?" he says, glancing at me. I swear Chris snickers under his breath as he tries to comprehend my presumed stupidity. Oh well, at least I've taken his mind off our earlier conversation.

"No, I really don't know," I answer honestly.

Chris turns his head my way, his green eyes zeroing in on me conspiratorially. "So, I think Jasmine likes Jeff. Like, a lot. And I think she doesn't like when he pays attention to you," he says proudly, crossing his arms.

I stare at him, digesting his words. Could that be it? She's been acting like this because of some trivial teenage jealousy?

"Well, that's crazy," I retort. "He's friendly and he helped me feel like a part of the group. Besides, I..." I catch myself. I don't really need to have this conversation with a ten-year-old.

"Oh, I know, I know," Chris says. "You like Aidan."

The fire in my cheeks burns all the way to my toes. If

mortification was a grain of sand, I'd be basking on a beach right now.

And just like that I'm done talking. No point in risking conversation that may result in further humiliation on my part. Shooting my arms over my head in an attempted stretch, I force a yawn. "I'm getting really tired, Chris. You must be too. Why don't we call it a day and get some rest?"

He smiles knowingly, but I don't care. "Goodnight, Quinn," he says before he rises and strides out the door.

Chapter 49

The night seems to last for days. My body keeps pace with the questions and accusations racing through my mind. I toss and turn with each new thought I have no way to resolve or confront.

Riley always got mad when I was rude to Jim. Was something going on between them that I didn't know about? But she was so willing to take the bikes and leave, would she really do that if she was planning something with him? Why didn't she tell me he gave her that note? How long did she have it?

Declaring defeat, I tiptoe out to the ball pit and curl up on its edge. Peering toward the colorful storefront window, my eyes trace the outline of a cerulean butterfly perched on a broad emerald leaf. With deepening breaths, my eyes drift to the yellow and black frog launching over a spiky seaweed-colored bush. The image seers into my mind as my body slackens and I drift asleep.

Sunlight spills into the large room, beckoning me to wake. I barely register movement above me when I hear, "I found her guys! She's at the ball pit!" The swoosh of a body landing in an unnatural mass of plastic reaches my ears. Squinting, I focus on Chris, who's happily swimming in the pool of balls.

Sitting up to stretch out the kinks in my back, I see Aidan trailing a limping Wes as he maneuvers himself to the kitchen area. Watching Wes' every move, Aidan's practically spring-loaded, ready to launch into action if needed. Jasmine calls out, "Come on, Chris. It's time to eat."

Flashing me a smile, Chris climbs out of the pit and motions for me to follow him. The combination of inadequate sleep and a lack of soft bedding leaves my muscles stiff and sore.

Rising slowly, I saunter after the group, joining them in the kitchen. Jasmine's spread a breakfast of churros and chocolate chip cookies on the table. It sounds a lot better than pizza right about now.

Scarfing down the sugary confections, we debate our next move. Without a car, it's a much slower go to Virginia. Jeff suggests that he take a recon mission to find us another vehicle, but Aidan and Jasmine don't want to sit around this place any longer. They want to start walking and hope we come across a car we can *borrow*. I wholeheartedly agree. Our trip has stalled, and I need to move forward.

Wes insists that he can keep up with us, emphasizing that he wants to get moving, too. The original plan was for the guys to drop Jasmine off at home and then trek to Key West for a vacation. Now their intent is to accompany me to Langley Air Force Base, safely deliver Jasmine to her home, and then begin their own journey home. *I guess I'm not the only one itching to hit the road again.*

Chris sits in silence, happily shoving cookie after cookie into his mouth. Blobs of chocolate gooiness cling to his fingers and around his mouth. Rather than disturb his obvious glee, we continue our discussion.

"You know," Jeff starts, rubbing his chin. "We were lucky we didn't get too far before we needed that First Aid Kit. Before we leave this place, we should probably look around and see if there's anything we should take with us." He eyes each of us and, seeing no dissent, continues. "We have to balance what we can carry versus what we really need, but it's worth a look I think."

"You're right," Aidan interjects. "We aren't really planning ahead, and we should be. Who knows when we'll find food again or bandages for Wes."

"Yes!" Chris exclaims. "We need to find cookies and bring them with us!" And just like that, the kid's back in the conversation.

Within the hour, our bags are loaded with water bottles, preservative-laden food, and every last bandage and packet of antiseptic gel from the First Aid kit. I can't imagine we'll be able to move at more than a snail's pace. Besides the extra weight burdening our backs and shoulders, we're all careful not to walk faster than Wes is able to hobble. He refuses any help, but our sluggish movement makes me antsy. I won't complain, though. His bandaged leg looks painful, and red blots are already bursting through the white gauze.

The overcast sky offers some relief from the sun's scorching rays, but humidity embraces every inch of my body. We follow the main road only until it branches off into a residential neighborhood. White posters decorate every fourth or fifth telephone pole. The stark black text printed on them instructs residents to seek shelter at designated local "safe zones."

Jasmine spreads her arms out in question, asking no one in particular, "Why would people here need a safe zone?"

Scratching the rough stubble adorning his chin, Jeff points in the distance. "If I had to wager a guess, I'd say that's why."

Chapter 50

The jagged remains of a bridge hover at the edge of land, the highway they once supported simply gone. Concrete support columns rise from the water, leaning like dominoes.

"I bet when that came down, it flooded parts of the town," Wes interjects. Jeff backs him up. "And standing water is bad news. Maybe they wanted to keep people away from the bridge and away from any water that may have washed ashore."

"Well," Aidan interjects. "If the town's all gathered at this safe zone, then maybe we can just borrow someone's house for a little while and no one will even notice."

Glancing at Wes, my heart stutters. A sheen of sweat glistens on his pale skin. He doesn't even try to wipe away the salty beads running into his pained eyes. The bandage Jeff so carefully affixed over Wes' gash bears more red than white. It's bled through. Without one word of complaint, he continues.

Slowly, the landscape of a neighborhood that ceased functioning on trash day appears. The acrid stench of decomposing food mingles with slightly sweet hints of dryer sheets and lemon peels. Torn garbage bags and fallen trash cans line the sidewalks, scattered rubbish dots lawns and the street.

Jasmine pinches her nose, and for once, I'm right there with her. "Guys, I think we should get as far away from here as possible," she suggests.

"But wouldn't a place like this be safer?" Aidan retorts. "I mean, if most people want to stay away from it, maybe that's good for us."

When Wes stumbles, Jeff rushes over to him and wraps an arm around his waist. "Guys, we *have got* to stop," Jeff says.

"Maybe one of these houses has more bandages in it," I say. "I know it's not as good as a store, but we might find something that could help."

"Yes! Now that's what I'm talking about," Jeff states. "Quinn gets it."

"Alright," Aidan says, glancing around. "Any house look better than the others?" Our eyes rove over the symmetrically-spaced structures that look like they were stamped from the same cookie cutter. Boxy two-story white homes sit just a few feet apart, their shutters and door color the only distinguishing features.

Chris points to a house with dark green shutters on the corner of the block. "How about that one?" he says.

Jasmine smiles and leans down to meet him at eye level, "That looks like the best one to me, buddy."

Eyes wide, my head snaps her way. It shocks me when she's

nice to someone.

We scuffle down the street, trying to keep with Jeff and Wes' slow pace. When we're two houses away, Aidan weaves through our little parade and walks backward so he can face us. "I'm gonna go on up ahead and look around the house. You know, make sure no one's inside," he says. Before anyone can respond, he turns and sprints down the street.

By the time we reach our chosen home's front sidewalk, Aidan finishes his inspection and meets us there. "It looks empty, guys," he says. "I think we're good, but let's go in quietly just in case there are any nosy neighbors around."

Aidan takes over shouldering Wes, so Jeff can dig out his knife. After a bit of maneuvering, he effortlessly snaps the lock and pushes the forest green door open, sweeping his arm out as if presenting the house to us.

Chapter 51

We quietly step inside, huddling in the living room that's just inside the entranceway, and strategize. In hushed voices, we outline our plan.

After locating a couch or chair to carefully deposit Wes on, Aidan will check the garage for a vehicle. Jasmine and Chris will find the kitchen and grab any food they can stash in their backpacks. Jeff and I will look for a bathroom medicine cabinet or closet, aiming to find ibuprofen, bandages, or really anything that might help Wes.

With a plan in place, we disperse from the huddle in groups of two. I follow Jeff as he strides through the living room and turns down a hallway. As we creep along the seafoam green carpet, three doors await us. Two on the left and one on the right. Jeff motions that he'll start on the left and I should take the right.

DARKNESS FALLS

My assigned room appears to be an office. As I peer through the open door, my eyes sweep across the room. An orderly wooden desk monopolizes the small space and framed certificates adorn the walls. Nothing looks useful in this room. As I turn to check on Jeff and see if he's found anything, my eyes catch a coffee-stained white mug sitting on the desk. Before I can wonder how long that's been sitting there, a small billow of steam drifts from its surface. My eyes widen in alarm. *That coffee is fresh.*

Scrambling back to the hallway, rising voices reach my ears. Each word sounds louder than the last, like an argument is escalating. *We are supposed to do this quietly.* Jeff jumps into the hallway, throwing his arms up in confusion. We advance toward the intensifying commotion.

The noise leads us straight to the kitchen. Jeff pushes the white swinging door open and plunges into the room. He stops so abruptly that I crash into him, which bumps him forward a step but stops my momentum.

Other than Wes, we're the last to arrive at this impromptu gathering. Jasmine, Aidan and Chris stand like statues while a middle-aged man fluidly swings a rifle back and forth, aiming the barrel at each of them in turn.

"Whoa," Jeff says. I'm not sure if he's talking to me in response to our little crash or if he's talking to the stranger.

"There's more of ya?" the man shouts as his eyes dart our way. His salt-and-pepper hair stands in tufts and his face twists in anger. His raging expression holds no compassion.

Jeff raises his hands in surrender and somehow manages to keep his voice steady and calm. "Look, we were just looking for

242

some medicine. We didn't know someone was here. We're really sorry."

The gun-wielding homeowner turns his full attention to Jeff. *I liked it better when he wasn't focused on anyone in particular.* "Oh, so it's okay to break into people's houses and steal stuff as long as they aren't home?" he taunts.

"No, no, that's not what I meant," Jeff starts, his hands still in the air.

"I know what you meant," the man shouts, aiming the gun at Jeff. Frozen with fear, I see slight movement out of the corner of my eye. Jasmine steps forward nervously.

"Look, we didn't mean to cause any trouble," Jasmine says in an uneven voice. Her hands twitch at her sides. When Chris starts trembling, I notice the silent tears trailing down his cheeks. "Please," Chris plead. "Just let us go. We won't come back. Ever."

As the man swings the gun toward Chris, Jasmine shoots out like a bolt of lightning, jumping in front of the boy. "Stay back!" the man shouts. His eyes transform from anger to panic as the burst of a bullet flashes in my ears. Just as quickly, his momentary panic dissolves into a satisfied glare.

An involuntary scream escapes me as my mind attempts to comprehend what just happened. Before the scream has fully left my mouth, Jasmine's body jerks back, her eyes wide with shock, before she crumples to the floor.

Chapter 52

Before anyone can react, the man roars, "Get the hell out of my house or there's more where that came from!" Venom spews from each word.

He just shot a person and he's not even sorry. Why is that the first thought to run through my head? We all snap into action, converging on Jasmine before this nut job changes his mind.

The tears swimming in my eyes distort Jasmine's prone form. Lying on the cream tile floor, her right hand clutches her left shoulder. Jeff and Aidan kneel down at her sides, trying to gently lift her. She starts to protest, asking "What the hell—" Jeff cuts her off. I can't hear his whispered words over the rush of blood in my ears.

"I said get outta here!" the man shouts again. I grab Chris' hand and pull him toward the swinging door, leading him through and then holding it for the guys and Jasmine. She lets out a squeal of pain as Aidan tries to support her injured shoulder.

The man follows us to the living room, rushing us along. As the guys lead Jasmine to the door, I grab Chris' hand again and pull him toward the couch. We're the only ones left to help Wes. Even with all the commotion, Wes lies still on the couch, perspiration still beading on his forehead. I shake him hard, but he barely rouses.

"Wes, wake up!" I pray he understands the urgency in my voice. "Chris, we have to lift him up. Now!" Just as Wes cracks an eye open, Chris and I lunge, lifting him from the couch. He groggily asks, "What's happening?" We don't bother to answer as we rush to the door. The guys are slow-moving with Jasmine, but they've made their way to the sidewalk by the time we catch up to them.

No one talks, we just stumble down the sidewalk away from the raging man's house. *This street must be more populated than we thought.* I see movement in some of the houses we pass. Curtains swish as neighbors back away from their windows. A toddler's cry is stifled as we draw nearer to a house with a red and yellow playset in the front yard. People see us, clearly in need of help, but they stay hidden.

Wind carries a few leaves and a discarded paper cup down the street. Maybe we're just as aimless. Simply following the path, we're pushed along.

The farther we go, the slower we move. After too many blocks to count, commercial buildings start popping up. Signs jump out at us, touting the best nail salon, mom-and-pop hardware store, and laundromat around. As we near the end of the first block of stores, Aidan points and calls out, "Look, look around the side of the building."

245

"Holy hell," Jeff laughs. "I think we finally found some good luck." Like a beacon of hope, the last storefront on our left bears a red and white sign reading Emergen-Sea Care Ambulance Service.

The last of my dwindling energy drains from my aching body. Adrenaline must have carried me this far, but now the weight of our situation and Wes' slack body slow each step.

Aidan and Jeff lead Jasmine to the curb and slowly lower her down. Her once-yellow shirt bears an apple-sized red blotch about four inches above her heart. Dots of sweat bead along her forehead and her normally dark skin appears pale. Aidan sits next to her, helping her stay upright. He talks softly and strokes her arm while Jeff dashes to the ambulance company's front door. He throws his backpack to the ground and starts rummaging through it.

Sweeping my gaze across the parking lot, I spot a trio of ambulances sitting dormant. I guess this place is out of commission. We could have really used medical help. But maybe if this place was in service, the ambulances would be out helping other people.

Chris and I slog the last few steps to the curb and lower ourselves and Wes down. Instant relief sweeps through my legs and back. Jeff pops the door's lock and slips inside the ambulance company. For a brief moment, Aidan's eyes meet mine, mirroring the anxiety and exhaustion that I feel.

"Wh-where are we?" Wes mutters. I'm so relieved to hear his voice that an answer rushes out of me. "We found an ambulance company, and we're going to find some medicine for you and clean up your leg."

"And we're gonna help Jasmine, too," Chris announces. My shoulders hunch and my head bobs as I cringe. I don't want to think about the bullet that either blasted through her or now resides in her shoulder.

"What? What happened to Jasmine?" he asks. *Why is he so out of it? Didn't he hear the gun go off at that wacko's house?* I look to Aidan, but he shakes his head. Wes doesn't need anything else to worry about right now.

"Oh nothing," I reply feebly. "Let's focus on getting you feeling better right now."

With that, Jeff pushes through the front door and kneels down between me and Aidan. "Okay, there's a back room with supplies in it, but it's a lot of cardboard boxes, and I can't figure out what's up from down in there." When we just stare at him blankly, he continues. "So, I found a bunch of keys, and I say we just go right to the ambulances and try to patch Jasmine up in there. Maybe we can even find something for Wes."

"Sounds good to me," I say. Aidan nods in agreement. "Okay," Jeff says. "Just stay put and I'll see which keys unlock which rigs."

Jeff jogs to the parking lot. Chris starts pointing toward the sky. "Look at those clouds. Do you think a storm's coming?" Puffy gray clouds swirl in the distance. Their cotton-ball curves are well-defined, casting the landscape in an eerie black-and-white scene. I'm not surprised we didn't notice it approaching. I know my eyes barely ventured higher than the pavement as we slowly trudged along.

Aidan answers him, "Yeah, buddy, I do. We should probably hurry."

247

Jeff moves from one ambulance to the next, leaving the keys dangling from the one he's managed to unlock. When he returns to us, he stops and scratches his head. "Okay, how about I help Quinn lift Wes and we take him to one rig. Chris, you come with us. Then I'll be right back to help Aidan bring Jasmine to another one."

As the wind gusts around us, Jeff and I lead Wes to the closest ambulance. Once we get him settled on the stretcher, Jeff takes off again. After a moment of eyeing our surroundings nervously, I will myself to conjure up some courage and take charge. Jasmine needs immediate attention. Aidan and Jeff have to tend to her. What happens in this truck is all on me.

Chapter 53

Chris stands mutely, his green eyes questioning our next move. After just one deep breath, I shake the jitters free and squat to meet him at eye level. Grasping his shoulders, I explain my plan as he listens intently.

Once we break, Chris sidles up to the stretcher and watches over Wes. His job is to make sure Wes doesn't roll off the side. I step to the wall and start rummaging through the organized compartments that run along it.

The truck is equipped with everything from latex gloves to alcohol swabs to all kinds of equipment I can't identify. My first mission is to find medications, any sort of painkiller.

As I start peering into white plastic bins resting on a metal rack, Chris calls for me. "Quinn, he's really sweating, and his breathing is kinda weird." Knocking a box of gauze patches to the floor in my rush, I hurry to Wes' side. His forehead still beads with sweat and his eyes are cracked open. I spy an elastic bandage on a nearby shelf and grab it, using it to dab Wes' face.

"Hey, you just take it easy. We're gonna help you feel better," I say, leaning closer to him. "How are you doing?"

"Been better," he says, shuddering as he tries to stifle a cough.

"Why don't you tell me everything that's wrong, and we'll see if we can find something around here to help." I try to keep my tone uplifting, but it comes out high-pitched and awkward.

"Well," he starts slowly. "I'm really achy and tired. I feel like I can't get enough sleep. And my head is killing me. The only time it doesn't hurt is when I sleep. So maybe it's a good thing that's all I want to do."

"Okay, that doesn't sound so bad." I instantly regret my words when he shoots me a questioning look. "I mean, I bet we can find medicine for that, that's all." I motion to Chris to stay close to Wes, and I return to my exploration.

As I rummage through a cabinet that's built right into the side of the truck, I hit the jackpot. Clearly-labeled bins line the shelf, and I take a moment to marvel at the organized manner of every item inside this vehicle. *I guess knowing exactly where everything is can turn seconds or minutes into lifesaving moments.*

I grab a small foil packet from the ibuprofen bin. That pretty much cures everything, I think. At least temporarily. Some of the bins are rigged with locks. Those must be the hardcore meds. *I think we can survive without them.*

Now we need something for Wes to wash these down with. I close the medication cabinet and walk past Chris toward the cab. There on the floor behind the driver's seat sits a waist-height refrigerator with a glass door. A few bottles of water stand at attention inside, along with labeled bottles of what must be medicines.

After freeing one of the water bottles from its refrigerated prison, I rush back to the stretcher. "Alright, Chris," I say. "Let's sit him up so he can drink and take some pills." Wes visibly perks up, but I'm not sure if he's more excited about the medicine or the drink. Chris and I flank each side of the stretcher and place our hands behind Wes' back. On the count of three we slowly lift until he's in a sitting position.

"Okay, Chris, I'll make sure Wes doesn't go anywhere. You help him with the water and pills," I instruct. Chris nods and gets to work.

After he's downed the pills Wes says, "Hey, I think these things recline. Can you adjust it, so I can stay sitting up?" I motion to Chris to switch positions with me. Wes strains to stay inclined while Chris concentrates on supporting him.

As I'm fumbling around just under where Wes' head previously rested, Chris speaks. "Hey Quinn, you should look at this. Wes has a bump on his back." I stand and follow his finger as he points to a spot right between Wes' shoulder blades.

"Wes, I'm gonna lift your shirt in the back, okay?" I ask.

"If you get me more of that water, you can pretty much do whatever you want to me," he responds, attempting a snicker that sounds more like a soft cough. I make a mental note to send Chris up front for another bottle.

I gently tug the white cotton T-shirt up to his shoulders, revealing his back. Chris calls out, "Hey, cool tattoo! I didn't know you had one!" Just as quickly as Chris' excitement inflates, my spirit deflates. A pea-sized black blob clings to Wes' back. It's perfectly centered within what looks like a black bulls-eye.

251

Chapter 54

At that moment, Aidan steps up into the ambulance. "Hey, Wes, how'd you get Quinn to undress you?" My face flushes as my eyes slide toward our visitor. I steal a glance at Chris, but he's still marveling at what he thinks is a harmless tattoo.

Wes releases a burst of laughter. It's an amazing sound. "Look at this bod, man. Can you blame her?" Aidan approaches and starts asking Wes how he feels. I take that moment to secure us a bit of privacy.

"Hey, Chris," I say, my eyes never leaving Aidan. "How about you go help Jeff with Jasmine and Aidan can take over for you here?"

"Alright," he says as he starts toward the door. For reasons I'll never understand, he seems to actually like Jasmine. And, I don't think he cares much where he is, as long as he's far away from any gun-wielding maniacs.

As soon as Chris is gone, Aidan steps beside me. His eyes widen as they land on Wes' skin. "So, what the hell, guys? What's up with my back?" Wes asks.

"Well, Wes, it seems you have a stowaway and he's pretty nasty," Aidan says. "You picked up a tick somewhere along the way and he's given you a nice bulls-eye ring."

"So, that's why the kid said I had a tattoo. Just swell. I probably have Lyme disease," Wes huffs.

Jeff appears at the open doors and starts climbing inside. "What's this tattoo I'm hearing all about?" he asks. His playful eyes quickly turn serious when he reads our expressions. We step aside and Jeff peers under Wes' shirt. He exhales and says, "Never seen one like that before."

While Jeff asks Wes some questions, Aidan pulls me aside and provides some background.

Leaning in, Aidan speaks quietly, "Jeff used to run with the local fire department in high school. He was never an EMT, but he spent enough time with those guys that he picked up a few things. It's not ideal, but it makes him the most qualified in this kind of situation."

"How'd it go with Jasmine?" I ask. *I would have no idea what to do with a gunshot wound.*

"I'd say he did a pretty good job of patching her up," Aidan says. "She took the bullet to her left shoulder just above her armpit. The bullet is still in her, but Jeff gave her pain medication and cleaned and bandaged the wound. Now we have to make sure it doesn't get infected until we can get her real medical care."

Jeff helps Wes recline on the stretcher and spies the surroundings. Apparently, at some point, I knocked over Wes' water bottle and totally forgot about getting him that second drink. Jeff grabs one and presents it to Wes. When his eyes land on the gauze patches I knocked on the floor earlier, he says, "Quinn, promise me you'll never go to medical school. Or nursing school. Or basically follow any career path that involves taking care of sick or injured people."

Aidan laughs but attempts a recovery. "Don't listen to him. You did just fine." I swear I still hear amusement in his words.

I roll my eyes and stifle an audible *whatever*. I'm just glad someone knows what he's doing. Kind of, anyway.

"Alright," Jeff says. "The first thing I need to do is remove this bloodsucking bastard. Can you guys look for something like tweezers? There's gotta be some instrument like that in here."

I jump at the chance to redeem myself. "I've got tweezers!" They both look at me like I just announced that I was a Victoria's Secret model, mild amusement meeting disbelief. Ignoring them, I rush to my backpack and start digging inside. A moment later, I produce my sparkly silver tweezers.

"Something in your bag actually came in handy," Aidan mutters, smiling.

"That's right," I respond. "You can thank my sculpted eyebrows for this!"

Jeff locates alcohol and swabs the tweezers. Then he motions for us to help Wes sit up and lift his shirt. He deftly removes the tick, effortlessly. He reaches over us and grabs a plastic zip-lock bag, releasing the bug inside and sealing it.

"Wow, Jeff," I say. "I'm impressed. You made that look really easy."

"Well, we always had dogs growing up and you know, they're

kind of tick magnets," Jeff explains. "I had lots of practice. And this was even easier because I didn't have to dig through any fur to get to it. Good thing it wasn't Aidan. Not sure I could have fought through that manly rug of hair on his back."

I bust out laughing and, for just a sliver of a moment, forget why we're even here.

Once both patients are stabilized, Jeff and Aidan step outside the ambulance for a breather. I visit the other ambulance, peeking in to see Jasmine asleep on her stretcher. Her face looks peaceful, as if the wound is already forgotten. Chris must have found a chair and dragged it over by the stretcher. He's curled up on it, his left arm dangling off the side, fingers tangled in Jasmine's hair.

I turn my back on the tranquil scene inside and slowly close the ambulance doors, wincing at every creak. I join Aidan and Jeff only to find that their conversation ceases with my approach.

"Hey, guys, what's up?" I ask.

"Well," Aidan says, running a hand through his hair. "We're thinking we should just stay put for the night. Sleep in the ambulances, lock the doors."

"But," Jeff continues for him. "We need some supplies. There's water in the rigs, but we could take this time to stock up on some more food."

"And we need a map. With this afternoon's excitement, we kinda lost track of where we are," Aidan adds.

The guys look at me as if they've asked a question that I'm supposed to answer.

"Okaaaaaay," I say. "That sounds good."

They turn to each other, silently communicating. *What the heck is with these two?*

"Guys, what is it?" I demand, losing my patience. "What are you sending to each other telepathically? Cuz I'm not tuned into your wavelength."

Rubbing his chin, Jeff answers. "Look, we need to figure out who's making the supply run and who's staying here. I think Aidan and I should go, and you should stay here."

I'm so tired, but the thought of Jasmine or Wes waking up and relying on me to help them is a way too overwhelming. *Plus, I don't need two guys to do everything while I stay behind waiting patiently.*

"I think I'm more qualified to go on the supply run," I say firmly, readying my stance for an argument.

"Oh really," Aidan says, crossing his arms. "And what are your qualifications?"

"Well," I start. "I can run really fast." They both nod in agreement. "And I totally suck at taking care of sick people." Again, they nod, but this time with more fervor.

Jeff cracks a grin and says, "She's got a good point. I mean, Jasmine and Wes are our friends. We owe it to them to not leave them in Quinn's care."

Aidan laughs. "Alright, Quinn, looks like it's you and me then. So, doc, anything in particular you need?"

"Just a map and food, man," Jeff answers. "I'll take a Big Mac, large fries, and a large Coke."

"Noted," Aidan mutters.

Chapter 55

Armed with mostly-empty backpacks, Aidan and I make our way deeper into town. We're definitely out of the residential area now. At some point in our sleep-deprived haze the houses became businesses and sidewalks became city blocks.

"So," I start. "Where do you think we should try?" The streetlights are dark, the buildings unlit. This patch of civilization must have lost power. A few ornamental trees dot the sidewalks. Thankfully, their branches are somewhat sparse, so the moonlight spells out a clear path for us.

"Check out that corner two blocks up," Aidan says, pointing. "Is that a hospital?"

The boxy building is all steel and glass. The contrasting sharp corners and the main entrance's rounded overhang make for a dramatic structure. Soft lights shine dimly from inside. There must be a back-up generator churning away in there.

"It's way too nice for a hospital," I mumble. As we near the first corner, a sign comes into view: Maritime Medical Center. I stop at the sight of movement through the top floor window. Pointing, I ask, "Aidan, what's moving up there?"

He stops and squints. "I think that's a person." Our questioning eyes slide toward each other. My next question tumbles out, "Do you think there might be a doctor in there? Or someone with actual medical experience? I mean, beyond Jeff's vast knowledge." A smile plays across his lips.

Our feet practically fly over the pavement as we dash toward the building. By the time we're just a few yards before it, the soft glow inside illuminates an adult's silhouette standing in the top stairwell like a guard. The stranger's stance screams male and he's clearly zeroed in on us.

We slow our pace, carefully watching him, trying to gauge his reaction. When we're standing almost directly below him on the sidewalk, the glint of his gun casts a minute reflection on the glass he stands behind. His eyes follow us as the hand holding the gun motions down the street as if saying "move it along." His other hand holds a radio or walkie-talkie to his mouth. *Clearly not interested in making friends.*

"Quinn, I think we should just keep going. Now," Aidan says quietly. I nod quickly and we both instinctually lower our eyes and keep our heads down, as if we can just melt into the sidewalk.

Aidan hooks an arm around mine and we walk briskly, like we have somewhere to be. He turns back a few times but doesn't report what he sees. I face forward, allowing my eyes to bounce left and right as we pass storefronts and cafes that no longer welcome visitors.

"Okay," Aidan says. "Let's think this through. People need food, water, shelter, and medicine. Where can we find food that hasn't been overrun by anyone else yet?"

He releases my arm as we distance ourselves from the medical center. We scan the buildings we pass, but thankfully, no one appears in any windows, which encourages us to relax a bit.

My mind races to recall places that serve food that I would never want to eat. Mall food court. Nah, too many resources, people would probably flock there. Gas stations. They're probably high on the hit list for looters.

The farther we walk, the more retail and entertainment options appear. The cell phone store won't be of much help. We pass a McDonalds and I question if we should check it out. That food has so many preservatives, it will probably outlast both of us. The smashed windows aren't exactly inviting with their sharp jagged edges, so we continue past it.

That's when my eyes catch an interesting shape standing atop one of the buildings up ahead. A giant white bowling pin comes into view like a beacon. A bowling alley. That could be our ticket. What would anyone want at a bowling alley now? The ones I've been to always had snack bars, but it's not the kind of place that I'd think about looting.

"Bowling alley!" I practically shout, pointing toward the sign. Aidan stops mid-step, contemplating my idea.

"I know I don't say this often. I've actually never said it before, but Quinn, that's a great idea!" He smiles, but I don't acknowledge the backhanded compliment.

We quickly scuttle toward the bowling alley, continuously

scanning our surroundings for any potential threats. Thankfully, our trek to the entrance doors is uneventful. The glass double doors are intact, and the interior is dark. When this mess first started, I was afraid to leave the trailer when it was dark outside. In this moment, I feel safer in the darkness. If needed, we can dissolve into the shadows.

"Okay," I start. "We made it. Now, how are we going to get in there?"

He motions for me to follow him as he runs behind the building. He stops momentarily for a quick examination of a side entrance. When we reach the back of the building, he tries the handle on another door, but of course, it's locked. "That was your big idea? Hoping they left a door unlocked?" I ask.

"Of course not," he says, his eyes searching the small parking lot. Or maybe he's avoiding eye contact. Doubt that he has any idea how we're going to get inside this place swirls around in my mind.

"Okay, maybe we should have sent Jeff on this mission," I say. "He's pretty handy with breaking and entering, you know?"

"Hey," Aidan says indignantly. "I'm handy, too." His eyes focus on a beat-up vehicle resting on four flat tires. As he strides toward it, he continues his thought. "And I have a plan!"

Chapter 56

"You know what this is," he asks, running a hand along the canary-yellow boat of a car. Shrugging my shoulders, I respond, "Some old junky car. Not sure how that's going to help us."

Slowly shaking his head back and forth, he makes a tssssk sound. "Quinn, this is a Chevette. It's so ancient that it actually has a stick antenna. You don't see those anymore."

"Aaaaaaand," I draw out. "Why do we need to know this?" I'm starting to lose my patience. We are supposed to be finding supplies, not admiring some ancient antenna.

"I've got skills, Quinn," he says with mock seriousness. "I'll get us inside that bowling alley. I can MacGyver us a way in there." I cross my arms and watch, still not understanding his strategy. The events of the day are wearing on me and my patience is dwindling.

Aidan deftly unscrews the Chevette's antenna, yanking it free from the wire hiding inside. His prize in hand, he strides around the building. I follow at a slight distance until he reaches the bowling alley's side glass door.

Positioning the thicker end of the antenna flat against the glass, he draws the ball back at a forty-five-degree angle aimed at the top right corner of the door. Stopping mid-movement, he throws a glance back at me.

"Hey," he starts sheepishly. "Why are Geologists great comedians?"

Rolling my eyes, I play along. "Why?"

"Because they know all the dirty jokes!" His broad smile mingles with his words and a chuckle escapes me.

Satisfied he's relieved some of the tension emanating from me, he turns back toward the door and releases the ball. As it thwacks the glass, I step back a few paces, anticipating flying spears shooting toward me at any moment.

My temporary fear evaporates when it appears that the antenna made no impact. He mumbles to himself as he pulls the ball back again, this time drawing it farther away from the door, the silver stick tensing as he stretches it.

The ball shoots toward the door in one spring-loaded motion. My hope dissolves as the point of contact absorbs the impact without even a shudder. Huffing out a frustrated sigh, I turn on my heel to go search for a rock. Right about now I'm ready to pretend that door is Slim Jim and knock it into tomorrow.

Raising my knee in mid-step, the slightest crackle reaches my ears. I spin around in time to see a lopsided, grapefruit-sized jagged hole where the antenna ball struck. A spiderweb of cracks snakes out from the point of impact. Aidan takes a step back, admiring his work; a moment later, the remaining glass spills to the ground.

After the briefest moment of basking in our success, Aidan steps through the door, crunching on glass fragments. I follow close behind him. The bowling alley is shrouded in darkness. I bump into Aidan when he stops suddenly, tugging his backpack off one shoulder and digging into it. I mumble an apology as he holds up a flashlight.

Sweeping the narrow beam of light across the large open area, we quickly locate the snack bar. Dashing behind the counter, we both shrug the packs off our backs and launch our search. Within minutes we collect bags of chips, candy bars, and hot dog buns.

When I yank open the white refrigerator door, no light illuminates its contents. The hint of chilled air confirms that I've broken the seal on whatever cold the refrigerator was harboring since electricity last shot through its cord.

Snatching a package of hot dogs, I don't even bother checking for an expiration date. These things would have probably outlasted dinosaurs had they been invented back then. Skipping the moldy lunchmeat and cheese, any hopes I had of feasting on a wrap tonight dissolve.

Attempting to find the perfect balance between everything we want to take with how much we can carry on our backs, Aidan sweeps the flashlight across the room one final time. Turning to me, he asks, "You ready?" I answer with a quick nod.

As we step through the broken door, a steady thumping sound echoes above. Aidan pauses, powering off the flashlight.

He silently raises a hand as if to say, "Hold up." Peering over his shoulder, my eyes catch a spotlight dancing across the parking lot, waltzing its way toward us. My feet betray me when Aidan shoves me back into the bowling alley's consuming darkness.

Chapter 57

Tripping over each other, we tumble in a tangle of limbs. In a roll-like maneuver, Aidan jumps to his feet and grabs my hand. Dragging me back behind the snack bar, we both slide to the floor just below the counter. *We haven't seen much of anything since we escaped the crazed man's house. Who's out there and what are they doing?*

The thudding sound grows louder. "What the heck's going on?" I whisper, unsure if he'll answer.

"That's a helicopter, flying awfully low," he says. "But what are they looking for?"

I shrug, realizing he can't see that small movement in the dimness I add, "I don't know, but I wanna get back to the others." It comes out whiny, but this little scavenger mission is taking forever, and my mind is flooding with worry. "What if it lands?" I ask, wrapping my trembling hands around each other.

"It won't land here," he says, too quickly to serve as genuine reassurance. After pausing for a moment, he continues, "Let's just wait a few minutes and I bet it'll move away." We sit awkwardly, which seems to render time immobile. My thoughts wander to my family, wondering what my parents would do in this situation.

A sudden raging curiosity washes through me, and before I can filter my thoughts, they seep out into words. "Have you talked to your family since all this happened?" I ask. Cloaked in the safety of darkness, any nervousness I might have felt for intruding is nonexistent.

His first reaction is a sharp intake of breath. After a brief pause, he speaks slowly. "Right after the crash, we all called our parents. They told us to stay put. My dad was going to drive down and meet us to get the car fixed."

With a deep sigh, he continues. "That was before we all realized how bad the pileup was. When we found the campground, my dad said that sounded like a good place to hole up. He said he'd come down for us as soon as the roads were cleared."

"But before the roads cleared up, there was a fracking accident," I interject.

"I don't know if that had anything to do with it," he murmurs, lost in thought, "but our phones stopped working, even the ones that had some charge left."

"So, you don't even know if he's on the way or not?" I ask cautiously, not wanting him to sink into the despair I feel each time I think of my parents.

"No, but I'm sure he's fine. They're fine. I'm just gonna finish what we came to do, and then I'm going home," he says confidently. "Hey, it's quiet outside again. Let's get out of here," he says, concluding the conversation.

Our walk back to the ambulance company is quiet. We move smoothly, melding with the shadows. Thankfully, no helicopters or raging lunatics cross our path. While a few vehicles sit idle along the curb, no vehicles are traveling the roads.

My aching legs quake as the ambulances come into view. My body needs rest. I'm sure Jeff has Wes secure, so maybe I can just sneak into a truck, curl up on a seat, and get some sleep.

Just as we reach the plaza, shouting cuts through the peaceful atmosphere. Wide-eyed, Aidan and I glance at each other before breaking into a full sprint toward the ambulances.

Following the source of the noise, we race to the second ambulance. Yanking open the door, Aidan steps inside while I follow closely at his heels. Silence befalls the vehicle and all eyes land on us, but it's clear that we interrupted a heated argument.

"Glad you guys decided to come back," Jeff says. "I've got an irate patient and I'm about ready to sedate her!" He glances at Jasmine as she narrows her eyes.

Tired and a bit out of breath, Aidan sighs. "Guys, what's going on?"

Jasmine sits up on her stretcher, a clean bandage protecting her injured shoulder. She attempts to cross her arms but stops and lowers them to her side instead. *That must have hurt.* "I'll tell you what's going on," Jasmine says angrily. "Jeff wants to put himself in danger. Again. And there's no point to it."

Though he tries to sound calm, Jeff's voice escalates as he presents his side. "Some asshat pointed a gun at all of us, *shot* Jasmine, and we're just going to walk away? I say we go back there right now and explain to him how a civilized society works!"

My mouth drops open. *He wants to go back there? Nothing good can come from confronting that guy.*

Aidan looks around the truck. "Where's Chris?" he asks.

When Jeff explains that Chris is keeping Wes company, Aidan suggests that I go check on the guys and offer them some of our newfound food.

Gladly, I agree. They can all duke it out while I share our treasure with the others.

Jeff stomps to the other ambulance in a few quick strides. His demeanor changes the moment he pulls the creaky door open.

Chris sits cross-legged on the bench seat next to Wes' stretcher. "Hey, guys!" he calls, throwing us a wave.

Wes slumps in the reclined stretcher, but his eyes are alert, and he bears a small smile. "Find anything good out there?" he asks me.

Shrugging off my backpack, I counter, "You tell me." Perching on the seat beside Chris, I dump the contents of my bag.

The guys gawk at the mound of snack bags.

When I showcase the hotdogs and their accompanying buns, a collective trio of sighs resounds in our small space.

Just as we spread our feast out on a clean sheet, the creaking door seizes our attention. "Jasmine!" Chris shouts as she carefully climbs into the rig, bolstered by Aidan. With unrestrained excitement, he bounces over to her side.

"Hey, buddy," she answers, wrapping her good arm around

his shoulder. "We heard there was food in here." As if suddenly remembering the hot dogs, Chris sprints back toward the spread and assembles his meal.

After exchanging some chitchat with Wes, Aidan and Jasmine grab some food and settle into the driver and passenger seats. Running a hand through his ruffled black hair, Aidan lets out a deep exhale and meets Jeff's eyes. "So, obviously we found food, but we had no luck finding a map."

Before Jeff can respond, Jasmine indignantly answers, "What do you mean, a map? What would we need a map for?" Focusing on my dinner, I let the guys handle this.

"Well," Jeff begins, "we kinda got off course today. I can point us south, but we still need to "old school" it with an actual paper map."

Cocking her head to the side, Jasmine challenges, "You underestimate me. I can still get us to Virginia. You find us a ride, and I'll get you there."

"You've got yourself a deal," Jeff says, smiling. "I guess we don't need a map when our firecracker is healed enough to navigate."

Once we've stuffed ourselves with sodium and carbs, we discuss our next move. When Jeff suggests we drive the ambulances the rest of the way to Virginia, Aidan details our trip to the bowling alley. Everyone listens intently as he describes the unfriendly gunman in the medical center. Audible gasps slice through the silence after he recounts the low-flying helicopter's spotlight roving over the bowling alley's parking lot.

Chewing on a fingernail in concentration, Jasmine asks, "What do you think they were looking for? It had to be the military, right?"

Jeff and Wes exchange a confused look. "Maybe they were just making sure people evacuated. You know, those signs we saw on the telephone poles?" We all nod slowly, processing the information.

"They could have been sweeping the coast for damage," Wes says. "With all this weather stuff going on and that bridge collapsing," he pauses to raise a hand in the air, swirling his finger in a circle, "maybe they just want to see what the area looks like, so they can send people back home."

"Why would they come at night?" a small voice questions innocently. "If they just came during the day, they wouldn't need a spotlight," Chris declares.

Chapter 58

After a thoughtful silence, we all give up trying to guess what's going on. I'm putting my faith in Chris. He'll probably figure it out before the rest of us do. With some debate, we settle on walking for the rest of our trip. While Aidan, Wes, Jasmine and I think it's too risky to call attention to ourselves, Jeff argues how much faster we'll get to Virginia if we drive. Eyeing the gadgets along the shelves and the machines tucked into the walls, Chris sides with Jeff. It doesn't much matter, though, since they're outvoted.

When Aidan questions if Jasmine and West are truly up for walking, they both adamantly insist that they are. Jasmine claims she can barely feel the bullet lodged in her shoulder, but the beads of sweat on her forehead say otherwise. Still, we don't have a better option right now.

With plans to continue our journey first thing in the morning, we divide up to get some sleep. Jasmine, Aidan and I trudge over to the other ambulance while Jeff and Chris stay with Wes. Curling up in the passenger's seat, my exhausted body accepts the upright position while my slowing mind craves a real bed. I easily drift into an uncomfortable sleep, and the day fades away.

The shrill creak of a door opening jerks me from a dreamless sleep. Eyes still closed, I can picture the body attached to the feet bounding inside our ambulance. Not that I need to wait for confirmation.

"Hey, guys, it's time to wake up!" Chris announces.

Rubbing the kinks in my neck, I respond with a noncommittal grunt.

Jasmine stirs on the stretcher, rubbing her eyes. "It's morning already?"

Chris smiles and answers her. "Sure is!"

I've never understood why anyone would want to smile this early in the morning.

Aidan stretches in the driver's seat, joints cracking as he straightens his arms and legs. "Are the others awake, buddy?" Chris' nod is enthusiastic. "Yep, they said it was time you got your butts up so that we can hit the road." Then under his breath he adds, "Since we have to walk."

Rising to his feet, Aidan steps toward Chris and ruffles his hair. "We'll get there plenty fast, even if we're walking. You'll see."

Once we've eaten and gathered all our belongings, we start, what I hope, is the last leg of our journey.

Jeff applied new bandages to Jasmine and Wes, and they both seem to be in good spirits.

Maybe just having actual medical supplies and medication, even though it's nowhere near the same as true medical care, has eased their discomfort.

Wes walks with a slight hobble and we keep pace with him. When Jeff and Aidan attempt to take Jasmine's bag for her, she firmly refuses. Hefting the backpack over her right shoulder, she makes a show of walking effortlessly.

As we tread south, the silence engulfs me. No birdsong drifts on the breeze, no bees buzz along beside us. The world is quiet. At least this little part of it. *Is this something new and strange or has it been this way since we first ventured on this journey? Have I been too caught up in my mind to truly hear anything outside of it?*

About two hours later, we pass through the graveyard of what appears to have been a copse of trees. Trunks as thick as my body litter the grass around us. Rich beige ovals sit where branches used to grow. Yellow and orange construction vehicles surround the massacre. They're immobile, and no one is around to drive them, but their destruction is complete.

As my eyes sweep over the area, I notice half a dozen cigarette butts and empty soda bottles littering the ground. The machinery and discarded trash lie in twisted contrast with the natural surroundings.

Jasmine speaks wistfully. "I bet this was really beautiful at one time."

Yeah, I think to myself, *now it's just dead limbs and logs. And trash.*

273

Jeff reaches out and touches her good shoulder. "And I bet it will be again someday."

With that, we continue. We've been travelling through wooded paths as much as we can. Besides trying to avoid others, the shade provides some relief from the intense heat of the day. I don't ever remember a June this hot.

"Have you noticed," Jasmine starts, "that we've seen more litter on this trip than wildlife?"

Aidan and Jeff chime in with their agreement.

Chris just plods along.

I wonder if he ever regrets coming with us.

"So, what do you think is going to end the world as we know it?" Jasmine asks no one in particular. Staring into the distance, she proposes possible answers. "A nuclear meltdown? An asteroid? Overconsumption of natural resources?"

"Maybe a giant crater will swallow us all up," Aidan suggests. His eyes grow wider as he looks around the group. "Maybe I'll be the one to discover it, and—"

Wes cuts him off. "We know you love rocks and all, but really, man?"

"Yeah, no way it'll be a crater. I'm gonna go with the zombie apocalypse," Jeff jokes.

After a quiet chuckle, Chris shares his opinion. "People."

Chapter 59

Realizing Wes hasn't spoken in a while, I steal a glance his way. My concern for him skyrockets. While I fully expect the sheen of sweat that covers his face, I'm startled by his sickly pallor. Without another thought, I blurt out, "Can we find a place to rest?"

Jasmine looks annoyed while Aidan and Jeff raise their eyebrows in question. They know I'm eager to get to the Air Force Base. And honestly, I could easily walk another four hours if it got me to Riley faster. Suggesting that we stop already is probably the last thing they expected to hear from me. I swear relief flashes through Wes' eyes.

Chris is the first to answer. "Yes! Let's find a place to sit. I'm tired of walking."

Except for Wes, everyone looks skeptical, even with Chris' glowing endorsement of my suggestion.

"Look, we must be getting close to Virginia by now. It won't hurt anything to take a break," I say.

Chris nods enthusiastically. The others exchange glances, but when they notice Wes' state, realization washes over their faces.

Jasmine refocuses on Chris as she cracks a smile and says, "I think that's a great idea."

While Wes, Jasmine, Chris and I park ourselves on some boulders lining the path, Jeff and Aidan scout ahead for shelter. An uncomfortable silence hangs over us. Chris digs around in his backpack and pulls out a crinkly bag of chips. Pulling it apart at the seams, he starts munching.

Wes sprawls out on the smooth surface and drapes an arm over his eyes. "Hey Jasmine," he asks. "How's that shoulder of yours?"

Glancing down at her bandages, she replies, "It's fine. Barely hurts anymore. How about you?"

I wouldn't expect any other answer from her. I have a feeling that even if she was in pain, she wouldn't show it.

"Feeling great," he chuckles. "Never been better." When quiet descends again, his breathing slows almost instantly.

A shaking tree branch in the distance catches my eye. The squirrel dashing across it gives me hope that some things haven't changed. It also reminds me of Snickers. I can't wait to see him again. The pounding thud of footsteps startles me, dissolving the mental image of my favorite fuzzy face.

Bursting onto the path before us, the guys are out of breath. Their eyes dance with anticipation when they see us. "Guys… we're really…close…to the…Virginia border," Aidan gasps.

"Yep," Jeff pants, clapping Aidan on the back. "We made it…to southern…Maryland."

Thrusting a crumpled white flyer toward us, the guys gulp deep breaths while we read.

By order of the United States Armed Forces, due to expected hazardous weather conditions, and to ensure the safety of residents, this area is under evacuation orders. Pack minimal belongings, such as medications, inhalers, and other medical necessities, and report to either Staunton Rescue Fire Station Number 1 or 2. Military personnel will be onsite to offer assistance and instructions.

"Come see what…we found," Aidan huffs, motioning for us to follow him.

Chapter 60

Once the guys catch their breath and wake Wes, we trudge along until we reach a clearing. As Jeff and Aidan lead us down a path that forks toward the street, I start scanning our surroundings. So far, we've managed to avoid mini marts and grocery stores because we thought they would be the first to be looted, and also have the most potential for hostile intruders.

A small cluster of houses comes into view. Their stone-faced exteriors remind me of cottages dotting the countryside. A breeze swirls around us, kicking up some leaves.

Jeff points toward our intended target, announcing, "I think it's cleared out. We watched the area and didn't see anyone come or go."

The slate gray home sits on the last lot in the small neighborhood. I'm guessing the guys chose it because of its proximity to the woods where we would pick up our path again.

It's also set off a bit from the other houses, giving it a more desolate feel.

Plodding down the narrow street, we are completely exposed if any neighbors bucked the evacuation order. Aidan walks right up the house's winding pathway to the front door. When he twists the knob and the door pops open easily, I know Jeff has worked his magic on it already. He must have unlocked it on their recon mission.

"Guys," Jasmine starts. "What are we doing? Someone could be in here." When she lifts her right hand to her wounded shoulder, I wonder if she even realizes it.

Aidan rushes to her side. "Hey, we checked every inch of this place. I swear, Jasmine, we wouldn't bring everyone here if we weren't sure it was empty."

Jeff strides over, placing a hand on her good shoulder. "Jas, this place has running water and strong walls. We'll be safe here."

Holding both Jeff's and Aidan's gazes for a moment, trust flows between the friends. She slowly nods and motions for the guys to go inside. We all follow.

The dusty-pink living room drowns in floral wallpaper. The stale décor is strangely inviting. Jasmine wrinkles her nose but follows suit as we investigate the other rooms. The single-story house is small. With only two bedrooms and one bathroom, I'll just wait to see how this plays out tonight.

Dropping our bags and creating an impromptu shower schedule, we make ourselves comfortable. Chris explores each room, looking for something more interesting than our meager possessions. Wes hits the shower first, and Jasmine checks out the kitchen, inventorying anything edible that was left behind.

Aidan and Jeff speak in hushed tones, probably talking about Wes' condition or how we're going to find our way to the Air Force Base.

With some time on my hands, I have my own priorities. The walk today barely tired me out. We needed to stop so Wes and Chris could rest, but I could have easily kept going. Now, I crave a run, as well as the mind-clearing energy it yields. With so little privacy, this may be my last opportunity for solitude in who knows how long. We all carry a share of the weight of our situation and the only thing that's going to help me forget for just a little while is a run. Even a twenty-minute jog will release some tension and remind me of what "normal" used to be.

Grabbing my bag, I lock myself in one of the bedrooms to change into my running gear. A crowd of peacocks stares at me from the sky-blue wallpaper. I push past my discomfort and undress. Showers have become a bit sporadic, so there's no way I'm going to wash up and then take a run.

Striding down the hallway, Aidan and Jeff notice my wardrobe change. "Hey, Quinn, what are you doing?" Aidan asks. At that moment, Jasmine enters the living room, just in time to observe our conversation.

"I'm going for a quick run," I answer. "I'll be back soon."

Jeff takes a step toward me. "That's not really a good idea." He rubs his chin and glances at Aidan. "I mean, we're guessing that no one is around, but we don't know for sure."

"We should all really stick together until we know it's safe," Aidan adds. Meeting their eyes in turn, I implore them to understand. "Guys, thanks for worrying, but really, I *need* this. I just need a little time to myself to clear my head. I'll be back before you even notice I'm gone." With that, I turn toward the door. As I'm closing it behind me Jasmine's voice rings out, "If she's going out, I'm going… "

I leave them to their next argument. Jasmine's fierce streak has only worsened now that the guys are worried about her. Apparently, that chip on her shoulder wasn't damaged by the bullet she took.

As I stretch my weak muscles, my mind plunges into a numbing state where my only focus is on each foot as it strikes the ground. After a proper warm-up, my mind shifts to autopilot and my feet take over. With each stride, exhilaration blossoms through my body.

The humid air plasters strands of hair to my forehead. Wisps cling to my cheeks. When sporadic fat drops begin to fall from the sky, I welcome the miniscule relief they bring. It's perfect. The perfect setting to let my stifled emotions bubble to the surface.

How different would life be if we hadn't left for vacation that day? Would all four of us still be alive? Would we be home together right now? My mind flashes through just a few of the life experiences snatched away from me in mere seconds. *I'll never shop with my mom for a prom dress. My parents won't see me graduate. My dad can't walk me down the aisle.*

With one big rush, I allow the surfacing anger, pain, and frustration to burst like a dam. Camouflaged by the rain, the tears flow freely. As my feet pound the path, each footfall boosts the last, slightly numbing the pain.

Shifting focus to the surrounding brush, I imagine the army

of trees swallowing me whole. *If I could just dissolve into the breeze, would I? Would anyone notice?* Stifling the spiral I've fallen into, I clear my mind of all thoughts.

After about a mile and a half, I turn around. I want to get back before too long, and my body is no longer accustomed to distance running. When I'm about a half mile from our camp, I slow to a cooldown pace. The rain has stopped, but between sweating and running through the brief shower, I'm soaked.

Within a few minutes, I stop entirely to stretch my overworked muscles. A few months ago, this run would have been just a warm-up. Maybe there will be time again for sports and hobbies when Riley and I get back home.

As I'm bent over at my waist, reaching for my toes, a deep voice startles me. "Hey there, beautiful." I jolt upright and turn toward the voice. As I suspected, it's no one I recognize.

Chapter 61

A twenty-something guy with long dark hair stands a few feet behind me. The smile on his face looks anything but genuine. Brownish stains adorn his otherwise white T-shirt, and his gray cargo shorts look weighed down. Beady eyes flitting up and down my body, his presence is unsettling. And the fact that he was able to sneak up on me so easily is disturbing.

"Um, hi," I say dumbly. I take a few slow steps backwards, away from him.

"What are you doing all the way out here?" he asks.

"I was just getting some exercise, but I'm done now, so I'm gonna get going," I say, hoping the nervousness in my voice isn't as audible as I think it is. I'd love to sound strong and confident right about now, but my vocal cords are just as scared as the rest of me. I start to turn away from him to continue on the path back to camp, but he calls out to me. "Hey, I'm Dylan. What's your name?"

The last thing I want to do is give this guy my name. "I'm... in a hurry," I sputter.

"You all alone out here? You need some help?" his sugary-sweet tone carries no sincerity.

"I'm good, thanks," I say, preparing to run as fast as my tired legs will take me. They're my only weapon out here. Turning on my heel, I raise a knee and plunge forward in a mad dash away from Dylan. Just two sprints into my escape, another man jumps out in front of me. I skid to a stop in my tracks.

This guy looks a little more clean-cut. His wavy brown hair must have seen a comb within the past few days and his shirt bears no stains. Although the navy V-neck T-shirt might just be good at hiding whatever it might have come in contact with. His tan shorts reveal muscular legs.

"No need to run off, pretty lady," he says. "I'm Hunter and it looks like you already met Dylan." He raises his hands in a *why not* questioning gesture. "We could all help each other in this new world." His toothy grin gives me a sinking feeling, like a rabbit caught in a trap. I'm sure that's what I look like to them.

Before either of them can say another word, my brain checks out and my body takes over. I bolt. I push right past Hunter and run as hard as I can. Without turning back, I hear them both laugh before the sound of feet hitting the ground carries to my ears. *Dammit. I knew they'd follow.*

I sprint straight back to camp. There's nowhere else to go and I can't be alone in unfamiliar surroundings when I run out of steam. Although the laughing has ceased, their labored breaths seem to be closing in on me.

Just as I'm rounding the last turn before the clearing, a blur crosses my path. A body slams into me—hard—and we crash to the ground, a tangle of limbs. An audible "oomph" accompanies the air that the collision knocks out of my lungs. A pair of deep brown eyes meet mine. Jasmine. She narrows her eyes and says, "What the hell are you doing?" My temporary relief at seeing a familiar face—even hers—evaporates when I hear a laugh.

"You've got a friend?" Hunter says between gulps of oxygen. Snickering, Dylan adds, "Looks like we got ourselves a double date."

Jasmine's eyes widen, and she jabs a thumb in the air toward the guys. "Who the hell are they?"

I answer her without taking my eyes off the sneering, leering men. "Trouble."

We both rise on shaky legs, clutching our aching elbows and wrists. We'll be sporting a few bruises from that collision, but I'm not as scared now. Even though we're not exactly friends, we've instantly become allies.

"Nice to see another pretty lady around here. We were just trying to get to know your friend here a little better and she high-tailed it away from us. Kind of rude if you ask me," Dylan says.

Hunter is happy to play along. "Yeah, we just thought we could all help each other. Looks like you got hurt out here," he says, gesturing to her shoulder. "I bet I could make that feel better." His meaning is clear. They can do whatever they want, and no one is watching. No one is enforcing laws. They see no value in civility.

Jasmine eyes me and then turns to the guys. She levels them with a gaze that was previously reserved for me. "Thanks, but we've got somewhere to be. We have plenty of friends, and I'm sure they're getting worried about us."

As she turns to go, Hunter takes a step closer and grabs her uninjured arm. "Oh really? Or maybe you're just bluffing. Maybe it's just you two lonely ladies out here, trying to survive on your own."

Dylan chuckles.

"Jaaaaasmine," a male voice calls out.

My shoulders drop with relief. I recognize that voice.

Jasmine responds, keeping her eyes on the strangers. "I'm back here."

Hunter releases Jasmine's arm and takes a step back. Both guys shift uncomfortably. They've suddenly lost their sense of humor now that it's not just two helpless women.

I've never been so glad to see Jeff. He smiles at Jasmine. "Hey, there you are." When his eyes land on me, he says, "Good, you're back. We were all wondering how long you were gonna be." His smile fades when he sees Dylan and Hunter standing awkwardly a few feet away.

"Hey, I'm Jeff. Who are you?" he says as he takes a cautious step toward the guys and extends a hand to shake.

Like a true slimeball, Hunter takes another step backward, avoiding Jeff's greeting. "We were just leaving. We came across your friend here running in the woods." He throws a brief nod my way. "We thought she was alone, but since you're all obviously together, we'll just be on our way." He shoots a side eye at his friend and they start to turn away.

Jeff places a hand on my arm. "Everything okay?"

I just want those creepy guys to leave. We can talk about what happened after they are long gone.

As all three of us watch the strangers slink away, I answer Jeff. "Better now."

Chapter 62

The three of us hike back to camp, Jeff firing off questions faster than we can answer them. I explain how the first guy appeared out of nowhere and instantly gave me the heebie jeebies, his creep-factor surpassed only by his vile friend. *I silently promise myself no more running alone until Riley and I are back home.*

Jasmine explains how she ended up in my flight path. When I left, she decided that she wanted some time alone too. At the ambulance company, she felt like a prisoner in a medical ward. When she announced that she was going outside to take a look around, Aidan and Jeff weren't too happy, but they knew arguing would be pointless. A few minutes after she left, the guys were already worried, so Aidan stayed with Chris and Wes while Jeff rushed out to catch up to her.

We talk until we reach our tiny stone castle. At least that's what it feels like—a physical barrier between us and the world.

Maybe things are no more predictable than they ever were, but having to face everything without my family around sucks.

Relief courses through my veins, slowing the adrenaline that kept my body in motion when those guys were chasing me. An involuntary shudder racks my body when I think about what could have happened if Jasmine and Jeff hadn't shown up. Even if I got away, I would have led those guys right to everyone.

As soon as we push through the door, Chris rushes over and wraps an arm around Jasmine. His smile reaches from ear to ear. Jeff pats his shoulder. When his eyes land on me, Chris throws me a small nod.

Hearing our grand entrance, Aidan appears. The apprehension on his face transforms into a smile when he sees all three of us are back.

He and Jeff greet each other with a high five fist grab. "Hey, glad to see you guys."

"Yeah, glad to be back," I say.

Sensing the unspoken words that hang between us, Aidan asks Chris to bring Wes some water and stay with him until he drinks. Rolling his eyes, Chris trudges off to the tiny kitchen and takes his time filling a glass. The four of us sit on the grey-green wraparound couch until Chris moseys down the hallway and disappears into the room we've designated for Wes.

As I settle into the cushions, my damp clothes cling to my skin, sending a chill over my body. *At least the rain gave me a brief shower until I can get a real one.*

Jeff makes a show of leaning back into the cushions and linking his fingers behind his head, elbows pointed out. "So, Quinn, tell us all about the two guys you tried to pick up today."

Aidan's eyes flash wide as he turns to face me. I grab a throw pillow and launch it at Jeff.

He and Jasmine burst into laughter.

My annoyance dissolves, and a relief-giggle escapes me. Being here, surrounded by what feels like some semblance of safety, I can laugh. I can forget what might have happened. For just a moment.

"What did I miss? What happened?" Aidan's had enough of being left out of the joke. We shake off our laughter and fill him in on the details. He listens intently, releasing a big sigh when we finish. "Do you think they followed you?" He glances toward the windows.

"Uh, I don't think so." I hadn't really considered that.

Glancing at me, Jasmine speaks up, "They took off. I think Jeff's raw masculinity scared them."

Jeff leans forward and steers the conversation serious. "They were pretty eager to break ties with us once they saw they were outnumbered. Are you thinking we should set up a watch tonight to make sure they don't try to take us by surprise?"

Aidan props his elbows on his knees and drops his head into his palms. "I don't know," he mumbles.

Jasmine rushes to his side and rubs his back. I focus on keeping my face neutral, even though my eyes are itching to hurl daggers her way.

In a hushed tone, she asks, "What's going on, Aidan?"

With so many things wrong right now, we anxiously wait for him to define exactly what's weighing on him at the moment.

"Guys," Aidan says. "Wes is in really bad shape. He's in a lot of pain and the ibuprofen isn't doing much. I don't think we have what he needs to get better." He presses a fist to his mouth and closes his eyes.

Jeff and Jasmine exchange a worried glance before Jeff speaks. He asks Aidan a series of questions. "Is he still shaky? Feverish? Headaches?"

Every answer is a yes.

Before anyone can say anything else, Chris runs out to the living room. "Um, guys, Wes wants you."

Chapter 63

We rise in unison, moving like a herd down the hallway. When Jeff reaches the doorway first, he turns toward us, holding a finger up to his mouth in a silent "Shhhh." We quietly shuffle into the room to find Wes asleep. When we all turn to Chris he just raises his shoulders and throws up his hands, whispering, "He was just awake and asked for you!"

With nothing else to do, we settle into the room. The guys carry some kitchen table chairs into the tiny bedroom and we each claim one. Within five minutes, Chris is kneeling on his chair, pushing the boundaries of balance. Jeff motions to him and leads the kid out to the hallway.

A few minutes later, Jeff returns alone. "I gave the kid a job," he says, shrugging his shoulders. "He was bored, so I told him to guard the house. He's making rounds, checking the doors and windows. Maybe that'll tire him out." As if on cue, echoes of small footsteps pounding the floor drift toward us.

At some point, I relax into the chair enough to fall asleep. My cruel mind flashes images of the day we drove to the beach. Raindrops pound the windshield and my window. My dad's gripping the steering wheel so tight that his knuckles turn white. My mom glances back at me, her eyes clouded with worry. A flash of red turns my attention to the windshield.

My body jolts forward, tearing me from the nightmare. Eyes flying open, I search my surroundings. Jasmine, Jeff, and Aidan watch me as if I'm a science experiment that just exploded.

"You okay?" Aidan asks. Smoothing my hair out of my face, I answer, "I'm good. Just had a dream. It was a little…intense." I'm grateful when a muffled moan shifts the attention from me. We all turn toward the bed.

Wes' head lolls back and forth as he emerges from a fitful sleep. Aidan rushes to his side. "Wes, man, are we glad to see you awake! You kinda scared us there for a little while." I can tell he's trying to sound casual, but his words are clipped, his timbre off. He scans the group, his eyes urging us to join him in acknowledging Wes' improved state, even if it is imaginary.

Jeff jumps to his feet, his chair clattering to the floor. As he takes a clumsy step forward, he loses his balance and crashes into Aidan's empty chair. His knees meet the floor with a crack.

"Jesus, Jeff. Are you okay?" Aidan's concern shifts from one friend to the other in a heartbeat.

Jasmine rushes over to Jeff, helping him up.

I avert my eyes, trying to avoid the awkwardness cutting through the already-charged space.

Jeff jumps to his feet and splays his hands out at his sides. "I'm fine. Just a little fall. I was eager to see my man Wes."

Wes finally speaks, his voice a raspy murmur. "Jeff, you dumbass. You just can't stand when all the attention isn't on you." And just like that, the tension dissipates. Leave it to Jeff to provide comic relief, without even trying, when we need it most.

The guys ease Wes up into a sitting position and offer him water. He gratefully drinks. Speaking quietly, he says, "This is getting worse, guys. Even with aspirin, my head doesn't stop pounding. And my muscles...I feel like I can barely lift my arms. This must be what Jeff's puny biceps are like." He pauses, flashing a pitiful smile. "I don't know if I can even get out of this bed."

With his words, the walls seem to close in around me. Anxiety skyrockets through my veins. I shoot up out of my seat awkwardly. "Guys, I'm gonna go check on Chris." Focusing on my feet, I exit the room as swiftly as possible.

I wander into the kitchen to find Chris perched in front of a window, intently scanning the backyard. He doesn't even hear me approach. *Not a very effective lookout. Maybe he really does need my help.*

"Chris," I say softly, placing a hand on his shoulder. My attempt to avoid startling him fails as his body jerks upright.

"Whoa, Quinn, I'm on outside guard duty. I can't keep watch in here too," he says.

"Sorry, buddy," I say, rubbing his arm in a way that reminds me of something Riley would do. "So, have you seen anything out there?"

"Nah. Nothing at all," he utters, his tone dejected.

"Well, maybe you just have too many windows to cover," I state, trying to boost his confidence. "I'm here as your second-in-command now. Why don't you assign me to a lookout spot and we can both watch?"

His posture straightens and he instinctively raises his chin. "Okay," he says enthusiastically. "You stay here in the kitchen. I'll check the front door and bedroom windows. Yell if you see anything!"

"You got it!" I attempt to sound excited, but I'm pretty sure it sounds flat. Either way, he doesn't seem to mind. He trots off toward the hallway while I turn toward the windows.

It takes only two strides to reach the windows of the galley kitchen. As small as this space is, it feels safe. Someone in our group is always just a room away and sturdy walls separate us from the outside world. Right now, that's enough.

Beyond the strong stone walls, thick clouds choke the ashen sky. Wind batters the backyard's flowering bushes and overgrown grass. Leaves, yanked from the smattering of lush trees by the wind's powerful grasp, toss and turn in the breeze. Turning away from the window, my eyes catch another door that I assume is a pantry.

Ambling toward the door, I focus on the wooden house-shaped key holder clinging to the tan wall right next to it. A set of keys on a silver Tree of Life keychain dangles from one of its hooks. A small smile tugs at my lips. *It must be.*

Twisting the handle, I gently pull the door open and wander into the attached two-car garage. One of the bays sits empty, but the other houses a gold Ford Escape. Betting that the home's residents loaded up in one vehicle, I'd say this one is up for grabs.

I pocket the keychain and stride back into the kitchen. I had better check my post again before Chris catches me slacking off.

Pausing at the kitchen window, I draw one lacey curtain away from the window and peer outside. After scanning the backyard, which is free of human or animal intrusion, my eyes drift to a roiling sky. It's mesmerizing.

Puffy gray clouds swim in an ashen atmosphere. Although they tumble slowly now, I fear those clouds will twirl in somersaults soon enough. In pursuit of a better view, I let the curtain slip from my hand, swishing over the pane until it falls back into place along the window's side.

I disobey my orders and stride toward the front door. Yanking it open, a rush of wind chases the hair off my shoulders, launching it behind me like a cape for just a moment. The breeze was subtle during my run. It's definitely growing stronger.

Stepping onto the winding sidewalk, my feet meander while my eyes rove. A mere three steps into the blustering night, the resounding thud of footsteps echoes behind me. I turn back toward the front door just in time to see Chris barreling through it. For a kid who probably weighs sixty pounds soaking wet, it sounds like a herd of elephants when he runs. "Quinn, it's getting really dark outside all of a sudden!"

Standing side by side, we both tilt our heads back, our eyes devouring the scene above. The dark swirling billows are mesmerizing. Leaning on each other to maintain balance, the sound of rushing wind fills our ears.

"Quinn! Chris! What are you doing out there!" Jeff calls as he bursts through the open front door. "Come on inside. A storm's a-brewing!"

With Jeff in the lead, we hustle inside, allowing the front door to abruptly halt the wind that was just chasing us.

Chapter 64

Inside, Aidan slouches on the couch. Jasmine sits next to him, her body melding into the cushions. They both look as if they've aged by a decade since they last sat here.

Chris excitedly updates Jasmine and Aidan on the current weather conditions. He seems to have forgotten his failed mission of guarding the house. That's probably for the best. Those creepy guys must have seen the storm coming and, if they had any brains, found a place to wait it out.

Jasmine and Aidan barely acknowledge any of Chris' words, but that doesn't deter him from embellishing his account of the brewing storm. When he finishes speaking, silence falls over the room. Jasmine stretches her legs and starts to rise. "Hey, Chris," she says. "How about you and I go round up some food? Let's see what we can find."

Without another word, he runs to the kitchen. As she trails behind Chris, Jasmine throws Aidan a knowing glance. My eyes shoot toward Aidan just in time to see the subtle nod he passes back.

Once they leave the room, Aidan leans forward, resting his elbows on his knees. He folds his hands, dropping his chin on the rounded steeple they form. His tired eyes capture the sadness seeping from his words. "So, Wes seems to be getting worse no matter what we do. Even Doctor Jeff here can't fix him," Aidan explains.

Jeff shrugs his shoulders. "He's resting but we *have got* to get him to that military base. They must have medical staff there. Someone who can help us. The sooner the better."

"Yeah," Aidan agrees. "We've got to move faster, but at this rate, he'll need to rest more than he'll be able to walk."

"Guys," I start excitedly. "I know how we can get him there. Fast."

I'm practically jumping out of my skin when the rush of words flies out of my mouth. "There's a car parked in the garage, the keys are hanging right there in the kitchen," glancing back and forth between them, I continue. "Let's just take it. Let's get the hell out of here and get to that base."

Running a hand through his hair, Jeff exhales a deep sigh and meets my eyes, "We already stole one car. What's one more? I think we should do it."

Aidan eases back into the couch cushions and rubs his forehead. "Yeah, you're right. We can't keep this pace."

I jump to my feet, digging into my pocket to retrieve the keys when Aidan raises a hand, motioning me to stop. "Quinn, I don't think we should leave right now," he says. "There's a storm out there and it's dark. Let's just wait until morning. At least we'll be able to see where we're going then."

As if on cue, thunder erupts in the atmosphere. Rain strikes the roof like pebbles. Tree branches lash the windows. Momentarily startled, thankfulness washes through me as I envision the house's stone exterior. At least we're safe inside this structure.

After a moment's hesitation, Aidan rises to his feet and takes a step closer to me. "Quinn, would you mind hanging with Chris tonight? Maybe just keep him busy and make sure he gets some sleep?" He nods his head toward the hallway. "That way the rest of us can watch over Wes tonight and just…be there in case he needs anything."

Reaching toward him, I squeeze his hand and agree without hesitation.

Jasmine emerges from the kitchen with plates of tuna and crackers. Chris trails behind her, carrying cups of water. They make a few trips between the kitchen and the bedroom, carting more food and drinks, before Chris returns to me alone.

He slouches onto the couch. "Well, Jasmine said I have to watch you tonight cuz they're too busy taking care of Wes." He jabs a thumb toward the bedroom.

"Gee, thanks," I say. "I hope it's not too much trouble for you." Seriously, this kid practically begged to tag along with us and now he's acting like *I'm* a burden.

"It's okay," he says reluctantly. "So, Jasmine found some food in the kitchen. You want anything?"

My stomach responds for me, loudly growling before I can affirm that I would love to see what food choices await me.

He snickers before raising his eyebrows and says, "Guess that's a yes."

As we enter the kitchen, the aroma of canned tuna engulfs the small space. The smell makes my nose crinkle. I'm not a fan of seafood or its distinct odor.

I quickly forget the offending scent when my eyes land on the cluttered counter, which is a treasure trove of food packages. Chris and Jasmine must have emptied every cupboard and drawer. A smile tugs at my lips as I scan the cans and boxes stacked atop the speckled white countertops.

Gazing longingly at cans of mandarin oranges, boxes of cereal, and pouches of beef jerky, my mouth waters.

"Well, go on," Chris says. "Dig in."

Since I have access to an actual sink and water, I take advantage of it and wash up before selecting my feast. Chris watches with fascination while I devour five strips of teriyaki jerky, two handfuls of Cinnamon Life cereal, and an entire can of fruit.

"Wow, Quinn," he says with awe. "I didn't know a girl could eat that much." I start to question why I always seem to get stuck with this kid when I remember where everyone else is. I place both hands on the bistro kitchen table and push myself up.

"I'm gonna clean up in here. Why don't you go use the bathroom and we'll get ready for bed," I say.

He gives a quick nod and marches out to the living room and down the hallway.

The house has a second bedroom, but I don't know if

Jasmine or either of the guys will need some space overnight, so we'll leave it empty. After wiping up my crumbs and tossing the empty wrappers in the trash, I search for bedding. The sole linen closet in the hallway holds all that I need. Loading my arms with pillows and blankets, I dump them on the couch and start building makeshift nests so that Chris and I can bunk in the living room.

When Chris is ready for bed, I make sure he's settled on his share of the couch before I venture down the hallway, pausing outside of Wes' door. The sound of muffled voices confirms they are all still awake, but I continue on to the bathroom. I care about Wes, but the most I can do right now is keep Chris occupied, so the others can focus on their friend.

Besides, tomorrow we'll get him to the base. I bet there are medical people there that can fix him all up.

Chapter 65

Within minutes of burrowing into the couch, the world fades away. Hazy images flit through my mind. Wes' strong jawline and thin lips morph into Riley's warm brown eyes and high cheekbones. The image of my sister vanishes as I'm running along a wooded path. Gnarled tree limbs reach toward me as my feet glide over the ground. I stumble to a stop when the creepy guys from my earlier run jump into the path.

Exaggerated smiles mask their faces as they reach for me just like the snaking branches. I twist to escape their grasp. My brain ceases to separate the dream from reality because I jolt out of the nightmare when my body lands on the floor.

Momentarily stunned, I swivel my head back and forth, assessing my surroundings. I'm in a living room. Chris is sleeping just a few feet away from me. The small house. We're in the small house and Wes is…sick.

A brief clatter pulls my attention toward the kitchen. I'm not going to sit on the floor for the rest of the night. I rise on unsteady legs and tiptoe toward the sound.

Entering the dark kitchen slowly, I just barely decipher Jasmine's trembling frame. My first instinct is to retreat, return to the couch, and pretend I'm still sleeping. As I take a small step backward, the floor creaks and Jasmine faces me.

"Hey," I whisper. "I was just coming to get a drink of water, but I don't really need it. I'll just go back to bed."

"No," she says softly, wiping her cheeks. "Go ahead."

With no choice but to follow-through on my lie, I stroll over to the sink, find what I hope is a clean glass and half-fill it with water. I lean against the counter uncomfortably, gently swirling the water around in my glass.

Jasmine sits at the table with her forehead propped on her hands. She startles me when she speaks. "I just can't believe this is all happening."

When I don't respond, she continues. "I'm so tired of all this. I just want to be home. I want this all to go away."

I step forward and join her at the table. "This has been the worst summer of my life. And it just keeps getting worse and worse."

She raises her head and looks me in the eye. The light is dim, but I believe she truly sees me for what feels like the first time. "Quinn, I'm sorry for everything you've gone through. I don't know what the hell is happening, but I can't take much more."

I reach out and touch her hand. "Me either."

Wrapping herself in a hug, she continues. "I just want to go home. I want to forget everything that's happened." She rocks forward and back slightly, as if soothing herself. "Nothing will ever be the same, Quinn. Whatever's going on, it can't just fix itself. And we sure as hell can't rely on humans to fix it."

"You know, I never thought I'd say this," I start with a half-smile. "But I think you're right."

After a short chat and a long cry, Jasmine retreats to the empty bedroom to get some sleep. I return to my couch nest. My thoughts drift to Wes. Although my brain is swimming in sadness, unloading some of the emotional weight I was carrying leaves me exhausted and I quickly succumb to sleep.

Chapter 66

The air is hazy as I slowly enter Wes' room. When I peer at his sleeping form, he whispers to me, "Help them, Quinn. Help them get home. Find Riley. And Quinn, I'll tell your parents you said hi."

Just as I'm about to reach for his hand, my body jolts awake. Gasping for breath, I take in the trail of pink roses on the wall and remember that I'm in the living room of the gray stone house. *It was a dream. It was just a dream. Wes is here, everything is going to be okay. I just really wish Riley, Mom and Dad were here too.*

Easing into alertness, my ears hone-in on the whispers of hushed voices slinking through the house.

I scan the living room, confirming that I am alone. Chris must have woken up and joined the others. The clanking of a spoon and bowl directs my attention to the kitchen. Standing, I rub my arms in a futile attempt to smooth the goosebumps that have erupted there.

Entering the kitchen, I find Chris sitting at the table, his head downcast, propped up by one angry fist. His other hand half-heartedly pushes a spoon around the half-full bowl of dry cereal. Jasmine and Aidan sit on his either side, slumped in their chairs, eyes downcast.

Jeff leans against the wall with his arms crossed. He stares off into the distance, not acknowledging my presence. Misery hangs in the air like one hundred percent humidity. Not one of them meets my gaze.

"Guys, what's going on?" I ask quietly. I don't really want to know, but I have to know. Sliding into the empty seat at the table, my eyes shift from one lethargic person to the next until someone answers me.

Aidan finally breaks the silence. "He didn't wake up." He pauses for a moment before adding two nearly inaudible words. "He's gone." In that split second, I tumble back into the funnel of despair that consumed me after the crash.

My meager memories of Wes' life flash through my mind. Him joking at the fire when we first met. Him showing us the bug-infested cabin. Him sneaking through the woods at the trailer park. After that, I was too consumed with myself to notice much of the personal hell he must have been enduring. I know this, though, he never complained. Not once. And, just like losing my mom and dad, I didn't get to say goodbye or even thank you.

After several minutes of quiet, Jeff finds his voice. "I'm gonna head out back and see if I can find a shovel or something." Chris jumps up from his seat, mumbling, "I'll help." No one is in any mental state to take care of a kid right now. Once again, I wish Riley was here with us. She'd be able to put Chris' emotional needs before her own.

Not sure what else to do, I clean up Chris' untouched cereal and spoon. I want to fill the emptiness of the room with words of sympathy and understanding, but I won't say I'm sorry. Sorry doesn't scratch the surface of what anyone is feeling right now. I choke on a sob when I realize that Wes' family doesn't even know that they'll never see him again. He left this life in a strange bed in a strange house and we have no way to tell his parents. Maybe the only consolation is that he was surrounded by friends right until the end.

The rest of the morning passes in a blur. The guys prepare a grave in the backyard while Jasmine creates a marker for it. Together we find some Sharpies and a small flat rock. She arranges her meager supplies on the kitchen table and focuses on the task. While she carefully scripts Wes' name in loopy letters, I wash the dishes and utensils we've used. Setting the clean dishes on a towel to dry, I start organizing the food Jasmine and Chris pulled out of the cupboards. Although, the more I think about it, we probably won't need it.

Turning away from the meaningless piles of food, I observe Jasmine's handiwork as she outlines a tiny jet on the stone, signifying Wes' dream of joining the Air Force.

Chapter 67

By mid-afternoon, we gather to say our goodbyes. Aidan and Jeff gently place Wes' body into the hole and Jasmine carefully positions the rock marker. Memories spill out of their trembling lips as tears stream down their cheeks.

In a soft-spoken and shaky voice, Jeff recalls meeting Wes in an ROTC Basic Course class. They ended up sitting next to each other and their mutual dislike for the professor made them fast friends.

Aidan remains silent as Jasmine shares her favorite memory of Wes, who became a regular fixture in Jeff and Aidan's dorm room. Jasmine lived in the same dorm and hung out with Aidan and Jeff often. She hesitantly welcomed Wes, although he sealed the deal on Halloween, when he brought a bag of Reese's Peanut Butter Cups for the group to share.

"How could you not like someone offering peanut butter cups?" she asks through an endless stream of tears. Aidan wraps an arm around her as she squeezes her eyes shut and shudders.

When silence greets us once again, dark circles shadow three sets of eyes. Their sluggish movements are punctuated by slumped postures.

Chris watches solemnly as we take turns expressing our final words for Wes. When Aidan reaches for a shovel to fill in the hole, I grab his arm. "No, you go inside and rest. Chris and I can finish up out here." I look to Jasmine and Jeff. "Please, let us do this. All three of you need a break."

Aidan flashes me a weak smile and nods his head once. When he starts walking toward the house, Jasmine and Jeff follow. I don't know how any of them are still standing right now. They were probably awake most of last night.

When Chris picks up a shovel and hefts it into the pile of dirt, I grab the other one and mirror his action. By the time we've returned all of the dirt to its original resting place, my shoulders and back throb. Placing a hand on Chris' back, I praise him. "Great job, bud. I'm really glad the others could go inside and rest. I couldn't have done this without you."

Peering up at me with dirt-streaked cheeks, he simply says, "You guys are all really nice. Even when bad stuff happens." Once again, I wonder what this kid's home life was like. As I meet his eyes, I hope he can't see the pity that lurks behind my smile.

After we stow the shovels on the back porch, I tell Chris to take a shower. The house must have a well because we have working water, it's just not heated. While he's in the bathroom, I gather some food for a quick dinner. There's no sign of Jasmine or the guys, so I'm guessing they went to the bedrooms and passed out. It's much deserved if they did.

Chris grumbles about the cold water all through our dinner, but I tune most of it out. The kid doesn't complain about much, and there's a lot to be unhappy about these days, so I just stay quiet and let him get it out of his system.

While he's rambling on, I remember something I saw earlier in the refrigerator. It's no longer cold, but it will still be a treat. Standing, I retrieve two cans of Sprite from the fridge. Chris stops mid-sentence, smiling and nodding. And just like that, he's forgotten his troubles.

We both crack open the warm sodas and enjoy the simple pleasure they bring. Once we've finished the last of our meal, I clean up the table and plates and send Chris to the bathroom one last time to get ready for bed. After I've tucked him into his couch nest, I take my turn in the bathroom, silently cursing every minute the cold water hits my body.

When I'm finally ready for bed, I crawl under my blanket and surrender to sleep as the emotional and physical exhaustion of the day overtakes my body.

Light filters into the small living room, prompting my body to wake from yesterday's nightmare. With the weight of reality still clinging to me, I stay right where I am, staring at the white ceiling with wooden beams. *That looks really nice. This was a good house to find.* My brain processes simple thoughts, as if fearful of delving any deeper.

"Guys, she's finally awake!" Chris yells from the room's entrance that borders with the kitchen. He steps over to the couch and plops down on his side of it. Jasmine, Jeff, and Aidan filter in from the kitchen.

"Morning, sleepyhead," Jeff says with a weak smile.

"Good morning," I answer.

Aidan rubs his forehead. His eyes still bear dark circles, and I wonder if he actually got any sleep last night. "So, Quinn, how about we all pack up and hit the road? There's nothing left for us here."

I meet his eyes and nod. I want to wrap my arms around him and tell him that it's okay to visit the dark abyss that's calling, as long as he comes back from it at some point. But I don't.

Without another word, Aidan stands and walks down the short hallway to the back bedroom. Jasmine turns toward the kitchen and disappears inside. Jeff takes a step toward Chris and places a hand on his shoulder. "Hey, buddy, you need any help packing up?"

"Nah," Chris answers. "I don't have much. It won't take me long."

"Well, after you have your stuff packed, go see Jasmine, okay? She'll put some food in your bag too. We're all gonna help carry extra supplies." Jeff clasps a hand on his shoulder and Chris nods in agreement.

"About that," I start. "So, I noticed a car in the garage. I say we borrow it and make it to Langley today." Jeff's eyes widen for just a moment as understanding dawns on him. "Best idea I've heard in a long time," he says.

An hour later, our belongings and a few borrowed food items are stowed in our backpacks. Jasmine is the last to filter out of the house. She pulls the door closed behind her so that we can start the last leg of our journey.

The Escape provides plenty of room for just the five of us. Overcome with defeat, no one cares about drawing attention to ourselves anymore. We all just want this trip to end.

Sticking to main roads, our trek is largely quiet. Grief hangs like an unrelenting cloud just overhead, clinging to every minute and hour. We pass other vehicles now and then, but I'm barely cognizant of the blurs rushing past my window. My only interest is in reaching our destination.

The sun is still high when signs for the Air Force Base begin appearing on the side of the highway.

Chapter 68

"Guys," Jeff says from the driver's seat. "I think we should hide the car. You know, go in on foot."

"I guess it wouldn't look too good if we showed up in a stolen car, huh?" Jasmine interjects.

Hotels and motels line the highway. Pulling into the Insignia Suites lot, Jeff parks the Escape in the midst of vehicles, effectively blending in with the surroundings. We quickly exit the SUV. I shoulder my bag and Riley's while the others leave their belongings. *Yeah, they can just hop back in here and drive to Jasmine's house after they're rid of me.*

As our feet pound the pavement, I realize this is the last walk we'll take together. Shaking the thought from my head, I focus on our short trek. The brilliant sun should be a warm welcome from the recent gloomy skies, but its blinding rays just make my head pound. Squinting, I tuck my chin down in a futile effort to block the glare.

Jeff calls out landmarks. "There," he says, pointing straight ahead in the distance. "See that? It's the air traffic control tower. We're almost there."

My feet slow as my nerves surge. What if Riley isn't here? Then what do I do? Will everyone hate me? While I think Jasmine hates me a little less than she initially did, what would she say if this trip was for nothing? What would Aidan and Jeff think? They went way out of their way to help me, and if Riley didn't come here after all…

"Hey," Jeff nudges my shoulder. "You ready to see your sister?" I nod awkwardly. "What, are you nervous?" Jeff prods. Afraid my voice will crack, I default to my standard response: a fast nod. Aidan moves to my other side and matches my pace. "Don't worry, Quinn, we're right here with you." I find my voice briefly. "Thank you. I really mean it. Thank you for everything."

Somewhere along the way, these people started to mean something to me. They made me laugh when tears threatened, they offered comfort when loneliness hovered, and they accepted risk when they could have just walked away. And now, that's what I'm supposed to do. I'm supposed to just walk into this base, find Riley, and make our way home.

As we near the fence surrounding the field, my eyes land on a tan sign that stands taller than me. Its black letters announce the U.S. Air Force. Next to the letters is the familiar v-shaped wing Air Force logo. It silently welcomes us to Langley Field. A twinge of sadness surges through me when I think of Wes. He was the only one who was excited to come here, and he never got to see it.

Within the fence, activity buzzes around the buildings.

Camouflaged soldiers walk casually amongst civilians. Middle-aged couples sit on plastic green lawn chairs, chatting as if the world isn't falling apart. Kids of various ages huddle together, flipping water bottles to see who can land one the farthest distance from the group.

Our movement draws the attention of two guards overseeing the main gate entrance. They greet us stiffly. "How can we help you?" As I open my mouth to respond, Aidan beats me to it. "We heard that this is kind of a safe zone," he says nervously. "That people could come here if they needed a place to go until things…um, settle."

With no hesitation, a stocky man with a badge identifying him as Mitchell responds, "Sorry, sir. This base is full. If you step over to this booth, we can process you and then direct you to the closest base that is accepting civilians at this time."

Jasmine has no qualms questioning the soldier. "What do you mean *process* us? If we can't come in anyway, we'll just be on our way."

Mitchell is starting to look bored. "Ma'am, regardless of this base's operating status, all civilians and military personnel onsite must be logged into the system and vaccinated to avoid spreading illness to the vulnerable populations within the region's military facilities." He barely looks at us as he speaks. He must have recited this speech a thousand times.

"We don't need to be logged or vaccinated," Aidan says, trying to sound casual. After spending the past few weeks with him, I detect anger brimming just below his calm exterior. "We're just here to drop our friend off and then the rest of us are heading home."

"Regardless of your plans, each base is required to log civilians that make contact. The information is shared across bases, so we can add your information here and then if you proceed to Fort Belvoir in Fairfax, which is the closest base still open to civilians, they'll allow you immediate entry."

He speaks with no inflection, no hint of a personality. This time I'm the first to respond. I point first at Mitchell, private or corporal or whatever he is, then toward the main building "Look, my sister is in there and I am not leaving until I find her. I don't care about being tracked or logged or whatever. I've come a really long way and I'm not giving up now." My tone is harsh, but I've been to hell and back and the only reason I'm still standing is so that I can find the one piece of my family that's left. If she's not here, I give up.

My outburst draws attention from those within earshot. Another camouflaged soldier strides over to us, obviously planning to take control of the situation. My eyes fly to his badge. E. Bowen. I guess there's more than one Bowen or else this guy's special enough to get his first initial on his tag.

"Is there a problem over here?" he asks. The guys must sense my inability to control brimming emotions because Aidan answers before I can. "No problem at all, sir. Our friend here lost her sister and word is that she's on this base. So, maybe we could just take a little look around?"

The soldier raises an eyebrow but before he can speak, Jeff jumps in. "Evan? Or is it Ethan? Maybe Edward?" He's trying to connect with this guy, but I'm guessing military people aren't the type to break out the jokes with strangers. Although, Jeff's got a good sense of humor and he was going to college to be a military officer, so maybe he's on to something.

"You may address me as Sergeant Bowen," the soldier huffs. *Yep, no room for casual conversations here.* He continues before Jeff can open his mouth again. "Follow me. We'll discuss this in private." Before anyone can respond, he turns on his heel and strides toward a nearby trailer. We all jump to follow him.

Sergeant Bowen leads us up a few metal steps to a white door. The trailer's gray metal siding makes it look like a temporary structure, not a permanent fixture. The only window on this side holds a black and white sign that reads Intake Office 3. I wonder how many feet have shuffled through this door in the past few weeks. Hesitating, I wonder if Riley's been in this trailer.

Chapter 69

The sergeant circles a cluttered metal desk and sits in the well-worn swivel chair behind it. He motions for us to sit at the folding chairs scattered throughout the room. We each pull one into a cluster across from him and settle onto the thinly-padded seats.

He leans forward with his elbows on the desk, rubbing his palms together. "So, as the soldier told you at the gate, this facility is at capacity but before we send you to another facility, we have to document your existence." He rubs his forehead. He doesn't seem nervous, more like he's allowing himself to take a much-needed breather.

"Look, sir," Jasmine says before he can continue. "Only one of us is interested in coming in. The rest of us just want to be on our way home. We don't want to be documented or vaccinated."

"I understand." His tone borders on conversational as he holds Jasmine's gaze. "But I do have to insist, ma'am, that you take a brief detour to our medical facility after I process you here."

Raising a hand to her left shoulder, Jasmine slowly nods. Quietly, she answers. "Thank you." Satisfied that he's addressed one issue, he moves on to the next.

"Which one of you has a family member here?"

I lean forward, eager to have this conversation. It's taken me what feels like a million miles and a billion days to get here. "Me. My sister, Riley Whelan, is here. Well, I think she's here anyway."

"And what makes you believe that?" he asks, his hazel eyes boring into mine. A quiet confidence radiates from his every word and movement.

Shooting a quick glance at Chris, I answer, "Um, well, my sister was kidnapped, and someone overheard the guys who took her say they were coming here."

"I can't guarantee your sister is here, but we'll do everything we can to reunite you with her if she is here." After he's temporarily addressed my need, thereby reducing the probability of any further meltdowns, his eyes land on Chris. "And you, young man, where are your parents?"

Panic jolts through me like lightning. How are we supposed to explain that we helped a ten-year-old run away from home? The words sound somewhat criminal in my mind. Seated in the chair next to Chris, Jeff leans toward him and throws an arm around his shoulder. "This is my little brother, Chris. After we drop Quinn off here, we're dropping our friend Jasmine off at home, and then I'll get both of us home to Mom and Dad." Jeff throws Sergeant Bowen an innocent smile.

The sergeant watches Chris' face for a reaction when he asks, "Is that true, son?"

Chris plays along like a pro. "Yep, Jeff's my big brother. Most days I wish he wasn't, but you know, like our mom says, you can't pick your family."

Satisfied, Sergeant Bowen tents his hands and addresses the others. "I need to take some information from you, and I do need to vaccinate each of you. Your cooperation is expected and appreciated." His intense gaze demands compliance. We all mutely nod.

One-by-one everyone provides the sergeant with their home address, except for Chris, who stays quiet and lets Jeff speak for him. I watch as Bowen enters everyone's details into his computer. Skipping me entirely, he stands and strides to a beige cabinet at the back of the office.

When he pulls open the squeaky metallic doors, shelves of vials and syringes greet him. He carries four of each back to his desk. After he types numbers from each bottle into the computer, he slips on green surgical gloves. As he preps each syringe, he announces who gets that shot.

I think the fight has faded from everyone because even Jasmine complies. Or maybe they figure this is the fastest way to get out of here.

Disposing of the medical waste in a marked box next to the cabinet, Bowen slips off the gloves and tosses them in a trash can. He returns to his maroon swivel chair and yanks open the top drawer, dropping Band-Aids on his desk.

"If you would like a bandage, help yourself," he says, eyeing my friends. "You," he points at Chris. I contain a huge gulp in worried anticipation. He reaches into another desk drawer and pulls out an item that he thrusts toward Chris. "Put a Band-Aid on your upper left arm and stick this lollipop in your mouth."

With a huge grin, Chris complies. He drops the empty lollipop wrapper on Bowen's desk. It blends into the community of paperclips, rubber bands, and crumpled papers already in residence.

Smiling, Jasmine's eyes slide from Chris to Sergeant Bowen. "Can we go now? We just came along to make sure Quinn got here safely."

Sergeant Bowen looks around the group and the others nod. "Well, then it looks like you've completed your mission. Take a moment to say your goodbyes, and then I'll have someone escort you to medical before you leave the base."

He pushes up from the desk and looks at each of us. "I'll wait right outside the door. When you're done, meet me out there, and we'll get you on your way. Miss?" He looks at me tentatively.

I nod to acknowledge him. "You can just have a seat and I'll be back in to get you situated."

With that he strides to the door and promptly closes it behind him. The others rise to their feet. Jasmine approaches me first. She probably just wants to get this over with and get outta here.

Her eyes gleam with a kindness that's never been bestowed upon me. She places a hand on my shoulder. "Quinn, I'm really glad you're going to get your sister back. Family should be together, and I'm glad this new world didn't keep you apart." I flash a watery smile her way. She said so much with those few words.

"Jasmine, thanks for sharing your family with me for a little while," my voice starts to crack at the last few words. I look around at each of them. "I really couldn't have done this without you all. I'll be forever grateful."

She flashes me a perfect smile and slowly turns away, heading to the door. Chris is practically bouncing on his heels. He's clearly going to burst if he doesn't speak next. "Quinn, tell Jim that he's an idiot. And if he wants to know who deflated his dirt bike tires a couple of times, well, it was me!" Proud of himself, Chris leans toward me and lets me wrap him in a hug. I start to chuckle, but it's one of those dangerous laughs that could morph into crying with no warning.

As my emotions crest again, I attempt to sabotage them. *Don't cry. Don't cry. This was the plan from the start. You and Riley go home, and they go their way. It's supposed to be just the two of us.*

Chris skips toward the door, calling for Jasmine. As he yanks it open and crosses the threshold, Jeff steps toward me. "Well, Quinn, I'm gonna miss seeing you in those running clothes." A burst of laughter escapes me. His smile quickly turns serious. "I'm really glad we met, and I knew we'd find Riley. You helped us just as much as we helped you get here. I wish you both all the best this world has to offer. Now go find your sister!" He pulls me in for a solid hug.

By the time I pull away, I feel a trickle sliding down my cheek. Jeff turns abruptly and walks away.

Suddenly, it's just me and Aidan. He raises his eyes to meet mine, and I swear I see a slight wave wash over them. He holds my gaze and says, "Until next time. If there is one." His weak smile does nothing to hide his sadness. I stand on my tip toes and lean closer to those gentle blue eyes and firmly say, "Until next time, Aidan. I *will* see you again." Relief briefly flashes over his face before he starts to slowly turn away from me. I step forward and place my hand on his shoulder to stop him. Before he can completely turn toward me, I crash into him, stretching my arms around his broad shoulders. I pull him close and whisper, "Thank you. For everything. This is goodbye for now, but we're not done yet. I'll find you as soon as I get Riley."

He turns toward the desk, scanning across its disheveled surface. Stepping around me, he grabs a pen and a notepad. With determination he says, "Quinn, I'm writing down Jasmine's last name. If you and Riley decide to catch up with us, go to Jasmine's house. I'm sure the sergeant can give you her address. Then we can head north together."

I nod quickly, thrilled that he thought of this.

"I'm also writing down my last name and my home address. If you end up staying here for a little while, you can still find me when you get back home. If you want to, that is."

The smile blazing across my face must say it all. When I snatch the paper from his hand, his eyes meet mine and flash to my lips. I forget to breathe as I anticipate what's coming next. I let my eyelids flutter closed as his lips sweep toward mine. He pauses there for just a moment and plants a gentle kiss.

Much too soon, the warmth of his soft lips dissolves. My eyes flit open and land on Aidan's back as he retreats to the door. *No! My mind screams what my mouth can't verbalize. Tears threaten to spill as he disappears through the door and out of my life.*

I hadn't really thought too far beyond what would happen when we got here. I knew I had to find Riley, but I didn't think that meant I had to give up everyone else. I swipe the tear trails off my cheeks and turn on my heel. I need to find Riley and get the hell out of here.

Maybe, if luck feels obligated to make up for some of the crappy recent developments in my life, we can actually catch up with the guys at Jasmine's house. We can say our goodbyes to her and then head north together.

It's all riding on one person, and I'm counting on him to find my sister, so we can get out of here.

Chapter 70

Sergeant Bowen clears his throat as he opens the door. He's probably trying to ensure he doesn't startle an emotionally unstable teenage girl. I desperately try to pull myself together in the mere seconds it takes him to walk around the desk. He sits and faces me, again motioning for me to sit.

"Now, young lady, what is your full name and what is your sister's name?" he asks.

I take a steadying breath. "Quinn Whelan. My sister is Riley." He jots down my words on the same notebook Aidan used to write my note. As that thought crosses my mind, an urgency surges through me. The faster I can get Riley, the sooner we can catch up with the group.

"And when do you believe your sister arrived here?" he asks as if we've got all the time in the world.

Before I can stop myself, I rise from the uncomfortable chair. "Sir, uh, Sergeant, I don't mean to be rude, but do you think we can hurry this along? If I can just get my sister and go, I'd love to catch up with our friends that just left."

He raises an eyebrow and motions with his pointer finger for me to take a seat. *So much for making my case.* After what feels like hours, but is probably only about twenty minutes, he finishes asking me more questions than an attorney doing a cross-examination. After I answer all of his questions, he turns to the computer and starts typing away.

Why the hell did he use pen and paper if he was going to type it all in a computer anyway? I sigh in frustration. When he glances over, my confusion must show because his fingers cease moving and hover just above the keyboard. "Call me old fashioned but this won't ever run out of electricity," he says as he taps the paper.

When he turns his attention back to the computer, its white screen reflects on his glasses. I can't decipher any images or words, so I study him. His brown hair is close-cropped but not buzzed. His chin is clean-shaven, but he sports a tidy mustache. *I didn't think military guys were allowed to have facial hair. Who knows?*

I glance around the messy desk, barely containing my impatience, as Sergeant Bowen continues entering information into the computer. Besides the random piles of papers and sticky notes, a single frame sits next to the monitor. A blonde woman smiles at the camera, her arm wrapped around a chubby black dog with a white muzzle. Just as I'm about to question how much longer this will take, he turns to me expectantly.

"Alright, we have three Rileys on the base right now. I'm guessing your sister is twenty-year-old Riley Masters."

Goddammit. I'm going to wring his weasely neck. "My sister is Riley Whelan, but the slimeball who took her is Jim Masters. He must have said that was her last name when they came here. And she's not even eighteen yet."

At the realization that we're both minors, he asks about our parents. My vision blurs as I once again fight to suppress brimming tears. *Everything would be so much better if they were here.* I choke out the only words I can form. "They're gone." I know he understands my meaning because he abandons that line of questioning and focuses on something else I said.

"So, you're saying she was brought here against her will?" he asks, eyebrows raised again. I wonder if they will be thin brown lines by the time he goes to sleep tonight. They're getting quite the workout today.

"That's exactly what I'm saying." I cross my arms. I know it won't help my case, so I fight the urge to stomp my foot and sulk until he believes me.

"Well, let's see what she has to say," he states simply. I knew Jim took her, but to say that she has his last name? I'm seething as he picks up a walkie-talkie and powers it on. He depresses a button and instructs the person on the other end to bring Riley to the Family Readiness Center. He starts to gather paperwork from his desk when the walkie-talkie emits a clipped beep.

Releasing a sigh, he answers the call with a simple "Go ahead." This time the voice on the other end demands the sergeant's attention.

"Bowen, clear your schedule for a meeting at sixteen hundred hours. Location to follow," the voice says. After a quick, "Yes, sir" response, the voice continues, sternly asking, "You alone?"

With no hesitation, the sergeant replies, "Yes, sir." He turns his back to me, but that does nothing to shield the words coming through the receiver.

"Seems we may have a situation out west. The Yellowstone Volcano Observatory reported increased activity that could lead to an eruption. That would directly impact aid currently diverted to this side of the country. We'll discuss this further at the meeting."

Glancing my way, silently willing me to keep my mouth shut, Bowen responds, "Understood, sir." He sets the walkie-talkie down and looks to me. "That conversation does not leave this room. Do you understand?"

"Yes," I reply confidently. "I really don't care what's happening out there. I just want my sister back, so we can go home." Pleased with my answer, he gives me a sharp nod.

As he rises from his seat, I mimic the action. "Ms. Whelan, I'd like you to affix a bandage to your upper left arm," he says, completely confusing me. "When you leave this office, you will act as if I entered your name and last known residence in this computer." He jabs a thumb at the monitor before continuing. "If questioned, you will confirm that I vaccinated you."

My awkward nod returns, and I pray he doesn't mistake it for a seizure.

Gathering his papers and walkie-talkie, he leads the way to the door. Just as he opens it, the clipped beep sounds again. With a bigger sigh than the last, he answers, "Go ahead."

"Sir, the lady you asked me to retrieve, her husband is demanding that he accompany her," the solider says uncertainly. Since arriving here, my moods have ranged from sadness to rage to diluted hope. The pendulum quickly swings back to rage.

"No," Bowen says confidently. "Just her. If he can't follow our orders, then I will personally explain what is expected of guests on this base." *I like the way this guy thinks.* With that, the conversation is clearly over.

"Thank you," I say quietly as he leads me out the door.

"I'm going to get to the bottom of this," he says tiredly.

"Well, I appreciate your help. I know this is probably the last thing you have time for," I say.

With that, he stops walking and turns to me. "If someone is being held here against her will, we're going to remedy that."

While I have his full attention, I take a chance. "Sergeant, can I ask you something," the words spill from my mouth quickly.

He gives me a tired nod. "Why didn't you vaccinate me?" Caught off guard, his eyes widen with surprise. Glancing around, he pauses momentarily and then leans toward me. "I am helping you because it's the right thing to do." He releases a deep exhale. "And, if you're going on the outside soon, I may need your assistance with something," he says quietly.

My questioning eyes meet his gaze, but he responds with a subtle shake of his head.

I'm not going to get any more information about this right now.

Sergeant Bowen slows as we reach a nondescript gray building. The stark white sign bears the words Family Readiness Center. Each step feels like I'm trudging through waist-high mud. Now that I'm this close to what I've fought so hard for, time moves in slow motion.

My eyes wander as we enter the building. *Does paint come in any other color than gray around here?* We continue to the door at the end of a stark hallway. Bowen pulls it open and gestures me inside. "Just have a seat in here. We'll bring your sister to you in a bit."

I pace the room. I'm not sure if time stands still or spins out of control. My jumbled nerves tingle. Finally, the door slowly swings open. Sergeant Bowen escorts Riley into the room. Other than an angry red scar on her right cheek, she's exactly as I remember. *It's really her.*

Riley's brown eyes swell with tears. Other than her hitched breathing, silence pervades the room. A single fat tear tumbles down her cheek before she springs forward, crashing into me. *My God. My sister. She's here. Home isn't 300 miles away in a boxy brick structure. Not anymore. Home is my sister.*

AUTHOR NOTE

Dear Reader,

First, **THANK YOU**. Thank you for sticking with an unknown author's cast of characters through their debut journey. The gang will be back again in book two of the series – *Chaos Ensues*. While there is not yet a release date, I will share updates on my website and a soon-to-be developed e-newsletter. Visit www.authoraefaulkner.com to learn more.

In the meantime, before *Darkness Falls* was even back from final edits, I began writing *Anguish Unfolds*, a novella featuring Riley. *Anguish Unfolds* begins at the campground where we last see Riley in *Darkness Falls* and it concludes when she reunites with Quinn at the end of book one. Watch for that if you'd like to find out what she's been up to before *Chaos Ensues* releases.

Again, thank you for giving an indie author a try. If you enjoyed the story, please leave a review on Amazon and/or Goodreads.

Creating a book takes an enormous amount of time, energy and effort. But I was not alone in this endeavor and I cannot express enough appreciation for the following people who inspired and supported me through this process. Warning: more THANK YOUs ahead.

ACKNOWLEDGEMENTS

Michelle Preast of Indie Book Cover Designs, your talent amazes me. Somehow you took my nonsensical gibberish and turned it into the exact logo and cover I had no idea I wanted! My characters look forward to future designs you create to package their story!

Beth Suit, my partner in crime and editing! I cannot believe how lucky I am to have you in my corner. You are a master at what you do and your feedback and insight helped me more than I can ever express. Many, many thanks for your kindness when sharing input!! Your mastery of the English language and the makings of a good book are invaluable. And, you connected me with Michelle, the most amazing cover designer!

Michelle Warren, thank you for the author-to-aspiring author feedback. Your suggestions early in the process helped to shape the story in ways that made much more sense and upped the tension! You really impressed upon me the value of a "cliffhanger-ish" chapter end!

Emily Angeline, Robin Asick, and **Beth Suit**, thank you for serving as beta readers. Your feedback made this story approximately 400% better than it was before you took the time to scrutinize it. While some edits were painful, all were necessary, and your input was invaluable. *By the way, have I mentioned that I'm working on a novella??? I'll be in touch.* ☺

Vanessa Anderson at Night Owl Freelance, thank you is not even close to enough. You provided me with just the right

CONT.

amount of encouragement and tough love at just the right times. You have been an amazing coach and guide throughout this process, and your wicked sense of humor made every step in the process better. I'm so glad fate brought us together. I would have given up before I even truly started if it wasn't for Wild Bill!

Friends & family members, thank you for your support through this process! **Carol, Cindy, Diane, Robin, Bob, Christie & Katie**, thank you for your encouragement every step of the way. Several times I envisioned your faces all scrunched up asking, "Why? Why would that happen?" as I was writing. It really helped – or at least I'd like to think it shows in the final product! **Alyssa,** thank you for inspiring my main character, Quinn. She proudly displays your strength and persistence. Here's hoping you never have to face anything like what happens in the story.

Aidan, Jeff, Dylan, Eric, Cindy, Robin, Emily, Rose, & Stacy, thank you for lending me names and personality traits. I hope you enjoy reading about your fictionalized selves and situations! **Diane**, even though she doesn't wear your name, your kindness inspired parts of Riley's personality.

And, last but not least – **Scott, Landon, & Aidan**, thank you for sharing your vast scientific knowledge and storyline feedback with me! Bouncing ideas off of you helped keep details a little more true to fact – even though this is fiction! I appreciate your input along the way! Thanks for joining me (and putting up with me!) on this time-consuming journey. ♥

ABOUT THE AUTHOR

A. E. Faulkner was born and raised in Pennsylvania. When she's not lost in a book, she loves spending time with her husband and two sons, especially while hiking, biking, or exploring nature. She loves *almost* everything about nature—ticks excluded, and one of her biggest fears is the repercussions we will face when nature can no longer tolerate human destruction. As such, she never tires of reading dystopian-themed tales. Stories about the end of the world absolutely fascinate her.

FOLLOW HER WORK

To learn more visit:
AuthorAEFaulkner.com

She can also be found:

Tweeting @AuthAEFaulkner

& on Facebook @authaefaulkner

To leave a Goodreads review, please visit
Goodreads.com and search for
Darkness Falls by A. E. Faulkner.

CPSIA information can be obtained
at www.ICGtesting.com
Printed in the USA
LVHW041326221219
641390LV00001B/63

DEATH BEHIND SILENT WALLS

BLYTHE BAKER

～

After her husband dies under suspicious circumstances, Victoria Sedgewick is drawn down a dark and spiraling path of family secrets. There, she uncovers a deception so deep it threatens to destroy everything she holds dear.

Will the private inquiry agent investigating her husband's murder complicate matters? Or might Mr. Branwell Keats prove to be an ally, as a growing shadow of danger looms over Victoria's household?

～

1

—————

The early hours of the morning were some of the loneliest. Even in a city as vast as London, one could feel entirely isolated in those long, dark moments after midnight. The glowing gas lamps along the streets flickered as I stood before my open window, and the sounds of a few distant voices and horse drawn carriages clacking against the cobbles drifted up to me on the wind.

The very tops of the trees in Hyde Park could be seen in the distance, between the other townhomes just across the street, their shapes nothing more than shadowy silhouettes in the darkness. Far away, the booming chimes of the clock tower at Westminster could just be heard echoing throughout the city.

*Already so late...*I thought. *How long have I been standing here?*

The bundle in my arms squirmed.

"Shh, now, Daniel, it's all right," I murmured in a low

voice, my eyelids heavy. "It's late now. You should close those eyes and go back to sleep."

I had stopped making any sort of sense almost an hour before. The baby having woken hungry, his nanny had crept into my room to wake me. She knew it was my wish to feed and care for my own infant as much as possible, peculiar though most would find such a habit in a lady of my station.

I had left the comfort of my warm bed in order to feed and rock little Daniel, all the while struggling to keep my eyes open. For some reason, however, the child remained wide awake and nearly inconsolable.

I had little idea what more I could do for him. I'd never had a child before, and seeing as he was only four months old, we were still learning how to get along with one another. There was still much about him that I did not know.

There was one thing I hadn't tried yet. I pulled open the windows in my bedroom and stood in front of them with Daniel laid against my chest, rocking myself back and forth. As the breeze swept inside, I hoped the change in temperature might relax him.

I hummed bits and pieces from different songs I would have no trouble recalling in the middle of the day, but the words would not come to me in the moment. I couldn't even be certain the infant heard anything I hummed, with his wailing and carrying on. It seemed the night breeze had not soothed him.

I found myself sinking down into the rocking chair, holding my baby tightly against me.

It wasn't long before I noticed my head falling backward against the chair, only to be jerked awake once again by further stirring and crying.

"I wish you could tell me what is wrong, Daniel," I said. "Are you still hungry – "

My question was interrupted when the door to the bedroom suddenly burst open.

I gasped, startled, and swiveled around to squint against the bright light from the hall that washed into the room like a flood.

"There's my two favorites," said a slurred voice, belonging to a shadowed silhouette standing in the doorway.

Annoyance flooded me, and I stood from the chair. "There you are," I said in a sharp tone. "Where have you been? It's nearly one in the morning."

"Sorry, my love," the silhouette said, stumbling into the room. "I didn't realize it was...s' late."

The light from the hall fell upon his face as he turned to look at me where I stood beside the rocker.

He was not very tall, with a mop of dark hair on his head that was in desperate need of a trim. His front teeth were crooked, but he rarely smiled anymore, so I wasn't sure anyone apart from me had noticed. His eyes, typically a lovely shade of steely blue, were red-rimmed and bloodshot, and it was clear he was having difficulty focusing on me.

"You've been down near the docks again, haven't you?" I chided.

"Oh, come now, Victoria...don't treat me that way..." he said, reaching out to grab onto the fireplace mantle beside me in order to prevent himself from falling over.

"Duncan, what have I told you about visiting those gambling halls and opium dens?" I snapped. "You promised that you – "

The baby whimpered in my arms, which drew Duncan's unfocused gaze.

"There now, my boy, it's all right," he said, reaching for the young child.

I took a step backward, moving my body to block Daniel from his view. "No," I said. "Not in your sorry state."

"He's only distressed because you're angry," Duncan said, gesturing clumsily toward the baby. "Here, let me hold him. Then you can get back to sleep – "

"I said no," I repeated. "Now please, go clean yourself up and get to bed."

"But I haven't seen you or Daniel all day…" Duncan said, taking a step toward me. His foot caught on the leg of the rocker, and he stumbled forward, falling on top of the cushioned ottoman at the foot of the chair.

"Duncan, this is ridiculous," I said, bouncing a now wailing infant in my arms, finding my patience wearing thin. "Go and take a cold bath. I shall ring for Warrington to come up and prepare one for you."

"I don't need a bath," Duncan said with a chuckle. "I just need to spend some time with my lovely wife and son."

"You can spend time with us tomorrow after you've slept off your indulgences for the night," I said. "How can you possibly think I would let you anywhere near Daniel when you cannot even look me straight in the eye?"

Duncan's face fell as he stared up at me. "You're

right..." he said, though his jovial temperament remained. "That might not be very good." He threw back his head and a bark of laughter escaped his mouth, echoing around the otherwise silent room. "Why don't you at least let me...let me help you," he continued, his words slurring together. "I could fetch his favorite blanket for you."

I had not thought of that. Perhaps it would soothe Daniel.

"Very well," I agreed. "But then it's straight off to bed with you."

Duncan grinned at me. "I promise I'll be better, Victoria. I promise."

My cheeks flushed pink. "You always say that...and look where we are tonight."

Duncan didn't seem to hear, for he was already making his way toward the door, his body swaying as if he were aboard the deck of a ship in a storm. He caught himself from stumbling by grabbing the door frame with a resounding *bang*.

"Don't you worry, Daniel...I'll be right back," he said, and he disappeared into the hall.

Exhaustion washed over me as I sank back down into the rocking chair and began to rock the baby once again.

It was not more than a moment later that I heard a gentle knock on the doorframe.

I looked up to see the face of our butler, Warrington, peering in at me.

I was surprised to see him outside my room at this hour and still dressed for the day in his typical dark suit. He was much taller than Duncan, though easily twice his age. His grey hair, well kempt, was trimmed close to his head, a sign of his time in the military as a young man.

"My apologies, madam. It was not my intention to disturb you," he said, his hands falling behind his back as they always did.

"It's quite all right, Warrington," I said. "You are not a disturbance."

"I heard, er, raised voices and wished to be sure all was well," he said.

The discreet phrasing was typical of the man. I was certain he knew as well as anyone what the source of the raised voices had been, but he would not say so directly. Evidently, my exchange with my husband had been louder than I realized.

"Everything is fine," I said. "No one has been injured."

"I also heard the baby crying," the butler continued. "Might I offer any assistance?"

"That is kind of you, but I don't know what there is to be done. Perhaps he is feeling unwell. It's so hard to tell, as young as he is. He cannot communicate well enough with me yet," I said.

"It is not unusual for young ones to sense any unease in the house," Warrington said, stepping into the room. He stooped to pick up a handkerchief I hadn't noticed just inside the doorway. It was Duncan's.

"The master has arrived home," Warrington observed unnecessarily, folding the handkerchief and setting it on the vanity beside the door.

"Yes, he's already made an appearance in here, as you heard," I said, unable to keep the hint of bitterness from my voice.

I wished my husband would listen to me when I asked him to cease spending nearly every night out late. Time and again he had promised he would give up his unfortunate habits, a promise that he never kept. Already, he had managed to squander away the inheritance my parents had given me and had even begun asking his brother for money, which the foolish man willingly gave. It was impossible to guess whether Hudson knew what his money was being spent upon. Duncan might well have fed him lies about investing the money in the new business he wished to involve himself in.

As if Duncan knows anything about steam trains or railways! It is just another daydream of his!

I stifled my anger and sighed. Perhaps Duncan was not entirely to blame. Perhaps it was my fault for failing to give him whatever support he needed. There was no sense in pretending our marriage had been formed for any reason beyond mutual convenience to both our families. Even the birth of our son had done nothing to create any great affection between us. Indeed, recently I felt that I almost loathed Duncan.

"He is worse than usual tonight," I found myself admitting to Warrington. "His speech is slurred and he is unable to focus."

Warrington nodded. It had become impossible for the servants not to know what went on in the house, of late. "Perhaps you would like me to send for the doctor in the morning?" he asked. "I believe he has been working with the master to help him cease the habit."

The habit, which we both knew he was reluctant to name, was opium.

"Yes," I said. "At least, that is what we agreed upon. Perhaps a visit from the doctor would be wise, though I am not sure how much he can do. Doctor Higgins did say that the desire for the drug would be overpowering, that it would be much worse before it was better – "

A terrible shriek cut through our conversation, the noise echoing down the corridor.

Ice swam in my veins as I stared up at Warrington.

What in the world was that?

We didn't wait to speak of it. Both he and I were rushing out the door before the last of the scream had faded away.

We weren't the only ones, either. Servants who had been delivering freshly laundered clothing or linens had stepped out into the corridor, staring down toward the last door at the end.

The nursery.

My heart sank until I remembered that Daniel was still cradled safely in my arms, though the scream seemed to have startled him enough to stop his crying.

"What has happened?" one of the maids asked, her hands partially covering her face.

"We heard a scream," said another. "Who was it?"

No one knew, but the blood surging through my veins kept propelling me forward.

Warrington made it to the nursery first, ducking inside.

He stopped short inside the doorway.

I stopped just behind him.

Over his shoulder, I saw the nanny, Eliza, standing huddled near the window. She was clutching the very blanket that Duncan had come to find, a simple linen that had been embroidered with tiny likenesses of birds and foxes.

Eliza's eyes were not on Warrington, or me, for that matter. They were fixed on something stretched out across the floor in front of the cradle.

I swallowed hard, but found my mouth was as dry as the blanket the nanny held so tight in her grasp.

Duncan lay there on the floor, sprawled out at an odd angle...his eyes wide open, and his body eerily still.

2
***

I paced the drawing room floor, back and forth in front of the bassinet. At least Daniel had finally fallen into a restless sleep, over the past hour.

I, however, was wide awake, and was quite certain that I would not be sleeping for some days to come.

"Can I get you anything while you wait, madam?" Warrington asked from near the door. "Perhaps some tea? Or a glass of water?"

"No," I said, rather curtly. "Thank you," I added as an afterthought.

I had changed into a maroon dress my mother had once given me for receiving guests in. Never had she guessed that I might, at one time in my life, have to expect the company of others at nearly half past two in the morning.

"Here, madam, allow me to arrange that hair of yours that does not wish to stay tidy." It was my housekeeper, Mrs. Bell, who had been with me so long she sometimes forgot I was no longer a child in need of minding.

She was a kind woman, if perhaps a bit gruff when things in the house did not go precisely her way. Sturdily built, she had wide hips and a broader set of shoulders. She was taller than I, with golden blonde hair the opposite color of my own dark tresses.

"Very well," I said, knowing she would force me into the chair whether I wished it or not.

I took a seat in the low armchair at the desk, and Mrs. Bell was there at once, already undoing the pins I'd so hastily clasped into my hair.

"Where could the doctor be?" murmured Eliza, who sat near the bassinet, where she kept peering inside to check on Daniel. She was a delicate young woman with wide eyes that always made her appear startled, and dark hair tied up in a knotted plait beneath a bonnet.

"I am certain he will be here soon," Warrington said, peeling back the curtain and glancing outside at the front steps. "The poor man was likely fast asleep when our messenger arrived."

Mrs. Bell, busy with taking down all of my hair only to put it back up the same way I'd had it before, sighed.

I knew what she was thinking without her saying anything. And it was the same thought on my mind. On all of our minds. How could this have happened to the master of the house? How could a young, healthy man have collapsed so suddenly without any warning?

After we had found Duncan in the nursery, no one was quite certain what to do. I had been so distressed I could not think clearly.

Fortunately, my loyal servants had sprung into action. Warrington had checked Duncan's breathing and felt for

a pulse. On finding none, he declared that my husband
was deceased and suggested sending for the doctor to
confirm it.

Not wishing to leave Duncan's lifeless body alone, I
had instructed several servants to wait in the room with
him, though I could not bear to remain there myself and
had moved to the drawing room.

I felt the butler's eyes on me even now, watching to
see how I was dealing with the shock. The realization
that Mrs. Bell and the nanny were watching for the same
reason kept me from dissolving into tears on the spot. I
felt that I had to display strength at such a time, though I
felt numb inside.

Daniel squirmed in his bassinet, and Eliza was on her
feet, ready to tend to him.

He was simply stirring in his sleep, however, which
was of great relief to me. I did not think my nerves could
handle a baby's cries at the moment.

"The good doctor is here," said Warrington, peering
through the window once again. He promptly stepped
from the room in order to answer the door.

I smoothed my skirts, preparing to receive the visitor.

Mrs. Bell and Eliza made as if to leave the room, but I
gestured for them to remain. The last thing I wanted right
now was to be alone.

The door to the drawing room opened and an
anxious looking man hurried inside.

Doctor Higgins, a balding man who looked to be in
his late forties, nearly dropped the medical bag he held,
as he attempted to dislodge the pocket of his frock coat
that had caught on the door handle as he came inside.

"My apologies, Mrs. Sedgewick..." Doctor Higgins said to me, straightening, and pushing his spectacles up the bridge of his long nose. "I came as quickly as I could."

"I appreciate your promptness, Doctor," I said, regarding him from my armchair. "I trust my messenger explained the situation to you?"

"Yes, and so has your manservant," he said, glancing over his shoulder as Warrington reappeared in the doorway behind him. "Most dreadful news."

"Indeed," I said woodenly, my thoughts too clouded to think of any further response.

"Where might I find the deceased?" he asked.

"This way, sir," Warrington said, gesturing down the hall toward the staircase leading upstairs.

"Right," Doctor Higgins said. "I shall go to him."

As I watched the last of his frock coat disappear from view, I licked my lips and did my best to retain my posture. It would do me no good to lose my composure now. I mustn't be overwhelmed by the situation or thoughts of what the future might hold next. Perhaps it was best to focus on the moment and try to understand exactly what had occurred.

"Eliza, what exactly happened when you entered the nursery, earlier?" I asked. "Or were you already there when my husband arrived?"

The girl, who was absentmindedly rocking the bassinet in order to keep little Daniel asleep, jumped ever so slightly when I addressed her. "Oh, I was already in the room when he walked in," she said, knotting her hands in her skirt. "I was laying out some clothes for the baby for the morning, and wondered if he might need something a bit cooler for tonight, as it was so warm in his room..." She looked down at her hands, her brow furrowing in worry. "As I was sorting through some of the baby's things, Mr. Sedgewick came into the room and seemed awfully...well, how do I put it?"

"Strange?" I asked.

"Quite odd, yes..." she said. "I was surprised to see him up so late. And he seemed almost as if he was walking in his sleep. He came into the room and nearly fell over the rug. He ordered me to give him the baby blanket, saying he needed it right that moment. I tried to do as he asked, but as I turned to look through the chest of drawers, he began to laugh rather strangely."

He did the same when he was in the room with me.

"And then," she went on, her eyes widening, flinching away as if she had seen something horrific. "There was a gargling noise, and the sound of something heavy falling to the ground. I turned and found him lying on the floor, and that is when I..."

"When you screamed, yes," I said. "Well, that was a frightening thing, of course. I am sorry you had to witness that."

Eliza nodded, and sank back into her chair, seemingly exhausted from retelling her story.

The door to the drawing room opened once again, and three servants stepped inside. Mary, a quiet house-maid; Adam, a young footman; and finally, Mr. Tulson, a man who seemed to have a knack for every sort of task around the house, and was invaluable in his own right.

"Madam," Mr. Tulson said, bowing to me, the other

two following suit. "The doctor asked us to vacate the room while he examines the master."

"Yes, of course," I heard myself murmur, my throat tight. "Thank you for sitting with him as long as you did."

"Certainly," said Adam, his large blue eyes fixed upon me. "We wished to do whatever we could."

"If I may say so, madam," Mr. Tulson said, smoothing his graying moustache. "The master returned home this evening at a peculiar time, much later than he typically does. Not only that, but he chose to enter the house at the back door down in the kitchen."

"Did he?" I asked vaguely, my gaze drifting to the drawing room window. It would be dawn soon, a new day that Duncan would never see.

"Perhaps he did not wish to disturb anyone," I heard Adam suggest quietly.

"Yes, that could be the reason," said Mr. Tulson.

"I did not see him pass through the garden, while I was out in the stables," Adam said. "I only knew something was amiss when I heard Eliza's scream through the nursery's open window."

"The stables?" I asked, before recalling that Adam's father had once had the charge of our horses back in my father's day. The young man might be a footman now, but he was still occasionally called upon to make use of his childhood expertise.

"Yes, madam. The mare had knocked over a basket of oats, utterly destroying it, and I'd spent the hour before that tending to the broken strap of a saddle. The master must have been quiet or I should have heard him arrive home during that time."

I would not say as much before the servants but the truth was the entire household had become all too familiar with my husband's odd habits and tendencies, as well as his way of creeping into the house at late hours. At first, I had thought nothing of his opium use, as Duncan insisted that he took it for nothing more than soothing his old knee injury. But then as time passed by and his dependency progressed, perhaps I did not wish to admit to myself what was clearly the truth, that he had taken a fancy to the stuff and to spending time with those who supplied it.

Mrs. Bell must have been following the line of my thoughts, for she huffed behind me. "It was that disgusting habit that ended his life. I have no doubt of it," she said. "Beg your pardon, madam, but he should never have put you through such worry all these years. As for associating with those men down at the docks the way he did...he had no business being there with such folk."

"That is enough, Mrs. Bell," I said wearily. "My husband may have had his failings but he is still—*was* still, the master of this house. I would appreciate it if you would remember that."

There was an uncomfortable silence before Mrs. Bell answered, "Yes, of course, madam. Forgive me."

I waved a dismissive hand. "We are all tired and not at our best, in this moment."

I turned to the others. "I suppose I must admit Mr. Sedgewick was not himself when I last saw him. His cheerfulness seemed almost forced, as if he was nervous or not entirely right in his own mind. He couldn't keep focused on me, and he was stumbling all over the room."

"It makes one wonder – " Mrs. Bell began, but her words were cut off when the door to the drawing room swung open once again.

Doctor Higgins returned, with Warrington trailing along behind him.

The doctor looked around at all of the staff surrounding me, as he pushed his spectacles higher up the bridge of his nose.

"You may say whatever you wish before my servants, Doctor," I said. "We are rather informal, like a large family here."

"I see..." he said, obviously finding the idea slightly eccentric but unwilling to remark on it.

"Please tell me about my husband," I prompted.

"Mrs. Sedgewick..." he said, his voice heavy. "It is as we feared. I regret I must confirm that your husband is indeed dead."

Although his declaration was not a surprise, it still felt strange to hear the words spoken out loud.

"He was alive such a short time ago..." I said.

"Yes," Doctor Higgins said. "It certainly happened suddenly. You have my deepest condolences."

"How?" I asked, the question suddenly rising up in my mind to blot out every other feeling.

"I am sorry?" the doctor asked.

"How did he die?" I asked. "I do not understand."

Doctor Higgins clenched his hands nervously, staring about the room, as if to avoid my gaze. "I...well, without further investigation, I cannot be perfectly certain, but given the evidence I have, as well as his condition when I examined him – "

"Doctor, please," I said firmly. "What caused my husband to die?"

He sighed, removing his spectacles. He procured a cloth from the inside of his coat and began to clean the lenses. "I suspect that his heart stopped," he said. "As there were no outward injuries. I should like to ask, however, what he was doing when he died?"

"He was retrieving a blanket for our son," I said. "He had just left my room to fetch it from the nursery."

"And was he behaving in a typical fashion?" Doctor Higgins asked.

"Heavens, no..." I said. "His speech was slurred and he was unable to keep his balance, seemingly drunk, though I could smell no alcohol on him. He arrived home quite late, as well. I suspect he came straight from some sort of opium den."

Doctor Higgins' face was grave. "I warned him that if he continued to overindulge, there could be fatal consequences."

"You are suggesting it was the drug which killed him?" I asked.

The doctor appeared surprised that I could speak of the matter so easily, but the truth was that I was not entirely shocked by what had occurred. I had warned Duncan time and again that this might happen. In a way, I had been prepared for tragedy and had time to numb myself to it.

It didn't matter how many times he had promised he would change, or how often he told me that he wanted to stop for Daniel's sake. None of that mattered, not when he was dead now.

"Is that your professional opinion then, Doctor?" I asked, smoothing the wrinkles from my dress once more.

"I – " Doctor Higgins said. "Well, as I said, I cannot be certain."

"I thought you were supposed to be helping my husband," I said, my eyes narrowing slightly as I regarded the medical man. "All these treatments you've been giving him over the past few months...it seems that none of them helped, did they?"

On seeing several members of my staff shift their wide-eyed gazes to the doctor, I realized perhaps I had been overly blunt. But was I not entitled to be, under such circumstances?

"I am terribly sorry, Mrs. Sedgewick," Doctor Higgins said. "You are absolutely correct. I promised you both I would help, and it seems that I was unable to do as I said." He straightened his collar, which was askew. "I feel as if I am responsible, in some way. I should have realized his condition was worsening, especially since I had seen him earlier yesterday."

I frowned. "You saw him yesterday?"

Doctor Higgins looked surprised. "Why yes. Just after two in the afternoon. I assumed he would have told you he was visiting me?"

"My husband did not always keep me informed of his business," I said slowly. "What was the cause for the sudden meeting? I thought your next appointment was a week from Thursday?"

"And it was," Doctor Higgins said nervously, staring around at all the pairs of eyes fastened upon him, each person hanging on his every word, expecting an explanation for why the master of the house had so tragically died. "He came to me a few days ago and asked if we could meet, as his spirits were terribly depressed of late and he wished to discuss his troubles."

"He did inform me that you had been trying a new technique with him, something called psychoanalysis?" I asked.

"Indeed. Fathered by a renowned Austrian neurologist, it is a treatment meant to help the patient discover truths hidden within his or her mind. I've been studying it somewhat myself, and your husband seemed to be making a great deal of progress," Doctor Higgins said. "But perhaps we began our attempts too late."

He ran his hands over his balding head.

"Mrs. Sedgewick, it may be too soon to say for certain, but I must tell you there exists a possibility that your husband deliberately took his own life, perhaps by purposely taking too much of the drug."

I took a sharp breath.

No...that cannot be, I thought. *Duncan would not end his own life. Of that much I am certain.*

I watched the doctor as he watched me, an apologetic expression on his face, as if he expected me to be offended at the suggestion.

"While I cannot agree with your suspicion, I do believe that something mysterious has happened here tonight," I said, getting to my feet. "My husband may have made foolish mistakes, but there remained hope that he could right them. I do not believe he was ready to give up on his life."

"Then what do you suspect, Mrs. Sedgewick?" Doctor Higgins asked.

A brief silence descended over the room as I felt myself arrive at a decision I had not even known I was struggling to reach.

"I am not certain..." I said. "But I intend to find out what it was that took my son's father from him."

3

I had to sleep after all that ordeal, knowing little Daniel needed me to be as rested as I could be, given the next few days would likely be busy with callers and possibly the police coming around in order to investigate the death.

On Doctor Higgins' advice, we had sent for the authorities to collect Duncan's body and see that all was done properly.

I knew his remains needed to be taken care of, as I had no intention of going into the nursery again until they were removed, but I still had other questions.

"The police?" I had wondered aloud to Warrington, after the doctor was gone. "Why would they need to investigate a man's peaceful death in his own home?"

"They will wish to eliminate the same possibilities that you have considered, madam," he said. "Perhaps there was indeed something suspicious about the master's death."

"You agree with me then?" I asked. "About something strange surrounding this whole affair?"

"I am as inclined to believe it as you are," he said kindly. "But if I may suggest, madam, perhaps it would be wise to consider all of this with fresh eyes and minds after a night's rest? I shall do my best to ensure you are not disturbed until you wish to be."

I sighed heavily as an unpleasant thought passed through my mind. "I shall have to inform my father-in-law of his son's death," I said. "But I suppose it does not have to be before I have had some rest. Tomorrow will be soon enough."

I retired to my room, but found that I could do little apart from stare at the rocking chair I'd been sitting in when Duncan had barged into the room only a few short hours ago. Even though a part of me was angry with him for allowing himself to reach the point he did, I was also saddened at his sudden loss. It would surely take time for me to absorb and come to terms with what had happened.

I couldn't deny the hard truth that I'd never truly loved the man. Our marriage had been one that my parents had encouraged many years ago, together with Duncan's family, before all the problems began. I'd found Duncan tolerable enough when we'd been introduced after my seventeenth birthday, but had never felt any great passion for him. Still, my mother had told me we would learn to love one another with time. Moreover, that securing my future in a fine house with a husband of good family was the surest path to happiness. Foolishly, I had believed her correct and agreed to the marriage.

I'd always hoped she would turn out to be right, but in all the time I'd been with him, my heart had never been moved by Duncan. Not even once.

Nonetheless...he was Daniel's father and I had meant what I said to Doctor Higgins and the others. I owed it to my infant son, and maybe even to Duncan himself, to discover the truth behind his sudden death.

I SLEPT for a few hours before Eliza came in with Daniel, who was ready to be fed once again. It seemed he could sense the unease sweeping through the house. He was even more restless than he had been the night before.

Realizing that I would not be able to sleep any further, I rose before eight that morning, and dressed for the day.

I must prepare for the possibility of visitors, even if I hoped our acquaintances would possess the sensitivity not to call with condolences so soon after the death. For that matter, Doctor Higgins had given his word that he would not tell anyone about Duncan's passing until I was ready to let it be publicly known. I could only hope he would keep the promise.

"But before making any sort of formal announcement, I believe I am going to have to inform my in-laws," I said.

"Yes, madam," Warrington said smoothly, offering me the morning post as I sat at the dining room table. The butler was accustomed to my habit of thinking aloud to him or to Mrs. Bell, as I rarely had anyone but the servants to converse with. Even when Duncan was alive, he had so seldom been at home.

I glanced at little Daniel, wrapped snuggly in his bassinet nearby. I was reluctant to let him out of my sight this morning, as if something terrible might somehow happen to him as well. Eliza, hovering in the background, kept constant watch over the sleeping child.

Adam stepped into the room, carrying covered trays of food, which he set down before me. It wasn't as if I had much of an appetite, but something about continuing my typical routine helped me to feel a bit calmer.

"I do not know how I shall go about doing it," I mused. "I feel as if a letter to my in-laws containing such sad tidings might be cold, whereas arriving in person may not be the wisest, either, given my responsibility to Daniel."

"If I may, madam, you cannot be expected to journey all the way to Yorkshire to deliver the news," Warrington said. "Surely a letter will be sufficient, perhaps hand-delivered by a servant, who will be able to answer any questions they may have."

"I would be happy to go," Adam said, stepping forward from his place along the wall. I looked over at the footman. Young though he was, he was never opposed to taking responsibility for various necessities around the home. Even eager at times. I remembered once when I was ill the previous winter, I asked him to fetch me something warm to help soothe my aching throat, and he returned with a hot kettle of water, along with all of the tea available in the house.

Warrington regarded him with a look of some relief. "Very well," he said. "It seems a good solution."

After breakfast, I sat down in the drawing room and composed a message on black-edged stationery to send to my in-laws. Then, Warrington handed the envelope to Adam and sent him on his way, the footman seeming pleased to be entrusted with such a responsibility.

"Do not worry, madam," he said before departing. "I shall take the next train to Yorkshire to deliver your message and return so swiftly my absence will hardly be noticed."

"I shall appreciate your speediness, Adam," I said.

My in-laws were not the only people I needed to inform of what had taken place. I composed a less personal message to be sent out to the newspaper. Duncan may not have been the most popular man in the city, but he held a relatively prestigious position, and there were many who knew him based purely on his marriage to me, and his father's status.

It is with deepest regret that we must announce the passing of Mr. Duncan Sedgewick. Letters of condolence may be sent to the following address...

I hoped the subtle suggestion of letters of condolence would make it clear that Mr. Sedgewick's widow wished to grieve in solitude and peace, for the time being.

A rustling sound made me look up from my stationery to watch Mrs. Bell, who was busily sorting books on my shelf. Duncan had left them disorganized after he had haphazardly looked through them some time ago in a mad search for information about some strange idea he'd had, something to do with steam trains.

With a pang, I realized that maybe he genuinely did want to change his irresponsible ways and become more useful to his family. Perhaps he had been searching for the inspiration to do just that.

It was nearly half past three when I sealed the letters to send to all the proper people in town.

"I suppose I should prepare myself for those inevitable visitors I am bound to have today..." I said.

"Surely you need not receive them, madam?" Mrs. Bell asked, shelving yet another hefty book, titled *The History of the English Railway.* She glanced past me to where Warrington hovered in the doorway, waiting to dispatch the last of my mail. "Mr. Warrington, you shall refuse all visitors today. And tomorrow, for that matter. Even that pesky Mrs. Harriet. *Especially* Mrs. Harriet." The glare she gave Warrington was not intended for him, but for the woman in question.

At a less tragic time I would have been amused by my housekeeper's protectiveness toward me and her feelings against my neighbor, Mrs. Harriet. She was right, of course. I was certain I could not tolerate Mrs. Harriet's antics, now more than ever.

"Will you send a note to Doctor Higgins as well?" Warrington asked me.

"For what?" I asked. "To ask him whether or not he realizes he was ultimately responsible for my husband's death?"

Both the butler and the housekeeper turned to look at me. Mrs. Bell's eyes were wide, and Warrington peered at me curiously.

"What do you mean, madam?" Mrs. Bell asked,

setting down the stack of books she'd collected from the floor. "Surely you do not think he somehow – "

"How can I know for certain?" I asked, shrugging my shoulders. "The man comes into my home and claims that Duncan took his own life, all the while having met with him earlier yesterday, completely unbeknownst to me."

"I did find that rather strange," Warrington said, rubbing his eyes with his thin, boney fingers.

"Doctor Higgins said his new treatment had been working," Mrs. Bell said. "He said the master had been making progress."

"Yes, but I have been aware of every session they have had," I said. "Every other Tuesday at two in the after-noon. That was our agreed upon time. And then the day Duncan died, they simply happened to have another session? How did that occur without my knowledge?"

"Perhaps Mr. Sedgewick went in to see the doctor without planning ahead," Warrington said, stepping closer, the light of the green-shaded lamp beside him reflecting off his pale face. "If he was considering taking his own life, as has been suggested, then maybe he would have wished to see the doctor without your knowledge."

I pursed my lips. "How many times must I say my husband did not take his own life?" I asked.

"If I may ask, madam, why are you so determined to believe he did not?" Mrs. Bell asked firmly, coming to stand before me. For a moment, I could almost forget she was my housekeeper and believe her to be my governess and myself a child about to be scolded. She continued, "We all know he was an unhappy man with unfortunate tendencies. He brooded around here, day after day, without any sort of motivation."

"Yes, and the only motivation he ever had was that terrible drug," I admitted. "That, and whatever it was he had convinced himself about investing in steam trains."

"Exactly my point," Mrs. Bell said, her brow furrowing. "He was never happy unless he was under the influence of opium. Perhaps he felt that was not a way he wished to continue living."

"Yes, I see your point," I conceded. "But I cannot say I believe in it."

I looked over at Warrington. "You told me yesterday you agreed with me that something strange surrounded his death. And I do not mean that he was the one who took his own life. Why would he have bothered to come in and see Daniel and me before wandering down to the nursery where he died, if he planned to kill himself anyway?"

"He never made any sense when he was under the influence of the stuff, did he?" Mrs. Bell said. "Perhaps he was not even aware of his actions at that point?"

"He was aware enough," I said. "He even...he even promised me that he would be better." For some reason, my voice caught in my throat. "Why would he make such a declaration if he knew he would be dead within the hour?"

Mrs. Bell didn't seem to have a ready answer, instead turning her head away, her eyes focused on the Turkish rug spread out along the floor beneath our feet.

"And not only that," I went on. "But he really did love Daniel...and in a way, I think he believed he was doing all he could to set himself straight for the baby, even if that progress never seemed evident to the rest of us."

No one could deny that Duncan had loved his son.

"What do you suggest as an alternative, madam?" Mrs. Bell asked. "Perhaps he unintentionally took too much of the drug."

"I suppose that is possible," I said. "But I would wonder how he had never managed to do so before. He once admitted to me that he needed to take more and more in order to feel the same sort of relief, which is rather troubling..."

"It seems to me that settles it," Mrs. Bell said. "As tragic as it was, it could have simply been no more than an accident."

"Or," Warrington interrupted, "someone could have forced him into taking too much."

Mrs. Bell turned and frowned up at him. "You ought not to encourage such thoughts."

"I am capable of forming my own notions," I reminded her firmly.

Mrs. Bell said, "Of course, madam, but you are in distress and have not slept properly, so it is quite easy to understand that you might be confused – "

"I am not confused," I said, getting to my feet, turning away from her. "Far from it. In fact, I am almost as certain about this as I have been about anything in my life."

"But to believe that the master was murdered –" Mrs. Bell began.

I whirled around, my dark skirts twirling around me. "Mrs. Bell, you must admit that this all very odd," I said. "Everything about his death is unsettling. The timing,

Duncan's attitude, his condition, the place where he died...even Doctor Higgins admitting that Duncan had gone to see him in secret yesterday."

"You keep returning to that piece of information, madam," Warrington said, his gaze curious as he watched me. "May I ask why? Do you suspect the doctor might be the one who killed him?"

"I am not certain," I said. "But why would they have met so suddenly when they weren't supposed to meet until the following week?"

"Didn't Doctor Higgins already explain that?" Mrs. Bell asked.

"What if he lied?" Warrington asked, looking between the two of us through his eyelashes, his chin dipped down near his chest.

Mrs. Bell glanced at me, blinking once, twice, considering the words.

"That is my fear," I said. "I simply find it very strange that they happened to meet on the day my husband's life ended. And it seems equally strange that Duncan did not mention it to me."

Mrs. Bell shuddered, rubbing her hands up and down the length of her arms. "What purpose would a doctor have in killing one of his own patients?" she asked.

"I have no earthly notion," I said, turning and pacing around to the desk. The stack of letters to be sent to the city officials sat waiting, holding likely many questions for those who would be receiving them. "All I know is that this entire matter is deeply disturbing..."

"Indeed it is," Mrs. Bell said, seeming to shake off the fear that had gripped her a moment before. "A death alone is unsettling enough, and now we have to consider it being a murder? By whom? Do we need to worry for your safety as well, madam? Or for the rest of the house?"

That was not something I had considered.

"Is Daniel in danger?" I wondered aloud.

Both Warrington and Mrs. Bell grew pale.

"We need to get to the bottom of this," I said. "If my son is in danger, then we need to uncover who is responsible for Duncan's death. Quickly."

A letter arrived at the house two days later.

Under my instruction, Warrington and the rest of the staff had spent that time refusing any visitors, of which there were not many. Daniel's nanny noted each and every one, peering out the windows. "Madam, do you suppose they are offended?"

"They very likely are," I said as I rocked Daniel, who had been sleeping well since the night Duncan passed. "However, I care little for what society thinks. I am a widow in mourning, after all. Can anyone truly blame me for wishing to be alone with my loss?"

Eliza allowed the drapes to fall over the window once more, returning to the pile of baby's clothing she had laid out across the bed to fold. "Oh, of course not, madam. It is absolutely terrible what happened here, and only two days ago." She lifted one of Daniel's outfits and examined it, ensuring it had been properly cleaned by the laundress. "You seem to be taking it awfully well, though, madam, if you don't mind my saying so," she said.

"Everyone downstairs is impressed by your calm composure."

I looked down into the little face of my son, and not for the first time, noticed the similarities he shared with his father. He had the same dark hair, the same soft brow and jawline. For a moment, I wondered if all of Duncan's innocence that had once convinced me he had some redeeming qualities had been passed to the baby when he was born.

In truth, our son was the best thing to come out of my marriage with Duncan.

It had taken me the full two days since his passing to realize the grief I had expected to eventually feel would never come. I had expected that after the shock of his death had worn off, I would begin to miss him. Instead, I found I had woken to a house where his bellowing didn't echo down the halls in the late morning hours. I would no longer fear how carelessly he seemed to hold Daniel. His bizarre morning conversations over breakfast about inane and unimportant matters would never happen again.

Guilt was all I felt, I realized in the deepest recesses of my heart. Guilt over *not* feeling sorrow at my own husband's death. Guilt that I would be perfectly happy to carry on alone. Guilt that I might even be able to find happiness now that he was gone.

"Yes, well, I am doing the best I can," I finally said in reply to the nanny, shifting Daniel to the crook of my other arm. "The best thing I can do for my son is ensure I remain strong."

Eliza gave me a sympathetic smile. "You're so very brave, madam."

Yet another pang of guilt struck me, like the string of a harp snapping beneath my fingers.

There was a knock on the door, which drew my eye. "Come in," I said, rising to lay the baby down in his bassinet beside my bed.

Warrington pushed open the door, peering inside. "I beg your pardon, madam, but a letter has arrived for you. I imagined you would wish to read this one as soon as it came."

Nervousness washed through me, though I tried not to show it. "Who is it from?" I asked, walking over to meet him as he stepped fully into the room.

He passed me the envelope, a look of concern on his face. "Old Mr. Sedgewick, madam."

My blood turned to ice as I stared at the envelope. "I thought they took the news of Duncan's passing rather well..." I said.

"According to Adam they did, yes," Warrington said. "He only just arrived back from Yorkshire himself a short while ago, so they must have dispatched this message immediately after he left them. Perhaps the letter will explain more."

I tore open the envelope and unfolded the paper within to find a very short, very definitive letter.

Expect us on Friday, July 23rd, before the noon hour. We should like to pay our respects to our deceased son and brother.

It was signed by both Mr. Erasmus, Duncan's father, as well as Mr. Hudson, his elder brother.

I looked up at Warrington, my brow furrowing. "They

intend to be here by Friday? That is only three days from now..."

"Just in time for the funeral, it seems," Warrington said.

"Their wish to be present is understandable, but somehow I had not expected them to come all this distance, it being such a small, private affair," I said, shaking my head. "But then, perhaps I should have realized that if my father-in-law has anything to say about it, all of London shall attend..."

"Shall I inform Mrs. Bell you would like rooms prepared for them?" Warrington asked.

I frowned, rubbing my forehead. "Yes. We must be accommodating, I suppose. They too have suffered a great loss."

I glanced sharply toward Eliza hovering across the room, as I recalled that servants were capable of a great deal of gossip. "I do not resent their presence, understand. It is only that my in-laws have a way of taking over a situation."

"Do not worry, madam," Warrington said. "I am certain they will be courteous and eager to cause no inconvenience. You, after all, are mistress of this house."

FRIDAY CAME FAR TOO QUICKLY for my liking. I spent the whole of Thursday night alternating between troubled memories of Duncan's death and dread of my difficult in-laws, so much so that I woke every hour, the lingering nightmares of cold faces and demanding voices fading as

I rose to check on Daniel. The infant was very nearly sleeping through the night now.

I dressed in a satin black gown, adorned with black lace around the wrists and along the breastbone and high collar. Even if I did not feel as grief-stricken as I should, as far as society was concerned, I was a heartbroken widow. It was unthinkable not to appear in full mourning, especially before Duncan's family.

I was downstairs, ready to receive my in-laws just before the clock struck noon. Warrington stood near the front door, hands clasped behind his back.

"Ah, madam," he said. "You are looking much better rested this morning."

"Thank you, Warrington," I said, as I went to stand beside him.

"Move along, now," came Mrs. Bell's voice from the top of the staircase.

I looked up and saw her shooing a few of the servants down the stairs, all of whom were dressed in clean, pressed clothing. Adam, Mr. Tulson, and a housemaid named Marie, hurried down the steps.

"Good morning, madam," they all said in unison, bowing or curtseying to me.

"Good morning," I said. "I trust we are all ready?"

Adam nodded. "All the preparations have been made."

A sudden noise outside drew our attention and I turned back to the door.

Warrington peered out the side window, and a low hum reverberated through him. "They are here," he said. "Their carriage has just arrived."

Under my tightly fitted corset, my heart began to beat hard against my ribs.

It was one thing to appear collected and in control before my household staff, but it would be another thing entirely to stand strong in the presence of my imposing in-laws. Would they somehow sense my regret over Duncan's death was not as intense as it should be? And what of the unusual circumstances surrounding his passing? I knew it was unreasonable, but a part of me could not help fearing they would hold me responsible for failing to somehow correct my husband's habits before they cost him his life.

I took a deep breath to steady my overactive nerves, and nodded for Warrington to pull the door open.

Warrington, in all his military precision, bowed deeply to the people ascending the steps that were out of my sight. "Good afternoon, Mr. Sedgewick, Mr. Sedgewick. Welcome to – "

"Yes, yes, you can spare us the pleasantries," came the raspy voice of my father-in-law, Mr. Erasmus Sedgewick.

He brushed past Warrington in all his haughty desire to be inside.

Duncan truly had been a spitting image of the other men in his family. The man scowling around the foyer was a thinner version of his youngest son, but had the same echoes of dark hair and a wide jawline. The hair around his ears had begun to grey and to thin around the crown of his head.

His chin, jutting outward, swiveled in my direction.

"There you are, Victoria," he said, coming toward me.

I nodded politely, doing my best to keep the appearance of graciousness written across my face. "Welcome, Mr. Sedgewick. I hope your journey was – "

"Glad to see you chose appropriate attire," my father-in-law interrupted sharply, as he regarded me from head to foot. "My son deserved nothing less than your full devotion and deepest mourning."

"Of course, sir," I said, keeping my smile fixed firmly in place. "All the proper customs have been observed. I am sure you will find nothing lacking in my *late husband's* home."

I knew he would not like to admit the home was mine but I could not resist the subtle reminder that at least it was not his own.

He grunted, the steely grey in his eyes the same shade as Daniel's. "Where's my grandson?" he asked.

"With his nurse," I said. "I could send for him if you would like – "

"No, that's quite all right," he said, not meeting my eye.

"He is doing very well, though he has been rather fussy as of late," I said.

"He misses his father, no doubt." Mr. Sedgewick declared.

"No doubt," I agreed. There was no point in explaining that my son was not yet old enough to be aware of the changes in the household, nor had he ever much enjoyed the company of his father.

"With your permission, sir?" Warrington offered, stepping forward. "Adam will escort you to your room so that you may rest before dinner."

"Very well," my father-in-law said. "My baggage is on

the carriage. And see that your man doesn't drop it. It's likely worth more than he is." He sent a scathing look toward the footman behind Warrington.

"Yes, sir," Adam said with a quick bow, and hurried outside to fetch the baggage.

Just then, Mr. Hudson Sedgewick, Duncan's elder brother, appeared in the doorway.

He was as burly in build as Duncan, though stood nearly a foot taller than my husband had. He might have even been considered more handsome than Duncan, with straighter teeth and a kind smile when he remembered to use it. I knew him well enough to be wary of him, however. When his father's business had expanded almost a decade ago, his head swelled right along with it. These days, Hudson was altogether too pleased with himself and could be rather insufferable at times.

"Ah, sister," he said, his gaze coming to rest on me. "Good to see you and all that."

"You as well, Hudson," I said. "I trust your journey was pleasant?"

"Pleasant enough, despite those buffoons we call servants," he said, glancing over his shoulder at the door. His eyes swept around to Mr. Tulson, who stood nearby. "You there, go out and fetch my things. I should like to get out of these traveling clothes as soon as I can."

"Of course, sir," Mr. Tulson said, bowing quickly before scurrying out after Adam.

"I am surprised you have yet to redecorate in here, Victoria," Hudson said, peering up at the chandelier overhead. "Between your inheritance and the money we heard Duncan was making, I thought you would have had some new portraits painted or the furniture reupholstered."

Already the criticism begins, I see...and what's that about Duncan making money? I suppose I should have suspected he would have fed them lies like that...

I did my best to keep my face smooth. "I'm afraid there have been other things on my mind recently."

"Yes, well, I suppose there would be..." he said.

Avoiding the conversation, it seems.

We were interrupted by my father-in-law suddenly speaking up. "Now that I think on it, I would much prefer a hot cup of tea to the solitude of my room. Butler, bring me something to eat in the parlor."

With that order, old Mr. Sedgewick turned and stalked down the hall toward the room in question.

"Of course, sir," Warrington said expressionlessly. "Right this way. Mrs. Bell will send in your tea."

"That old bird?" Mr. Sedgewick asked. "I'm surprised she is still living."

His words echoed after him as he continued on his path.

"I shall join you, Father," Hudson said. "Some refreshment sounds excellent after such a long journey."

I knew it would be best if I were to accompany them. Unpleasant though the task may be, as the hostess, I needed to be where my guests were and keep them content.

Reluctantly, I trailed down the hall after them.

"Coming along, Vicky?" my brother-in-law asked, glancing over his shoulder. "I thought you might pass on it."

"What sort of hostess would I be if I were to neglect my guests?" I asked, smiling stiffly.

The parlor absorbed the light of the morning sun so that the leather armchairs beside the fireplace were warm and inviting. Naturally, Mr. Sedgewick and Hudson took those seats as if they were the masters of the house.

I, myself, took an upholstered wooden chair beside the table in the center of the room, not displeased with the distance between us.

"Thank you, butler, you may excuse yourself now," Mr. Sedgewick said, waving dismissively.

"I would prefer Warrington remain," I corrected quickly. "In case I require anything."

It would do no harm to remind the man exactly whose servants these were that he was ordering around.

My father-in-law arched a brow but did not protest.

Hudson cleared his throat. "Father, I suppose we should discuss the matter at hand," he said.

Mr. Sedgewick folded his hands together in front of himself, and sighed. "I suppose we could, though I had hoped to wait until after the funeral..." He locked eyes with me, and a sober expression settled over his face. "First of all, we would like to know what happened the night that Duncan died. Your letter was vague, and I would very much like to have the story straight before the funeral tomorrow."

I stared at him, considering. It was only natural that he should wish to know the details of his son's death. I could see no reason not to reveal them to him, but I knew it would be unwise to reveal my full suspicions on the matter. Without proof, my concern about the manner of my husband's death would seem like nonsense. My in-laws would be only too glad to dismiss my worries as the overwrought fears of a foolish woman.

"Very well," I said. "Duncan came home late Sunday night. I was awake, feeding and rocking Daniel, when Duncan stumbled into the room. It was clear from the moment I saw him that he had been down to one of the opium dens he favored so much – "

"What?" Hudson interrupted, leaning forward. "What is this about opium?"

I stopped, and glanced between them. *This again?*

"Do not encourage her, Hudson," Mr. Sedgewick said. "Victoria has expressed these...imaginings once before."

Imaginings?

"Whether or not you believe it does not change the truth of my words," I said, narrowing my eyes. "Your son was an opium addict, and an avid gambler, who spent nearly everything you ever sent us – "

"Enough of that!" Mr. Sedgewick snapped sharply. "Enough. I will not hear you besmirch the name of my son. Especially so soon after his death. Why are you insistent on telling such tales? Don't we already have enough to grieve over, all of us?"

I did not have a chance to respond, before Hudson cut in. "Calm yourself, Father. I'm sure she means no offence. Perhaps her grief has driven her to hysterics. She cannot accept that her husband is gone, and so is imagining these things – "

"I assure you, I am perfectly rational," I said, raising my voice ever so slightly, trying not to let my growing anger boil over.

This is a temporary arrangement, their being here. I must keep calm in their presence. They are guests only until the funeral. It makes perfect sense they would wish to know what happened, and given our lack of knowledge of the situation, it should be easy enough to keep the story truthful and yet save myself any more of this pointless bickering.

Mr. Sedgewick tugged on the bottom of the silk vest he wore beneath his jacket. "I am surprised at you, Victoria. Allowing yourself to develop such silly suspicions about my son. Do you have any idea how difficult a life he lived? How much his mother and I sacrificed for him and his brother so they could enjoy comfortable lives when they were older?"

My face remained unchanged, even as my mind raced.

"There were times when I feared we would starve," Mr. Sedgewick said with a sweeping, dramatic gesture. "My income allowed for only the most basic necessities, in those days. It wasn't until I stumbled upon what was perhaps my greatest business idea that I began to see the light at the end of the tunnel."

Not only had I heard this story nearly every time I saw my father-in-law, but I also was well aware of how untrue it all was. *If it were not for the kindness and generosity of* my *father, Mr. Sedgewick, you would have remained in your troubled circumstances.*

"You did the best you could for us, Father," Hudson said with a firm nod.

"Indeed I did," Mr. Sedgewick said. Then he turned back to me. "Not that I expect you to understand, Victoria. What with your family's estate houses and grand dinner parties..."

I adjusted my skirts, not allowing his jab to settle into my heart. The truth was he was right, in a way. I could not understand the sort of difficult past he described, nor did I wish to. Not theirs, anyway.

It is quite possible that after the funeral, I will not have to see much of them again. What would tie them to me after all this? They have little interest in Daniel, what with Hudson already having a child of his own. As the eldest son of an eldest son, that child will surely be the one to inherit the Sedgewick family fortune...what little of that there may be in the future.

I was eager for the next few days to be over with, and even more eager to excuse myself from this conversation.

"Mr. Sedgewick, if we are quite done quarreling about the differences in our pasts, then could we please discuss what it was that you wished to speak of?" I asked. "I assume it is about the funeral arrangements?"

My father-in-law's brow furrowed. "No, actually. Hudson and I merely wish to inform you that we will be hiring a private inquiry agent to look into the matter of Duncan's death."

I stared at them, startled. A detective? But wouldn't that mean –

"Do you suspect his death was not natural?" I asked, keeping my face as expressionless as I could manage. *How strange that they should share my own suspicion, when I have yet to speak of it to anyone outside my staff...*

"We do indeed," Mr. Sedgewick said. "My boy was a young man in prime physical condition. I can hardly imagine that he would have died so young from a sudden internal illness. He was fit as a fiddle."

I held my tongue. *He was anything but...nevertheless, it is quite interesting...*

"Hudson and I agreed that something else must be at play," Mr. Sedgewick said, leaning back and jutting his chin once again. "That someone must have killed him."

I drummed my fingers against the inside of my arm. *It is striking that they, too, believe something is amiss in all of this. I never thought I would see the day when we were in agreement.*

"What makes you so certain of that?" I asked. "Perhaps it was nothing more than an accident of some sort."

"That may be. It was certainly the opinion of the police inspector I spoke with before coming here," Mr. Sedgewick said. "But I cannot rest until I know the truth. And so, when the inspector did not take my suspicions seriously, I knew I must privately hire a man who would."

I kept my face smooth at the revelation that my in-laws had already attempted to involve the authorities.

The inquirer shall arrive some time after the funeral," Mr. Sedgewick added.

"He will arrive here?" I asked, surprised. "I wish that I had been informed sooner."

"Surely if you had been informed, you would not have refused?" he asked, a subtle edge to his words, his steely eyes glinting.

He does not believe I have the means to refuse.

I folded one hand over the other, making my gaze as hard as his. "It is not a matter of refusal but of courtesy. The last I knew, this was my home and Duncan was my husband. I am sure you must see that I should have a say in the matter."

"We wish you to feel at ease with the arrangement, of course," Hudson said quickly.

"But do not forget the reality that it is I who supports you and your household here in London, now," my father-in-law said, his lips twitching briefly upward as if to soften the plainness of his words.

I winced at the reminder but could not deny it. Much as I wished it were otherwise, my circumstances now left me and my infant son dependent on Duncan's family.

"As I am certain you are well aware, someone must be responsible for the upkeep of this fine house," Mr. Sedgewick said. "Since your parents, and now your husband, have all passed on, you have no sources of income, I believe?"

I swallowed, shifting in my chair. "I have my parents' inheritance," I lied.

"Which Duncan informed us you spent every bit of," Hudson said. "He did not blame you, of course, as you were accustomed to such an extravagant lifestyle in your youth."

My eyes widened. I had not realized Duncan had invented such a story to explain away to his family his own poor use of my inheritance.

"Naturally, I will support you, as my late son would have wished," Mr. Sedgewick continued. "I should like you to continue to have the luxuries that you so enjoy..." His eyes slid over me to Warrington, who stood behind my chair. "Such as your loyal servants. It would be a pity if you were to lose any of them."

There was no obvious bite to his words, and yet I sensed they were a threat.

I was trapped. I had no other choice. They had pinned me against the wall, and there was nothing I could do about it.

Mr. Sedgewick had been sending Duncan and me an allowance since we had been married, and had even increased it after my parents' deaths. Its assistance had allowed us to continue to pay our bills and our staff. I'd done the best I could to stash away as much of it as possible without Duncan's knowledge, because if he had access to it all, I had no doubt he would have spent it on his vices.

"I see you are beginning to realize the precariousness of your financial situation," Mr. Sedgewick said. "But do not fear, my daughter. I shall not let harm befall you. All you must do is respect our wishes and continue to receive our help as your family...as Daniel's family."

He knew precisely what to say, didn't he? If he hadn't mentioned Daniel, I might have given some argument. But I was not too proud to realize when I had been bested, at least for the time being...

"Very well," I said. "You have my cooperation. I only hope this inquiry agent of yours may shed some light on this mysterious matter."

5

I was no more than a child when I realized I would marry Duncan one day.

My father, a clever businessman, had a great love for people and was quick to befriend Duncan's family soon after meeting them and to help Mr. Sedgewick along in his own growing business. The better our two families came to know one another, the more obvious it became that all parties hoped for a union that would cement all of our interests.

Duncan had quite the temper, even as a boy. We never got along terribly well, but my mother assured me that one day we would understand each other, that he simply needed time to grow into a man, that all young boys had far too much energy and far too little respect for others.

The trouble did not start for us until the health of both my parents deteriorated...a sudden illness that medicine could not cure. They died, one soon after the other.

Shortly afterward, Duncan's mother sickened and died, as well.

Thus, we were both left brokenhearted, each of us having lost something. And in that loss, much of our true selves began to show. When the buffers of kindness had been taken from us, my parents and Duncan's mother, there was no one left to deflect the tension that naturally fell between us.

And now here I was, standing beside the casket of my dead husband, a man whom I had never truly loved, and who never loved me.

The morning of the funeral had arrived. The sky was bleak, which seemed far too poetic for my liking. The winds blew against the side of the house, causing the shutters outside the parlor windows to rattle. Daniel protested the sound rather heartily, and refused to be dressed in his black mourning clothes that Mrs. Bell had sewed for him.

"He senses the tension," Mrs. Bell said to me as I bounced the infant, trying to soothe him before the mourners arrived. "He will be right as rain come this afternoon."

"I certainly hope afternoon arrives quickly," I said.

"I know, madam, I know..." she said, her eyes unwillingly darting to the nearby casket, which I had insisted remain closed. "You will get through this. You have the support of the entire staff."

She excused herself to help prepare the rest of the food that Mr. Sedgewick had ordered to be offered to those coming to pay their respects.

I did not have to wait much longer. Warrington

appeared in the doorway to the parlor a short time later, a troubled look on his face.

I nodded to him, and passed little squirming Daniel to his nanny, who had come in to fetch him.

Eliza smiled as she wrapped Daniel up in a swaddling blanket and left the room, his tiny cries echoing down the hall as they departed.

I wished I could hold him as a comfort, but knew that wouldn't be wise. Not with the expected number of guests who would want my attention.

"Are people beginning to arrive?"

Mr. Sedgewick stepped into the parlor, dressed in a suit so elegant I thought he might have been setting out to a ball instead of to the funeral of his youngest son.

He did not wait for a response to his question. "I think Hudson and I shall stand on this side," he said. "Duncan was my son, after all."

I didn't argue. Custom dictated that I was the one who should stand nearest the casket as his wife, but what did it really matter?

Warrington only allowed a few people into the parlor at a time, for which I was grateful. There were quite a number I was pleased to see at first; my cousin Madeline and her husband, my dear friend Samantha, and another old friend Dorrings and his wife and children. Warrington likely thought sending them in first might help put me at ease. He was correct.

Then other guests came in who I was less familiar with, but recognized all the same. Business partners of my father, who offered condolences to both Mr. Sedgewick and I. A few I had never met attended, explaining they had known my father and wished to offer their respects in his daughter's time of grief.

I thanked them for their coming, careful not to betray the growing desire in me for the funeral to simply be finished so that I would be able to move on with my life, and step away from the casket I was all too aware of beside me.

Every once in a while, I'd catch Warrington's gaze over the heads of people he allowed in as others left. My butler was keeping a close eye on me, ensuring I was not overwhelmed or too distraught.

Mrs. Bell, too, came in and out of the room a few times to offer me something to drink or eat. The look in her eyes told me she was asking after more than my need of refreshment.

It was not until nearly two hours had passed with people streaming in and out of the parlor that a voice caught my attention.

"Mrs. Sedgewick?"

"Yes?" I turned my face up to the person who had spoken my name.

A man who was probably in his early thirties, easily a decade older than I, stood before me. He was tall, with dark hair that could have fallen below his ears, but was instead swept back atop his head. A narrow mustache covered his upper lip, and a black top hat was clutched in his hands.

"I apologize if I startled you," the stranger said. "My name is Branwell Keats. I am the private inquiry agent your father-in-law hired."

"The detective?" I asked, a prickle of annoyance

running down my spine. So this was the man who had been hired without my knowledge to investigate my husband's death? Under ordinary circumstances, I would have been glad of his assistance, but the fact he had been employed without my consent still rankled.

"It is a pleasure to meet you," I said, masking my irritation. "I expected to see you sometime after the funeral, when we might be able to discuss things at greater length."

"Indeed," he said. "I thought the same, however Mr. Sedgewick insisted on my coming today, as he said he and his eldest son would be leaving shortly after. He was uncertain whether he would have the chance to meet me before leaving."

"Ah, I see," I said. "Well, I am thankful for your help, sir. Losing my husband has been…" I wasn't quite sure what I could say that would not sound like a falsehood.

"I understand," he said. "I should not like to disturb you long, as I can see the line behind me grows ever longer."

I peered over his shoulder briefly. "Indeed it does," I said.

"When shall I return to the house to speak with you again?" Mr. Keats asked.

"Oh, I will be available most of this coming week," I said. "Speak with my butler at the front door. Mr. Warrington will know the best time to schedule our appointment."

"Very well," Mr. Keats said, inclining his head. "Fear not, Mrs. Sedgewick. We shall discover the truth behind what happened to your husband."

"I certainly hope you can," I said. "And my staff and I will do our very best to assist you in your endeavor. Whatever you may need, we can happily provide."

"I shall need nothing," he said. "I have been conducting investigations for the past fourteen years, and in that time, I have found that I require very little, aside from the honesty of those I am assisting."

"And you shall have it," I said. "Of course."

"Very good," he said. "I must introduce myself to your father-in-law, now. My condolences."

He bowed his head once again before stepping in front of the casket, giving it a lingering glance, and then approaching Mr. Sedgewick, who he towered over.

"Are you ready for tea, madam?"

I looked up and saw Mrs. Bell had stepped between me and another couple waiting to greet me.

I blinked at her, suddenly very weary.

"Yes, Mrs. Bell, I think I am," I said. "And a chair to sit would also be quite welcome."

She waved over her shoulder at Mr. Tulson who stood near the door. "Fetch a chair, would you?" she asked him quietly.

He nodded and scurried away.

She looked back at me and leaned in a little. "If you don't mind my asking, madam, who was that gentlemen here a moment ago? The one leaving the room now?"

I turned to see Mr. Keats stepping out of the parlor, his black top hat still in his hands, nodding at other guests as they passed through into the room.

"Believe it or not, Mrs. Bell, he is the detective that my father-in-law has employed," I said.

"Quite the charming man," Mrs. Bell said.

"Perhaps," I said. "He certainly seemed polite enough. We shall see for certain, when he comes by next week to investigate Duncan's death."

Mrs. Bell pursed her lips. "Yes, well...I suppose we have no choice, do we?" she asked, eyeing Mr. Sedgewick warily. "We shall have to endure this invasion of privacy."

"Indeed," I said, my lips twitching in amusement at her habitual use of the word "we" to refer to the entire household. My housekeeper often seemed to think she was a part of the family – and I would have it no other way.

I said, "We have little choice, so we might as well make the best of it."

Mrs. Bell nodded as Mr. Tulson arrived with a chair.

"If you would like to rest your feet, madam, I'll clear some of the guests away," Mrs. Bell said. It sounded more like an order than a suggestion. "Don't worry, this ordeal is almost over. And then we will get to the bottom of what really happened."

"I certainly hope so," I said.

———

"Now, the inquiry agent promised he would send me letters after each development in the investigation," My father-in-law said the next morning as Warrington helped him to shrug on his riding coat. Not that he truly needed one, given the bright sunshine and warmth of the day, but I certainly would not stop him if he wished to make himself uncomfortable without reason. "Please see to it that he does not forget."

"Of course," I said as evenly as possible.

Warrington smoothed the shoulders of Mr. Sedgewick's jacket before brushing off some stray dust and debris.

Mr. Sedgewick asked him, "Is the carriage ready?"

"Yes, sir. All packed and inspected, as per your orders," Warrington said.

"And everything's as it should be?" asked Hudson, who had come lumbering down the stairs, Adam trailing after him with his enormous traveling case.

"Not a thread out of line, sir," Warrington said pleasantly. I was beginning to think he was almost as pleased about them leaving as I was.

"Good," said Hudson. "Well, see you next time, Vicky."

With nothing more than a wave of his hand, he strutted out the front doors and down the steps, his boots crunching on the gravel drive.

Some might have been offended by his lackluster departure. I, on the other hand, was relieved.

"It pains me to have to warn you, Victoria, but I will anyway," Mr. Sedgewick said. "I must not hear again of you frivolously spending the allowance I send you. If I do, I shall have no choice but to reduce your income and expenses."

I bit back the denial on the edge of my tongue and simply nodded my understanding. I could not challenge my late husband's claims about my frivolous spending without implying he was less than honest with his father.

Mr. Sedgewick said, "Well, good day, Victoria. I shall be in touch."

He took his hat from Mr. Tulson's outstretched hands, and set out through the main door.

I maintained my composure and waved after the departing carriage until Warrington closed the front door.

He came to stand beside me, and together we waited for the blissful sound of the wheels spinning in the drive before the *clack, clack, clack,* of horse hooves on the cobblestone street indicated that they were, indeed, on their way.

My shoulders sagged, and I let out a long breath I'd been holding.

The butler said, "If I may say so, madam, I thought you maintained your calm quite well while they were here."

"I'm certainly glad you think so," I said. "There were far too many moments where I would have liked nothing better than to be weeping over more than one grave yesterday..."

Warrington smiled. "Would you like breakfast served, now?"

"Please," I said. "I thought they might never leave."

I started down the hall, where I could hear Daniel's happy cooing from inside the dining room. Eliza had brought him down so I could feed him as soon as Mr. Sedgewick and Hudson had left.

To my surprise, however, I was stopped in my tracks by a knock on the front door.

I looked back toward the sound. "Perhaps they forgot something?" I wondered aloud.

Warrington made his way over to the door, his brow furrowing.

I hesitated, a knot tying itself around my chest, squeezing tightly. *They were supposed to leave. How am I to have any peace if they refuse to go?*

Warrington pulled the door open, and his voice echoed down the hall. "Mr. Aubrey. What a pleasant surprise, sir."

My heart sank as I heard the name.

"Good morning, Mr. Warrington," said the voice on

the steps that I recognized far too well. "I was hoping I might speak with Mrs. Sedgewick for a moment."

I froze, contemplating hurrying down the hall to the dining room. Warrington would invent some excuse for me, surely.

But what on earth is he doing here?

"I am sorry, Mr. Aubrey, but she is not taking calls at the moment." Warrington said.

"It's quite all right, Warrington..." I said, making up my mind and starting toward them. The sooner I spoke to my guest, the sooner I could be rid of him and back to having the peace and quiet that was constantly being robbed from me. "I shall speak with him briefly."

"That's very kind of you," said the man standing out on the front steps.

A thin, sickly looking man, Mr. Aubrey always looked as if he had narrowly escaped some sort of tragic death. And the smile he frequently wore, the one where his golden front tooth would glint plainly for all to see, always held secrets and mischief that made me distrust him all the more.

He pulled his ratty grey bowler hat from his head, his dirty auburn hair falling over his forehead, and bowed deeply. "Mrs. Sedgewick, what a comfort it is to see you looking so well, even at such a sad time."

"You are too kind, Mr. Aubrey," I said, my voice doubtless betraying that my feelings did not match my words. "May I ask to what I owe this visit?"

"I came to offer my deepest sympathies, of course," he said, placing the bowler hat back atop his head. I noticed a long scratch over the bridge of his nose that hadn't been there the last time I had seen him. "I meant to stop by yesterday for the funeral, but – it was yesterday, wasn't it?"

It took every ounce of my strength to keep my expression patient. "Yes, it was yesterday. I was rather surprised that you did not come to pay your respects when all the rest of London seemed to show up."

"Yes, I fear I was...indisposed," he said, the sunlight gleaming off his golden front tooth as he grinned up at me. "I have come to apologize for my absence."

"Thank you, Mr. Aubrey. A note of condolence would have been sufficient," I said. "You needn't have come all this way to tell me in person. However, your thoughtfulness is appreciated."

I nodded farewell to him and gestured to Warrington to close the door as I moved to walk away.

"No, but it was necessary," Mr. Aubrey said, stepping swiftly inside the foyer before he could be shut out.

I frowned at him. "Oh?"

"Of course," he said. "Duncan was one of my closest friends. How could I not come and pay my respects to his lovely widow?"

"You mean he was one of your best customers," I said, my patience coming to an end and my eyes narrowing to dangerous slits.

Mr. Aubrey's face fell. "Mrs. Sedgewick, I don't understand what you could possibly mean by – "

"Do not think me a fool, sir," I said. "I am well aware of my late husband's weaknesses..."

Mr. Aubrey scratched the side of his face, his eyes wide, but he would not meet my gaze. "I am afraid, Mrs.

Sedgewick, that I do not know anything about such matters."

I sighed at his refusal to admit the truth. "I think it is time for you to go, Mr. Aubrey."

"All right, very well," he said, his smile faltering as quickly as it had appeared. "I admit Duncan and I would go out and enjoy the occasional drink together. What's the harm in a man spending time with his friends?"

"The harm came when you introduced my husband to a habit he could not break away from, so that he felt his life meaningless without it," I said.

"Oh, come now, he wasn't that bad," Mr. Aubrey said. "I've seen other men who practically live down there at the docks – "

"What happened the night Duncan died, Mr. Aubrey?" I asked. "And if you do not give me an answer that I like, I shall have no choice but to report your possible involvement to the authorities."

He threw his hands into the air. "Steady now. There is no need to get anyone else involved in our otherwise pleasant conversation..." He glanced toward my butler, and when Warrington did not move to push him back outside, he pulled a handkerchief from his pocket and began to dab at his forehead. "Now, what was it you wished to know?"

"Duncan came home last Sunday in a bizarre state," I said. "I know he had visited one of the opium dens down at the docks. He didn't deny it when I accused him. I could tell he had taken the stuff. He'd been miserable for several days before, and when he returned home, he was all too happy to spend time with both Daniel and I."

"Well, that's good, isn't it?" Mr. Aubrey asked. "Why condemn something that makes him wish to be with you more?"

"It was the middle of the night, Mr. Aubrey..." I said through gritted teeth. "In what world would that be ideal?"

Mr. Aubrey snapped his mouth shut. "Oh, I – I see," he said. "What makes you think that I saw him the night he died?"

"Because I assume he saw you down at the docks," I said.

"Well, he certainly did not," he said, folding his arms. "I haven't been there in weeks. Months, even."

"Really?" I asked. "When was the last time that you met with Duncan?"

"Oh, I suppose it was...well, let me think. I suppose it was last Thursday. Yes, Thursday, at a public house."

My eyes narrowed further. "You would do well not to lie to me, Mr. Aubrey. I know full well that my husband was at home with me last Thursday."

"Oh, then perhaps it was Wednesday," he said. "Yes, that must be it."

I shook my head. "You dig your grave further. We dined with my cousin and her husband that evening."

"Well, then I – " he said. "Mrs. Sedgewick, I was not with Duncan the night he died. I do not know what happened that night."

"Then why am I having such difficulty believing you?" I asked.

Mr. Aubrey licked his lips. "If I may be so honest – "

"I would certainly appreciate it, yes," I said.

He hesitated as Warrington stood up slightly straighter in the background, giving off a convincing feel of someone who would have no trouble escorting Mr. Aubrey from the house with little effort.

"I did indeed wish to come and offer my condolences. Despite my shortcomings, Duncan was a friend of mine. And – " He hesitated. "And I was also hoping that I might be able to collect something that belonged to me. Something that I had allowed Duncan to borrow recently. "

I frowned. "I have no knowledge of this. What is it that was borrowed?"

"I – I would know it if I saw it. If you would simply allow me go up to his room and – "

"Absolutely not," I said. I would not put it past the man to steal something if I allowed him to creep upstairs unsupervised. "There is no proof that anything in this home belongs to you."

"But what about my item?" he asked.

"Until you can explain to me what it is, and what its purpose is, then it remains here," I said. "And that is even if you are telling me the truth in the first place."

Mr. Aubrey's eyes flashed but he held his temper in check.

"Well, no matter," he said, adopting a sudden casualness that was obviously forced as he waved a dismissive hand in the air. "Perhaps I was mistaken after all."

"Perhaps you were, indeed," I said.

He gave me a sweeping bow. "Au revoir, Mrs. Sedgewick. I'm certain I shall see you again soon."

"I doubt that, Mr. Aubrey," I said. "You and I move in very different circles."

He shrugged, went out the door, and wandered down toward the sidewalk, whistling through the gap between his regular tooth and the gold one.

"I must admit, madam..." Warrington said as we watched Mr. Aubrey tip his hat to a young woman with a parasol walking her poodle. "I've never much liked the man but something about all this feels...well, rather strange."

"I'm glad we are in agreement, Warrington," I said, folding my arms. "Everything about his visit was bizarre. He is hiding something, that much is certain."

"I am worried this will not be the last time we see him here," Warrington said.

"I fear you may be right," I said. "We may face more unwelcome visits, at least until we discern the truth about what happened to Duncan."

7

It was brought to my attention that Mr. Branwell Keats, the private inquirer, would be coming to begin his investigation on Monday, August the first. When I woke that morning, I found I was slightly nervous to have a stranger poking about in my home.

"How can I even be certain that this Mr. Keats is who he says he is?" I reflected aloud. "How do I know that my beloved father-in-law didn't simply hire someone to spy on me?"

"Good heavens, madam. Surely he would not do such a thing," Mrs. Bell said as she set down a tray with a fresh pot of tea in front of me for breakfast. "Isn't it possible that he is just an investigator like he claims to be?"

"But how can I know?" I asked.

"I've heard his name around the city, madam," Mr. Tulson said, setting down a small silver egg cup with a perfectly cooked egg resting inside next to my tray of tea. "At least within the past few years. He's made something of a name for himself."

"Truly?" I asked. I might have known I could look to my servants for any gossip that might surround the man.

"Oh, from what I've heard, he's rather unsuccessful though," Adam said, bringing a piece of toast with a side of strawberry jam and setting it down before me. "It's been said that he fails as often as not."

I looked up at Adam. "You see? This is precisely what I was worried about."

"You must have been hearing about someone else," Mr. Tulson said, giving Adam a flat look. "I've heard that Mr. Keats is one of the best. Mr. Sedgewick was right in hiring him."

"I'm not so certain," Adam said, shrugging. "I have also heard that he is excessively greedy in his fees."

"That matters little to me, as I am not the one paying him," I said. I sighed heavily, staring down at the food that I no longer had an appetite for.

"Fear not, madam," Warrington said, sweeping into the breakfast hall. "I have done some investigating of my own into this Mr. Keats."

He set down a newspaper before me, pointing to a photograph at the top right of the second page.

The black and white face of the same man I had met at the funeral was framed within it.

He was actually somewhat handsome, which I supposed I wouldn't have noticed the day of Duncan's funeral. The serious look on his face displayed his depth of thought. At least, one would assume that. Perhaps he thought of nothing more than what sort of meal he would order for dinner that evening. His strong cheekbones were prominent in the photograph, and as I studied it, I also noticed his furrowed brow, his eyes intent and staring ahead.

The article beside the picture was titled, *The End of The Line.*

"It's about a crime he solved recently, but it also speaks of his wit and work ethic," Warrington said, running his fingers over some key lines. "He has done very well for himself over the past few years, even being brought on by the city police for some more important cases."

"Has he now?" I asked. "I am surprised that my father-in-law somehow managed to employ someone so capable. I'm almost annoyed."

"This is from some weeks ago," Warrington said, indicating the date. "I imagine Mr. Sedgewick saw his name in a more recent edition, and thought of him straight away for his son's death."

"I suppose that makes sense," I said. "And it certainly makes me feel better."

"How so, madam?" Mrs. Bell asked, pouring some of the fresh tea into a cup for me.

"Simple," I said. "My father-in-law's good fortune was nothing more than chance. He merely happened upon Mr. Keats' reputation in the paper, not because he searched and searched for the perfect candidate."

"I told you, lad," Mr. Tulson said, giving Adam a smug look.

Adam blushed and scuttled from the room.

"Well...I suppose it's all right as long as he really is who he says he is," I said. "My fear now is that he will find nothing."

"And what if he does not?" Mrs. Bell asked. "If I may ask, madam, would that really be such a terrible outcome if the master's death ended up being nothing more than an accident?"

"I suppose not," I said. "Of course, it would be the better of the two possibilities, the alternative being that he was murdered."

"Indeed," Warrington said. "If the cause of death was nothing more than natural, then the household can simply move on."

"Move on...." I murmured into my cup of tea.

I wondered what, exactly, moving on would look like for me. Would I remain dependent on my in-laws forever? It seemed likely, as I could not imagine any other means of support for a lady of my station.

Unless, of course... It was far too soon to contemplate the possibility of remarriage, although I had to admit to myself it would be the simplest way out of my dilemma, ending my reliance upon Duncan's family, while also providing a father for my young son. Moreover, at my age it would be expected by everyone. I was far too young to remain alone for life.

I was not, however, eager to risk the possibility of another unhappy union. Certainly it was better to remain as I was, at present. There was no hurry to "move on" as Warrington phrased it, not when I would remain in mourning for some time to come anyway.

"You ought not to speak of such things, Mr. Warrington," Mrs. Bell said. "It is unwise to speak of the dead, especially so soon after their departing..."

"Perhaps my husband's spirit can come explain to me

what happened the night he died..." I said, glaring up at the exposed beams around the ceiling, watching the glinting lights in the chandelier overhead.

Mrs. Bell shuddered, as though fearing it was a real prospect.

"Mr. Warrington, he has arrived," came Adam's voice through the open door to the dining room.

Warrington bowed to me, and excused himself from the room.

I crumpled up my napkin and threw it on the table. "These visitors do not have any consideration for the most basic rules of etiquette. These early calls...my father never would have stood for them."

"Times are changing, madam," Mrs. Bell said. "The earlier to work, the more money there is to be earned."

I frowned, taking a regretful bite of my toast.

I refused to rise, even for the detective, and instead continued on with my breakfast until Warrington reappeared.

Perhaps seeing me still at the table, instead of properly settled in the drawing room, would remind the caller of the earliness of the hour. He ought to be aware of the inconvenience he caused.

"Madam, Mr. Branwell Keats has arrived," Warrington announced.

I wiped my mouth and settled the napkin back into my lap. "You may send him in," I said, picking up my teacup and taking a sip. I frowned. It was rather cold, now.

Mr. Keats' top hat entered the room first, quickly

followed by the rest of him. As he had been at the funeral, he was dressed in a sharp suit of olive green.

He removed his hat as he straightened, and inclined his head toward me. "Good morning, Mrs. Sedgewick. My apologies for disturbing you so early, but a great many things have come up since we last spoke, and my day is already very full."

I set down my teacup, and looked at him, my gaze stern. "It's quite all right, Mr. Keats. Would you care for some tea before you begin your task?"

"No, but thank you very much," he said. "As I said, I do not have a great deal of time. Would your butler care to show me where Mr. Sedgewick was found dead?"

I looked over at Warrington. "I do not mind showing you myself," I said.

My visitor nodded. "Very well."

I waited for Mr. Tulson to pull the chair out for me before I stood, and led the way from the room.

"I apologize in advance, Mr. Keats, for the state the room is in," I said as we reached the bottom of the landing leading upstairs. "I have yet to step foot in this room since that dreaded night…"

"That's quite all right," Mr. Keats said. "I certainly do not blame you for not wishing to visit the place."

"My maids have kept the nursery in decent order, though I have contemplated moving all of my son's items back into my bedroom. I am not comfortable with him sleeping in the same room that his father…" I allowed the sentence to linger, unfinished.

"I understand," he said. "No need to explain yourself further."

We reached the landing of the next floor, and a chill ran down my spine.

I haven't been able to bring myself to look down this hall, not even once. My mind has played that scene in the nursery over and over again and I cannot escape it.

"It is just down here," I said, my heart beginning to beat rapidly.

The door loomed at the end of the hall, and for a moment, it was as if the entire floor beneath me shifted.

"Madam, are you all right?"

It was Warrington, who had come to my side in a flash. It wasn't until I looked up into his concerned face that I realized I was leaning against the wall, clutching at my chest.

I blinked a few times to clear my mind. "Y – yes," I said.

Mr. Keats stood near the doorway to the nursery, his top hat held in his hand, watching me warily.

"My apologies, Mr. Keats," I said, stepping away from the wall and smoothing the wrinkles from the front of my dress. "I have not been sleeping terribly well this past week."

He nodded. "Of course. There is no need to apologize."

"Come along, Mr. Keats, the nursery is right through that door," Warrington said. "Mrs. Bell, perhaps you had best stay with the mistress."

My housekeeper appeared, as if materializing out of thin air. She joined me, as I watched the two men disappear beyond the open door.

"Good heavens, madam, what happened?" Mrs. Bell asked. "I have never seen you so pale."

"I am not certain..." I said, laying a hand against my perspiring forehead. "I never thought a room could distress me so."

"Perhaps it would be best if you remained out here," Mrs. Bell said, wrapping an arm around my shoulder and guiding me back down the hall. "We shall find you a place to sit down – "

I stepped out of her hold, finding my resolve. "No," I said. "I am not a child, to indulge in foolish fears. I must go in there. He may have questions for me that only I can answer. Besides, I should like to know exactly what it is that he is looking for, or what he might be hoping to find that could help him discern whether or not it was indeed a murder."

Mrs. Bell gave an exasperated sigh but did not dare lecture me. "Very well, madam. I shall fetch you a cool cloth. Do not hesitate to sit down if you begin to feel dizzy once again."

I gave her some sort of vague word of promise, and then made my way back down to the nursery.

I shouldn't be so frightened. This is my son's room. The room itself did not kill Duncan. He could have just as easily died in my bedroom when he'd come to see Daniel and I that night. Would I be as frightened of that room as I am of the nursery?

I took a deep breath, attempting to slow my racing heart.

Yes, I think I would have been as frightened. I never would have wished to sleep in that room ever again.

I needed to be brave, though. For Daniel. I needed to learn the truth of what happened to his father.

As I stepped through the doorway, I expected a cold chill to pass over me, perhaps as Duncan's way of telling me he was there, watching me. Not that it was a comforting thought, not in the least. But I expected there to be some sort of recompense for my lack of grief in the past few days.

When nothing happened, I looked around, almost confused.

The room was precisely as we had left it on the night he died. The stack of blankets that Eliza had been folding had been moved, as we had used them since Duncan passed, but nothing else had been touched.

The chair I had fallen into out of shock was still askew, pressed up against the bookshelf beside the window. The rug where Duncan had collapsed was wrinkled and the right corner was still overturned. The cradle no longer stood against the center of the far wall; instead it had shifted off to the left, likely when Duncan had grabbed it in an attempt to catch himself as he fell.

There was no blood, no dents or scratches...no evidence anywhere that a death had taken place.

Nothing apart from the memories that pulsated in my mind as clearly as though it was all occurring again right this instant.

"Tell me again, Mr. Warrington," Mr. Keats said, standing off to the side of the room, surveying the crumpled rug on the floor. "He came in here to find a blanket, and the infant's nurse was here, doing some tidying up?"

"Yes," Warrington said with a nod, standing beside

him with his hands behind his back, glancing every few moments over at me. "That is correct."

"I should like to question the nurse," Mr. Keats said. "Is she available?"

"I am not certain," I said. "She was tending to my son while I was having breakfast."

"We should certainly speak with her," he said. "She was the one who saw him die, wasn't she?"

I winced, but told myself there was no point in speaking around the matter. The details of the death would have to be plainly discussed if this man were to do his work here.

"Well, yes," Warrington answered his question. "We all came running in here, and the nanny looked as if she had seen a ghost."

"She was in here alone with him, and no one has yet questioned her?" Mr. Keats asked. "Has anyone noted anything suspicious in her behavior of late?"

"Eliza?" I asked, incredulous. "I do not know what you are implying, but she never would have – "

"I beg pardon, Mrs. Sedgewick, but all possibilities must be considered in cases such as this one, however unlikely they may seem. For example, can you prove to me without a doubt that during the time the nurse was alone with him she didn't somehow find a way to injure him, and then scream to alert the rest of you?"

My brows rose. "It was not something I had considered, no."

I did not add that the reason I had not considered it was because it was too far-fetched to imagine. Eliza the nanny as my husband's murderer... The suggestion was ludicrous. Perhaps my father-in-law had not chosen the right man for this investigation after all.

Though I did not speak my doubts aloud, the detective seemed to sense them.

"I am not saying it happened in that way. Most likely it did not," Mr. Keats said. "But it is important to keep our minds open to all the options. Sometimes the least likely suspects are those who we need to be most wary of." His gaze moved to Warrington. "Fetch this Eliza for me, will you?"

She was easy enough to locate, tending to Daniel in my bedroom just down the hall. Warrington found her and brought her down to the nursery.

I watched the hesitation in her face as she, too, stepped inside. Had she not been in here since that night, either?

She isn't guilty. The look on her face tells me enough. Besides, what advantage would she have if she were to kill Duncan? I can see no point in it for her. And that's to say nothing of the fact that there were no obvious wounds on him...

"Eliza, I presume?" Mr. Keats asked. His face took on a very sober expression as he surveyed the girl. "I have some questions for you about the night that Duncan Sedgewick died."

Eliza's face turned the color of ivory, and her bottom lip trembled. "Y – Yes, sir. Certain – certainly, sir."

"Here, I will take the baby," I said, stepping forward and scooping Daniel out of her arms. "It is all right. Mr. Keats only wishes to know what went on that night, nothing more."

Eliza nodded, but her eyes remained wide.

"I have been told that you were in the nursery when the master of the house died. Is that correct?" Mr. Keats asked.

"Yes, sir," Eliza said. The front of her apron had been stained, and I noticed one or two of her dark curls had come loose from beneath her bonnet, likely pulled free by little Daniel's grabbing fingers.

"What can you tell me about what was happening before Mr. Sedgewick entered the room?" Mr. Keats asked.

"I was folding some of the baby's clothing and blankets," she said. "It had – it had been raining earlier in the day, so I couldn't take them off the line and bring them up, as they had not dried. It wasn't until after I had finished my supper that I went out to check them and found them ready to bring in, so I did, and – "

"Rambling, Eliza, will not help me to believe you any more than I already do," Mr. Keats said. "Please keep the information relevant. Why were you up here as late as you were?"

"I am often awake late, sir," Eliza said. "It is my duty to check in on the mistress and young Daniel at least once before I make my way to my own bed. When I checked in on them around eleven, the baby was awake and very cranky. So I decided it was best for me to do what I could to help the mistress and be available for her if she needed me."

Mr. Keats' head swiveled around, his grey eyes landing on me in a questioning manner.

"That is all correct," I said, bouncing Daniel in my

arms, until the infant cooed happily up at me. "She did indeed come in around eleven, and checked on me every half an hour afterwards."

Mr. Keats nodded, returning his attention to Eliza. "Please continue with your story, Eliza."

She nodded, and I noticed her hands trembling behind her back. "Yes, sir. It was...around one in the morning, I believe, when I was in here finishing folding the clothes and blankets I had brought up from the clothes line, still waiting to see if the mistress would need me to take the baby for her, when Mr. Sedgewick came in through the door..."

Mr. Keats' brows shot upward as she hesitated. "And?" he asked.

"He...well, sir, I don't really know, but he was certainly behaving strangely. He stumbled into the room, nearly tripping over the armchair there, by the door. He laughed, but it sounded harsh and strange, as if he were entirely out of his senses. It – well, it frightened me."

"Did he speak to you?" Mr. Keats asked.

"Yes," Eliza said, shrinking inward on herself. "But he wasn't making much sense. He was laughing so hard, thinking it amusing that he tripped the way he did. Then he asked me for the baby's favorite blanket, which I had folded and had already set aside. He had an odd look in his eyes and was breathing heavily. I told him I would fetch the blanket for him, and when I turned around to reach for it, I heard him begin gasping for breath. I looked back and saw him fall against the cradle, but it wouldn't support him, and he tumbled to the floor, and... that's when he stopped moving."

"I see," Mr. Keats said, taking long strides out into the middle of the nursery, his eyes taking in the room once more as if with fresh eyes. "Would you say he fell about here?" he asked.

"A little further over," Eliza said.

"Very well," Mr. Keats said.

I watched as he began to inspect every inch of the room; the cradle, the rug, the wall, the chair. He ran his fingers over each surface, every once in a while allowing himself a contemplative, "Hmm," or an, "Ahh."

"What is it that you are looking for, Mr. Keats?" I asked, shifting Daniel to my opposite hip.

"A sign, of course," he said. "Of anything amiss."

"How could you know if it was amiss or not?" I asked. "You have never set foot in this room in your life."

"Quite true," he said. "But there are tells that are the same, no matter where they are. Such as this," he said, pointing to a scuff along the foot of the chair. "This was caused not by Duncan's fall, but by the edge of a broom. See the way the scratch is rather deep?"

He then knelt down beside the cradle.

"And here there is a scuff that looks to be from a bracelet," he said. "Perhaps yours, Mrs. Sedgewick? Or perhaps Eliza's?"

Then he ducked his head down beneath the cradle and peered underneath.

"And what do we have here?" he asked, reaching beneath and pulling something out.

"Likely nothing more than a toy, Mr. Keats," I said.

"Is it?" he asked, righting himself and holding his find in the air before my face.

It was a small, brown bottle with a label fixed to the front. Duncan's name was written across it in a neat, tight script.

Beneath it were instructions to take two doses, twice a day; once in the morning and once before bed.

And beside the instructions was yet another name.

Doctor Higgins.

I certainly was not the only one startled to find a bottle of medicine underneath the cradle in Daniel's room. Especially when it was a bottle I had never seen in my life.

Mr. Keats seemed to think it was of importance to the case, but also insisted that he had overstayed his time at our home that morning.

"But how can you possibly make any progress with what little you have learned?" I asked as I followed him down to the foyer.

"I've learned a great deal more than you may realize," Mr. Keats said, replacing his top hat on his head. "It is all about looking at the information that others fail to see."

He promised he would return within the week to continue with his investigation, and that he would, of course, be reporting everything he discovered to Mr. Erasmus Sedgewick when he found anything of note.

I didn't like the thought of his reporting information to my father-in-law about what went on beneath my roof, but I knew there was no help for it. It was Mr. Sedgewick, and not I, who had hired the detective and who would pay his fees. Besides, deep down I wanted to know the truth, perhaps even more than my father-in-law and Hudson did. Duncan had been my husband, after all.

THE QUESTION on everyone's minds that afternoon and evening was the medicine bottle that had been discovered.

Warrington seemed just as surprised as I was about it. He assured me he had never seen it before.

"How could Doctor Higgins have prescribed him something that I was completely unaware of?" I asked. "It does not make any sense."

"It could very well have been a part of his therapy, madam," Mrs. Bell offered. "Doctor Higgins did say that they had been making some progress."

"I do not know if this sort of medicine could truly count as progress," Warrington said, picking up the bottle from the desk in the drawing room, where Mr. Keats had set it down hours ago, on his way out. Warrington examined the bottle, swirling the dark glass around, the liquid sloshing against the sides. "There is no name on the label, no description other than how often to take it."

I said, "Perhaps if I smelled it, I might be able to deduce what it could be."

"Would that not be dangerous, madam?" Mrs. Bell asked. "We have no earthly idea what it could be. What if you became ill after smelling it?"

"I fear Mrs. Bell is correct, madam," Warrington said.

I frowned. "If it was potentially dangerous, then why did Mr. Keats not take it with him?" I asked. "If it might have been evidence, wouldn't he have wished to remove it?"

"I think Mr. Keats would consider the doctor himself as part of the evidence, but maybe not the bottle," Warrington said. "Even still, he instructed me not to lose it, in case he wished to inspect it again."

I leaned back in the desk chair, glaring at the bottle as Warrington set it back down on the desk. The fireplace behind me crackled merrily; the night was cool, despite the fact it was only the first week of August.

"What I do not understand is why this was in Daniel's nursery in the first place," I said, glancing over at the bassinet beside my chair. The baby was stretched out inside it, his little fists resting to either side of his head. I watched the steady and rhythmic rise and fall of his chest for a few moments, assuring myself that he was sleeping peacefully. I didn't wish to wake him with my angered words.

"That is something I have wondered about, as well, madam..." Mrs. Bell said, folding her arms. "What if it rolled out of the master's pocket the night he died?"

"I have thought the same," Warrington said. "But the maids are so efficient at keeping the entire house spotless, it seems quite odd that one of them did not discover it sooner."

"I agree, Warrington," I said. "Which is why I have decided that I am going to go and see the good doctor for myself. I shall ask him precisely what this medicine was, and if there is any chance that it killed Duncan."

"You wish to see the doctor yourself?" Mrs. Bell asked.

"Why, of course," I said, looking up at her incredulously. "A strange medicine just happens to appear in the place where my husband died? That cannot be coincidence."

"But would it not be safer for you, madam, to leave this with Mr. Keats and his expertise?" Warrington asked. "One would imagine the detective has come to the very same conclusion you have, and that he will surely go and speak with the doctor on his own."

"When he has time, I'm certain he will," I said. "But I wish to know what happened now. I want to put this all behind me. Can't you see? The longer this takes, the more awful I feel about it all, and the longer it will be until I can have peace."

Warrington and Mrs. Bell looked at one another over the desk, but both must have known there would be no dissuading me in this matter.

"You may make the arrangements for me in the morning," I told Warrington.

"Very good, madam," he said in a tone that implied it was anything but.

I decided I would be arriving at the doctor's under the pretense that he would be seeing Daniel, instead of me. I felt a little uncomfortable using my son in such a deceptive way, but I knew it was the swiftest way to get Doctor Higgins to see me.

Warrington managed to arrange an appointment with the doctor on Friday morning, which seemed later than I would have preferred, but I had little choice in the matter. Naturally, the medical man had other patients to tend to.

Until then, all I could do was wait...

A HANSOM CAB dropped Daniel and I off in front of the doctor's office at half past nine that morning. I had brought Eliza along to help carry the sorts of small necessities required when traveling with an infant.

"Just pretend with me," I instructed the nanny. "And it will go smoothly."

"But, madam – " she said, nearly tripping over the curb as we stepped up from the street. "I am terrible at lying."

"How are we lying?" I asked. "We came to visit the doctor, did we not?"

"But the baby is not truly in need of medical attention," she said. "He is quite healthy."

"Indeed," I said. "But there was no other way to ensure that Doctor Higgins would see us."

Deep down, I shared her concern that the doctor would uncover our deception. Still, I was far too determined to hesitate at the bending of a few rules.

The doctor's office was located in the third floor of a corner building on the opposite side of Hyde Park from where I lived. It was a busier part of town, where many people conducted business during the weekdays. I watched a man carrying a stack of newspapers taller than him stumble and fall, sending the papers flying into the air above him like birds taking flight. A woman stood before a cart across the street, passing some coins to a man who seemed to be surrounded in a field of wildflowers. A cab passed by, the horse's hooves clattering noisily across the cobbles of the street.

"Come along, Eliza," I said. "We must get to the doctor's office."

The stairwell up to his office was narrow and rickety. We passed by an elderly gentlemen who clung to the railing as he coughed so hard and so loudly that I was very nearly certain he would bring up his lung.

I held Daniel close as we continued to wind our way upstairs.

The door to the clinic was propped open, with the words *Doctor Higgins, Physician* scrolled across the glass in peeling letters.

The waiting room was very nearly full, with only a pair of chairs vacant beside the receptionist's desk. *No wonder he could not see us until today...*

It was almost an hour before my name was called to go back and see Doctor Higgins.

He waited for us in a room down a short hall that had no windows. A cabinet stood along the far wall, and a metal bed with nothing more than a thin blanket draped across it filled the empty space.

"Ah, Mrs. Sedgewick," Doctor Higgins said politely. "And your infant. Please, won't you come in?"

I stepped nervously into the room, followed by Eliza, who now held the baby.

"I have a note here that you wished for me to look at some problem with little Daniel?" he asked, looking up from the paper he referenced on the counter. "Though it doesn't say what it is, precisely…"

"We did not come for Daniel, Doctor Higgins," I said, reaching into the pocket of my coat. I pulled the brown glass bottle from inside, and held it out to him. "I came to ask you about this."

Doctor Higgins' eyes widened as he looked from me to the bottle. He pulled his spectacles from his face and set them on top of his head. "What is it?" he asked.

"A bottle we found in the room where Duncan died," I said, passing it to him, trying my best not to bristle with anger. *How could he have forgotten about it already?*

He examined the bottle, bringing it close underneath his nose, squinting as he read the words that he himself had written across the label.

"Oh, I see…" he said. "I very nearly forgot I'd prescribed this for him."

"What is it, exactly?" I asked.

"It is a mild sedative," he said. "Nothing too strong. Something I thought might help him to sleep through those cravings he would have for the opium."

"Could this have been what killed him?" I asked. "Could he possibly have taken too much of it?"

Doctor Higgins held the bottle up to the light, peering through the glass with one eye. "I don't think so, no…" he said.

"Why do you say that?" I prodded. "It was found only a short distance away from where he died."

"It could not have killed him because he never took any of it," Doctor Higgins said, setting the bottle down on the counter. "I gave this to him the day he died, when he came to see me that morning. But from the looks of it, he didn't take a single drop. I could measure it back out, if you would like me to, if you do not believe me."

I frowned, but he met my gaze easily. He seemed far less flustered than he had the night he'd come to the house after Duncan's death.

"Mrs. Sedgewick..." he said, folding his arms. "May I ask what is the real reason you came to see me today?"

"It was the medicine," I said. "Truly."

Doctor Higgins' face screwed up in question. "Something tells me you believe I might be responsible for your late husband's death in some way. Am I correct?"

I wasn't sure why it was startling to hear the suggestion from the man himself. I was caught entirely off guard and could think of no response but the truth. "I – " I began. "I do not know. I have wondered, certainly, especially after hearing you had met with him earlier that day, and then finding this medicine..."

Doctor Higgins' face reddened slightly but, if he was offended, he hid it admirably. "I can understand why the thought crossed your mind. But please believe me when I assure you I would never do anything that might cause harm to one of my patients. You have my word on that."

But isn't that exactly what he would say, even if he were responsible? Whether it was a case of accidental incompetence or deliberate malice, I can hardly expect the man to admit any responsibility for what happened to Duncan...

Doctor Higgins sighed, as if reading the doubts written across my face. "Though it troubles me to say it, you are not alone in wondering if there might be anything suspicious behind Mr. Sedgewick's death," he said. "He had a tendency to spend time in the wrong sorts of places with the wrong sorts of people. Who knows who he might have crossed? It could have been nearly anyone."

Is he being genuine or merely trying to deflect my suspicions in a different direction?

It was impossible to know. Still, I had to ask, "What do you think killed him, Doctor? You have had some time to consider. What, in your professional opinion, seems most likely?"

The medical man rubbed the back of his neck, and replaced his spectacles onto his slender nose. "After consulting with several other physicians and examining my own notes on the patient's history, I cannot escape the conclusion that it looked a great deal like an overdose of opium."

"You still believe it was nothing more than an accident, then?" I asked. "That he simply took too much of the stuff?"

"That is likely the cause, yes," Doctor Higgins said. "Of course, I cannot guess whether he did so deliberately, or whether someone else might have forced or encouraged him..."

My gaze sharpened. "You are saying some enemy might have convinced him to consume more than he wanted in hopes that it would kill him?"

Doctor Higgins looked uncomfortable, even though it had been his own suggestion. "It would probably be best not to indulge in such speculations."

"Yet even you have concerns about the dangerous company he kept," I reminded him. "You said yourself that he may have crossed someone. How could I prove that happened? Or even learn if it did?"

"You may not be able to," Doctor Higgins said. "Apart from recalling how he behaved when he returned home on the night of his death. He died rather quickly, rather suddenly, correct?"

"Yes," I said. "It was all very strange."

"The dosing must have occurred relatively soon before he went home, then," Doctor Higgins said. "That much of the drug could very easily stop the heart, or cause asphyxiation, or any number of maladies that would cause the body to cease functioning properly..."

"In the past, I have seen him become ill or sleep for long periods of time," I said. "But I never saw him stumbling like he was that night. It was as if he had somehow gone further than he ever had before. He was in the worst state I had ever seen him."

The doctor nodded.

"The question, I suppose, is whether he took the deadly amount willingly," I continued. "Or whether he was tricked or coerced in some way."

"I wish I could be of more help," Doctor Higgins said with a sigh. "But I fear this is one of those cases where the final answers are unknowable. That being so, I would urge you, Mrs. Sedgewick, to put all these dark questions from your mind. It can do you no good to ponder such matters now and your late husband would not have wished you to distress yourself needlessly."

Was there anything suspicious in the doctor's desire to push the matter aside? Or was he sincere in his advice and sympathy? I could not decide, but either way, there was nothing to be gained in allowing him to see my doubts.

"Thank you, Doctor Higgins," I said. "You have been most helpful. And now, I believe we should go, as it seems you have your hands full here today."

"I certainly do..." he said, and the exhaustion showed for a brief moment on his face. "No matter, though. I take great pride in helping those in need."

"I'm sure that you do," I said, though I could be sure of no such thing.

Eliza and I left the clinic a few moments later, and were back out on the busy street.

"I am sorry you didn't get any answers, madam," Eliza said as we made our way toward the hansom cab. "I know you were hoping for more."

"On the contrary, Eliza," I said as I stepped up inside, and turned to reach for Daniel. "I believe I managed to uncover some rather valuable information."

"So he believes it could indeed have been the opium that killed Duncan," I told Warrington as he served my dinner that evening. "Of course, we always suspected that as a potential cause of death but he told me today that he has spent some time conversing with other physicians since, as well as looking through Duncan's past medical history. It seems the doctor has been thinking about it a great deal, and has developed a suspicion that Duncan could have been tricked or coerced in some way."

Dinner that evening was a delicious stew, prepared by our home chef, Corbyn. Everything he made was always delectable, and I looked forward to each meal knowing it came from his jolly kitchen.

Adam set down a basket of freshly baked bread beside me, and I smiled at him. "Thank you, Adam."

"Of course, madam. Of course," he said.

Mr. Tulson stepped between him and me and set a hot bowl of stew down before me. Tendrils of steam floated in the air above the rich, dark broth, and bits of carrots and potatoes bathed in the thick, almost gravy-like liquid.

My mouth watered.

"Well, it would certainly be difficult to prove if that is truly what happened to the master," Warrington said from his station beside the door. "I can easily imagine an environment where someone who did not have his best interests in mind might convince him to take more of the stuff."

"The question I would have is whether the deception was intentional or not," Mrs. Bell commented, seemingly having set aside her distaste for the topic. "What if it was nothing more than one of his companions chiding him, telling him he had to prove himself to be a man in some capacity? If this person was as overcome with the drug as the master was, then how could we ever get a confession out of him?"

I delicately sipped the broth from my spoon, and felt a little better already. I had been so distracted all day that I had scarcely remembered to eat until now.

"I see you are warming to the idea that this might have been more than an accident..." Warrington said, arching an eyebrow at my housekeeper.

Mrs. Bell glowered at him as she refilled my teacup with hot, steaming tea. "Perhaps I am," she snapped. "And yet, we could all very well be chasing shadows."

"Indeed we could be," Warrington said.

"It seems a great deal more sinister if someone of sound mind convinced him to take more of the drug," Mr. Tulson said, stepping back away from the table, a clean napkin draped over his arm, ready should I need him. "It is difficult to imagine someone intentionally convincing a man entirely lost to himself to take even more of the stuff, knowing full well that it would ultimately kill him."

Adam who had just walked back into the room from the kitchen, tripped over the edge of the rug, the bowl of roasted veggies in his hands soaring across to the wall and spattering against the wood paneling.

"Good heavens, man," Mr. Tulson scolded. "What do you think you're doing?"

"I'm terribly sorry, madam," Adam said to me, staggering to his feet. "I'll have it cleaned in no time."

I spared him a brief glance as he hurried from the room. It was not surprising this morbid subject was disturbing to some of the servants. I did not greatly enjoy it myself, but I did not have the luxury of ignoring the facts simply to keep the household calm.

I looked back over at Mr. Tulson. "I've been having the same thought on the matter. Who could have looked Duncan in the eye, and willingly sent him to his grave? It seems awfully vile. Particularly because my husband had a tendency to be rather...trusting and persuadable, shall we say? Someone could easily have fooled him."

"Yes, but who?" Warrington asked. "There could be dozens of suspects down at the docks who might have known him."

Suddenly losing my appetite, I set my spoon down. "And I imagine they will all behave just as Mr. Aubrey did. Evasively and dishonestly."

Warrington nodded. "I fear that is so, madam."

Aggravated, I gritted my teeth. "How am I supposed to

find who is responsible for this?" I asked. "If no one will answer my questions, and I cannot be certain how he died in the first place…"

"There are many questions to ask," Warrington said. "I hope you will not mind my suggesting this, madam, but one I keep wondering about is whether or not the master owed someone money?"

I sighed, leaning back in my chair. "You never need worry about offending me with the truth, Warrington. I am as aware as anyone that my husband was prone to reckless behaviors. That he might have borrowed money is not something I had considered, but you are right. What if he did owe someone money? His tendency to gamble leads me to believe that he couldn't possibly have always won. In fact, I do not think he ever did, hence he spent my parents' entire fortune."

"But if he did indeed owe someone money, wouldn't they have come to call already?" Mrs. Bell asked. "That is, assuming they thought a grieving widow would be easier to collect from than the living debtor himself."

Warrington pondered for a moment. "Yes, I imagine they would have appeared by now…" he said. "Though it is possible they have been watching the house for the appropriate time to strike."

"To strike?" I asked sharply. "Whatever do you mean?"

"He means nothing, madam," Mrs. Bell said quickly, rounding on Warrington with a firm look. "There is no cause for alarm. This is all purely speculation, and it seems to be a stretch at that."

"We must consider every possibility," Warrington said, seemingly unfazed by her response.

She gave him one last, hard look before turning back to me. "I wonder if it would not be someone who was better acquainted with him, someone he would see regularly."

"Such as the doctor?" I asked.

She nodded. "He seemed a far more likely suspect, didn't he? Given his direct connection to the master."

"Perhaps," I said. "He could easily enough have been lying in all he said to me, trying to point suspicion elsewhere, before ultimately discouraging me from looking into the matter further. However, the more I think on it, the more I wonder what good killing Duncan would really have done him."

Adam returned with towels and a waste bin, and began to scrape the vegetables from the wall, where they were now collecting in a wet, cold pile near the baseboards.

I turned my attention back to Warrington. "The only motive I can think of is that the doctor might have wished to hide his failed attempt at the new therapy he had been testing on Duncan. He did say it was a new treatment and implied he was not entirely experienced with it. I suppose it might damage his reputation if an unsuccessful experiment became known to his other patients."

"That seems a plausible theory, madam," Warrington said. "Even though he proved to you that the master did not take any of the medicine he'd given him, that doesn't necessarily prove the doctor did not injure him through some other means."

I frowned. "Yes..." I said. "I fear we cannot cross Doctor Higgins off the list of those who might have wished my husband harm. But to be perfectly honest, I am less inclined to think it was him, and instead think it might be of interest to speak with Mr. Aubrey once again. Something about that man has always seemed strange to me. He is a most untrustworthy character."

"It is difficult to imagine such a questioning would prove fruitful," Mrs. Bell said, shaking her head. "Mr. Aubrey would never cooperate. There would be no way to ensure we managed to get the truth from him."

I smirked at her habitual "we", amused as the idea of my sturdy old housekeeper physically shaking the truth out of the devious Mr. Aubrey.

Then I tapped my finger against my chin, peering into the stew bowl before me.

Mr. Aubrey believed he had the upper hand with me because of his way of life. He lies, steals, and cheats every day. I doubt he would expect any sort of manipulative behavior from a helpless widow in my circumstances, would he?

"Perhaps I could get him to tell the truth if I were to speak his language," I said.

"What do you mean, madam?" Warrington asked.

I nodded to myself, the plan already taking shape in my mind. "We must summon him to the house, Warrington," I said. "Tomorrow would be best, of course."

"Truly?" Mrs. Bell asked. "That wretch? In your home?"

"Yes," I said. "And I intend to show him all the hospitality that someone in my position is capable of."

"It is dangerous, that's what it is," Mrs. Bell said to me the next day, frowning whenever she happened to be in the same room as me. "You are going to lure him here on the presumption that you do indeed have some item of his. Surely, madam, you have considered all the violent ways he might react when he realizes you are merely trying to coerce him?"

I rolled my eyes toward the ceiling, lowering the book I had been trying so very hard to read. Daniel had finally fallen asleep after a fussy morning, and I wished for nothing more than a few moments of peace and quiet before Mr. Aubrey arrived.

"Yes, Mrs. Bell, for the last time...in order to make someone like Mr. Aubrey listen to me, I must first draw him in with something he wants. By the time he realizes I do not truly have the thing, what can he possibly do about it? As for the coercion, if he will only understand anger and hostility, then that is what I must use."

Mrs. Bell pursed her lips as she waved a feather duster over the brass sconces. "I am quite concerned."

"Yes, I know," I said, my eyes returning to the page in front of me, reading the same line almost a dozen times. "You've made it plainly clear."

"Madam? There is someone here to see you."

I looked up and saw Warrington standing in the doorway, his steady gaze on me.

"He's here already?" I asked, closing the book and glancing at the clock on the wall. It wasn't even eleven in the morning.

"No, madam," Warrington said, hands held behind his back. "It is Mr. Keats."

My eyebrows rose. "Mr. Keats? What does he want now?" I asked.

"He has not informed me," Warrington said. "Shall I see him in? Or shall I tell him you are not accepting calls today?"

I bit down on the inside of my lip. *If Mr. Keats has made progress with this matter, then certainly I desire to hear about it. But if he is still empty-handed, and he happens to be here when Mr. Aubrey arrives, then I might very well lose my chance to speak with Mr. Aubrey. Especially if Mr. Aubrey knows that Mr. Keats is a private inquirer...*

Although the detective's mere presence could ruin my plans, I could not resist my curiosity to learn what information, if any, he had uncovered about Duncan's death.

"You may let him in," I said. "But he must keep it brief. We have other important company coming today."

"As you wish," Warrington said with a bow, and started back toward the front door.

Mrs. Bell arched a brow, and I could not be sure whether her stern expression was for Mr. Keats or Mr. Aubrey. "Perhaps that man has finally come with an answer," she said. "And we can shoo Mr. Aubrey away before he even steps foot inside this house."

"I hope so as well," I said. "It would certainly save us a great deal of frustration, wouldn't it?"

Warrington reappeared a few moments later, Mr. Keats right on his heels.

He swept into the room with an elegant, confident grace that gave me pause. Whatever his work might entail, he certainly had the bearing of a gentleman. It was no wonder even clients at elite levels of society felt comfortable dealing with him. Whatever his own background, he had obviously studied our ways and adapted to fit them.

I tipped my chin up ever so slightly as he bowed.

"Good morning, Mrs. Sedgewick. I am pleased to see that you are home."

"I am always at home to those who might bring me important news," I admitted. "It is only to tiresome visitors who have nothing to say that I am out."

"Well then, I am honored you do not suspect me of being one of those," he said, his lips twitching at my honesty.

I offered a stiff smile in return. I must not forget this man worked for old Mr. Sedgewick, not for me. "That remains to be seen," I said. "I hope you have not paid me a visit merely to exchange pleasantries?"

"Certainly not," he said. "I have news regarding the death of your late husband."

"Do you?" I asked. "Would you care to sit?"

"Thank you," he said, as I gestured toward one of the tufted, blue armchairs beside the low table where I had been playing a game of chess with one of the servants the evening before.

Mr. Keats sat and placed the black top hat which had been tucked under his arm onto the table beside my game.

"You play chess?" he asked.

"I do," I said. "And I'm rather good at it, though I say so myself."

"I fancy myself a player as well," Mr. Keats said. "I seem to have a skill for anticipating the next move of my opponents."

"Perhaps it has something to do with your line of work," I said charitably. "You investigate crimes and other sensitive matters, after all. That surely requires foresight."

"I suppose it does," he agreed.

Mrs. Bell stepped forward to ask me, "Shall I fetch some tea, madam? Perhaps you and the gentleman might have a match?"

"Oh, no thank you," he said, in response to my inquiring look. "As much as I would enjoy a rousing game, it has been made clear to me that you are expecting guests soon, and I do not wish to intrude. Besides, it would be quite the disgrace if I were to interrupt the already close game that seems to be still under way here."

"Very well," I said. "Perhaps we had best get to the news that brought you to my door."

"Yes, of course. I am certain you are anxious to hear what I have learned," Mr. Keats said. "And it is good news, I assure you."

"That is most refreshing," I said. "I feel as if all I have heard recently is bad news."

"Indeed," he said. "After my initial inspection of the site of Mr. Duncan Sedgewick's death, and after we stumbled upon that bottle of medicine, I took it upon myself to go and speak to Doctor Higgins about the liquid in question."

I had already assumed as much, but nodded for him to continue.

"In a positive turn of events, the doctor seemed pleased to discuss the medicine, and gave me a full report on all of the treatments he had been trying with your late husband. I received detailed lists of appointments they had kept, including what had occurred at each one. He explained to me that the medicine he gave Mr. Sedgewick before he died had been nothing more than a mild sedative to help him sleep when his opium cravings became too strong. I asked him if he could verify the amount of medicine Mr. Sedgewick would have had to consume for it to negatively affect him, and he told me there was no need. He showed me the bottle, saying he had obtained it once again."

"Yes, that makes sense," I said. "Because it was I who brought him the bottle when I went to ask him a few questions myself."

Mr. Keats paused, his eyes narrowing slightly. "I beg your pardon, but *you* went to speak to Doctor Higgins?"

"Yes, of course," I said, feeling suddenly defensive. "Why shouldn't I? He was my husband's physician, after all. Why wouldn't I be curious about the fact that a bottle of medicine I had never before seen was in the same room where he died?"

"Well, naturally, to be curious is one thing. But to then go and take the investigation into your own hands is another matter entirely," Mr. Keats said. "Mrs. Sedgewick, you must realize that your late husband's death could be part of a much deeper, much more sinister plot than we even realize at this point. And if you are to go around asking for information, you may very well find yourself in a dangerous encounter."

"I am well aware of all that, thank you," I said, my chin tilting higher. "But as Duncan's wife, I feel as if I have a right to know whether or not – "

"You most certainly do," Mr. Keats said. "And no one agrees more than I. However, do not underestimate what people in your circle may be capable of. If someone, most likely a person you know, went so far as to deliberately cause your husband's death, what makes you think they would not do the same to you should they learn of your curiosity?"

I frowned. "They would have to be fools to think I wouldn't be interested in Duncan's death."

"Yes, but it would also be foolish to traipse around the city without caution, asking questions that anyone might be able to overhear," he said. He leaned in more closely to me. "Do you realize that this person may be watching you very closely? If the culprit suspects you know more than you should, then he or she will not hesitate to react."

I swallowed, my throat becoming dry. It was true that I had not seriously considered the possibility. But I was not about to let him know that.

"I do not wish to imply you are incapable, Mrs. Sedgewick, because I am sure you are an intelligent woman. But may I ask you to be patient and allow me to investigate this entire matter for you?" he asked. "I have a great deal of experience in resolving questions surrounding these sorts of tragedies –"

"Crimes," I cut him off.

"What?"

"If my husband's death turns out to be the result of a deliberate act of malice, it will be a crime," I said. "Not a mere tragedy."

"Yes, of course," he agreed. "But there is a point I wished to make."

"Your point, if I'm not mistaken, is that you wish for me to keep out of the way and leave the investigating to you."

"I had not intended to put it so harshly."

"But the sentiment, however phrased, is ultimately the same," I guessed.

"That is true," he admitted. "But it is not my own convenience I think of, only your safety. I promise that I will do my absolute best to find your husband's killer, if such a person exists. I know it may be frustrating to just sit and wait, but it would be best for you. A lady in such a position as yours should not sully her mind with vile matters like death and murder. And that is why your father-in-law hired me. He wished me to do this so that you would have peace of mind, and so that no one in your family need be placed in harm's way."

Can that be true? Does Erasmus truly have my best interests at heart?

I wondered if Mr. Keats also suspected Mr. Aubrey. He spoke of dangerous people who might be watching me, people who would not hesitate to cause me harm. Mr. Aubrey certainly seemed to fit the description of a devious character. The only trouble was that it was difficult to take him seriously. As a potential murderer, Mr. Aubrey did not strike me as very threatening. But then, perhaps it did not require terribly sharp wits or a great deal of courage to kill a man like Duncan.

If I told Mr. Keats about Mr. Aubrey, then he could certainly investigate him for me and determine whether he might be our villain. I wouldn't have to interrogate the man like I've planned.

However...

How can I be certain that Mr. Keats would get at the truth? He's an inquirer, the exact sort of person that Mr. Aubrey would likely flee from, the sort of person even Mr. Aubrey would be clever enough to lie to. At least if I were to question Aubrey, I might catch him in a trap he does not expect. Or he might confess all to me, because of his friendship with Duncan. Guilt could very possibly work in my favor with him.

"I realize this must all be very difficult for you right now," Mr. Keats said. "Naturally, you are still terribly distressed at your recent loss."

Was it my imagination or was there a hint of doubt in his gaze, as if he questioned the depth of my grief?

"Naturally," I said, keeping my voice devoid of emotion.

He couldn't possibly know. How could he guess that I do not mourn my loss as greatly as most widows would?

I considered what he had been saying to me. He was correct, of course. This was his profession. I had never before investigated any death, let alone that of a family member. I had no understanding of stealth or proper conversational techniques to receive the answers I wanted. Mr. Keats might well be able to resolve this matter if I were to simply let him.

But something in me rose up. *A challenge, perhaps. My father-in-law thinks I am incapable. None of this is Mr. Keat's fault. He simply happens to be caught in the middle of this ever growing feud between old Mr. Sedgewick and me. He intends to keep his control over me very clear, even after his son has died.*

Well, no more. I shall get to the bottom of all this on my own. Erasmus can waste all of his money on Mr. Keats, only to find it was entirely fruitless. And that will be the end of it.

"Trust me when I say that I understand what you are going through more than you know," Mr. Keats continued.

I blinked, his words soothing some of the anger toward old Mr. Sedgewick growing within me.

"Thank you for your understanding," I said.

Mr. Keats smiled, but it was a rather sad smile. He then took up his top hat from the table. "I thank you, Mrs. Sedgewick, for your hospitality. Your conversation has been most engaging, as always. I shall be in touch with any new information I happen to find."

"I would appreciate that," I said, with a polite smile.

I did not disclose that the last thing I intended to do was to simply sit and await his reports.

M r. Keats took his leave and departed the house, leaving me relieved at his absence. The man seemed almost able to sense my thoughts at times and I did not wish him to sense them now.

"He was very kind, madam," Mrs. Bell said. "It's clear he wishes to protect you."

"Either that, or my father-in-law wishes to do nothing more than exert his control over me once again," I said. "That is the most likely reason why he hired Mr. Keats in the first place."

"No doubt you have already considered this, madam," Warrington said, having entering the room. "But as he was the late master's father, he may be genuinely concerned that something sinister befell his youngest son. Perhaps he merely wishes to find out the truth in the best way he knows how."

I scowled at my butler's irritatingly rational sugges-tion but could not argue with the logic of it. There was denying old Mr. Sedgewick possessed affection for his sons.

I walked to the window to peer down on Mr. Keats as he descended the front steps of the house and disappeared down the sidewalk.

Exactly how to deal with you, Mr. Keats, is a question I will have to decide at a later date.

IT WAS HALF past noon when our expected guest arrived at the house. I had sent Daniel away with his nanny, the infant seeming content enough to cuddle with her while I was busy.

"Good afternoon, sir," Warrington said, opening the door wide. "Please, won't you come in?"

"I certainly will," came the cheerful sounding voice of Mr. Aubrey. "Mrs. Sedgewick wrote in her note that she found something in her husband's bedroom that didn't look as if it belonged to him. I assume she has entrusted it to you?"

"I'm afraid not, sir," Warrington said. "But I am sure you can ask her about it when you see her in a moment."

I stood just inside the doorway, waiting with a smile fixed upon my face. I mustn't tip him off too soon.

"Welcome, Mr. Aubrey," I said. "How good to see you."

Mr. Aubrey stepped inside, looking around the lavish foyer. "Thank you, Mrs. Sedgewick. It's very kind of you to – "

Warrington closed the front door behind him with a definitive *click.*

Mr. Aubrey looked over his shoulder, as if slightly uneasy upon realizing his means of exit was now barred by Warrington standing before the door.

"I thought you might like to join me for luncheon," I said, gesturing down the hall as I began to walk away. "You must have something to eat before returning to whatever it was you were doing before you came by."

"Oh," Mr. Aubrey said. "I thought I might just stop in and pick up my item from you – "

"It's down here," I said. "In the dining room. Won't you join me?"

He stared at me for a long, hard moment.

Of course he does not believe me, not after the way I treated him when he was here last...

"If you would rather not stay, that's perfectly all right," I said. "I simply thought you might enjoy something after coming all this way."

"Well..." Mr. Aubrey said, glancing once more at the closed door. "I suppose a small morsel wouldn't hurt."

I smirked as I turned away.

I entered the dining room and took my seat at the head of the table. It still felt strange to sit there, after watching Duncan occupy the spot, day after day, during the years we had been married. Adam appeared from nowhere to push my seat in for me, before quickly withdrawing into the shadows with another server to await my needs.

Mr. Aubrey looked around him at the gilded mirror hanging over the fireplace, the silver candlesticks, and the crystal chandelier overhead. When his gaze returned to me, there was speculation in his eyes. "Quite the place you have here, Mrs. Sedgewick. I regret to say I have never before been inside your home."

"A circumstance I am happy to finally put right," I said with a smile. "I am glad you like the design. Duncan was rather proud of this house as well. It is really too bad that we never saw the fruition of our dreams here together, isn't it?"

"Indeed, it is very sad," Mr. Aubrey said, reaching out toward one of the chairs.

A servant stepped forward quickly and pulled it back for him. "Please allow me, sir."

"Oh, all right," Mr. Aubrey said, slipping into the chair. He flinched a little in surprise when the servant then draped a linen napkin over his lap.

He has never been in a dining room like this before. Of course he hasn't. He has never rubbed shoulders with genteel society, unless it was to pick their pockets.

"So...about my item," Mr. Aubrey said. He seemed unsure where to put his hands, so he clasped them tightly in his lap. "May I see it?"

"Of course," I said mildly. "But first, perhaps you would be so kind as to answer a question that has been on my mind."

"A question?" he asked.

"Yes," I said, and my tone became less genial. "Perhaps you can tell me what happened the night that Duncan died?"

Mr. Aubrey's face fell. "I – I have already told you," he

said, sounding a good deal like a small boy caught in a lie. "I didn't see him that night."

"Yes, you did say so before. But the trouble is that you were *lying* to me, Mr. Aubrey," I said calmly.

The room fell silent, the ticking of the clock above the fireplace becoming unnaturally loud in the stillness, as I took a long sip from my glass of water.

Best to give him a moment to worry.

As my guest opened his mouth to protest the accusation, I cut him off by continuing. "You were lying then and you are lying now," I said. "It is of no matter how I know this. I have sources I do not choose to reveal, but the point is that I do know. And I do not take kindly to falsehoods, especially about such an important matter concerning my late husband. I am sure you can appreciate that."

I made a small gesture with my hand, and at once, my servants closed the doors to the dining room, positioning themselves in front of them.

Mr. Aubrey turned and stared at them.

Another servant, likewise, went and stood in front of the door into the kitchen.

"What is all this?" Mr. Aubrey asked, standing up, his chair sliding out from behind him and nearly toppling over. "Mrs. Sedgewick, what is the meaning – "

Again, I cut him off. "Mr. Aubrey, I was kind to you, I thought. Reasonable, even. I asked you questions and expected that you would answer me honestly. And yet, here we are, and you have not done as I wished."

Mr. Aubrey's face paled, and he glanced back and forth between the doors behind him and me.

"Surely you do not mean to hold me here?" he asked. "You cannot possibly. You wouldn't dare."

I gave him a steely look. "I mean to do precisely whatever is necessary to get at the truth."

"I...could report you to the authorities," he suggested halfheartedly.

"You could, once you eventually made it past my servants," I agreed. "But that would require you to draw the attention of the authorities to yourself and your activities, something I suspect a man like you would be most reluctant to do. Instead, you can save yourself and me a great deal of time by merely doing what I want."

I couldn't blame him for looking dismayed. Our cordial meeting had taken a very unexpected turn. I could see him weighing his options, judging whether he could break past my servants, and probably wondering how undignified he would look in the process.

"And what is it that you want?" he asked, much more warily.

Good. He is looking for the easiest way out.

"You already know the answer to that question," I said. "I want you to tell me what happened on the night of Duncan's death."

He hesitated, and I noticed the sweat droplets standing out on his forehead.

"All right, very well," he said suddenly, resuming his seat and nervously adjusting the top button on his shirt. "It is hardly worth making a fuss over. I have kept silent merely out of respect for Duncan's wishes."

I hid a satisfied smile. If I must coerce a man, it

seemed I had chosen the right sort, one who gave way easily under pressure.

"Were you with Duncan that night?" I asked.

"Yes," he admitted, dropping his eyes to the table. "I thought it would spare you distress if I said otherwise, something which Duncan would have preferred... But yes, I was with him."

"And?" I asked when he wasn't any further forthcoming. "Tell me exactly what happened. Spare no details."

"He came down to the docks and met me outside an establishment we sometimes frequented," Mr. Aubrey said. "As was our usual arrangement, he paid me, and I passed him the drug he sought. I followed him inside, and he and I indulged together."

I nodded, unsurprised. This much I had expected. "Then what?" I prompted.

"We were there until just before eleven," he said. "And then we parted ways. I give you my word I know nothing of his activities after that."

"How can I trust you?" I asked. "That leaves the two hours before he came home unaccounted for."

"I realize that," Mr. Aubrey said. "Nonetheless, it is the truth."

"And about the opium you provided him that night..."

"It was no different than usual," he said. "I didn't give him any more than I usually did. In fact, I've been trying to give him less, in order to have more for other clients..." He frowned. "It wouldn't have been enough to kill him."

I sighed, sitting back in my seat to consider the man across from me. He might have some sort of motive to hide the truth, but I was beginning to doubt he possessed the wits or courage to do so.

"Very well, Mr. Aubrey," I said. "I shall allow you to leave for now. But know this. If my sources investigate your claims, and they tell me you were not where you said you were that night, then you will realize just what I am capable of. Do I make myself clear?"

"Perfectly," he said, dabbing at his shiny forehead.

I was glad he was convinced, because I was not at all clear in my own mind as to what I could do if he did prove dishonest. The fact that my "sources" were fabrications designed to frighten him left me with few options.

But there is no need for him to know that.

"Good," I said, gesturing to my servants to step away from the doors. "You may go."

"What about the possession I came to retrieve?" he asked uneasily.

"Mr. Aubrey, I have no doubt that there exists among my husband's belongings some borrowed money or other valuable items you would like to help yourself to, but I have come across no such items, as of yet. I pretended otherwise only as a ruse to bring you here."

His face reddened and he wasted no time in leaving, after that. Hopping up from his chair, he scurried out through the doors as quickly as Warrington and Adam opened them.

I sagged against the back of my chair, sighing.

"Now there is an entire two hours that are unexplained, unaccounted for..." I said to myself. "What am I to make of that?"

S ocial obligations kept me busy over the next few
days. Of course, I could not go about a great deal
in society so soon after Duncan's death, but my
cousin Madeline insisted on having Daniel and I over for
a small, private celebration of Daniel reaching five
months of age. And after that, one of my father's old
friends was retiring from his business and invited me to a
quiet dinner party to mark the occasion.

It was early in the morning of August the twelfth that
I was enjoying a peaceful breakfast with Daniel when
Warrington appeared, carrying a letter on a silver tray
for me.

"Why do you look so dismayed, Warrington?" I asked,
plucking the letter off the plate.

"It is from Mr. Sedgewick, madam," Warrington said,
concern written across his face.

My stomach clenched. "What could he possibly want
with me now?" I muttered.

Perhaps my father-in-law had finally decided to send along the delayed funds I had been expecting.

I peeled open the envelope.

There was indeed money inside, but far less of it than usual.

My dear Victoria, the letter began. *I have taken a great deal of time in pondering the following matter, and would like you to know that I did not arrive at the decision lightly.*

Having considered all the properties that I am responsible for and the fact that I now have more than one household to support, I have realized some sacrifices need to be made.

"Sacrifices?" I reread, alarmed. "But this – this is a pittance!"

There are no longer three of you for me to support, so I am sure you will agree that you will not need quite as much assistance as before. With little Daniel being as young as he is, no doubt his needs are small. And I am sure your own lifestyle and entertainments will become less lavish while you are in mourning.

My hands trembled as I read those words, and I felt all of the confidence I had mustered recently melting away. My father-in-law had long held the threat of reducing our allowance over our heads when Duncan was alive but he had never, until now, actually made good on the threat.

I glanced at the fine furnishings around me, at the elegant stitching of my somber but fashionable gown, and knew that I had no idea how to survive on a reduced income.

Then I thought of my father-in-law living in the big, fine house on his Yorkshire estate, a man who had no shortage of wealth, subtly lecturing me about economies. The letter wrinkled beneath my fingers as I squeezed the paper, sudden anger flooding my veins.

I realize this will come as a shock, but I do hope you know that I have your best interests at heart, and that I am going to continue to take care of you and little Daniel, no matter the financial burden to myself. Of course, some adjustments may need to be made in order for you to continue living in that large house, including releasing some of your staff, but I'm certain a woman as clever as you will find a way to manage –

"What nonsense! I snapped aloud, tossing the letter aside. "This isn't about him lacking the funds, it is about punishing me. He never liked me and, now that Duncan is gone, he feels free to show it."

Warrington, who had been waiting patiently before me, looked unsurprised at my sudden outburst. "I take it the news is not good, madam?" he asked.

"You may as well read the letter for yourself..." I said, indicating the partially crumpled sheet of stationery on the floor. "It involves you." I glanced around at the other servants in the room. "It involves all of you, really."

"All of us?" asked Eliza, who hovered nearby with a sleeping Daniel in her arms.

"Yes, my dearest father-in-law seems to think that just because my husband is dead, I do not need more than half the allowance he had been sending me up to this point," I said.

"But the requirements of running a large London house do not change greatly with the subtraction of one member," Mrs. Bell pointed out.

"He feels the baby is too young to have many needs,

and though he did not say it, much of our expenses were due to Duncan's careless spending..." I said. "The point is that I might have to consider letting some staff go."

I saw nervous glances exchanged between Mrs. Bell, Eliza, and Adam, who stood near the doorway. Warrington remained expressionless at the news but I had known him long enough to guess at his thoughts. My butler was steady and calm, like a deeply rooted tree unchanged by the raging storms. I needed him to manage my household.

"I need all of you," I found myself admitting aloud.

"We would never leave you, madam," Adam said quickly. He looked around at the others. "I would happily take a cut in wages in order to keep my place and remain on staff."

"He is right," Eliza said. "Other work is always available but I have never been treated as well in any other house as in this one. If you will permit it, all of your servants would likely take reduced wages rather than lose their positions."

Mrs. Bell nodded her head. "Of course we would. I have served your family since before you were born, madam, and I mean to go on doing the same."

"As do I," Warrington said with a bow.

I looked from one face to the next, moved by their loyalty.

Nonetheless, I had to be sensible.

"As much as I appreciate your loyalty, the matter is not as simple as that," I said. "Every mouth under this roof has to be fed and there may come a time when I can scarcely cover my own needs and Daniel's."

"Perhaps it will not come to that," Warrington said. "It has not yet, and if it does, we can adapt as the situation requires."

"But what if that is old Mr. Sedgwick's plan?" I asked. "For the money to completely dry up? What if he intends to put me and my son out on the streets?"

"I doubt he would do anything so injurious to his reputation," Warrington said.

He was right. My father-in-law was a proud man and allowing his daughter-in-law and infant grandson to go hungry would scandalize polite society. The story would be on the tongue of every gossip from here to Yorkshire. Besides, he was not as greedy as all that. And I had to remember that, for all his faults, Erasmus did care for his family.

"He will look after us...as long as he can use his wealth to control us," I said, slamming my hand down on the table, making the crystal clink together precariously. "He has long resented that my family had so much more than his did. Now he wishes to remind me that I have come down in the world, even as he has risen. Jealousy drives him."

The room fell silent, as I took a deep breath and tried to calm my thoughts. "I must...I must find a way to set this right. I will not allow that man to hold such control over me. Which means I must find a way to become less dependent upon him. If I earn income of my own, then I will be less reliant on his good will."

It was a strange thought, for I had never before contemplated the idea of earning my own bread. I was not born or raised to consider such a need, my wants having always been supplied by others. Even now, I could not decide whether the thought of becoming financially independent from my husband's family was exciting or frightening. Probably, it was a little of both.

A sharp rapping on the front door out in the hall cut through the tension in the room like a blade.

There was a moment of silence and then Warrington disappeared to go and see who was at the door.

I glowered at my plate, a heaviness settling over my shoulders that I had not experienced in some time. "What am I going to do?" I wondered aloud.

"You will think of something, madam," Mrs. Bell said. "I am certain of it."

I wallowed in my sorrows for a few moments before Warrington returned to the dining room, yet another letter in hand. "A messenger just brought this one from Mr. Keats, madam," he said. "It seems he has more information."

"Perhaps some good news?" I asked, taking the letter from him.

The servants returned to their work, fetching my breakfast, while I unfolded the letter and began to read.

Mrs. Sedgewick. I have not discerned the exact identity of the villain yet, however I have reason to believe your husband's death may have been deliberately caused by someone in your own home.

"What?" I breathed, reading through the words once again.

I have spent many days investigating some men who seemed to know the late Mr. Sedgewick down at the docks. They may be villains, but their stories have all checked out and they were surprisingly open about the deceased and his habits. Unfortunately, this turned out to be nothing more than a dead end.

It appears that your husband had few business partners, as most of his money seemed to come from his father. I had nowhere else to turn but to those he saw on a daily basis.

I managed to speak with a few of your staff while you were out the other day, and while I did not get any definitive answers, something rather strange seemed to be happening the night of the murder. I intend to return as soon as I am able and question each of your staff in full for further information.

I trust you are well, and I will be in contact again soon.

I stared down at the page. He thought it was someone in the house with me who had killed Duncan?

I stared around at the servants in the room, just as I had a few moments before, but with a fresh set of eyes. What if he was right? What if it was one of the members of my own household?

I'd certainly never considered it before, but why hadn't I? They would have had the closest access to Duncan, and it would have been easy enough to act on their intentions...

And yet, what possible motive could any of them have? Most of them had been with me for a long time and I had always been satisfied with their service. It was difficult to accept on so little information that one of the people I counted on for the day to day management of my home could be capable of such a deep betrayal, let alone fathom a reason for it.

My mind went around in circles. Perhaps Mr. Keats was mistaken. After all, I hardly knew the private inquirer, whereas I knew the people around me much better than he did. Then again, was it not the detective's business to discern this sort of thing? Why should I trust my instincts above his, when I had no experience of such dark matters as violence and deception?

"Madam?" Adam asked as he returned to the table, a bowl full of porridge in his hands. He peered down at me with concern. "You look distressed. Are you feeling unwell?"

"I am fine, of course," I said, folding the letter and hiding it in my lap. "Perfectly all right."

What was I going to do?

13

I t was time for me to take matters into my own hands. As much as I would have wished for help, I knew I needed to push forward on my own.

I can trust Warrington and Mrs. Bell, can I not?

I snuck a glance at my faithful butler, who was standing nearby. Always watchful for my smallest needs, always ready to serve, always quick to shield me from any unpleasant knowledge or painful task. He had never failed me in any way that I could recall.

My gaze moved to Mrs. Bell, certainly an unconventional housekeeper in some ways, a woman who almost forgot her place at times and assumed a role that was more maternal toward me than servant-like. At times it was as if my house was hers, my family her own. And yet, how could I not trust someone who had been so near at hand for so many years, always determined to protect me from the slightest hurt or inconvenience?

Yes, surely I can trust the two of them. I must be mad to

think otherwise for one second. If there is any truth to this report against my staff, it must be one of the others...

I thought I could trust them all, and yet the inquirer had shed light on something I had never considered. Was I too blind? Was I unwilling to look at what was right under my nose?

Not any longer, I won't be. In order to get to the bottom of this, I need to question everything and everyone I know.

I decided not to send a return message to Mr. Keats, out of fear that one of the staff might see me and wonder what I was doing. Possibly that person might even report my message to others. I realized that would very likely spoil my plans.

I needed to tread carefully. My initial intention to solve this matter had been born out of a sense of duty toward my late husband and toward Daniel, so that I could give my son the full story when he grew old enough to ask questions about his father's death. And yes, maybe my determination had been hardened by a slight vindictiveness toward my father-in-law, for his interference in my life. Perhaps I had wished to prove I had no use for the private inquiry agent he had hired, that I did not require his meddling to uncover the facts about what had occurred beneath my own roof.

But now, it had all become more than that. With the knowledge that a murderer might well be living under the same roof as me and my son, I knew that this person needed to be found as quickly as possible. We might all be in danger here. Well, all of us except the killer...

I went upstairs and tucked Daniel in for a nap after a good feeding. I instructed Eliza to keep an eye on him.

"Are you going out, madam?" the nanny asked innocently.

I hesitated at the simple question. Was I to do this from now on, every time a servant asked me anything, always wondering if there was an ulterior motive for the question?

I shook my head at the notion. I was being overly suspicious. If no one else in this household was trustworthy, at least I could be sure of the person who spent the most time with my baby, watching over him. Couldn't I?

"I – " I said. "No, I am not leaving the house. I simply need some time alone with my thoughts. All of the sorrow and difficulty of these past weeks is finally starting to sink in, and I...I need a little time to gather myself."

The girl nodded sympathetically. "Of course, madam. You must take as much time as you need. And don't you worry about the little master here. I shall look after him as if he were my own son. I always do."

For some reason, her words sent a shiver of apprehension down my spine, instead of comforting me, but I shook off the feeling. I was being foolish now, seeing sinister intentions and hidden meanings where there were none. I could not afford to let my fears chase away my good sense. Daniel had always been perfectly safe in Eliza's gentle care and he would remain so.

Or would he?

I knotted my hands in the fabric of my dress as I marched down the hall.

Don't allow yourself to be too sentimental, no matter how

long a servant has been here. That is precisely what will prevent you from seeing the truth.

It was a difficult balance, to avoid jumping at shadows, but also to question what I had thought I knew about all of these people I came into daily contact with.

The nursery was just as I had left it the last time I was there. I had asked the maids to leave it be during the investigation, in case Mr. Keats needed to look at it again later.

Insisting the door remain closed, Warrington had given me the key to ensure that no one could get in. Had he also suspected that one of the staff could have been involved in Duncan's sudden death? If so, why had he said nothing to me? Perhaps he did not wish to distress me with a mere suspicion that could well prove false.

Or did he have some motive of his own for discouraging anyone from entering the room again, a guilty conscience or something to hide?

I shoved the uncomfortable question down deep, but it continued to gnaw at the edges of my mind.

I stepped inside, the lock giving easily with the turning of the key. I hoped I could one day have Daniel's cradle removed from this place, as well as some of his toys when he grew bigger. It seemed wrong for him to sleep and play in the same space where his father had died. Eventually, I would have one of the spare bedrooms cleared out for him, as a new nursery.

For now, I examined the room. I searched everything as thoroughly as we had the day that Mr. Keats had come to inspect the space. Frustratingly, but unsurprisingly, I found nothing new of note. Had I really expected it to be that simple?

*If only I had the eyes to see the missing pieces in the same way Mr. Keats seems to...*I thought, struggling to my feet as I stared around the room once again. There was nothing strange. Nothing beneath the cradle, nothing underneath the chair, or the rug. Nothing looked unusual or out of place.

After an hour of searching to no avail, I decided to make my way down the hall once more to Duncan's room.

It was across the hall from my own bedroom, but I had rarely visited the place. Duncan had tended to keep his things untidy and did not like the servants to clean often, preferring his privacy. As such, I rarely disturbed him when he shut himself away in there, sometimes for days at a time.

As I reached out for the door knob, I felt as if I were intruding, even though Duncan was no longer alive to know the difference. I shoved the feeling aside and continued.

It smelled of dust and stale drink in the room as I pushed the door open. It was as messy within as I had expected, with clothing strewn about on every surface. Letters and other various documents were piled in a leaning stack on the desk at the far end of the room beneath the window. Slivers of sunlight peeked out from behind the edges of the thick drapes that were drawn shut, their narrow beams illuminating dust motes that danced in the air.

I wrinkled my nose. The room reminded me of him, and it was not in a pleasant way.

I threw open the drapes and stared around at the disgusting space, its details now revealed by full daylight.

Setting my hands on my hips, I sighed.

This is going to take an eternity to sift through.

It did indeed.

I looked over everything he owned. Every letter, every paper. The first thing I managed to find of note were love letters from two different women I had never heard of, but whose existence I had always suspected. The letters were undated, so I could only guess whether they had been written recently or whether he had kept them from before our marriage.

Either way, I felt strangely detached as I sorted through them, as if they had little to do with me. Duncan and I had never pretended any great love for one another anyway, and I had always believed I was not the first or last woman in his life.

Could either of these women have had some personal motive for killing him?

It was hard to guess, but I decided it was unlikely, as Mr. Keats had made no mention of them as potential suspects. Surely he must have uncovered their existence and relation to Duncan, and yet he had said nothing of them to me. Was that merely to spare the feelings of a grieving widow, or because the affairs were not relevant to the case? I did not know Mr. Keats or his methods well enough to be sure.

Still, I dismissed the love letters for now, setting them aside and moving on. There were a number of overdue payment notices from several debtors. That aroused my suspicions briefly, until I considered that a debt holder had little reason to kill my husband. After all, with Duncan dead, the chances of collecting on the debt likely sank lower, rather than increased. Besides, a few minutes later, I discovered a note from Mr. Aubrey congratulating Duncan on escaping his debt. It seemed the chief person to whom he owed money had himself been arrested by the police for some minor crime or other, freeing Duncan from the need to repay him for the time being.

I sighed and moved away from the papers. It seemed I would find nothing truly revealing in them, nothing that would incriminate any of my husband's friends or associates, let alone members of our own household.

I checked the pockets of his waistcoats and jackets, finding only dirty handkerchiefs and a fistful of spare change.

It was nearly dusk by the time I sat in the middle of the room, entirely exhausted, and realized I was not going to find the answers there.

"You certainly had enough secrets, Duncan…" I said into the emptiness. "But none of them worth killing you for."

I decided it was best for me to give up for the time being. Mentally and emotionally wearied, I needed a rest. At least I now had a little more information to digest, even if I could not see at the moment how any of it was terribly useful.

I went to look in on Daniel, but found that Eliza had already fed him and put him back to sleep.

So much for my silly misgivings. He is as safe under his nanny's care as he would be under my own...

I eyed the servant with new appreciation, feeling slightly guilty for the suspicious thoughts I had entertained about her earlier. "Thank you for sitting with him, Eliza."

"Of course, madam. What use would I be if I did not do my job?" she asked cheerfully.

I was hungry but did not wish to go through all the trouble of having a formal meal that evening. Now that I always dined alone, I sometimes thought it was hardly worth the servants taking the time to set the table. Perhaps in future I would go to taking dinner on a tray in my room, at least occasionally.

For now, I slipped down the back stairs and wandered down to the kitchens to have something small. It was not as if I had much appetite after reading some of those letters of Duncan's...

In any house, kitchens were some of my favorite places to explore as a child. I had loved the way they always smelled like baking breads and sweets, and how in the autumn the burning wood warded off the cold encroaching from outside. Even as an adult, I appreciated the comfort such spaces brought, though I did not visit them often anymore.

I stepped inside and found Corbyn, our cook, whistling away in front of the stove against the far wall in the corner. He was a large man with almost no neck, and a mop of ginger hair that seemed to curl with a mind of its own. His hands, the size of a bear's paws, skillfully worked a ball of dough out on the counter in front of himself, his tune quickly turning into a sea song.

"*Onward we sail, fast as she goes, 'til the ocean replies, and puffs and blows –* "

He looked up as I sat down in one of the stools nearest him, ready to listen to his songs as I so often did when I was younger.

His broad smile split his face, and he threw back his head and laughed. "Well, look what the cat's brought in. It's grand to see you, Miss Victoria."

Unlike the rest of my servants, he had never adapted to my married name or picked up the formalities of serving in a large house. He was the same simple and jovial man today that he had been years ago.

He went on. "I was mighty surprised when you didn't order dinner tonight. Is anything amiss?"

"Not at all," I said. "I was simply too tired to face a large meal. Besides, it's been too long since I've looked in down here."

He grinned again. "Are you hungry? Can I feed you anything?"

"Something small would be all right," I said. "I do not have much of an appetite these days…"

His bushy, orange eyebrows drew together in sudden concern. "You mustn't starve yourself now, Miss. Little in life is worth harming your health."

I knew it was as close as he would come to voicing the opinion that Duncan was not deserving of my grief. It was well enough known that my husband hadn't had the respect of the entire household, and I had always sensed that Corbyn in particular had not thought well of him.

The big man set a bowl of soup and a spoon before me, and I sipped lightly. It was delicious and soothing. Exactly what I needed to clear my mind from all the suspicions and questions that had been chasing themselves in circles all day.

I looked up at Corbyn, and a thought occurred to me. "Corbyn, I don't know if anyone has already spoken to you or not," I said, thinking of Mr. Keats. "But can you tell me of anything unusual that happened on the night Mr. Sedgewick died? Were you awake? Did you see anything strange?"

"Strange? Oh yes indeed," Corbyn said, sitting down in the stool beside mine. "The master decided to come in through the kitchen entrance that night. I can only guess why..."

I knew exactly why, I thought. Duncan undoubtedly hoped that if he crept into the house stealthily enough, I would already be asleep and wouldn't lecture him about the lateness of his return. A plan that became pointless, of course, when he soon forgot it and wandered in on me and Daniel upstairs.

"I was still awake, preparing a roast for the next evening, because it needed to cook all through the night," Corbyn continued. "That's how I saw him come in by the back door."

"That is more or less what Adam and Mr. Tulson told me," I said. "Though Adam did not see him arrive, of course."

Corbyn's brow furrowed. "How could he not? The lad came in through the kitchen just moments after Mr. Sedgewick did. He could hardly have missed seeing him.

I don't think the boy noticed me off in the pantry, though, because he was sneaking all quiet, as if not to disturb anyone."

My gaze sharpened. "Is that so? He told me he had been working out in the stables when he heard the nanny's scream through the open nursery window."

"The stables?" Corbyn asked. "He couldn't have been there. He was in the stables earlier in the evening, yes, but as I said, he was in the kitchens right after Mr. Sedgewick came home. Where he went after that, I don't know."

I frowned. "Why would he tell me he was out in the stables, if it wasn't true?" I asked.

"I've no notion," Corbyn said. "Perhaps he was referring to earlier?"

I shook my head. "That's not what he said..."

Corbyn shrugged. "I wouldn't think too much on it, Miss Victoria. That boy doesn't have his head on straight sometimes. The death and all could have frightened him into misspeaking."

"True..." I said, chewing on my lower lip in thought.

But why should Adam be nervous enough to misspeak when no one had accused him of any wrong-doing? As far as he knew, the master of the house had been suddenly taken ill and passed away. There was no cause for anyone who believed the death to be natural to go inventing false explanations of where they were when it occurred. Why would he deny having seen Duncan that night?

There was only one way to find out.

"Thank you, Corbyn, for this delicious meal," I said,

staring down at my half-eaten bowl of soup and a plate of barely touched mashed parsnips. "I'll be happy to finish it tomorrow, if there's any left."

He smiled. "It's all right, Miss Victoria. There are some hungry pups out back that might be happy to have a bit of what you enjoyed tonight. Why don't you go get some rest? You look as if you could use it."

"Thank you, perhaps I will," I said.

But as I swiveled around off the stool and headed out of the kitchen, I knew the last thing I would do was get any sleep tonight. I had much to lie awake and ponder...

14

The next morning, I decided to head down to the stables and inspect them for myself. After all, Duncan had passed by them on his way through the garden to the kitchen door, hadn't he? Who was to say he had not entered them or lingered outside their doors, that night?

Of course, it would not be consistent with Adam's claim that he himself had been in the stables at the time, but perhaps the servant had stepped away for a short time and missed Duncan. Or perhaps Adam had been lying altogether about where he had been. If I could not trust my staff, as Mr. Keats' message had implied, surely that might include Adam as well? Especially in light of his having lied about not seeing Duncan entering the kitchen, when Corbyn seemed certain that he had.

I waited until most of my staff went about their chores, including Adam, who seemed busy with instructions from Mr. Tulson on waxing the floors in the foyer.

Knowing I wouldn't be disturbed, I slipped out the

door of the kitchen when Corbyn's back was turned, and made my way across the back garden.

I looked out for anything unusual as I crossed the muddy ground, any footprints that seemed out of place, any small scraps of fabric caught in the hedges, any item of Duncan's that might have been dropped on the night he died. I did not know exactly what I hoped to find, anything out of the ordinary, I supposed. But I saw nothing that struck me as suspicious, and so I moved on into the building itself.

Our stables were small and most of the stalls stood empty, as we only kept one horse nowadays, a concession to the times and the ease and affordability of hansom cabs. In my father's day, he had kept a carriage and four horses, but it was difficult to justify such expense any longer.

I found my mare, Brookmire, peering out over the door to her stall, anxiously waiting for me.

"Hello, girl," I said, hurrying to her and laying my hand on her nose.

She snuffled into my hand, a contented sound, and waited for me to rub the side of her face, which I happily did.

"I wish now more than ever that you could talk, old girl," I said, leaning in close and whispering to her. "You might have the exact answer I need to unravel this whole mystery..."

I found a few dried apples, which she accepted with great excitement, and then turned my attention to the rack that held her saddle.

I had not been riding for some weeks now. In fact, I

was almost certain I hadn't taken her out since before Duncan died. It had been on that outing through Hyde Park that the saddle strap had broken.

I reached up and touched the leather, recalling that Adam had said he had mended it.

With a small tug, however, the broken piece came undone again.

So he lied about repairing the saddle that night... Or perhaps he simply did a poor job of it?

There was one other place that I still had to look.

The basket of oats stood nearly to my waist. Hand-woven and beautifully made, my mother had ordered it made as a gift before she had died, as a way to encourage my riding habits.

I knelt down beside it and ran my hand over the inter-woven thin, wooden strips.

Each and every one of them was where it should be, as if the basket had never been damaged.

Adam said it had been destroyed that night...and that was why he was out here when Duncan returned. He said he never saw Duncan come home.

And yet...Corbyn said that he had followed Duncan inside.

So who was lying to me?

My heart began to beat faster as I looked around. I was still entirely alone, but I suddenly felt as if the footman might be around the corner, waiting for me.

Why in the world would Adam have done anything? He's younger even than I and has very little experience of the world. What would turn the thoughts of one so young toward violence? What could inspire him to take Duncan's life?

Surely there must be some innocent explanation for the evidence building before my eyes.

The sound of a door opening at the far end of the stables startled me, and I threw myself into a gap in the wall between Brookmire's stall and the rack of saddles.

Relatively well hidden, I peered through the straps of the saddle and saw Adam at the far end, muttering to himself under his breath.

"...waxing the *entire* foyer today? He must be mad..."

He tossed a mop aside forcefully, and then sagged against the wall.

He continued to mutter, though much of it was too quiet for me to hear, until I distinctly heard him say my name.

Victoria...

I could not recall him ever addressing me so to my face. Before my marriage, I had been "Miss Victoria" and later "madam" or "Mrs. Sedgewick," but never just "Victoria". He said it as if we were social equals and somehow better acquainted than we truly were. As if we were friends.

I held my breath as he stepped closer to me, still mumbling as he rummaged through one of the shelves of baskets, looking for goodness knew what.

I frowned as he cursed under his breath, slamming one of the baskets further to the back.

This was a side of him I had never before seen. I was used to the respectful, devoted worker that he always was, someone who leaped to help, someone who went above and beyond what he was instructed to do.

Was this who he truly was? An angry young man, bitter and harsh?

"...Not that Victoria would think it of me," I heard him whisper. "Would she, Brookmire? No, she would never think me foolish or – "

He stopped suddenly, and stared around.

I bit down on my lip so hard I tasted blood on my tongue. Attempting to shift my position as one of the stirrups of the saddle had been digging into my side, I had caused the floorboard beneath my foot to creak slightly.

Adam's gaze searched the room, his eyes darting back and forth.

"Brookmire, was that you?" he asked, taking a few steps toward me.

The mare, as if in response, whinnied, shaking her gorgeous grey mane. Her hoof scuffed against the bottom of her stall, making nearly the same sound that my own foot had against the floor.

I sighed with relief. *I know you don't understand what you just did, Brookmire...but you very well may have saved me from an embarrassing moment. I cannot imagine how I would have explained my presence here...*

Adam seemed satisfied as well and turned away, walking back down the hall he had entered through.

I had never been that far, but I was aware it was where some of the staff had their living quarters, as there were not enough rooms in the big house itself.

Adam began to hum, low and out of tune, from one of the rooms at the end of the hall.

I chanced a look out from my hiding space, and found the coast was clear.

It would be best for me to make my escape now, before he notices me.

And then I heard his voice again, echoing down the hall so faintly that I could barely make it out. Was he speaking to someone else? To himself? Or perhaps rehearsing a conversation he meant to have later? I strained my ears to hear more.

"Oh, Victoria...if only this unpleasant business could be put behind us. Then perhaps I could – "

Whatever he said after that was lost as Brookmire began to whinny once again.

I glowered over at the wall separating her from me. *So much for your help...*

Now I had no choice but to see what he was up to.

"...If only you knew what it was doing to me...how it was killing me..." Adam continued.

I frowned. He might only be conversing with an imaginary version of me, nonetheless, it was entirely inappropriate for him to do so in such a way. He was a footman and I was mistress of the house. It seemed that, when he was alone, he forgot the roles we both occupied.

I straightened and marched down the hall, for a moment thinking I would remind him of his place.

He returned to his humming, and I stopped short as I came to the open doorway and peered inside.

The room beyond was quite cramped, with nothing more than a bed, a small desk, and a tiny window overlooking the back garden. As sparse as the furniture was, it astounded me the amount of clutter that filled the space.

And it was not just any sort of clutter.

Hanging from the wall was a shawl of deepest blue.

With a start, I recognized it as a gift I had received for my eighteenth birthday. Made of handwoven silk and dyed with the petals of my favorite irises, it had been nearly six month since I'd seen it. I had thought I'd lost it on an excursion to the center of London.

Atop the desk rested a pair of white gloves, the finger-tips stained pink from the juice of strawberries. My cousin Madeline and I had gone berry picking nearly two summers ago, and I had left the gloves out to dry in the sun, only to find them gone the next morning. I had assumed Mrs. Bell had taken them to clean and had never been able to get the juice from the cloth.

On the bedside table, there was a glint of gold. As I focused on it, I realized it was a pocket watch that had once belonged to my father. A memento of his, one of the few things that I had kept after his death, I had assumed when it went missing that Duncan had stolen and sold it for money. I had accused him even, and when he denied it, we had quarreled.

Silence pressed in against me, as I considered the meaning of all these items of mine collected together and stored in what was apparently Adam's living quarters...

The humming had stopped.

Not until I looked up did I realize that Adam had spotted me standing there in the doorway. His wide eyes searched my face, his own having drained of all color.

For a moment, all I could do was stare back, dumb-founded.

"Miss – Miss Victoria," Adam exclaimed, a nervous hitch in his voice. "I – What are you doing here?"

I contemplated turning around and running away but knew that with my heavy skirts hampering me, I would not get far. I must try a different tactic.

"I think the better question is what are *you* doing, Adam?" I asked. My voice was steady, but sharp. "All of these things, *my* things, belong in the house. How in the world did you come by them?"

Although I sounded calm, my heart was pounding in my ears. In this moment, I could think of only one interpretation for my servant's actions, and it was a dangerous one. I was acutely aware that we were alone in a somewhat isolated location. But if I kept distracted and on the defensive long enough, surely some of the other servants would wander out here, eventually.

Adam looked all around the room. "Oh, all these? It's

– well, of course, madam, it isn't at all what it looks like –
"

"And what might that be?" I pressed. "Tell me, Adam, what does it look like? And how, exactly, is it not what it seems to be?"

He took a step backward, bumping into the chair at his desk, sending it skidding into the wall behind him.

"Well?" I asked, glancing pointedly over at the gloves resting on the desk once more. It seemed that my strategy of intimidation was working, for now. "I am waiting, Adam."

Even as I spoke, my mind was still racing to make sense of the situation. Could it be? After all my wondering, searching, and agonizing, I had stumbled upon the identity of the killer almost by chance?

But Adam...how could it have been him? One of my most loyal servants...

It seemed that Mr. Keats was correct in his assessment of others. *Sometimes the least likely suspects are those we need be most wary of.* How right he had been.

"I would like an explanation for how my things came to be here," I prompted further. I took a step toward Adam, making no attempt to hide my displeasure at his betrayal.

He stumbled backward away from me. His hands grazed against the bottom of the shawl hanging from the wall, and my anger spiked.

I reached across to the wall and yanked it down, the nail holding it in place tearing a hole in it several inches long.

"Do you see what you've done?" I asked, my voice

growing in volume. "This was a gift from my mother before she died. And you hang it up here as if it belonged on some sort of – some sort of shrine!"

Somewhere in the back of my mind, I wondered if I should be calling for help, instead of confronting him. But anger had taken hold of me now. All the days and nights of fear and frustration since Duncan's death had been building up to this moment, and I could no longer hold back my emotions.

"I – I'm sorry," Adam said, looking cornered and desperate. "Please don't tell anyone. I never meant to distress you – "

"And how could stealing my things and hoarding them not distress me?"

"I meant no harm," Adam protested. "I just – I just – "

He seemed out of breath, like a man who had been running a long way, rather than one who remained trapped inside a small room.

"He – he never treated you well," he said, his gaze become distant and crazed. "He never treated you as you deserved."

I hesitated. "...Duncan?" I asked.

Adam's eyes snapped over to me, and I saw a nearly hysterical glint in their depths. There were no traces of his usual cheerfulness, no evidence that he had ever been the pleasant, dependable servant I had always known him to be.

"It was wrong...so wrong..." he said, running his fingers over his face. "He had everything he could ever have wanted, and he – he did nothing but torment and abuse you. And then you had your son, and he was even worse – "

Though he was right in his assessment of Duncan's behavior, I wasn't ready to openly agree with him. In fact, Adam's sudden change in manner seemed so strange, so unrecognizable, that it unnerved me. It almost did not seem real.

"Why did it matter to you how he treated me?" I asked. "Why should it have anything to do with you or your duties?"

"Surely you already know the answer to that..." Adam said. "Miss Victoria, don't you see?" His eyes grew wider, so wide I thought they might leave his skull.

He took a step toward me, and a shiver ran down my spine.

"Miss Victoria...I have loved you for all these years. Everything I have done has been to protect you – "

"Adam, have you taken leave of your senses?" I asked, genuinely shocked.

"No..." Adam said, a flush rising in his cheeks as if he were intoxicated. "In these past few weeks, I have never been surer of myself. I am a hero...and I have saved you, Miss Victoria."

I took an uneasy step backward. It was one thing to suspect him of killing Duncan, but now that he seemed on the verge of admitting it, I found myself unprepared to hear the words.

"I assure you, Adam, you have done no such thing – "

"I certainly have," Adam said. "You do not know the truth, for if you did, you would be grateful to me. You would love me for it."

"Adam – " I began, but my foot caught on the hem of my dress, causing me to stumble backward.

As Adam moved forward, I could not be sure if he was coming to help or harm me. He no longer looked like himself. His eyes, now glassy, seemed lifeless and vacant. A smile stretched across his once handsome face, parting his lips and revealing teeth that seemed ready to snap.

I sidestepped out of the room so quickly that I collided clumsily with the wall across the hall. My blood pounded in my ears, and the room spun.

"Stay away from me," I ordered him, grasping at the wall to stay upright.

My fingers closed around the handle of a broom, and I immediately yanked it off its hook on the wall. In one swift swipe through the air, I had the end of the broom pointed at Adam's chest, forcing him to keep his distance from me. It was a sorry excuse for a weapon, but I was in no position to be particular.

"What did you mean that I would be thanking you for what you did?" I asked. "What happened?"

I already knew the answer to that question, or thought I did, but would always be in doubt until he truly confessed. However I dreaded the answer, there was no escaping my need to know.

Adam's smile stretched further up his face, and he took hold of the opposite end of the broom with both hands. "I was the one who disposed of your husband, of course."

My breath caught in my throat, but I could not afford to be paralyzed with emotion. Not now.

I nodded, trying to slow my racing heart. "Yes...of course you did. Tell me about that."

"I only wish I had been clever enough to think of it from the start," Adam said obligingly. He offered a laugh that made the small hairs on my neck stand up. "I certainly could have saved myself a great deal of agony... but more than that, Miss Victoria, I could have rescued you from so much pain, from so many secret tears."

His words chilled me. Adam was not some stranger who had happened to stumble into my life. No, he was intimately aware of my day to day, someone who had been present to witness many of the most painful events in my life. Even at times when I had imagined myself alone, in moments that I had assumed were private, how much had he seen? How often had he been there, listening at the other side of a door?

Of course I had thought all of my staff trustworthy. I had made no great effort to hide things from them. They were loyal to me, after all, there to serve and help me. If I could not trust them, who could I trust?

And so, Adam had seen me quietly grieving over the loss of my marriage, the loss of my son's father, well before Duncan had actually died.

"You are saying that you killed my husband?"

I asked it as calmly as I could from the other end of a broomstick. I must make him say it aloud, I must leave no doubt.

Adam nodded. "Brilliant, isn't it?"

"But why?" I asked. "How could you do something so
– "

"Courageous? Right?" he asked, pulling the broom,

and myself, closer to him. "I enacted justice that was long overdue."

"How?" I repeated.

"Oh, well that was easy," he said. "I knew of his weakness for opium, so I was already prepared, merely waiting for the right moment. It came when he returned home that night and I recognized he already did not have his wits about him. I lured him here into the stables, where I offered him more of the stuff. I promised it was a special kind, which it was, because it was laced with poison…"

My grip on the broom became weak, my hands trembling. Maybe I had not exactly loved Duncan, but it was still difficult to hear his end described so gleefully.

"After he took the stuff, I asked how he felt, and he said he felt better than ever," Adam continued. "I followed him back into the house to be sure he made it. I could hardly have him collapsing so close to the stables, could I? He made it in through the kitchen all right and well…we know the rest."

I didn't even know how to respond. What could I say to such a story?

"You…" I said, and realized my voice was shaking slightly. "I never thought you capable of planning such a thing…"

"Well, of course I cannot take all the credit," he admitted. "If I had not been told that with the master alive you and I could never be together, then I might not have gone through with it."

"What do you mean?" I asked, confused. "Are you saying someone suggested the idea to you?"

Adam turned his gaze to me, a light returning to his

eyes almost as if he were coming out of a stupor, as if he were just seeing me for the first time.

"I…" he said, removing one hand from the broom to run his fingers down the side of his face. He left angry, red trails behind as his nails scraped against his skin. "I don't know. Someone sat next to me at the pub one night. He bought me a few drinks and we fell to talking. I suppose I told him my troubles and he gave advice. I never…got his name."

"But this person definitely encouraged you to commit a murder?" I asked.

Adam's fingers seemed to have a life of their own. His nails dug into his skin, and blood began to bead up on the surface, streaking across his cheek as he continued to run his fingers over it. "He told me that if you found out – oh, it would be bad if you ever found out, that you could never find out – "

"Adam, listen to me," I said, trying to calm him. "This is important. Did the man you spoke with know specifically who I was? Who Duncan was? Did you tell him who you worked for?"

Adam didn't seem to hear my questions. He stared around wildly, his other hand letting go of the broom.

It sent me backward, further down the hall. The broom handle flew from my grip as I fell against the wall, attempting to steady myself.

"No – no, this is bad," Adam ranted. "You – you shouldn't know the truth. You have to forget it. I cannot let you know that I killed him. Why would you ever love me if you knew I had killed your husband?"

I wouldn't ever love you, you fool, not if you were the last person on this earth.

The dangerous glint in his eyes warned me, so that I turned around, drew my skirts up to my knees, and ran.

"No!" he shouted. "No, you cannot – you must not tell *anyone* what I told you!"

It didn't matter. I had every intention of leaving this place and finding help, if only I could get out in time before he caught me.

I raced down the length of the hall, trying to reach the door at the end. *Just a bit farther – just a bit farther –*

Something yanked on the back of my skirt, causing me to pitch forward.

I flailed outward with my hands and managed to grab onto the latch of Brookmire's stall.

The startled mare bucked and neighed as I struggled to free myself.

"You must not, Miss Victoria," he said. "You cannot go and tell anyone – "

I tugged myself forward as hard as I could, and the force of my pulling managed to undo the latch of Brookmire's stall.

The door flew open, knocking me clear to the ground.

Immediately, the thunderous sound of horse hooves and the whoosh of air as the mare leaped over me made me curl into a ball. I covered my head with my arms, half expecting to be struck by a hoof.

Brookmire landed on the other side of me, and I looked up through the dust to see the panicked animal rearing on her hind legs, hooves flailing.

Adam screamed in fear. "Brookmire, no – "

He was cut off by a squelching *thump*, like the sound of a cracked watermelon, followed by the heavy *thud* of his knees striking the floor.

From where I lay in the dust, I watched as his body collapsed to the ground, a bloody wound on the side of his head, where Brookmire had struck him.

The horse landed on the ground between us, shaking out her mane, and then ambled away to sink her nose into a basket of oats.

I could do nothing except lie there trembling...all the while becoming far too aware of the metallic tang of blood in the air.

"Can I get you anything, madam? Perhaps some tea? Or a fruit tart?"

I looked up from the book I had been trying to distract myself with, a riveting tale about a man's adventures around the known world by railroad. I smiled wearily at Warrington as I closed the book, my finger holding my spot between the two pages. "No, thank you. I'm quite comfortable here, just grateful for the peace and quiet for now."

Warrington glanced over at the bassinet beside me. "It appears little Master Daniel has finally fallen asleep?"

I nodded. "Yes. I think all the commotion here this morning is what troubled him so."

"Very likely," Warrington said.

"Is Mr. Keats still here?" I asked.

"Yes," Warrington said. "He wished to speak with you one last time before he departs."

"Very well," I said. "And Brookmire? Is she all right?"

Warrington nodded. "Yes. She has been moved to

Myers stable down the street for the time being, and we have ensured that she has been cleaned and calmed."

My stomach clenched, but I forced a smile regardless. "I'm pleased to hear it."

Warrington looked thoughtful. "You know, it's quite remarkable how she stepped in to save you like that, madam," he said. "She must have sensed his intentions, and known you needed help."

"Yes, well, we mustn't attribute too much intelligence to the instincts of an animal," I said. "She was likely only startled into flailing out. Still, I suppose in a way I owe her my life, don't I?"

"I suppose you do, madam," Warrington said.

He fell silent for a moment then, and I knew we were both thinking of Adam.

"I never would have expected him to be capable of such a thing," Warrington said.

"Nor I," I said. "It was all so strange, like a bad dream..."

Corbyn had found me as I stumbled back into the house a short while after Adam had been struck by Brookmire. I had no earthly idea if Adam was alive or not, but I had no desire to stay and find out. Corbyn had helped me to the parlor, where I summoned the other staff and explained to them what had happened.

The doctor had been called to the house, as well as the authorities, though none had stayed long. Just long enough to collect Adam's lifeless body and hear my explanation of events, which to my relief, they did not seem inclined to doubt.

Mr. Keats was sent for soon after, as I hoped he would

examine the evidence and confirm my story to the authorities, should they later require further convincing.

"You were right after all, it seems," I had said to the inquiry agent, on his arrival. "It was one of my own staff, someone I had expected to be loyal to me 'til the end."

Mr. Keats had given me a grave look. "Unfortunately, it is not uncommon for this sort of behavior to occur in those who are closest to us."

"How did you work out that the danger came from within the house?" I asked him.

"By eliminating other possible sources," he said. "I knew that I only needed another afternoon, perhaps two with your staff, and I would uncover the truth."

After that, he had gone out to the stables to inspect the scene and whatever evidence the police may have left behind. I did not choose to accompany him, as I knew I would not wish to return to that place any time soon. It felt strange to know that there were now two places in my home that would forever be tainted by death.

"You know, Warrington..." I mused now. "If we are not careful, people are going to start claiming this house is haunted."

My butler offered a hint of an amused smile. "Perhaps they will, madam. That ought to keep the ruffians away."

I laughed, surprising myself. I had assumed it would be a long time before I could make such a sound again, but already relief seemed to be easing the dark clouds that had settled over me since Duncan's murder.

Footsteps out in the hall drew my attention, and Mr. Keats appeared in the doorway.

He tucked his hat beneath his arm before ducking into the room.

"Are you finished with your inspection, Mr. Keats?" I asked.

"Yes," he said. "And I discovered everything precisely as you described. I found your belongings in the footman's room, as well as a rather bizarre journal that I will not be sharing with you out of respect for your sanity."

A shiver crawled down my spine. "Very well. I shall defer to your discernment."

He nodded, pocketing the small, leather bound book. "I spoke with the police on their way out and they told me the cause of death, trauma to the head, was quite clear and was also confirmed by the doctor you summoned. At least the four-legged killer was cooperative."

"My horse will not be punished, will she?" I asked.

"It is unlikely the authorities will pursue anything like that," he said. "The animal was protecting her mistress, after all. Unless you feel threatened by her, I see no need to do anything other than perhaps give her a few extra sugar cubes at dinner."

He gestured to a chair beside me.

"May I?"

"Of course," I said, setting my book down on the side table nearby.

He took his seat. "So, what gave it away?" he asked.

"What do you mean?" I asked.

"That the killer was your footman," he said. "How did you figure it out?"

"Well...I spoke with our cook, and after hearing his

story from the night Duncan died, I realized that what he said and what Adam said did not match. For instance, Adam claimed that Brookmire had knocked over her basket of oats, ruining it. He also claimed to have repaired her saddle. When I went into the stable to verify the truth of his words, I found he had lied about them both. Then I happened upon his room, which was filled with my belongings. Once he saw that I had seen the evidence, there was no stopping the events that were put into motion."

Mr. Keats nodded. "I see. It is fortunate you survived your confrontation with him. It could have quite easily ended a different way."

His words were neutral but his tone seemed to imply that I had been reckless in my investigating.

My face flushed with annoyance. "I am aware it was dangerous, but I was as cautious as I could be under the circumstances. I merely needed to discover the truth, for my own peace of mind."

He refrained from commenting on that, instead changing the subject. "There is one other thing I wish to ask you about. You said the killer made mention of another person, someone who encouraged him to commit the murder in the first place. Is there anything more you can tell me about that?"

I shook my head. "No, it was not really clear to me what he meant. Whether this other person knew our family, or whether they offered their 'advice' randomly, whether they sought Adam out, or if it was only a chance meeting... Adam died without shedding light on the details."

"It is a shame he did not survive," Mr. Keats said, his gaze fixed on a distant spot on the wall, his brow furrowed together in one long line. "I would have liked to investigate his claims, and there are many questions I would have had for him."

"I know," I said. "They are questions that eat at me, as well."

The detective looked at me more closely, and I felt uneasy under his steady gaze, as if he might somehow read my thoughts. "I hope you do not feel responsible for your servant's death, Mrs. Sedgewick?"

"Of course not," I said, smoothing my skirts. "I am not as silly as that."

He looked unconvinced. "Because it would be very natural, you know, and often people do feel unwarranted guilt after surviving an attack. It would be an understandable feeling, but believe me...you were doing what you had to in order to protect yourself. As for him, he chose his own path the moment he decided to take your husband's life."

I shifted in my seat. "Thank you, but I do not need reassurance, Mr. Keats. As I said, I am at peace with the situation."

"I am glad to hear it, Mrs. Sedgewick."

Perhaps it was something in my voice that gave the lie to my words, but I was left in no doubt that he knew the truth, whether I wished to admit it or not.

"You needn't call me that," I said quickly, to change the subject. "I was 'Miss Victoria' before my marriage and, now that my husband has passed, it is a name that feels more natural to me."

He inclined his head. "I shall remember that...Miss Victoria."

He then stood, and turned his hat around in his hands.

"I must take my leave. The police have removed the body and I have taken the liberty of asking your staff to tidy up the place. If you were to go out there, you might not even realize anything had happened."

"I appreciate the thought, Mr. Keats, but I am quite certain I will never be able to step foot into that stable again without thinking of what occurred there today."

He nodded. "Quite so. I bid you good day, Miss."

I nodded in farewell, and he turned and walked out of the parlor.

I waited until he was out of sight before allowing the polite smile to slip from my face.

There remains something more to you, Mr. Keats, than meets the eye...

My mind flickered for a moment to the unresolved matter of Adam's mysterious acquaintance who had encouraged Duncan's death. Would anything more ever be heard of that matter or was it forever put to rest? I thought of Duncan's friend Mr. Aubrey, who lacked courage, and of Doctor Higgins, who lacked motive. I even thought of my own father-in-law and brother-in-law, neither of whom had any cause to wish ill on their own flesh and blood. And last of all, I thought of the clever Mr. Keats, who worked from the shadows and seemed to know things he should not.

Then, I shook my head. I was worrying over problems of my own invention. Duncan's killer had been captured and I had no more reason to fear. If I let myself go on considering such dark matters, I would soon become suspicious of Warrington and Mrs. Bell...again.

I let out a heavy sigh, looking over at Daniel in his bassinet. Still sleeping quite happily, it seemed.

"Warrington," I called, and the butler quickly appeared at my elbow.

"I have decided I am in need of a brief retreat, perhaps at my parents' old place by the sea," I said. "A few weeks with the salty air...there might not be anything better."

"Shall I make the travel arrangements?" he asked.

"I think so, yes," I said.

He nodded and turned toward the door.

"Warrington," I said, and he stopped, turning to look back at me, questioningly.

"Our friend Mr. Keats has stirred up a thought in my mind..." I said. "What sort of income do you suppose a private inquiry agent earns?"

"I could not hazard a guess, madam, but I suppose a man of his unique skills must command a generous fee," Warrington said. "Is there a reason you wish to know?"

"Perhaps. As it turns out, I seem to have a skill of my own for getting to the truth of things. It makes one wonder whether I might not resolve my own troubles by solving those of others. After I return from the seaside, of course."

I walked to the front window and pulled back the drapes. I peered down just in time to see the straight-backed figure of Branwell Keats striding off down the crowded sidewalk.

"Yes…" I said aloud to no one in particular. "There must be many potential clients in London who would like their delicate inquiries conducted in an inobtrusive manner. And if my skills and wits prove equal to the task, my financial dependence upon my in-laws may soon be at an end."

My eyes narrowed as the detective's coattails disappeared around the corner. "Prepare yourself, Mr. Keats, for competition."

Warrington cleared his throat, reminding me that he was still in the room. "You really mean to pursue this… trade, madam?" he asked hesitantly.

"I do," I said, my resolution growing.

"But if I may ask, madam, where do you intend to begin?"

I turned to smile at him, a sudden excitement coursing through me. "Where all good mysteries begin, of course," I said. "Right underneath our noses."

Continue the mysterious adventures of Victoria Sedgewick with "Death Under Wrathful Skies: The Victoria Sedgewick Mysteries, Book 2."

BLYTHE BAKER

DEATH
·· UNDER ··
WRATHFUL SKIES

THE VICTORIA SEDGEWICK MYSTERIES: BOOK 2

ABOUT THE AUTHOR

Blythe Baker is the lead writer behind several popular historical and paranormal mystery series. When Blythe isn't buried under clues, suspects, and motives, she's acting as chauffeur to her children and head groomer to her household of beloved pets. She enjoys walking her dogs, lounging in her backyard hammock, and fiddling with graphic design. She also likes binge-watching mystery shows on TV. To learn more about Blythe, visit her website and sign up for her newsletter at www.blythebaker.com

Made in the USA
Columbia, SC
25 July 2024

39309031R00102